YEAR OF MIRACLES

Also by CE Murphy

YEAR OF MIRACLES

COLLECTED TALES OF THE OLD RACES

C.E. MURPHY

a miz kit production

MKP

YEAR OF MIRACLES
ISBN-13: 978-1-61317-130-1

Editor: Betsy Mitchell / betsymitchelleditorial.com
Cover Art: Tara O'Shea / fringe-element.net

for Katrina Lehto

Author's Note

The author would like to suggest that the
OLD RACES UNIVERSE books are best enjoyed
in order of publication, which is as follows:

HEART OF STONE
HOUSE OF CARDS
HANDS OF FLAME

BABA YAGA'S DAUGHTER

YEAR OF MIRACLES

KISS OF ANGELS (forthcoming)

Contents

THE THING WITH FEATHERS

SHE WAS BORN OF SECRETS: of whispers at a well, and a white stone rubbed for luck. She was born of the hope for a child, the first blush of love, the thanks given when illness passed and health returned. They said, later, that she was the first human woman, created of clay and risen from the earth, and half of that was true: she had sprung fully formed from the earth, but it had been humanity itself that gave her the power to live. She came with boons, when she rose: she came with the touch that begot a child where none had come before, with the knowing hands to raise grain from the soil, with the herbal wisdom that sent sickness scurrying away. She carried the elements of her magic in a box, and inscribed her mark on the forehead or arm or belly of those who sought her out, until they named her for what she was: Anesidora, the girl who gives the gifts.

She might have stayed where she was birthed, and been mother to a people like no others: all strong and gentle, untouched by disease or sorrow, but the world was wide, and its varied souls called to her. She learned she could not cross any stream wider than her stride, and so circumvented rivers: climbed mountains, crawled through jungles, entered deserts, and ran freely across plains. She found people wherever she went, living in the most extraordinary of places, and shared her gifts with them, freely, generously, joyfully, for she knew little other than happiness in her wandering ways. She traveled half a world this way, and found that when her path crossed her own, that her spirit had lingered on: she had become Gaea and Shala, Iusaaset and Prithvi, all the daughters of the earth who gave gifts to their mortal progenitors. Or perhaps they were not her reflections at all: perhaps they were the names of her sisters, born of magic in the way she had been, though she never met them. Her kind were few enough to begin with, and most were born of darkness.

She was old, if goddesses could be said to age, when gods and their sons began to come to light. Old when those gods, the Titans, the sons of Titans, began to swim the seas and touch the skies, when they took on form and walked the earth as she did. But not as she did: never in all her years had she heard of a god being born of secrets. Only goddesses came from the earth, and their own children were daughters, almost always. She had daughters herself, and had let them go long ago; they, more than others born of secrets, might have become Shala and Prithvi and all the others. Perhaps she had known that once and forgotten; it was a thought new and familiar all at once, and Anesidora knew herself as one who did not linger on philosophy.

The gods she met gained names later, in legend and in history, or changed their names to suit the times, as her own name would change. The two she remembered best, and loved the most, were as taken with intemperate humanity as she, making them alike as brothers and different as men could be.

The taller one was Prometheus, scarred from giving fire to man, but the other, Epimetheus, was perfectly formed and more beautiful. He was slight and black-haired, with eyes that glittered like star-lit nights, and his skin, sun-brown, carried summertime's warmth beneath it.

Prometheus, red-haired, jade-eyed, and as pale and cool of skin as Epimetheus was brown and warm, played at an air of noble suffering—what he had done to serve man! What horrors he had undergone, for the benefit of mortals!—while Epimetheus darted about like a bee seeking pollen, always intrigued by the moment. He angered easily and forgot that anger even more quickly; he spoke the thoughts in his mind and in doing so released them; he could not be contained or reprimanded for what he had done, for its memory had always already left him. He was her favorite of the two, for that reason: she lived as immediately as he did, only reminded of the past by moments of synchronicity.

He ran across an ocean for her once, or so he claimed: the great wide stretch of water she could find no way around, no matter how far she walked, and she had walked across the ice and back again in her time. Perhaps he lied, but he returned with an armful of plants and herbs she had never seen, and the lingering scent of sunshine burning into unfamiliar earth. There were humans there, he told her: beautiful and brown-skinned, often small but strongly built, with wide noses and wider smiles, as if they were Anesidora's children all. Their elders were striking, with grey and white grizzled hair, and their children sun-streaked blonde. Some of the plants he brought back, when mashed and mixed with dirt, made for colors subtly different than she had found in other lands, and she would not let him paint them on her: they would have meaning for those far-off people she had never met, and she had no wish to disrespect them.

He was quick, though, faster than any mortal man could be, and in the space of a breath she was painted anyway, white like a spirit, with red on her feet to tie her to the earth, and blue on her palms to reach the sky. Epimetheus was so pleased she could hardly be angry with him, and that night she took him as her lover, while he still smelled of the rich distant earth she had never seen. Prometheus sulked, somewhere in the distance, and Anesidora laughed at that. Laughed more at Epimetheus's smug delight, but taught him, some little while later, that her favoritism would not be held by possessiveness: Prometheus was entirely different, and no less entertaining, as a lover. Then Epimetheus sulked and Anesidora laughed again, drawn back to him because he *was* her favorite, and knew now not to parade that as a prize.

And so they went: she was inconstant and did not care, for no man could hold a goddess for long, though Epimetheus brought her gifts from all the world over to win her attention back for a time. Mankind had fire, given to them by Prometheus, but the other creatures of the world had gifts Epimetheus claimed to have laid at their feet. Stealth for the cats, cunning for wolves, strength for the rhinoceros, speed for the horse. Wisdom for the elephant, and when he spoke of that, Anesidora laughed again, and wondered would it not have been—well, wiser!—to offer men wisdom, but no: Epimetheus lacked foresight, and had given all the gifts away before he came to man.

"So your brother has given them fire," said Anesidora, and as ever, Epimetheus frowned a moment before recalling red-haired Prometheus to mind.

That was how it was with them, Prometheus had once said. They traveled, together and apart, and had done so for as long as the sun had risen, but Epimetheus had no better memory than he had foresight. Each time they parted for too long and re-met, Prometheus was like new to his beautiful brother. Epimetheus's constant ability to recall Anesidora, that her memory was a constant within him, was against the grain of who he had always been. *He has never met a goddess before,* Anesidora had replied, and Prometheus had bowed deeply, kissed her fingertips, and retreated with a secret smile upon his lips, to—in time—give fire to humankind.

"He has," Epimetheus agreed, and, remembering now, looked pleased. "And paid for it: you've seen his scar."

"I have," Anesidora said drolly. "So he is scarred for his gift, and you had none at all left to give them? You're a poor sort of guardian, my love. Gods and their children should be more careful."

Scorn took the stars from Epimetheus's eyes. "Gods are of human make. We are more than that."

Carefully, dangerously, Anesidora murmured, "I am of human make, Epimetheus."

"And we are more than that." It was Prometheus who usually wore arrogance, so easily it could be mistaken for charm. Settled on Epimetheus's shoulders it took his beauty and made it strange, as if his very flesh was changeable and could mold to disdain.

Anesidora was not afraid: nothing save the secret that had birthed her could undo her from the world, but she was stricken by the change in him, and brightly curious, and unfamiliarly offended, for men worshiped her and even the sons of gods should not show contempt. "What more, then?"

"We are the secrets." Epimetheus swayed with his whisper, and in the fading sunlight made shadows against the earth. Impossible shadows, his hands twisting beyond convention, but it was the dance of beasts he drew with them that held Anesidora's gaze even when she wanted to look upon the dread wrongness of his fluid bones. "We are old, older than men, older than the gods men have made. Anesidora, sweet child, the girl with all the gifts, you are old for what men have wrought, but we are so much older still."

Secrets crawled from his shadows: serpentine and sinuous, winged beauty that struck a chord in the very core of her: *dragon*, that thing was called, and its father lay coiled around her own mother's body, the heart of the earth. The dragon's watery brethren, the sea serpents, swam with dolphin-women and soul-eyed seals who shed their skins to look like men, and in the skies other creatures flew with the dragon: stone men whose visages were solemn to look upon, and feather-winged women whose fragile male children were nurtured carefully and still most often lost. Giant shuffling beasts, so fur-covered they could only live in the highest, coldest places, and desert-loving breezes that could shift to beautiful, brightly-bejeweled men: on and on the shadows went, giving lie to what had once been truth, that man was the only and most thinking animal that walked the earth.

They were not quite terrible, the things that she was shown. Not themselves: they might have drawn her to them as humans did, save for the thing that wrapped around their ankles, slithered and twisted between them and hunted them from time to time. Only rarely, though; only rarely, for the other beasts, the cunning wolf and the stealthy cat, the wise elephant and the quick horse, they were easier, and mankind the most satisfying prey of all. All of humanity knew there were dangers in the night: what better feast than one that understood it was being eaten?

"What are they," Anesidora whispered, and Epimetheus, so beautiful and deadly, sneered.

"They are Old, and my kind is the father of them all. You think yourself a goddess? You are only a witch. I've listened to the secrets on the wind and killed a dozen like you. Your blood is sweeter than humanity's, rich and full of magic."

"And is that why you've wooed me?"

As quickly as it came, the darkness in Epimetheus vanished: vanished into astonishment, as though the monster had never even lurked beneath. "Not at all. Why would I do that? I saw you and I loved you."

An anger, unfamiliar, heated Anesidora's chest. "To covet

is not the same as to love, Epimetheus. Coveting is a wish to possess, and you know that I am not to be owned." As she spoke to him, the earth her mother spoke to *her*, and these things rose to bind him: iron, earth, wood and water. Coarse and pitted iron, raw from the depths below them and formed by the power of her will alone into a shroud. Trees leapt to her call, shooting branches and tendrils that wound around him and pierced his skin, begetting a scream each time. They plunged him deep into the ground, and rain fell to weigh the earth until he struggled in a slurry, and Anesidora stood above him all the while.

His beauty was gone, the darkness of his hair and the brown warmth of his skin both turned to ichorous black. His jaw gaped, muscle stretching like tar, and within it his teeth were gashes of night, ready to raze. His voice ran high and thin, forced from a throat not meant to speak: *no one*, he said. *No one looks upon my true form and lives.*

She leaned close, close enough to taste the rankness of his breath and to look into the flat rage of depthless eyes, and from there whispered, "I have. I will tell the world, Epimetheus. All of your secrets, all of you demons who hide in the night. I will release you from the hidden places you have stayed within, and I will name you all, that man might know you and be ready to stand against you. I will show them how to kill and capture you, and in that, I will have put something into your box of secrets that you can't control. There will be hope for mortal man to end you, and that hope will plague you, demon, until the very end of time."

She left him there; walked away without looking back, and carried on until his thin screams faded with distance. Farther still, until the earth beneath her feet no longer reverberated with his cries, and beyond that until she admitted to herself that the weariness in her body was more than the fatigue of travel. She sat then, for a month beneath the changing moon, to ask herself whether she wanted to carry the demon's child. The moon gave her no guidance, pulled her neither one way nor the other, but its clear silver light on its brightest night cast the world into starkness, bright and dark, and in those sharp lines she saw the hope she had threatened Epimetheus with.

She was not human, but she was of human make, and Epimetheus was another thing entirely, ancient and alien. The child growing within her walked between her world and his, could be what neither of them were, and what she might need to protect her progenitors. Satisfied, she rose from where she sat, and, shaking off the stillness of a month, walked again, until a deep and warm crevasse in the earth, a cave marked with the scars and bones of old life, called to her.

There she stayed, watching the depth that the sunrise could stretch to, until the morning came that she squatted to bear her daughter. The breaking day showed the girl to have Epimetheus's beauty in her black hair and ebony eyes. Her skin was red ochre beneath its brown, as if the paint Anesidora had once been adorned with had become part of the child, and her name, she told her mother under that first light of dawn, was Ushas.

All children grew quickly, but none moreso than the children of immortals, for whom time's passage means nothing. It seemed an hour until Ushas crawled; a day until she walked; a week until she ran, and a month until she stood tall and strong and brown and lovely. In the wake of that passage of days, goddess and daughter came from the caves, birthed anew from the earth, and went once more among the people.

Wherever they went, Anesidora was revered, but Ushas worshiped: her beauty and comfort with humanity surpassed Anesidora's, her laughter and her memory for faces making her more of the people than the goddess could ever be. This was as it should be, as it must be, if she was the harbinger of hope to the world, and Anesidora, pleased, let herself age as she had never done before, becoming the storyteller, the shaper of worlds, and shaped her daughter's story as the loving protector goddess.

More, Anesidora named the demons in her stories. She set them loose in the world so that all mankind might know them in the night, and spoke too of the hope that came with day. It took no magic to make humanity look to Ushas as that hope, for they could see in her, and therefore in themselves, the strength and the darkness that would protect them from the demons known as the Old Races.

From one settlement to another they went, on and on, the world and time over, and where they went, their memory became history and their history became legend, until legend was myth, and known in the very bones of the mortals whose lives they had touched.

Prometheus found his tattered brother long before that: found him while history still lived in the minds of men, not yet relegated to generations past. Found him screeching and struggling still, held in the earth's grasp, and, sighing, said to him, "What have you done, Epimetheus? Try to remember what you've done."

"Try?" Even Prometheus had not often seen a hint of Epimetheus's true form; in that shape, even mangled by bonds, he could hiss any word, spit it from his throat with sibilants and hate. "I will never forget."

"I doubt that," replied Prometheus, and sat down to wait. He could wait nearly forever, and Epimetheus had always loathed the keeping of secrets; they were there to be exposed, for a creature who neither recalled nor forethought could see no reason to hide them. But neither was his brother inclined to confess, this time: Prometheus sat for months, perhaps years, under the barrage of Epimetheus's screams and rage, until the truth slipped free.

"I told her. I told her everything about the Old Races. She was so complacent, so smug in her godhead, and I told her that she was only a witch, and the least among the magic of this world. I told her who and what we were, and she promised to tell all humanity in return."

Prometheus raised a jade gaze to the bound vampire, and laughed without kindness. "And this least of magics has bound you. You fool. Epimetheus, you utter fool. You'll undo us all."

"Not if I kill her," he snarled, and at this, Prometheus rose.

"She's a witch, brother. Their secrets are hard to find, and even if you eventually find it, the damage will have long been done."

Epimetheus lashed at him, spitting, snarling, but could reach no farther than his bonds would allow him; Prometheus, who was difficult to hurt anyway, had no reason to flinch. "I think I'll let you stay here a while, my friend. Perhaps it will teach you the value of forethought. How long do you suppose I should be gone?" He glanced skyward, as if the changing moon and stars might tell him, and murmured, "A year or more, I imagine. You are, after all, very impulsive, and I can't think that less time would make any sort of impression. Be well, brother. I'll come back for you after a while."

He did, long years later when he had found the trick to releasing Epimetheus's bonds. Another witch; it could be nothing less, not where human magic was involved, and that was a thing Epimetheus had never learned. Another witch, and he put away the thought of the price he had paid, the knowledge he had given up in order to secure the witch's services. She broke the bonds Anesidora had cast, and

Prometheus sent her away before the last of the magic holding Epimetheus unwound. No one looked on a vampire's true form and lived, though witches were nearly impossible to kill, but still: she did not deserve to die, or to be threatened, for helping them, and so Prometheus sent her away before Epimetheus was free, that she might live a little while longer.

Perhaps Epimetheus would hunt her as he had hunted others, but that was beyond Prometheus's purview, and not his concern. For his own part, he was prepared to fight when at last the emaciated and enraged vampire was free: fight as the price for *his* part in Epimetheus's long captivity.

Instead he stood astonished as Epimetheus dropped to the earth, panting, then rose with rage in his eyes, and turned his back on Prometheus, walking—walking! When he would run before!—silently into the night.

Centuries passed before Prometheus saw him again, and then he hardly knew the face that had been his brother's. Slight in form: that much had not changed, but what once had been flawless beauty had mutated to plainness, attractive only in motion, and that for the charisma that could not be wholly squelched in fathomless eyes. His scent had not changed, nor the fluidity of his actions, but thoughtfulness sat about him like a cloak now, slowing his behavior, weighing it in a way that Prometheus had never seen before. Indeed, were it not for the scent, Prometheus might not have known him, and as so often was the case when they had been long parted, neither did Epimetheus seem to know him. Prometheus greeted him as he always had: "What name should I call you by?" and was given a look of consideration in exchange.

"What name would you call me by?"

Here, perhaps, he made a mistake, for when he offered the name of longest ease, "Epimetheus, and I shall be Prometheus still," a glitter of recognition came into his brother's dark eyes, though it went unremarked beyond, "Epimetheus, then," and then a pause. "There is a woman."

A smile flashed across Prometheus's features. "Tell me about her."

Ushas, called Aphrodite, called Hausos, called by many other names, commanded men with nothing more than a smile; men and women too, as her love and beauty knew no bounds. There were those who said she changed her face to suit the one who looked upon her, that she could not be less than perfection, for she reflected what they found most beautiful in their hearts. The brothers thought otherwise, for they saw the same woman, but it was not to her that Prometheus was drawn, but rather to her older copy: her mother, whose white hair was still threaded with brown, and whose eyes and mouth had lines of wisdom and joy written around them. She was beautiful too, brown as the earth, graceful as wind bowing the branches of trees, and with a deeply rooted strength that spoke of things greater than mortal man borne within her. They called her Pandora now, and upon seeing her, Prometheus spoke a single word to Epimetheus: "Don't."

"I think I must."

"There are very few *musts* thrust upon us, being who and what we are, Epimetheus. Don't," Prometheus said again, more softly, more intensely. "It will not end well."

"I think I must," Epimetheus repeated. "I am compelled from beyond memory, and I think I must." A sly smile showed flat human teeth; before, his teeth had curved, not so sharply as Prometheus's own, perhaps, but they had never before lied about what he was. "Call it impulse, and own that it is mine to embrace, *brother*."

Hesitation curled through Prometheus's heart. "You do remember."

"From time to time." The snarl faded from Epimetheus's

lips. "From time to time, and not well. I remember the hot sun on the plains, and the endless quest for a drink in the desert. Lizards," he spat. "Nasty things to taste."

Prometheus smiled, but said nothing, and Epimetheus went on uninterrupted. "After the desert, hunting. I saw others like me, once in a while. They rushed in, deathly fast; they panicked that which they chased, be it bird or beast or man. It seemed...wasteful. I began to insinuate myself instead, creeping closer until the prey came to me."

"Be it bird or beast or man," Prometheus said softly, and Epimetheus nodded.

"They all came to me, and with patience I feasted better than I ever had before. I watched the others of my kind, and saw they had no patience at all, and sometimes...I remembered. How I had once been like them, and how I had changed." A shudder ran through him, more profound than any man could ever sustain. His bones were fluid inside, his face, a dripping mask, before the plainness he had adopted came to steadiness once more. "I prefer not to remember. I believe I was happier then."

"Yes," Prometheus said, knowing it to be ill-advised, but gambling on the honesty. "Yes. I believe you were. But you were very foolish, brother. Very dangerous. To all of us."

"Yes." Unusually sibilant, that word, and the silence that grew up around it carried hunger as he watched the distant shadows and shapes that made up Pandora, who had been Anesidora. "I remember her. She has made me, Prometheus. She has made me into what I am. I might have forgotten, or ceased to care, before, but now I see and think too clearly, and for that I want revenge."

"It's too late for revenge, Epi. We're long since the stories they tell at night to frighten and awe one another. We're part of their subconsciousness now. No revenge will eradicate that."

"Then let it be justice, instead."

Prometheus sighed. "The purpose was to teach you forethought, Epimetheus. What good is it if you use that forethought to plot your own doom all over again? I say it again, brother: do not do this."

"And I say again that I think I must."

"Then on your head be it." Prometheus transformed, which he had not done in long and long and long again. The wound on his side said as much, scarred tissue never shifted often enough into dragonly mass to heal. In the thunderclap of shaken air, he flung himself skyward, a sinuous red slash against the blue, and a warning for Anesidora and all the world to see. Epimetheus sneered after him, and went among the mortals to stalk his prey.

He had searched: for centuries and more he had searched for the secret that was her birthright, but witch's secrets were hard to come by. Only the Old Races, or another witch, might live long enough to have been there when a witch was born from the earth, and should one witch betray another, she would surely die for it before a year was out. The wind-borne djinn, and the steadfast gargoyles: they were most likely to catch the birthing of a witch, and know the secret that gave her power. But *most likely* and *always* were nothing alike: since his captivity, he had learned the birth-secret of only one witch, and that one was not Anesidora.

Nor did it need to be, in the end. He could not *destroy* Anesidora without her progenitive secret, but with another witch captured by *hers*, he could ensnare the one who had once captured him. She watched for him, did Anesidora: she watched for the beautiful and charming boy he had been, and never looked at all for the plain and considering man he had become, much less for one of her sisters to come calling. He only let himself be seen when the magic was already working: human magic, so raw and rough beside the elegance of the Old Races, and so dangerous to them. She had caught him in her working of earth and water and wood and air; he did not wish to return the favor. Only stone, for the earth she had been made from. Under his witch's command blood turned to marble and ate its way outward, until a block much larger and rougher than he had expected stood where she had been. He was content to leave it there, where man would pull it apart in time, and thus end Anesidora.

He let his captured witch go, a thing he never would have done before. That was a gift and the curse of forethought: that he could see that he might have use again for a witch he could command, rather than simply indulge in the pleasure of her magic-rich blood. As vengeance went, it lacked, but justice: he rather thought he had meted justice, and that had a certain satisfaction of its own.

He left Anesidora, a frozen block of stone, and though he would not forget, neither could he foresee, not fully, not wholly, not enough.

His mother, they said, spat on the earth when she saw she had borne a son, and walked away from the babe, left him mewling on the ground. His father was the man who found him, a soft and gentle-hearted soul, who took the crying child into his home and gave him a life. He was an easy child, quiet, introspective, concerned from his earliest days with beauty, as though it was a puzzle to be unlocked. His manner of unlocking it was to sculpt: bits of soft wood as a child, graduating to mahoganies and oaks as he aged, bringing depth and form from the dark wood until it all but breathed with life.

A merchant uncle, sensing burgeoning talent, came home from a long journey carrying soapstone as a gift for his nephew, and carried away again the objects of his efforts: horses striding from foam, owls peeking from hollowed branches, bulls whose whitened eyes stared with arrogance at the viewer, all to be sold at generous prices. Some portion of that he returned to his nephew, along with more stone, which seemed his natural element, with a grace and finery unmatched in his woodwork. The boy worked, a stripling to a youth to a man, and in his manhood was much sought after for his art, and, as his wealth grew, for his prospects as a husband.

But no woman pleased him; this he publicly attributed to the sight of so many wanton females in the streets of the city. Privately, he conducted his affairs with other men discretely until the day came a beauty said to be the goddess Aphrodite herself brought him a block of stone, and bade him carve a woman from its depths. For this, she said, anyone his heart desired might be his, and no man would tell him differently.

He sat with the stone for a week; a month; a year. He learned its textures, its colors, its strengths, and when he knew it well enough he began to carve. A sculptor might say that the image lay within the piece already; that all he did was remove the pieces that did not belong, but he felt it more strongly with his lady of stone than he ever had before. Long before she was complete, he gave her a name: Elise, who was sworn to the gods, and he whispered to her the truths about who he desired, and how even a goddess could not give him what he wanted. She became his companion as she emerged from the stone, until the beauty he had been consigned to create took on a more human cast. She smirked, did Elise, a fulsome smile of fond amusement curling her lips, and the gesturing hand she offered was playfully inviting. There were elements of perfection expected in a master sculptor's work, homages to the current fashion of comeliness, and yet he could not bring himself to condemn his masterpiece to the slim athletic lines that more recalled a man's body than a woman's. She came from the marble plump and strong, powerful as a discus thrower, confident of herself. He showed her to no one as he worked, knowing she would shock with her strength, and afraid that, should Aphrodite hear how he did not honor *her*, but found another woman in the stone to reveal instead, she would refuse his payment, and he knew now what that payment must be.

For a month, and then three, Elise stood in his work space when she was done, for he could not bear to be parted from the friend he had brought forth from marble. He went to her in the mornings and told her of the world beyond his door, of his friends, of his family, of his lovers, and he bid her good night each evening when he left, happy to go on forever in such a way.

But it could not be: Aphrodite came to him in time, and asked—asked, did not demand—to see the sculpture. Heart in palpitations, he led her to Elise and cowered in a corner, expecting each breath to be his last as she saw what he had made of the marble. Round and round Elise she went, examining her for flaws, frowning in thought, murmuring beneath her breath, until finally she turned to him with a smile that blossomed as if from the heart of the earth itself, and said, "I knew I had chosen well with you. Name your heart's desire and it will be yours."

"She is." Simple words that sent him quaking through and through. "She has become my friend, mistress; she has become my closest companion. Only let her be mine, and I will ask nothing more of you at all."

Curiosity lit Aphrodite's eyes. Curiosity, and sorrow, and she murmured, "That may be the one boon I cannot grant, Master Sculptor. That choice is hers, not mine, but here: you have brought her from the stone she was captured in, which was a thing I could not do. Had I tried, she might have shattered and been lost to the world, and with her my heart and so too all the hope of mankind. Let me do what I am made to do, child of the blood that captured her, child of the earth that bore her." She turned then to Elise, and reached forth to grasp the statue's welcoming hand as a daughter might capture her mother's.

He knew magic, of course; any artist did. But what he knew, and what transpired betwixt goddess and statue, ran deeper than any magic he had ever touched. Color suffused Elise's hand at Aphrodite's touch: earthy brown, darker than the goddess. It swept Elise, life's blood flowing beneath marble's surface, until her palms and lips pinkened, until her thick hair softened into its myriad curls, until the smirk on her lips blossomed into a full smile, until she stepped free from her marble base a living thing to embrace the joyful goddess beside her.

He fell to his knees: of course he did, being no fool. He heard Aphrodite, now proven a goddess without question, murmur a name to his Elise: *Mother*, and knew he knelt before the daughter of Titans. He bowed forward, put his forehead to the ground, and only prayed that he might not be smote for looking on them both.

Elise's touch was warm and familiar in his hair, and her voice the rich laughing thing he had imagined. "Stop; stop that. Have we not become friends, these months and years as you've unbound me from the stone? Come, rise, be my friend still. Be my daughter's friend as well, and fear nothing from us."

"Gods are not so kind," he whispered, and would not look up.

He heard the smile on her lips, heard wryness in her answer: "Then perhaps I am only a witch, and not a goddess after all. Please," she said, more softly. "My gaze has been fixed all the while we have been together. Let me at least look on you, my sweet friend."

In the end, he could refuse her nothing, and lifted first his eyes and then all of himself, to sit back on his heels and look up at what he had, and had not, wrought. Goddess or not, she was made to be worshiped, all lush heaviness and sensual power.

Were she any other she would make him uncomfortable, with her closeness, with her nakedness, with her confidence. He knew her too well to be disturbed by those things, yet wondered that he could even bring them to light, when all he knew of what most men wanted was what the world admired as fashionable beauty that she did not reflect. "You *were* in the stone," he said uncertainly. "Not in the way that sculptures are, but caught there. By magic?"

"By magic." Elise knelt to be with him, and at eye level she was less overwhelming, if for no other reason than he no longer gazed up at her like a supplicant. Her eyes were distant, as if she called a faded memory into place. "There will be a reckoning for that magic, in time, but Ushas promised you a gift, one within my power to grant. I'll stay, if you wish it. Your friend and companion, for releasing me from the stone. I'll ask nothing of you that you don't wish to give, nor take offense when you find love elsewhere. I'll watch you sculpt, if you'll allow it, and care for you when you are sick and old."

"Why?"

"Because no one else could have freed me, and human lives are not, in the end, so very long. I can stay a while, without regrets."

"Mother," said Aphrodite, whom Elise called Ushas, and Elise shrugged one beautiful round shoulder.

"You think of me as flighty, daughter. As drawn from one shining moment to the next with no thought for what I've left behind. I am. I was. But I've been in the stone a very long time, my child, and stone is nothing but patient. Human lives are not so very long," she said again. "Revenge can wait."

"Stay," he blurted, and flushed as Elise smiled at him. "As long as you want to," he bargained. "For the rest of my life, if you wish it, but only a day if that's what your heart prefers. Come back if you can." His own heart was full, an ache that rolled through him slowly. "Come back if you want. But only stay if you desire it, Elise. Friends...do not hold each other back when they need to go, and I have never had a closer friend than you."

Aphrodite swore in a way that goddesses of love surely were not meant to, and stomped off to the sounds of her mother's laughter. Elise stayed, for days; months; years, until the morning came that he awakened beside the man who had been his lover for a full year that day, and recalled the memory of Elise's kisses on his cheeks sometime in the night, and the whisper she had left him with: *You will be remembered. Past history, past legend, into myth: you will be remembered as the sculptor who brought stone to life. I will see that it is so. Live well, and be happy, my sweet Pygmalion.*

She wore a feathered cloak, and walked with the jar balanced atop the braids on her head, always swaying to keep it steady. Demons lay within the jar; she knew, because she had put them there. Demons of speed and fire, of stone and air, of water and sky and wings. Hope, too: hope had come forth from the jar, and now wandered the world seeking a vengeance that she herself no longer desired. Instead she had painted the jar with the demons' likenesses, to hold them in place, and she had painted a creature with wings around its neck to represent the daughter who had left her in the name of revenge. Then she had stoppered it with wax and straw and string, and carried it until she no longer knew why, then carried it longer still. She left behind what she was and what she had been as she walked; she had never been a being meant for contemplation, and the world was warm and bright and inviting. She walked until she was weary, and walked on still; she walked as though she searched for something, trusting she would know it when she found it.

He found her climbing a mountain, the jar tied neatly to

her hip. How he had come there, she could hardly imagine: a plain man, dressed conservatively, standing on the rock above her and offering a hand. He had not, she was certain, been there a moment before, but she herself had been born of stone, and it seemed probable that he too had. She took his hand and let him help her up; up to what proved to be the mountain's crest; up to a view that took in half the world, and if she turned the other way, the rest of it.

He said, "Anesidora," in a strange voice, and she looked at him, puzzled, then smiled.

"My name is Elise. I don't know you."

"Do you not?"

"No," she said, and if there was a lie in the words it lay so deeply buried within her that no one, man or demon, might hear it.

"Elise, then. You remind me of someone."

"You loved her."

"Oh yes. And I hated her. I am," the man said to the distant horizon, "fickle like that."

A smile creased her lips. "Most of us are. Which was stronger?"

"I would have said the hate."

"And now?"

"Now I know she made me what I am, which is far more than I could have been. I owe her an apology for what I did, and a plea for forgiveness."

"Would she grant it?"

Softly, softly, softly so: "I do not know."

Elise tilted her head thoughtfully and offered the jar. "I think this is for you."

He took it with a bitter laugh at its weight. "Yes. Of course it is. Do you know what it is?"

"Heavy," she replied, "and filled with demons."

"No. The demons have escaped. Only their likeness is

there, Elise."

"Well, that will never do." She examined the fragile feathers of her cloak and smiled as an implacability that had slept within her reawakened. She was not, perhaps, made for contemplation, but neither was she made for forgetting, not in the things that ran deepest, and demons ran as deep as her mother the earth. "Wait a moment."

It only took a moment, winding herself in the cloak, calling the feathers to her skin. It took little more than that to shiver off the heaviness of a human body, and to become strange and small and winged. She fluttered in the air before him, quick and light and lithe, and saw agony stretch taut in his eyes before it snapped into loss. Then she dove deep into the jar, straight through the wax and straw and string, and in the darkness curled a smile of satisfaction. The trouble was that she loved him still, the demon called Epimetheus; did she not there would be no vindication in taking herself away from him in such a way; did she not, there would be no hope to leave him, fragilely ensconced within the jar. He could not undo human magic; he would have to tend to her, and tend to all the demons of the world, and tend to hope, that he might one day be forgiven.

She ought, she thought at the last, she ought to have mentioned Ushas, and her anger, but no. Like Epimetheus, she rarely thought far enough ahead, and now his voice, softened and distorted by the jar, was the last thing she heard before she willed herself to sleep: "Elise," he murmured. "Elise. Very well, Elise."

A demon climbed down the mountain, carefully, slowly, carrying the jar as a mortal might, and named himself Eliseo.

SKINCHANGER

"THE HIDE MUST BE FLAWLESS." She'd said it a dozen times, a hundred times; no one scolded her for it. Not after the long-past parting from the pod; not after the perhaps-more-agonizing departure from the sea. Its scent, the taste of fish on the air, the wind brusque with salt, the soothing murmur of waves shifting sand, the cries of gulls; all of those memories pierced the heart with loneliness, with loss and regret: but in the end, the greater loss, the driving fear, was the inevitable death of their people.

They had already, long since, spread around the world, clinging to coasts where humans also lived. Even the coldest and most inhospitable shores, where sense would dictate no one would stay unless they must, were peopled with humans, and in those far frozen places the humans had stories of seal-people, whose titles were as varied as the people who saw them. They were all born from sightings, distant or near, of one of the sea-dwelling Old Races, just as the tales of siryns and sea monsters were.

But those mortals didn't just tell stories about the selkies. They hunted them, too; they hunted *seals*, and even when the stories held the shapechangers in reverence, even when it was forbidden or considered ill luck to slay one, they still died under a harpoon's thrust, and mostly, no human ever knew that they had struck a creature more human than beast.

Ellu did not, could not, know if others had given up on the sea and sought a different path. Not even all of her pod had; at least half couldn't bring themselves to leave the water, despite its risks, but nearly half of them *had*. Eight or ten here, ten or twelve there; they had found a shore and shed their skins, and begun walking with the ocean at their backs. Perhaps her tribe were the only ones so desperate; perhaps the rest of the selkie race would scorn and cast out those who were willing to try anything, even becoming something else, to ensure their survival. No matter; they had cast themselves out already, by trying, and if exile was the price of their people living on in some way, in some form, then it was worth the risk.

It was worth the risk, especially, because she carried a child, and it would be easier by far for that infant to be born to a land-animal form than the seal shape it was naturally destined for. They were grateful, Ellu's little band of explorers, for the rivers and ponds and lakes they came across, and for the massive inland seas they sometimes found. But their selkie forms were never meant for the land; their grace and power came to the fore in the water, and the deeper into the heart of the continent they came, the more vulnerable they felt without their Old shapes to rely on.

Ellu's child would not feel that fear. She knelt before the cat's skin, large and sleek and black with patterns of spotted dapples buried darker within the black, and brushed her fingers over its spine one final time. It had been skinned delicately, singles seams split where necessary, and no other cut made, so that it resembled, as closely as possible, the seal skins that the selkies shed when they shifted. It had been killed by a strike through the eye, straight into the brain. The roof of the mouth was the only other way it could have died; anything else left flaws in the hide and rendered it useless. They knew this from trial and error, and the horror of realizing the lucky ones merely rejected the broken skin. The unlucky ones—Ellu shuddered, and put it out of her mind. Too many things could go wrong, too many things often *did* go wrong; they had been eleven when they set out, and were seven now, with only one of them successful in the skinchanging. It had to be approached with calm certainty; anything else, and again, it would go wrong. There were so many things that could go wrong.

"Ellu." Nattor, father to her child and the sole survivor of the skinchange, put his hand on her shoulder. "The hide is flawless. We've checked it dozens of times. Still, if you want to wait—"

"No. No, I wish I'd done it before I caught, but I won't put a child through the pain. If I do this now—"

"We don't know," Nattor said quietly. "We don't *know* that the change will settle into the child too, Ellu."

"But we do," Ellu whispered. "If we're caught in human form when we give birth, the child is born in *its* human form. I'll make the skinchange and give birth in the new form. The child will be born a kitten and will survive. Will *thrive*. It must."

"And if you're wrong?"

"I'm not wrong. I can't be wrong." A gut-knotting confidence swept the words, and before she lost that, Ellu lifted the heavy jaguar skin and wrapped it around herself. Nattor, seeing her decision had been made, lifted her seal skin and placed it over the jaguar's as swiftly.

Ellu did not even have to think, to begin the change, and then she *could* not think, as pain, red and sharp as knives, swept her and dragged her down into darkness.

Nattor stood back at a small distance, the rest of their tiny tribe farther back still. He had experienced what Ellu now went through, and, watching it from the outside, didn't think he would have the bravery to try it, having seen it first.

No; that was untrue. He had seen the failures, all of them ending—ultimately—in death: Jessel, the first to try and the first to go mad, had murdered poor gentle Adiff, and had finally died at his own brother Merro's hands, a necessary action to save the pod. Olle had simply not survived, had been too weak to undergo the dreadful change, and the last of them, Hennth, Nattor had killed himself, before the madness overtook her. So many deaths made watching what would surely be—had to be—a success no easier. The selkie skin writhed, squirming and shoving and pressing, trying to reach the woman beneath the jaguar skin. Normally the shift was the work of an instant, no more to be considered than the donning of a coat, but a coat was meant to go on over layers. Selkie skins were not. It struggled, crushing Ellu with its urgency to become one with her and yet unable to touch the skin that would meld so naturally with it. It fought the jaguar skin, though *that*, at least, lay passively, not yet imbued with a magic of its own, and unable to resist the selkie skin's increasingly desperate attempts to finish the transformation.

It happened all at once and with hideous slow clarity, the way the selkie skin finally succeeded in sinking through—*through*! As if the jaguar skin was viscous water, permeable with enough determination!—through the jaguar skin, *absorbing* it as it went. Or being absorbed by; it was truly impossible to tell which, save for the fact that when the change finally came, came with the pop and squeal and snap of bones and muscle forced into a new, unnatural shape, the beast left on her belly on the earthen floor was a jaguar, and the shredded remains of a selkie's skin and fur drifted to the ground around her.

Ellu crouched flat, ears back and her tail lashing, lips curled back to reveal deadly ivory canines. Her eyes, strangely golden now, glowed with fear and rage, and every glance she gave to the little group of gathered selkies fought between seeing them as friends or prey. Her breathing came hard, ribs expanding and collapsing rapidly, and her claws were extended, every muscle in her body torn between flight and attack.

Nattor remembered that too, the savagery of the new shape, how alien it had felt. Still felt, in some ways, when he clamped his jaws on the throat of a deer or pig and leapt with appalling ease into a tree, dragging the carcass with him. Still felt, when even in human form he opened his mouth wide to scent like the cat did, or his night vision startled him with its clarity. Their child would be born to those things, would find them natural, but long as he might live, Nattor thought they would catch him out, make him feel unfamiliar in his own body.

Then again, it had only been months, not even a year, since he had taken on the jaguar form, and a year was no time at all, to any of the Old Races. They had traveled so long and so far before desperation and discomfort had driven them to try what—so far as they knew—selkies had never tried before. What no Old Race, save perhaps the vampires, could do: shed one skin for another. Even if it had been their plan when they left the waters, the act of actually doing so, of going through with such a dramatic decision, had been harder than they had expected; not until they were dying already, starving, diseased, weak, were they able to even push themselves to try, and then the first attempts had gone so badly.

Ellu had already come through the worst of it: she was whole, and a jaguar, not some mangled wreck caught between the forms, nor some mad creature whose change had only been half successful, and wretchedly tied to the pull of the moon and tides. Nattor dropped to all fours, rolling onto his back even as he changed to jaguar form, and scented Ellu's awareness, her sharp fear and confusion. The animal part of her wanted to run; she was female, and gravid, and he was male and large and strong. But he was submissive, too, and even the beast recognized that, while the Old part of her soul fought to establish dominance over the wild animal whose form she had accepted.

He heard the shift of soil and leaves beneath her foot as she pushed one forward, the smallest testing motion, and a knot inside him loosened. Every padded step forward meant a triumph of sentience over the beast, and when she stopped above him, huffing through half-bared teeth, he rolled his chin upward, exposing his throat so she might—and she did—bury her nose in the familiar scent of him.

The return to human form came quickly then, a shuddering change that left her clinging to his furry form. Nattor shifted as well, chuckling as he wrapped his arms around her, and smiling in relief as the others of their little pod gathered close. "We can do this," he said to them in a low voice, in a rumble close to his jaguar growl. "We *will* do this, and we will live, selkies no more, skinchangers all."

The child grew up lithe and slim, with long bones and a lightness of foot, things that were not, broadly speaking, of selkie nature. A people born to swim cold seas tended toward a certain density of bone, of muscle; to breadth rather than height, and to a sturdy heaviness on land, none of which Nallu shared at all. She was positively fearless of heights, though every other member of her skinchanged tribe remained wary of them despite their new forms being suited for them, and of more predatory instinct than any of them save Ellu, whose fierceness came, Nattor thought, from the profound urge to protect her child.

Rilla, another of the women, had become pregnant in her jaguar form and remained that way with an unusual stubbornness; it felt wrong, she said, to shift to mortal form while gravid, a thing which Nattor had never heard a selkie woman say. But she was selkie no more, and whatever they had made of themselves, perhaps this was different, too. That Rilla gave birth to a *litter*, to *three* cubs, was *certainly* different; no one in the history of the Old Races had ever had a triple birth, and twins, even among selkie, were vanishingly rare. Rilla was overwhelmed by the very thought; Nallu, at nine or ten years or age, was filled with phlegmatic delight, and aside from the nursing, cared for the cubs with more confidence than their mother showed. She carried them by their scruffs, dropped them from heights and jumped on them, taught them to hunt, guided them silently through the forests until they could walk three paces behind an indigenous hunter without ever being noticed, tussled with them, disciplined them with swats that sent them rolling across the jungle floor, and shared with them a certain feline humor that their parents were never quite able to achieve.

By the time they were half grown, ten or twelve years of age, all of the adults save one, Merro, had taken jaguar form; it had taken that long to acquire flawless pelts, and Merro was the most reluctant, the most fearful, of the selkies to try the change. Nor could he be blamed for it; it had been his own brother who had tried the change first, and failed, and Merro who had felt the obligation to hunt his mad sibling to the earth and slay him. Nattor had gone with him for the hunt, both of them with skin crawling at their napes and flinches overtaking them at every sound in the night, for they knew they were out of their depth hunting in trees and plains, but when they caught the mad one, Merro had forbidden Nattor to make the killing blow, for all that the gesture was meant to spare Merro pain. It wouldn't, he had said; bad enough to live with the responsibility himself, but far worse to have to look on Nattor's face every day and know that Nattor had struck his brother down. Nattor thought now, as he had thought then, that it had been a mistake to agree, but it would have also been a mistake to disagree, so Merro's reluctance to change his skin was the price to be paid, and Nattor could hardly blame him for that.

Nallu brought the pelt back for Merro: flawless beyond compare, for she'd hunted the beast in jaguar form, giving it nothing to fear until she was on top of it, and in human form but with immortal strength she had strangled the beast, so that no part of its hide was broken from the outside, not even an eye, not even the roof of its mouth. She skinned it with a reverence familiar to Nattor from watching the small tribes of local humans, whose appreciation of the lives they took and survived on bordered on holy; if more humans accepted their place in the chain of life so gracefully, the Old Races might not be driven half to extinction and all to hiding. He was proud that Nallu had learned that respect, and prouder still that she went to such trouble for the uncomfortable elder in their pod. *Pride,* Nattor thought: they had not been a pod for a very long time indeed.

It was in Merro to refuse: Nattor saw that in his gaze, but the single remaining selkie was as touched, as honored, by Nallu's gesture as Nattor was, and in the end Merro couldn't bring himself to insult the first skinchanged child of the Old Races. He accepted the pelt, the gift of it, and under the brightness of the moon, for he couldn't bear to try the change in darkness, he underwent the struggle of skinchanging.

It could never be Nallu's fault that it failed, but still, she felt responsible.

She'd heard the stories, of course, of the hard first attempts, of how they hadn't understood the importance of a flawless hide, of how one of them had simply died in the attempt to change her skin, her body twisted and mangled beyond measure. How another, Jessel, had wholly rejected the change, unable to come near completing it; perhaps fear had driven that failure, or perhaps the pelt was just too damaged. Jessel, Nallu knew, had left the group after his failure, unable to contemplate belonging when he could never taken on the shape his brethren had chosen. Perhaps he'd returned to the selkies, where he could at least be among his people, even if they, too, were ultimately dying. And the other two, the two for whom the change had *seemed* to succeed..they were the ones who had to be hunted down, and now Merro was the prey, as well.

His scent was wrong. From the start, his scent was wrong, sick and sweet and thick, like infection. Nallu trembled every time she smelled it, and so did the cubs—more cubs now, because Dennir had bred too, two more babies, and if they were going to breed like this, six children inside of twenty years, they might single-handedly replenish the Old Races themselves—the cubs all shied away from Merro after the change, but the adults didn't, and Nallu, for the first and last time in her life, didn't trust her own instincts, but theirs.

It was hard on him, but it had been hard on all of the adults, and Merro was the most fearful of them, and so that it took days for him to come out of his new jaguar form seemed normal enough. That he stayed in human form the next weeks distressed no one save the children, who—to the amusement of their parents—watched him warily. He had retained his human shape for their entire lives, the seal form being entirely inappropriate for the sweltering jungle; why they should be bothered now befuddled them all except, perhaps, Ellu. Nallu crept to her mother in the dark of the moon, whispering, "Merro isn't right," to her in the velvet depth of the night, and

Ellu gathered her close, wrapped about her like she was a kitten, and breathed, "How not, cub?" in her ear.

She listened, as Nallu whispered her concerns, her distaste at Merro's scent, the way his movements seemed wrong now that he was skinchanged but wore human form. He had grown bolder, it was true; he climbed trees now, a thing he had never done before, and the others thought he embraced the jaguar, even when he didn't wear its shape. He seemed to be more content in the jungle now, but he watched the sky as if he expected something from it, and when Nallu came to the canopy top to visit him, if she did so without warning, he looked at her with a wildness in his eyes.

"Mother," Nallu whispered into Ellu's soft black fur, "he needs to die, before he kills us all."

"We don't kill our own, cub," Ellu murmured in return, but they both knew it to be a lie, and the warm weight of Ellu's head settled on top of Nallu's for a moment. "You're sure?"

"I would bet my skin on it." A more serious oath couldn't be taken; Nallu felt the breath hold in Ellu's chest, and then the pain of it releasing.

"I'll tell Nattor."

"If you do, Merro will hear. If not from Father, then from a whisper on the wind, Mother; you know that. That's why I'm here, in the night, whispering against your skin." Nallu unwound, rising to all fours, and looked down at her mother. "I'll take him away and do what needs to be done. You must take the pride somewhere else, Mother. Anywhere else; it won't matter that he can track you, only that you won't be here in the moment, if he should escape me and return to slay you all."

"You don't know what they're like, Nallu. The moon-bound, you don't know the depths of their madness. You shouldn't go alone."

"Mother," Nallu said gently, "you are fierce, for what you are, but I, I am not like you."

"No," Ellu agreed after a moment. "No, you're not. None of you are, perhaps, you Skinchanged children. I wonder what we've done, with you."

"Found a future," Nallu said, and went to kill a monster.

It was not, could not, be so easy; first there was finding him in the treetops, where he watched the star-filled sky and the creeping moon. It had grown to more than a sliver by the time she found him three nights later, and crawled into nearby branches to purr, "You've become a cat, Merro. Hunting and watching from on high. The pride misses you, when you're in the heights. I've wanted to hunt with you." She put hesitation into her voice, a worry that she didn't feel: "Did I do well with the pelt? I wanted you to like it. To feel strong in it. Do its instincts speak to you?"

"Powerfully." That he answered surprised her; that he spoke so certainly surprised her even more. "So powerfully I hardly dare shift to the new form. The cat is nothing like the seal, little one. We are predators in the sea, it's true, but not such deadly ones. Many things hunt us. Very little hunts a jaguar."

"I have nothing to compare it to, but Mother and Father have told me how strange it was to them, at the beginning. I think Mother has come closer to embracing it, but you feel it more strongly, I think. More naturally?" Nallu stood, stretching herself long on the wide branch. "I know a hunting ground a few days away. Pigs and tapir and deer, and...other prey...lies in wait."

The sharpness of his slit-eyed gaze made her skin shudder, fur ruffling everywhere. "Other prey?"

Nallu turned her gaze on him, calm and cool. "What good is tooth and claw if not employed against the one true enemy the Old Races have?"

A spasm of angry hunger passed over Merro's face, pulling it into cat-like anticipation for all that he still held, fully, his human form. "You would hunt humans?"

"I do hunt humans. Mother and Father would not approve, and so I do it far away, and wash in the vast river, and hunt fish and alligators to take the scent away after, but what child of the Old Races would not, if they could?" She leapt lightly from her sturdy branch to a slimmer one nearly fifteen feet away, claws digging in as it bounced and trembled under her weight, then steadied to let her creep closer to the tree's trunk. She let her voice linger, keeping challenge from it but imbuing it with all the arrogance she could, and the arrogance of a cat was a wonderful thing. "Do not follow, if you do not wish. Only do not tell the others; keep my secret safe, Merro."

She began to climb down, nose first, claws deep in the bark and wood, and heard, before she reached the ground, the sounds of a not-quite-mortal man cascading down the branches and trunk of his own tree. She landed lightly and began to pace away, just slowly enough that she could be caught; within minutes Merro walked at her side, fingers brushing and bunching at the loose fur between her shoulders. "I know the instinct to hunt is weaker in human form," Nallu murmured. "I will keep the pace for you, that you can fight it until it is finally time to give in."

"I didn't know," Merro said, "that any of us would understand me so well."

"I knew that I needed to bring you, of all of us, a pelt," Nallu answered, and they went silent into the night.

They walked for three nights, the moon turning from quarter waxing to bordering full; Merro watched it more and more intensely, and the scent of sickness in him rose until Nallu could barely breathe it, but she kept her mouth shut, refusing to let herself open wide and gulp down the terrible scent, refusing to hack and cough it away. There would be time to spit later, time to cast soil over his foul remains and stalk away from it with her tail upright and her whiskers alert. First there was the hunting ground, and in many aspects, she had not lied.

Swathes of forest had been burned by the humans whose distant high stony pyramids looked down over the land as if their occupants were gods, though they were not even so close to gods as the Old Races were. They were only mortal, strong and capricious and deadly even to their own kind, much less to those who walked in two shapes, but only mortal was enough: they, after all, had conquered the land, made their mark on it in ways that her own people had never considered. Crops grew in the burned fields, maize and manioc and squash, and where the fields had grown for two years or three they now lay fallow, ready to be planted in another year with beans or chilies that would ask different things of the soil, and give back elements to make new crops grow stronger. Nallu had watched them plant in this way for years, had seen how crops weakened or thrived depending on how well they were rotated, and had seen men die for failing to change a field's crops before its output fell.

And because the forest was clear, animals came to hunt and steal human crops and linger curiously at the edges of where fire had visited. There was easier prey than that, too, in the kept flocks of turkeys and the packs of dogs that were a food staple for the mortals, but even they hunted for most of their meat, and Nallu preferred not to risk her own hide by encroaching so closely on their more domesticated meals.

She did not, though, hunt the humans at all. They would have been easy enough, working their fields, carrying water, harvesting crops, and other jaguars—true jaguars, not skinchangers, not Old Races—*did* hunt them, occasionally.

Sometimes this was seen as a portent from the gods, a warning; others it was taken as an affront, and the offending beast was hunted to the death. Nallu couldn't tell what caused one response or the other, and even if she had been minded to hunt humans, that would have stopped her.

Merro, though, hung at the edge of the forest and all but slavered, watching the strong men and women working the fields, and Nallu made herself rumble a laugh as she placed one large paw on his human foot to stay him. He curled his lip, looking down at her, then forced his features back to calmness and retreated into the forest. "Tonight," he said, and Nallu, thinking of the moon's rounding belly, growled an assent. Perhaps it would be wiser to strike now, before the moon change took him, but it seemed unfair.

Unfair and, perhaps, a little dull: she had only heard stories of the moon-shifters, and wanted, selfishly, with cat-like curiosity, to *see* it; to see the madness overtake one of her kind, and to observe the dreadful change, so unlike their own quick and subtle shifts to a second form. She was first among the pride to be born to the jaguar form; she was strong with it, certain with it, and had confidence in her ability to best any half-formed creature born of magic gone wrong. *Wisdom* would have been crushing his throat the very night she led him away from the pride, but in truth, she hoped it could be blamed on the humans. Never mind the necessity of it; it was always easier to accept that humans had killed one of them, rather than one of them turning on their own, no matter how tainted they had become. Nallu prowled farther from the forest's burned edge, leaping upward to catch a high branch; behind her, Merro leapt with nearly the same ease, all the stranger in his human form. They settled into crooks and Ys, Nallu languid in the afternoon heat and Merro more alert, gaze on the unseeable fields, nostrils flaring as he caught the scent of human sweat and flesh. After a while Nallu drowsed, certain she would need her wits about her come moonrise, and too naive to dream how much.

The howl that wakened her was as she'd heard humans describe a panther's shriek: a woman screaming, shrill and sharp and scared. The pride screamed like that from time to time, not as often as a true cat, but this was something different still: jaguars screamed with rage or threat, but this carried pain, as deep and wide as a river.

She came to her feet fully awake, balanced in the crook of her tree, waiting to see if she should fight or flee, though the thinking part of her knew already that she would fight, that the screams came from the last of her pride to change, from Merro, who was foul with magic gone wrong.

He had fallen—fallen, she thought, not left in any controlled manner—to the jungle floor, and writhed there like a living sack of broken bones: they poked and shivered under his skin, breaking and setting, their pops audible even from the height she watched from. She crept downward, gagging on the smell of sickness, and, hunched low, watching from a nearby branch, knew she had been wrong to hesitate in the name of curiosity.

Every member of the Old Races had a human form to complement their natural shape, and the transition between one and the other was quick, painless, awe-inspiring. Air erupted and collapsed when the changes came, the switch was that sudden, but that familiar sound—not so great among the selkies and now the skinchanged jaguars, but vast for dragons—that pop of air was nowhere in evidence as Merro struggled with his change.

There was no transitive state for the Old Races; they were one or the other, human-seeming or alien indeed. Merro shuddered between the two stages: a tail, long and bony but unfurred, burst from his coccyx, fur raced up his spine and spread over his shoulders into a rough mane unlike anything a jaguar sported, but giving nod to the thick hair he wore as a human. His shoulders sharpened, not broadening but gaining a new feline musculature; his head changed shape piece by broken piece, smashing human features together with a cat's, until neither dominated and both looked wild with pain and rage. His nose furred up, short soft cat-like fuzz, and followed around to ears that were wholly jaguar on a mis-shapen head. The fur carried on down his arms, which thickened into long-fingered paws so large a swat from them would break most creatures' necks, and that was before claws erupted from their pads, longer, straighter than any true cat's. His knees stretched and bent, massive paws too elongated for a natural beast making deep impressions on the soft earth as he crouched in a manner all wrong for a cat and too animal for a human, and through it all he screamed in pain and rage.

Nallu watched all of this, and still was unprepared when he came for her.

It happened all at once, the leap from the ground into the trees, and his uncoiled energy sent him far higher than even she could jump. He slammed into her, his weight knocking her from the branches, and they fell a terrible distance, Nallu screaming fear as she fought to whip around and catch the earth with all four feet instead of her spine. She failed: Merro kept her from twisting, and landed on top of her with a triumphant yowl. Pain splintered through her and she shifted to human form without thinking, letting the shift take the damage away.

"Stupid, stupid little girl," Merro snarled, words distorted in his strangely shaped mouth. "Did you think I would believe your sweet stories? Did you think I would go alone into the woods with a killer? Do you think any true selkie could slay his brother, no matter how sick he had become? I nearly slew Jessel, it's true: I laid his throat open that he might bleed, that I might return to your pathetic father with blood on my hands and the scent of death on me, but we caught him under the bright moon, stupid child. What did not kill him could be healed by the shifting, and heal he did, under the strength of the moon. He has been so patient. *So* patient, with only Adiff for company—"

"Adiff," Nallu gasped. "Adiff died—"

Merro sneered. "Jessel never killed him. Only changed him, made him like Jessel. Adiff knew. He understood that he hadn't failed in the change, only that *they* wouldn't understand, the tribe, the pod, the *pride*. So Adiff pretended, he passed it off, and he left, but never far, oh no, never far. Near enough to watch without being scented, near enough to be taken in by Jessel, near enough to come to me when I took the moon-change too. Only poor Hennth died of it, was slain by your *father*, who didn't understand, only feared. But look at me, at us, look at our *strength*, idiot child."

How *she* was the idiot, when *he* was the one who released her, rising up to show the whole of his tormented half-changed shape, she neither understood nor cared. She only moved, shifting blindingly fast in the moment of his vulnerability; no smart prey ever exposed its belly. But of the two of them, only Nallu thought of Merro as prey, and he could not control the shifting in order to save himself by changing from one form to another, when her claws split open first his guts, and then his throat. He fell, too surprised for pain, and she closed her jaws over his bleeding neck, squeezing the life from him. He struggled once, claws arching toward her, but with more violence than she knew she had within her, she placed a paw on his chest and ripped his head from his body, to be certain he could not ever rise again. Quick, easy, almost painless. She hacked blood and turned her back on the body, flipping dirt over it dismissively.

That would have been well enough, then, had Jessel and

Adiff not been hiding in the forest.

Ellu took the pride away, as Nallu had asked. Took them, knowing that Nallu went three days south, six days north and west and north again; took them through rivers and across treetops, into caves where water dripped and rubbed scent away, made them travel in the rain despite their hatred of it, until they had left behind the temples and found humans who lived only in small tribes, with no great cities yet built. She took them, and she told them why, and then she alone returned, in all the same small uncomfortable ways that would allow as little scent to be traced as possible. Twelve days there and back again, with time to rest between; half a moon. If Nallu had not returned, Merro would be at his weakest, as far from the moon-change as he could be, when she found him. And if she could not find him in the dark of this moon, then there would be the next, and the next, and the next, until his taint was wiped from the earth and her daughter, the first born skinchanger, was avenged.

Vengeance was not, perhaps, the Old Races' way. Neither, though, was to cast off what they had been and make themselves into something new; neither was to change skin only at the moon's pull, and to become something neither Old nor new, but a monster, and so Ellu chose vengeance, if she should need it.

Nallu's scent was so strong at the old dens that it had to be purposeful: she had marked it again and again, making certain it would last through the rain, through the wind and through time. Enough time, at least, and even through the *other* scent, familiar and yet impossible: Jessel, long since returned to the oceans. In *his* scent, Ellu could catch the sickness Nallu had spoken of with Merro, and the damage he had taken: blood and viscera mingled with his musk, and all of it fresher than Nallu's scent. She followed them both, prowling stiffly, warily, for many days to the east, and found them doing battle beneath a full moon.

Nallu, in combat, was beautiful to watch: she shifted fluidly between one form and another, healing hurts that Jessel's monstrous bulk could only retain. He was fast, though, impossibly fast, even for one of their kind, and Nallu only held him at a stand-still, neither of them gaining or losing the overall fight. Jessel had reach on Nallu, too; that, and he had twice her lifetime of practice in the moon-changed shape, time enough to learn and embrace its madness.

Ellu crouched low to the ground, her belly against leaves, and edged forward one paw at a time, not even her tail lashing with anticipation. The wind was against her, bringing their scents to her and keeping hers away from them; she only needed a moment's opportunity. It came in a moment of Nallu's weakness; she shifted to scamper away, but in her human form caught a foot on some unkind branch that laid her flat, and Jessel pounced.

So too did Ellu, landing atop both of them with her full weight. Jessel was driven downward, on top of Nallu, whose protesting whimper might have been a howl had she any breath left to make one with. Ellu's paws wrapped around Jessel's chest to hold on as her jaws closed at the back of his neck. Thick neck, heavier and stronger than any normal beast she'd ever hunted, but his scream of rage bought Nallu the moment *she* needed. She flashed back to her jaguar form and struck, opening Jessel's throat and ending his scream. Ellu crunched her jaws tighter, shaking his foul form until the bones cracked, but when she would let go, Nallu hissed a denial and clamped her own jaws onto his shoulder, pulling. They braced themselves against the earth, hauling the monster into pieces, and only when he lay dismembered did Nallu collapse, falling back into her human shape.

A bite leaked at her shoulder, not deep, but unhealed; that

should not have happened. Ellu stepped forward to lick it and received a belt across the cheek for her efforts, as strong a blow as any full-grown cat might give, for all that Nallu lay wheezing in human form. "Don't lick it. It's full of his poison."

Ellu shifted, shaking off the blow, and ended speechless, gazing at the wound. Nallu chuckled dryly, low sound that might have come from her other form, then sat up in the muck of mud and blood to roll the damaged shoulder, wincing. "He had me. You saved me. You're not even supposed to be here."

"Did I also fill you with his sickness?"

Nallu shrugged her other shoulder and glanced at the big moon. "If I were human, yes. They can pass it through biting, though almost none of the inflicted survive. But I have magic in me already, and am born to skinchanging. I suppose we'll see in a month. You'll bind me. If I go mad, you'll slay me."

"I'm your *mother*!"

"And you came after me, so the duty will fall to you." Nallu rose carefully. "I want water to clean this. Salt water, I think. It feels right. We're not more than half a day's walk from the shore." As they walked Nallu told the story of Merro and Adiff, the latter of whom she had slain easily; his sorrow over Merro's death had left him too angry to fight well, and even Jessel had been unable to keep him from running to his death underneath Nallu's claws. "Jessel," she said in a rough and rueful tone, "Jessel was harder. Thank you."

"Thank me if the sickness isn't in you."

"I'll thank you anyway," Nallu said, and they went to the water. Nallu had never seen it before, not the whole of an ocean; Ellu's heart broke to see it, and yet she could do nothing other than laugh when her cat-born daughter curled a lip and touched the rolling surf as though it might be dangerous as a snake. But in time Nallu knelt in it, washing the wound. Ellu helped, and when Nallu retreated to the safety of shore, Ellu struck off into the waves, swimming strongly, in love with the buoyancy and taste of the sea. She returned only reluctantly, when Nallu rose a second time to come into the water herself, scrubbing her shoulder with a mixture of pain and relief. "It hurts, but in a clean way," she said, and Ellu thought that was how returning to the ocean felt to her, too.

The wound had seeped and bled and pulsed unforgivingly as they had walked through the forests toward the sea, but by nightfall the blood seemed clearer, a stronger red, and though Nallu washed it mercilessly several times the next day, and the day after that, it began to show signs of healing. Flesh knit back together, full motion returned, and there came a morning when Nallu groaned and rolled over, stretching once, then shifting to her jaguar form for a more luxurious stretch. Ellu froze, watching her, and after a moment so too did Nallu, before her lips pulled back in a cattish grin. They both looked forward to the filling moon with less fear, the, and on the first night of three no madness rose in Nallu, nor on the second, nor on the third and final night. They waited another month, then a third, before Nallu said, "Jessel believed there were others. He could feel them, he said, in the pull of the moon."

"Others? Other skinchangers?"

"Others who had tried skinchanging and had it go awry. Other skinchanged as well, I imagine; you can't be the only ones who struck out in desperation, looking for another way to survive."

Ellu tilted her head, an ear twitching. "Could we not be? It was so extreme, bordering on madness."

"The survival of a species requires madness." Nallu stood, padding some little distance to stare sightlessly at the sea; she had never, despite Ellu's cajoling, come to love the water the way her mother did. "The pride is safe?" She had asked before; asking now needed no real answer, and neither did she wait for one. "We do not *have* to go back. Not right now."

"You think we should look for others."

Nallu turned her head. "And hunt the moon-changed. That more than the other, I think. Skinchangers can care for themselves, but the moon-changed are dangerous to both us and the humans."

"They're driving us to extinction, Nallu," Ellu murmured, but the reprimand had a smile in it. "Must you save them?"

"They'll drive us even faster if they're certain we're more than tales," Nallu argued, and rolled her shoulders, bones pointing high before relaxing again. "Forget the humans, then. Tell me that the hunt isn't good."

"The hunt is good." Ellu's smile settled more fully, and she rose to meet her daughter on the shore. "Where do we begin?"

"I don't intend to swim across the ocean," Nallu said with a sniff, and so they turned and walked together, to where the land could take them.

ST GEORGE & THE DRAGONS

AT THE HEART OF THE River Seine, a dragon. Spoiling waters, fed on sheep, but in thrall to maidens fair. Daughters, never wives; a treasure trove, until the daughter is the daughter of a king, and a kingdom is bereft.

A saint with sword and cross: a princess saved, and a dragon slain. He is Quirinus, he was Perseus, Marduk, Tahrun and Thor; and his dragons Cetus, Tiamat, Illuyankas and Jormungandr. He has slain dragons for a thousand years, and will slay them a thousand more.

"He is a menace!" Outrage, rumbling like thunder through caverns near a shore. Well enough, that: there was little thunder to be had in this land, and the roar of a dragon's fury might at least be mistaken for heavy seas. Or they could be if the seas were heavy at all, but beyond the cavern mouth they lay serene and calm, cerulean skies reflecting on still waters.

"He is a mortal." Insouciance, uncaring; even boredom. Not at all the desired emotions, when the question at hand is the survival of a species. But the water was very blue, a jewel in itself, and there should have been a way to claim it.

"He has murdered one of us!"

"It happens from time to time." Hardly the right answer:

new outrage rose from some twenty throats. Janx sighed and turned from the view. Mediterranean blue could neither be equaled nor captured, and the beasts at his back were losing patience. "For the third time, will you not take human form to hold this discussion? How do you think they *find* us, these dragonslayers? They listen for storms where the sea is calm, they follow stories to cities of gold, they come to where legend claims virgins are sacrificed to mighty wyrms, and there we are, awaiting them in all our ancient, vulnerable glory. Humanity's guise may be distasteful, but it will also save your lives."

He had made the argument countless times over countless years, and it had fallen on countless deaf ears. He, at least, took his own advice: lanky with red hair cropped close to his skull, and a beard too tidy and sharply pointed to meet the approval of Roman matrons. There were, after all, limits: he couldn't bear the thought of his own fine features hidden behind one of the curly monstrosities worn by the wealthy. But details of fashion aside, with his skin warmed to gold by the sun's caressing touch and jade eyes, Janx was by all immediate appearances human. His brethren knew better; they could sense his dragonly mass, shuffled to some unreachable spot until it was needed. That he chose to wear a human shape did nothing to undermine his presence.

But they, all of them, kept to their serpent forms. It had taken months to find caves large enough to hold them when they would not shift, and even so there was sinuous life to the walls as they moved and made minute way for another. They did not, as a whole, bear each other's presences well; dragons were large, and largely solitary because of it.

Large and greedy, and all the more solitary for *that*. "Virginity," Janx muttered, "is a stupid thing to treasure anyway. It doesn't last, you know."

"Nor do treasure troves." One of the dragons—a young

one, no more than twenty or so feet in length, and nearly as blue as the seas outside—shifted the balance in the caves by releasing his dragon form. Two of the much larger, much older dragons slipped into the space the boy had been using, and one gave Janx a baleful look, as though the extra room to stretch was unwelcome.

"Toka." Janx watched the boy come forward, less graceful than he should have been in human form. His beauty distracted from his awkwardness, though: he had hair so black it glimmered blue, and eyes of heated sapphire. Bold child, all things considered: bold to have come at all, when this was tacitly a meeting of elders, and bolder still to side with Janx, who said, "Thank you," with genuine sincerity. "Thank you for seeing sense."

"Sense? Sense to claim treasure doesn't last?" Biru, as large as Janx himself—perhaps larger—and white as snowfields, with shadows gone to glacier blue beneath his scales—spoke for those who had no intention of seeing Janx's point. He had named Quirinus the dragonslayer a menace, and would gladly flatten the foolish child who dared disagree with him.

Coltish in human form or not, Toka was confident enough to face a dragon at least six times his elder with a shrug nearly as insouciant as Janx might offer. "Scrolls burn, gold melts, virgins die, shells shatter, stones crack. Treasures don't last, dragonlord. But we might be able to if we're careful."

Biru thrust his head forward, dwarfing the boy. White whiskers danced on thin streams of smoke, Toka half-immersed by them, but although he would make no more than a mouthful for the older dragon, he stood his ground. Janx lingered on the idea a moment, wondering what would happen if a dragon in dragon form ate a dragon in human form. Reversion, he expected: all the Old Races reverted to their true forms on dying, and a mouthful of brave infant would be a bellyful not even Biru could digest.

The same thought, perhaps, occurred to Biru. He snapped his attention to Janx, pale blue gaze cold enough to take warmth from the Mediterranean air. "Will you let children argue your cause now?"

"It's possible I should have begun with the children." Janx sat, wrapped arms around a drawn-up knee, and knew Biru loathed his casual air as much as the political stance he'd taken. "They might be more adventuresome and less hidebound. But there are so few of them." The last words were soft, so soft that only one of his own kind might have overheard it. Toka, at only a few centuries old, was a rarity, even for a race that bred slowly. There were a dozen or so more his age, but none younger, and that was unusual again, even for a race that bred slowly. Janx beckoned the boy over, letting Toka sit in his shadow before he addressed the ancient white dragon. "How would you have us win, Biru? Things are different now. There are millions of humans, and some may still worship us as gods or divine creatures, but they have the tools now to kill us."

"Not easily."

Exasperated, Janx curled his lip. "Nothing kills the Old Races easily, but we *can* die. And there are not so many of us—*none* of us, not just we dragons, but the Old Races as a whole—that we can afford to lose ourselves to idiotic confrontations with mortals. There are reasons we agreed to the laws that govern all of us, or have you forgotten, Biru?"

There was fire in those icy blue depths after all: anger flared in Biru's gleaming eyes, and beside Janx, Toka took a soft breath. He was too young by far—by eons—to remember the council that had convened to decide the fate of the Old Races.

There had been so many of them, then. So many wonderful beings, from the female-dominated harpy tribes to the dragons' sea-serpent cousins. Siryns and gargoyles, djinns and dragons, the slow-shuffling yeti and the shore-dwelling selkie.

Even the vampires had come to the table. Of course they had, because Janx was there, and Daisani would never stand for *him* to have a hand in the shaping of a future when Daisani himself did not. They had met at the southern tip of Africa, peoples from all over the land and seas, in what was to be their last great gathering. No one had quite known that then, but neither had they *not* known it: otherwise the shyer and less populous races would never have come. It had taken weeks simply to decide who would sit at the table and speak for each race.

Janx had not been chosen.

It would have rankled, had it been a surprise. But even then—*even*, as if he had not been old, venerable, ancient, by then—even then he was too independent, too unpredictable. Too close with the vampire called Daisani, for all that their relationship was known to be a rivalry. *Daisani* had been chosen, despite all those things. But then, Daisani called himself the master of his kind, and Janx had never known anyone to dispute that, not in all the years they had been together.

Biru, of course, had been chosen in Janx's place. Stauncher, more conservative, perhaps older, but certainly more ferocious in declaiming human strength and extolling dragonly survival. He had agreed to two laws: no war amongst the Old Races, no telling humans what they really were. But he had put forth the third, and argued for it passionately.

No interbreeding. Not with other Old Races—a dangerous prospect at best, as the half-breed children were new creatures entirely rather than half of one parent and half of the other—and not, most especially, with humans. Purity at all costs.

Even if that cost was extinction.

No wonder, Janx thought sourly. No wonder Biru was so fond of virgins. Purity at all costs. And tender meat, perhaps, but cattle were more filling and didn't scream or argue against their fate. "There have never been enough of us to rival them," he said on a sigh. "There are fewer of us now. We can't win. Playing at being them is our only choice for survival."

"There is sleep." Rabn, another ancient, whose scales seemed dyed by the very spices she treasured. It was said she slept in a bed of saffron, and that she had done so since the last great meeting of dragons. It seemed likely.

And sleep *was* an option, was always an option, but Janx's nose wrinkled with distaste. Still, he liked Rabn more than he liked Biru—he liked swimming more than he liked Biru, for that matter—and so he tempered his response with politeness. "Even if a council decided we should all sleep, there would be no way to enforce it."

Biru sneered, expression all in his voice; dragonly faces were not meant for such displays. "Nor is there any way to enforce us keeping to a guise of humanity."

"Tell that to Quirinus."

Toka, ill-advisedly, laughed. Biru snapped forward, snake-like strike to assuage his dignity.

There was never, Janx reflected later, any real danger. Not to an infant. Not from Biru, who, for all the poor choices he had made, was truly determined to see his race survive. Not, in truth, from any one dragon to another, because as a whole they took the laws of their kind seriously. No war amongst the Old Races: it was engraved in the gargoyle memories, written in stone as literally as could be.

In the moment, though, there was no consideration for Toka's realistic fate. In the moment, if Janx was to be completely honest—which, to be fair, he rarely was—in the moment, Toka's safety was of monumentally little importance to him. It was the challenge that he responded to: the boy had taken Janx's side, and deserved protection for that bravery. Even that, though, was posturing. Janx had disliked Biru for longer than either of them could remember, and that, *that* was why he broke his own habitual rule, and transformed.

Toka no doubt took more damage from Janx's transformation than he would have suffered at Biru's whim. Sitting so close to Janx, he was knocked aside by the concussion of mass returning, by the sudden excess of spitting red dragon face to face, nose to nose, flame to flame, with a white behemoth every bit as large as he. The blast of transformation knocked Toka a visible distance across the caves, until his slim human form crashed into Rabn and fell to the ground.

Extraordinarily, every other dragon in the cave slammed into human form, giving the two ancient dragonlords room to fight. Winding, writhing, hissing, they circled one another in the space allowed. Tight circles, red yang and white yin, because even with the others in mortal form, the caves lacked the size necessary for freedom of movement. That was just as well: transforming had been foolish, had thrown down a challenge, and there was no real way to win. They would never fight to the death, and fighting to defeat would humiliate Biru—because Janx never supposed *he* might lose—and humiliation would be more costly than death. Biru might, through slow patient persuasion, come to see sense, but not if he fought Janx and lost. It would make him not just a rival, but an enemy, for all time.

And time was very long indeed, for dragons. Janx bared his teeth, smoke huffing between them, then grim with self-denial, forced himself back to mortal shape.

Biru went still, a river of frozen ice at the heart of a cave. A solitary dragon winding around a tall red-haired man, and surrounded on all sides by dragons who could hardly be distinguished from humanity. Hardly: like Janx, their colors were saturated, Rabn's hair as orange as her hide, and her skin silt brown. Each of them met Biru's angry gaze, but none of them returned to their dragonly mass. It was not a vote for

Janx's path in the way Toka's transformation had been. Instead it was a demand for speech instead of sparring, and Biru, recognizing that, snarled aggravation and finally transformed.

He was startling, in human form. Not an albino; his pale eyes remained blue, not tinted pink, but the whiteness of him was unrelenting. Snowy hair, not so much worn long as unbothered with, and wrinkled skin that might have been Nordic mountains, all white peaks and valleys. Hawked nose, cragged cheeks, long fingers with no suggestion of warm blood running beneath the nails. His skinny frame should have looked fragile and instead warned of a terrible, unrelenting strength. Men made kings of those like Biru, and once, they had made gods of him.

For a wrenching moment Janx's frustration with Biru's determined blindness disappeared. Unforgiving regret rose in its place, a regret for what had to be. No wonder Biru had no use for pandering to humanity, when his presence said so clearly that he could rule it. No wonder Janx was such a thorn to him: a dragon who most often showed a playful face, who danced and laughed with humans instead of cowing them.

He bowed, more than just dipping his head, and meant it with respect. Biru would never see it that way: he would see mockery and triumph if he saw anything at all, but for a rare occasion the approbation was sincere. When he straightened, though, Janx made sure it was with a smile, because it would never do for Biru to imagine Janx meant the respect too deeply. Rue, gratitude, a hurry to move on; those were the emotions in the smile, and Janx spoke before anyone had time to take offense. "Thank goodness. We would have fished the sea dry to feed us all as we were."

Comical expressions of horror swept every one of his brethrens' faces, even youthful Toka as he stood and dusted himself off. Not one of them could imagine a desperation of hunger that would drive them to *fishing*: virgins, no doubt, were more readily available. Janx cast a look of amusement at his own feet, then arched his eyebrows as he met Biru's pale gaze. "What," he asked again, "would you have us do?"

"Gather." Biru's human voice was deeper than expected from his frail-seeming body. "Gather, and as one lay waste until the lands and skies are ours again."

"Under your command." A question without mockery, though Biru eyed Janx a long hard moment before nodding. Janx sighed and withdrew to a rocky outcrop where he could sit. "And when you say as one, you mean we dragons, or all of us?"

Surprise in the white dragon's gaze, and that was part of the trouble. He hadn't considered gathering all the Old Races, only his own people. He lacked the vision to do the job right, and without vision, only desolation lay before them. "They would come to you," Janx said idly. "As many of our people, at least, who could be called to a single banner at all, would come to you. You hold that place among us."

Biru's surprise faded into suspicion, but Janx spread his hands. "You stood for us at the last council. You're respected. I may disagree with you, but I can see the regard you're held in. I'm arrogant, Biru, not a fool."

That, at least, cracked Biru's stoicism. His, and others: a hiss of laughter ran around the caves, easing tension. Toka exhaled, soft sound of relief, but that was an emotion Janx would never allow himself. Not that he needed to; fear of what might happen during a council of wyrms had never been a concern of his. It was beyond the caves in the world outside that he saw danger. "There are too many of them," he said quietly. "You must know that."

"I cannot accept it." Stark words from a stark being, and a rumble of agreement from more than half a dozen chests. Rabn, though, shook her orange hair and took a single step closer to Janx. Emboldened, others did as well: two more females and a violet-eyed male whose interest was clearly more in the females than in Janx's position. It didn't matter, so long as he chose a side. A fourth female, younger than the others, stood indecisive a moment, then took quick strides toward Janx. Fina, her name was; Fina, whose black hair ran to the other side of the spectrum from Toka's, and had red highlights instead of blue.

That made all the females, then, and of the four who had come to the council, three had borne eggs. Young Fina had not, but she might wish to someday, and a war against humanity would reduce her choices for a mate. They would be thinking that way, Janx suspected, rather than coming to his side because of his charm and wit. They were no less likely or eager to fight—or to eat virgins—but this slight handful of them, at least, saw sense in remaining hidden.

Biru, though, had more supporters. The rest of twenty dragons stood with him, though one or two looked uncertain as all the females joined Janx. Too late, though; lines were drawn, and Biru's resonant voice was soft. "We will have war."

A flight of dragons marred the sky. Dozens, more than Janx had ever seen at once in his life, and those years were far too many to count. It took so much anger to bring them together. So much fear. They had come from so far, from the ring of fire that birthed them all and from the lonely stretches they had individually flown to, each settling in their own territory. But they were together now, united in a common cause against mankind.

It had taken years simply to find them all: the stupid youth who had set it all off had long since died, and been venerated as a dragonslayer. Biru had been unswayed by the detail; there would be others who came for their people, a fact which seemed incontrovertible as the arrowhead of vast beasts made their way across the sky. War on the dwindling Roman empire; that, and only that, would satisfy their anger. Biru himself was visible, a long white cloud against the blue sky. Janx thought of transforming and flinging himself skyward, to make his argument one last time, but stayed the impulse. Laws or no laws, so many of them against one of him might turn out badly for him. Besides, the lake was blue, almost a jewel in itself, and the color would last far too little time if Biru's war came here. Better to enjoy it before it was poisoned or stained with blood.

"What are they?"

The girl at his elbow was not to Janx's taste: too slim, too wide-eyed, too *young*, though nearly everyone was young in comparison. But there was something in her question, a hitch of wonder and hope, that mortals all too rarely voiced when the Old Races were about, and so he answered rather more honestly than Biru might have wanted: "Dragons."

She laughed uncertainly. "There are no dragons. And if there were, the stories say dragonslayers have killed them all."

"Then they must be very large geese."

"Colorful, too." Toka joined them, and the girl giggled as she closed the distance between herself and the youthful dragon. Sabra, that was her name; it fell out of Janx's head as soon as he remembered it, each time. He didn't belong here on the shores of Lake Seline; it was Toka's territory, and the girl his prize. But Toka had caught sight of him winging south, away from Biru's advance, and had invited him to visit a while. Undragonly behavior, that, but the boy was young and Janx had, after all, had some hope of reforming the young. He could hardly complain if he'd succeeded.

"One has broken away." Thin tension came into Toka's voice and Janx glanced skyward again.

"It's the lake. The color is...enviable. I'm not surprised someone couldn't resist."

"This territory is *mine*."

Sabra laughed again, this time with a note of warning. "Surely you mean it's my father's, Toka."

It had been nearly two decades since Janx had felt a flash of sympathy for Biru's disgust at considering a mortal-style existence. He felt that same impulse now, watching Toka's lip curl and smooth so quickly the moment disdain was barely notable. The boy said, "Of course," and Sabra smiled, peace restored.

Restored within her heart, at least. Resentment still lingered around Toka's sapphire eyes, tightening the skin there. By human standards the land, the lake, the kingdom, was held by Selinus, Sabra's father, but Toka had claimed it long before Selinus had come to the throne. The whim of a passing man to name a country his own would have meant nothing, had his daughter not been lovely.

Raven-haired, doe-eyed, still too slim for Janx's tastes, but appealing in Toka's eyes. He had become a man for her, his trove of wealth making him an appealing mate, were it not for the secret he kept. And he would not keep it a moment longer, if the great monster beating down from the sky thought to make this land its own.

Janx put a hand on Toka's shoulder, staying him. "Don't be hasty."

"He intrudes on—" Toka broke off, glanced at Sabra, and finished, "On occupied territory."

"And right now he has no idea it's occupied," Janx pointed out. "Nor will he if you...remain calm."

Toka bristled, all youthful outrage. He understood clearly enough; dragons sensed each other's transformations, not their simple presence. Still, the impulse was to change and protect, not to let calmness prevail. "And allow him to take—Selinus's—land?"

"It is a dragon." Sabra sounded cold, all life lost from her words. The beast—sable and cobalt in color, but not one Janx knew by name—landed on the lake's far side, large enough to be clearly visible even at the distance. Sinuous, with long wings tucked against its sides, it was a wyrm indeed, and dipped its head to drink from the lake. "The river feeds our lake there," Sabra went on, voice smaller with each word. "It will poison us, as they do in the tales."

"That's very likely," Janx agreed. Toka bristled again, all but hissing, and Janx tightened his hand on the youth's shoulder.

"My people will die." Just a whisper from the girl, who turned to look at Janx as she spoke. He nodded, and color drained from her face, but her voice strengthened. "The tales say dragons prize virginity."

"Some do." A ludicrous answer by all reasonable standards, but Sabra nodded as well, then clutched Toka's hand before breaking away, slim shoulders straightening.

"Then I will bargain with it. I will bring it a virgin princess, and in exchange for that gift I will ask it to leave this place in peace. Will it agree?"

Absurd fondness for a girl he didn't even like bloomed in Janx's chest. "It might."

Sabra nodded again, swallowed hard, and stepped off the pavilion overlooking the lake. "Do not tell my father where I've gone. Not until after. Not until it's too late to stop me."

"Sabra—!" Toka finally found his voice and sprang after the girl, only to come up short as she turned, an imperious hand lifted.

"You will not stop me either, Toka. You should know that I love you, but I love my people more. I could do nothing less and still hold my head high." She walked away a second time, leaving Toka stunned and silent at Janx's side.

"That," Janx said after a long moment, "is a fine young woman, Toka. It would be a pity for her to get eaten."

"I thought you didn't like her." Such a faint, mortal protest. The weak objection of a child to its elder when there was nothing else to say.

Janx smiled. "That was two minutes ago. Things have changed since then. Stop," he said more sharply, and for the third time put a hand on Toka's shoulder to keep him from chasing after Sabra. "You won't save her. That cobalt monster will snap you in two, and eat her for dessert."

"Our laws will protect me." Uncertainty in the boy's voice as the dragon across the lake kicked up a spray of water, then settled deeply into the earth. "I cannot leave her to die."

"No, and I suppose neither can I. Not now. Damn Biru, anyway." Janx glanced to the sky, to the phalanx of dragons winging their way toward the horizon. "This will end badly, all of it. Not just today but every day until this nonsense has stopped. Where do they think dragonslayers *come* from," he demanded again, uselessly, then put the thought aside. "There'll be knights and warriors on the road, following Biru's flight. I'll fetch one, and we'll try to save the girl."

"How? We can hardly fight to the death, and she's so fragile."

"Let me worry about that. Stay here. I'll send Sabra back to you, and you'll see me no more."

Janx himself would not have obeyed the command, but Toka did, diminishing in the distance as Janx strode away from palatial grounds to the nearest road. People streamed along it in both directions, the wiser ones heading away from the dragon flight, the less wise, toward it. Romans and Syrians alike, north and south alike, spreading color everywhere: rich shades of wealth and drab tones of poverty, but the poor were of no use to Janx. That was true enough to be written down, he thought, then snapped his fingers irritably at a northern-bound rider who wore a soldier's garb and carried a helm that looked like it had seen war. "You. Do you have a name?"

The man drew up, expression stern with slight offense. "That is no way to speak to a Tribunus. I could have you crucified. Who are you?"

Janx waved threat and question alike aside with a *ffft* of disinterest. "Do you have a name? Have you any fighting experience to go along with that sword and helm?"

Tension spilled over the man's face, but pride was stronger than insult. Posture improving—and it had been excellent to begin with—he said, "I am Geōrgios, and I have been a guard at Nicomedia, sir. I am no stranger to war."

"Geōrgios. Good. You're handsome enough, Geōrgios. Strong nose, a lot of hair, good skin. You're Syrian yourself, aren't you? Your coloring says so. Let me see your teeth."

Geōrgios bared his teeth before he thought, then flushed with angry color and pressed his elbow against his short sword's hilt. Janx clicked his tongue, ignoring the new threat as easily as the last, then nodded. "You'll do. Come with me, Geōrgios. I'm going to make you immortal."

They were impossibly large, dragons. Thirty paces in length, this cobalt-sheened beast, and its body blocked the river with coils to spare. Thin wings, long with slim, delicate-looking fingers holding membranes apart, looked too fragile to bear the animal into the air, though he'd seen it fly himself. Whiskers thick as river reeds quivered around its face, testing the air. Short and powerful legs, glittering claws washed in the river water. A watchful creature, ready for his enemies. Ready, too, to sup on the small woman who had so bravely come to bargain. She had lost the bargain already: a chain held her ankle, and the dragon held the chain's other end.

There was no purpose in words, only in action. He knew where to strike, which the dragon never expected. Knew to be fearless and rush it headlong, even through the roar of fire that heated his armor. Knew to ignore the metal sticking to his skin, and to race up the beast's nose: it was so large he could do that, a quick step between flared nostrils and then a sword held high, a sword falling, a sword plunged into the black-as-night eye that stared up at him in astonishment.

One blow, one hot splash of blood. Screams unlike anything men could make. A vast body, splashing in the river, thrashing, dying. Poison blood spilling forth, but it would dilute, and no harm would come to Sabra's people. *She* was yanked side to side as the dragon died, even fell deep into the water, but she found her way free again and never, ever screamed. Few women would be able to remain silent. Few men, for that matter; the death of a dragon was not an easy thing to see. This was one to watch now; there would be others. A flight of dragons in the sky promised that. They would have war, until the last of those willing to fight had died.

As this one was now dead. The dragonslayer threw off his helm and wiped sweat from short, matted red hair. Stared at the blood and the offal and the elongated body that seemed so much smaller in death, and not for the first time, whispered, "*Damn* you, Biru. Damn you."

He struck Sabra's chains away, set her free, then turned to the more important duty of transforming. Becoming the enormous red winged lizard that was his true form, and taking the nameless dragon's body away. Far away, to the heat of volcanoes, where it would return to the fire it had been born from. He had done this ugly duty before, and would do it again, for he is Geōrgios the Saint, he was Quirinus, Perseus, Marduk, Tahrun and Thor; and he had slain foolish dragons for a thousand years, and would slay them for a thousand more.

THE DEATH OF HIM

SHE WAS HUMAN, AND SHE would be the death of him.

That, of course, was true as a rule. Humans poisoned the seas, overfished the waters, bore children until the land couldn't feed them, and bred more still after that. Their numbers increased visibly by the year, while even the most populous of the Old Races bred slowly. Humans would be the death of them all, sooner or later.

But Róisín would be the death of him sooner, for she lay beside Eoin under the high late summer sun, and took his hand and put it on her belly and whispered, "Da," beneath his ear.

Blood rushed Eoin's head and made his hand cold against her stomach, but the fool's grin spreading across his face belied the shocking lurch of his heart. "You're sure," he breathed back, and was rewarded with a nod.

"Since Beltaine," she murmured, before her own grin split her features. "Since May Day, sure as night. My blood should be on me now and it's not come twice. Will we be handfasted at midsummer, Eoin? Will ye be your babby's da?"

He said, "I will," without hesitation, then rolled on his back to stare at the starless sky. "I will if you'll have me, Róisín, but there are things I should have told you."

She pushed up on her elbow, grin faded to a smile,

eyebrow raised in warning. "You'll not tell me you've a wife and children already."

"No. That would be...easier. Come down to the water with me, Róisín. Come down to the water so we can talk." Eoin stood, heart pounding, and offered her his hands.

She took them, eyebrows still vocal: lifted in question now, but her smile stayed in place. "Last time you brought me to the water, it wasn't to talk."

It wasn't, of course, and it hadn't been, because graceful as his people were on land, it was nothing to their ease in the water. He might have seduced most women on land, but Róisín had caught his eye with her dark brown eyes and deep red hair, and he'd wanted, of all things, to be sure of her. So he'd taken her to the sea, to the element he'd been born in, and she, who could not swim, had trusted his arms until she could entrust his heart.

She came again willingly enough, down to the quiet bay where small boats were tied to large trees, and laughed when he stripped away his white wool shirt and dropped his brown wool pants. "I thought it was talking you had in mind."

"It is," he said, "and it isn't. Róisín, sit, and be calm if you can. This is a thing I should have told you—shown you—before, but I..."

Expressive eyebrows rose again and he sighed, taking a bristling fur from beneath the roots of one of the ancient trees. "But I fell in love," he said, mostly to the fur, and made himself look back at the girl sitting curiously on the sand. "Róisín, will you believe this, that I love you, despite all the strangenesses that may come to pass?"

She tilted her head, pretty and thoughtful. There was no curl to her hair, but unbound from its braid it fell in waves past her elbows, and she twisted a strand around a finger as she replied. "Sure and let me think. It's most of a year you've come courting. Since Midsummer last, and you bearing gifts each time you've come. And you're from so far down the coast as Galway town. No man comes such distance without reason, Eoin. I'd hope it's love, for me da's got no money or land for you to wed." Humor slipped away. "You're worrying me, Eoin."

"If worried is all you remain, we'll be well." Fur gathered in his arms, he went to the water's edge. Róisín stood again as he took his distance from her, and this time he didn't ask her to sit, only said, "Your people have seen us often enough to have stories of us, Róisín. You'll know what I am in the moment of change."

She began, "Change?" and he slipped his secret over his shoulders.

Rough fur slithered and wriggled against his skin, fitting into place, changing the body that lay beneath from man to beast. It was painless, instantaneous, extraordinary: colors changed, dimming until what human eyes knew as blue and green were dominant, all-important water shades that they were. His eyes were adapted for low-light hunting beneath the sea; it was easy for him to see Róisín's shock in the island twilight. Her hands were pushed against her mouth, eyes large and dark above them, and acute hearing caught the high soft sound of alarm stifled behind her hands. She took quick steps backward, and he did not follow. Couldn't, not easily: seals were not meant to travel on land, though they were all but unchallenged in water. At least in Irish waters, where the toothed whales rarely swam.

She stopped when sand turned to rock beneath her feet. Stopped, and that was a good sign. Eoin remained still, animal heart chasing at too fast a pace, and when Róisín took a single step forward again, he nearly dropped in relief.

A single step, then half a dozen more, though she stopped a good ten feet away. He was tall in human form, as tall as his seal body was long, but his mass was considerably greater in the shape he'd been born to: twenty stone as a seal, to perhaps fourteen as a man. No one knew where the size went, when the change came on them; that was part of their magic, the magic of all the Old Races. His people were the least of it: dragons of impossible size were no larger than men, in their mortal forms. Still, a full-grown seal could kill a man with little effort, and Róisín was wise to keep her distance.

She knelt in the sand, slow incremental drop, and finally took her hands from her mouth and whispered, "Selkie."

Then, only then, did Eoin dare transform back. Inside an instant, from seal to man huddled within a seal's skin, and rue bubbling up within him. "Aye, selkie. It's not from Galway I've come."

To his astonishment, Róisín laughed, then knotted her fingers against her mouth again. "My clan lives on the islands," he said into her silence. "Dozens of us, as large a clan of Old Races as might be found."

"How can we not *know?*" The question burst out from behind her hands and was silenced again. Her knuckles would be raw from the chewing, if he couldn't answer everything quickly enough.

"You do know. Enough to name me," and there was a truth his people didn't like to consider: that they had taken on the name humans had given them. Even amongst themselves, they were the selkie, just as their desert enemies were human-named djinn. "Enough to tell tales, even if they're at most half-believed. It's against our laws to tell you about ourselves, Róisín. We are few, and you are so many."

"What happens? What happens if you tell?"

Eoin shrugged within his seal skin. "Exile. It's not our way to kill our own."

"Then you could come to me. Live with me and the babe—" Róisín went white and put her hands over her belly, another question in the action.

"I don't know," Eoin answered softly. "It happens from

time to time that one of us loves one of you, and leaves the clan, but children...children are forbidden, too."

"What would they do? What will it *be?*"

Eoin shook his head once, not liking the answer to the first. Their laws were against killing one of their own. They had no edicts about the lives of humans. As for the second, he murmured, "Half of us, half of you. Perhaps the blood would run true. I don't know."

Róisín dropped her hands from her mouth and stared at him a long while before speaking so quietly he knew instantly it hid rage. "So I've nowhere to go, then. I cannot come to your home, nor can I go back to mine. What would I tell me ma when I birthed a *seal?*"

"You'll birth a human babe," Eoin said. "This, at least, I'm sure of. We have to leave the water sometimes, and our women have given birth on land in mortal form. They've a harder time of it than they would in the water, but it's happened."

Blank curiosity filled Róisín's round features. "What happens to the children?"

A smile quirked Eoin's mouth. "They turn seal the first time they're washed. Not just wiped clean of the birthing fluids, but submerged. From then they can peel their skins away," he said, shrugging his, "and change at will. We grow up faster than your kind do."

"And die younger," Róisín said, but Eoin shook his head.

"No. We live...a long time. Sickness takes us sometimes, but more often violence. The Old Races are hard to kill."

Her gaze was hard again, hard and dangerous, though there was little an unarmed human might do to damage him. Little save break his heart, at least, but that had always been a risk, and was not, in the moment, Róisín's concern: "*How* long?"

He shrugged a second time, resigned. "Forever. We don't age, and we breed rarely." He held his breath, let it go, and whispered "I am the third youngest of my clan, and I've seen some hundred thousand tides."

The number was too large, meaningless to her, and she only waited until he had made sense of the tides and years himself and offered, "A hundred and thirty turns of the season, perhaps?"

Even that was too much, though it was easier than the count of tides. Róisín looked at him wordlessly, taking it in, and finally said, "My grandfather died an old man with seventy winters, Eoin. An *old* man."

"I know."

To his surprise, she nodded. Then she stepped back, leaving the mark of her weight in the sand, and pointed at the sea. "I'd see you go, and I'd ask that you don't come back to my home."

"Will I look for you here?" he asked softly.

Róisín's mouth twisted. "In sixty tides," she said, and pointed again at the sea.

Eoin slipped his skin back on, and if a seal stopped in the low choppy waves to watch her go, she did not see it, for her back was turned and her stride home certain.

"Is she worth it, Eoin?" A dark seal shape broke surface and became a girl, her hair slicked back with water. "You've been here every night for thirty. How can she be worth it?"

He lay on a flat rock just at the water's surface, moving only when surging tide lifted him. Megan folded her arms on the stone, holding herself in place. From shore she would seem a seal's head, poked above the water, and Eoin little more than that, though he transformed to mortal form as well. They had language as selkies, but the clicks and chatters carried better under water. In the open air it was as easy to talk as humans, though a good deal colder. Still, they could stay in the water far longer than any human might survive. His child, if Róisín had kept it, would have that gift as well, even if the transformation was beyond its reach.

"Yes," he said to the seal girl, but without looking at her. "Come out of the water, Megan, if you're going to scold me. She's worth it, yes. She's worth everything. She carries my child."

Megan came out of the water, seal-dark eyes were black with worry. Her hair was a pelt in itself, shining and sticking to her shoulders and spine, and she had the fine lithe body of a woman born to swim. They were age-mates, she and Eoin, and she the daughter of a clan lord, which she reminded him of, as if he could forget: "You watch your tongue, Eoin. That's near to treason, and me da—"

"Would be well pleased to send me away," Eoin said dryly. It was only half truth: no tribe of the Old Races was eager to lose its young, but Eoin spent too much time with humans to make any of his clan comfortable. "It's happened before, you know. We leave the clan for them, from time to time."

"Tsha!" Megan silenced him with a gesture, glancing around as if someone might have overheard the words. "It's nothing to be proud of."

Eoin shrugged. "We live alongside them. We fish the same waters, till the same earth, sleep beneath the same stars and sing the same songs. Why should we not love them when love comes along?"

"We are *Old Races,* Eoin."

"And we're dying."

Megan's teeth snapped together, sharp as a seal claiming a catch. "How dare you say such things."

"Because you and I and Amber, are the youngest in the clan, and even Amber's seen a hundred turns of the seasons. We may not die easily, Megan, but we'll still die out if no young are born."

"They'll be born again." She flattened her hands over her

belly, though, and glanced away.

Eoin's heart twisted. They'd lain together—and both of them with others, as well—often enough that kits should have come of it. Others, older, had left their clan to join new ones, and sent others back to join theirs, all in hopes of waking the spark of life that would bring children to the tribes. Megan *should* have caught, and Eoin should have been a father half a dozen times over, but almost the only children they'd ever seen had been human.

"If she's kept it," Eoin whispered, "I'll break every law we hold dear, and bring her and the baby among us. It's idiocy to do otherwise, when we *know* we can breed with them."

"They'll kill her, Eoin."

"Me first."

Megan fell into shocked silence and lapping waves filled it up, ceaseless, comforting, uncaring. "Then why bring her to us," she finally said. "Why not go to her people, and risk less?"

"Because *her* people aren't dying. If she'd come to us, Megan, if the others saw a *child*, a child of our blood—"

"Half our blood."

"A child who could make the change—"

"They'd kill it."

"Would they?" Eoin lifted his head, not caring if from shore he might be seen as a man. "Would they, Megan? Would *you*?"

He saw it in her face, in the naked sorrow illuminated by a falling sun. She tried to hide it, tried to offer some hesitation, but couldn't even make herself speak the lie. She only shook her head no after a moment, then clenched her fist as though trying to take back a confession. "But others would," she said without certainty. "My father."

"Would he, if you brought him a grandchild and wouldn't say who the father was?"

Pure astonishment wiped all other expression from

Megan's face. Astonishment, then hope, then hope betrayed. "If the child couldn't make the change..."

"We don't know, though." Eoin looked again toward shore, then back at Megan. "We know what happens when one of us breeds with another of the Old Races, but if we mate with humans, who knows?"

"Stay away," Megan whispered suddenly, sharp and full of desperation. "Stay away with your human, Eoin. Stay away until the baby's born and *learn*. Find out if the blood breeds true. Then tell me, and if it does..."

Anticipation seized Eoin's breath, but Megan said, "She's here," and slipped back into the water. Eoin turned away, knowing she wouldn't surface within eyesight, and saw Róisín's slim figure at the break between stone and sand. Waiting, hands tense by her sides, and did not relax until Eoin strode out of the sea a man. Then her shoulders fell. "You came."

"I thought it less likely you would than I. I've—" He broke off, but Róisín's mouth curved.

"You've been here every night, haven't ye? The fishermen have spoken of it, a seal waiting on the sea like a lover forlorn. I said a month, Eoin."

"I didn't want to miss you."

Her smile broadened and she took a step forward. "It's glad of it I am. Hearing the story of the seal helped me to decide."

He didn't move. Couldn't, he thought, not unless his life—or Róisín's—depended on it. "And what did you decide?"

"That there are no houses on the selkie islands," Róisín said pragmatically, "and I can't be living in the sea."

Eoin's jaw clicked shut, then opened again to release a startled laugh. "So you can't. I hadn't thought of it, Róisín. I hadn't thought of—"

Hadn't thought, he saw now, of what it might truly *mean* to pair his life with hers, or to pair his people with hers. They were wild, the selkie, wild in a way that others of the Old Races were not. The other sea creatures, the vast serpents who were cousins to dragons, lived solitary lives, and the siryns whose shapes were half-man at all times, made cities and villages beneath the waves. Not so the selkie, who lived in seal pods on the sea-broken stones of barren islands. To do less was to default to the human form, as did the otherwise-ethereal djinn, and which the selkie had long disdained them for.

Eoin would have his people become more like the djinn, and thought that might be the worst of the sticking points, even beyond the purity of bloodlines. "I'll build you a house," he offered, "halfway between sea and sky, and in time it will become the heart of our peoples' first village."

"Build it," she said, "and I'll come to your hearth, and my brothers will bring us grain from their fields to fill our bellies until you've the way of the land about you."

Dismay struck so hard Eoin felt his expression go comical, even before Róisín laughed. "I'll fish for us all, your brothers and mam and da," he blurted, "but don't ask me to farm, Róisín, or we're sure to starve before the winter is out."

"And how will a man with no skill for the land build me a house, I ask?" Róisín came to him, her hands extended, and squeezed his own when he took them. "That pelt of yours, Eoin, is it warm?"

"Warm enough to keep the water's chill away."

"Then share it with me, and come morning we'll find our spot of land. My brothers," she said drolly, "can teach you to build a house." And later, nestled in his arms, in the warmth of a seal skin that would never transform her, she murmured, "Your own people, Eoin, what do they say? Are you exiled forever?"

"No," he answered, knowing it might be a lie and yet somehow certain of it, "No. Not forever."

Seals, with their single pups and small sleek heads, had an easier time of birthing than humans did. Róisín's mother was there, thank the tides, and two aunties and half a dozen daughters and Eoin himself, stuck into the corner of the small house he'd learned to build. They chattered and laughed among themselves, breaking only when Róisín's bellows drowned them out, then began again, while Eoin sat agog in the corner and was as glad to not be much needed. The cursing and sweating and hobbling about with pain, crouching into a birthing squat and swearing and standing up again, had been going on for hours, for most of a day, and the best any of the aunties and daughters could offer was, "The first is usually hardest," until Eoin himself could take it no more. He elbowed through the women to reach Róisín's side, there to murmur, "Do you want them all here, Róisín? My people birth more...privately." It was the wrong word; seals had little concept of privacy. But they would and did retreat to give birth, not relying on a dozen others to help them.

Róisín, who was human, managed a short laugh and blew a strand of sweat-damp red hair away with a puff of breath. "Me ma and aunties would be enough, but you know what it is I want, Eoin? Water," she said, mystified, before he could ask. "A bath of warm water to dunk myself in and push until the baby comes, but that would drown the babe, would it not?"

"They're born in a sack of water already," Eoin said. "I don't know why two minutes longer would drown them when their birthing sac didn't. But the water, Róisín, if the blood breeds true..." His voice dropped with the warning, and his wife gasped another laugh around a ripple of pain.

"It's bred true, I'm sure of it, and that's why I want the water so."

"I'll get it for you," Eoin said with determination, "if you can tell me how to get all these women away."

"Out, so!" Róisín's bellow bounced off the little house's stone walls. "Out, all of ye's! The air's too thick to breathe and it's dying for a breath I am! Out, and come back when the birthing's done!"

In two minutes they were gone, all of them save Mairéad, Róisín's mother, and she herself stood arms akimbo and gave them both a withering glare. "I've never heard such madness as a bath for a birthing woman. Don't look at me so, I heard ye's clear enough."

"My people do it all the time," Eoin said, which was not untrue. They would take shallow water or shore, whichever seemed safer in the moment, and the pups were no worse the wear for either birthing spot. Surely a human infant would be safe as well. "Have we anything deep enough for Róisín to squat in?"

"A cow's trough at home," Mairéad said dourly, and spluttered outrage when Róisín said, "Get it." But she went, and Róisín sagged into Eoin's arms a moment before sighing and whispering, "Get me to the sea, then, I'll freeze me arse but I'm not waiting for her to go to the village and back again. The aunties and all will have gone with her, it'll be only the two of us and the babe."

Her shout had cleared the room. Eoin thought it wisest not to argue with a woman who could do that, and scooped her into his arms to bring her to the shore.

Seals awaited them. Half a dozen or more, barely in the water when they approached, though all but one scampered into the bay's safety. Megan remained, her pattern of faint spots distinctive to Eoin's eye, and he kissed Róisín's hair reassuringly as he waded into the water and toward Megan. "A friend," he murmured. "As good a midwife as you could ask for."

Róisín huffed acceptance, then shrieked as Eoin lowered her into the water. "Brigid's tits but it's cold! Oh holy *mistress* but I'll be frozen through and through!" Complaints turned to a growl that rose from her depths, and Eoin caught her beneath her breasts, offering support as she crouched and shouted at the world.

Megan shed her skin mere feet away and came forward in time to lift a startled, soaking seal pup from the water. Róisín went limp with shock as Megan, eyes shining, ran a fingernail down the pup's belly and split its skin to reveal a squalling, outraged human boy.

Róisín's shock fell away. She took the babe, curled him close even as Eoin lifted them both and carried them from the water. Megan followed a few steps behind, the baby's seal skin clutched safely against her chest. "Glendyr," Róisín whispered. "His name is Glendyr."

Megan gave Eoin a curious glance, but he was smiling. "Of the valley and water," he whispered in response. "A fine name, my rose. A fine name." Then he lifted his eyes to Megan, who folded the seal skin and, offering it to him, nodded once.

The blood bred true.

Half a dozen selkies, females all, went into the sea with that knowledge held close to their hearts.

Glendyr was preposterously weak and slow to grow, by selkie standards. Their children were born and lived their early lives as seals: Glendyr lived his as a human, only occasionally slipping into the skin that was his heritage. Selkie pups might nurse for three months, or four; Glendyr was at the tit for over a year. He swam naturally, even in human form, but it took a full turn of the seasons before he walked. Eoin watched with astonishment through all of it, equally horrified and delighted at the child's slow growth. Selkies kept closer to their parents than seals, forming a more lasting bond, but even so it was nothing to the years of dependency a human child had on its parents. Glendyr *needed* so much, so constantly, that it seemed incredible he could survive at all. But he did, and thrived.

Within a year, Megan came from the sea and Eoin built her a house of her own, and then more as other selkie females caught with human fathers and birthed children in whom the blood ran true. In five years Glendyr had a brother and a sister, and the selkie exiles had a village at the river's mouth, standing small but strong between two worlds.

The eighth summer, the warriors came.

None of them, not even Eoin, recognized them for what they were, not in the first minutes. Familiar faces, long-since unseen. Mostly males, coming out of the sea with their skins already set aside. Coming out of the sea with such weapons as the selkie used in human form: spears and nets, knives and sharp shells. Megan was the first to shore, the first to greet them, her smile wide.

The clan chief, her own father, gutted her.

She fell, blood spilling bright and red against the sand, and the children, screaming, ran for the water. Ran for the safety of the waves, the one place human fighters could never catch them.

Later, Eoin still did not know how Róisín did it. How she was there so quickly, when the selkies were among the slowest of the Old Races and humans were by far slower still. But she was there, red hair flying loose from its plaits, and she went not for Megan, not for the selkie warriors coming from the sea, but for the children who saw nothing of danger in a pod of seals splashing in the waves. Her voice rose and carried, sharp over the sound of screams: "High land, high land, not the waters at all! Get ye's to the hills now, go, go on with ye's, go!"

Glendyr, as red-haired as his mother and wise enough to listen, spun on his heel and grabbed the two nearest children to drag them with him. He was oldest, most respected, most adored by the younger pups, and they wheeled after him like sharks chasing fish. The smallest of them who could walk, the toddlers, were close enough to the village that their mothers scooped them up and ran while human fathers, knowing what their wives and children were, went to face the males on the beach with sword and shield and rage.

Róisín, between sand and sea, snatched the last of the children from knee-deep water and sent them running after Glendyr before turning to the oncoming selkie with all the courage of a warrior herself.

She saw it, Eoin thought. She saw the sleek-headed spear that caught her in the chest, though when it was thrown it had been intended for her back. Saw, but could not escape: its force collapsed her in on herself, arms flung forward as her shoulders caved, as her feet left the earth, as her spine bent and she fell. She had saved the children, and died facing her enemy.

Much, much later, Eoin thought she would have liked that, his bold and beautiful Róisín, but in the moment he thought nothing, only felt the pain of life going out of him, and ran to do battle.

"Eoin. Eoin, wake up. You've slept two days, and your children need you. Wake up." Familiar voice, but the wrong one. Eoin opened his eyes slowly, saw the thatch of his rooftop by the dim light of embers. Saw Megan sitting beside his bed, thin-lipped with grief and worry.

"You should be dead," he said after a time, and touched his own chest, his own belly, his own thigh: places where he remembered, almost, that pain had scored him. Not so deeply as the hollow in his chest, the emptiness of where Róisín had been, but deeply enough that life should have fled his body. "I should be too."

"Glendyr." The name broke from Megan's lips. Eoin sat up, stomach clenched with fear, and his age-mate, his oldest friend, wiped tears away and put her hand on his shoulder. "No. No, I'm sorry, I didn't mean that. He saved us. He got the children to higher ground and came back to the village to get our skins. The fighting was over then, I think. It was so fast, and you were..."

Her silence was louder than any words. Eoin had only sketchy memories, images of violence. He had seen seals fight one another at mating season, even kill one another. He had known the same capability, the same astonishing strength and potential for rage, lay within a people who shared so many aspects with the sea mammals, but had never imagined it within himself.

"Our men," Megan said, "they fought well, they protected the children, but some of them have left now. You're the only male who has left the clan," she said awkwardly, as if it was explanation enough. "We females aren't as strong as you. We frightened them, I think, with our strength, but you terrified them."

"But the warriors struck me down." Almost a question. The idea that his mortal friends had turned on him was too much to bear, in the fresh raw shock of survival and loss.

"My father," Megan said bitterly. "The same as he did me, and we would both have died, and most of the others as well, if Glendyr hadn't brought our skins so we could change." She swallowed. "My father and his warriors were less fortunate. They'd left their skins safely in the sea. By the time the others brought them..."

Shifting healed. They all knew that; it was part of their longevity, and more, it was part of what made the Old Races so very difficult to kill. It also, perhaps, had led the clan chief and his warriors to overconfidence: they would have imagined they could retreat and heal long before a puny army made mostly of mortal men might ever do them real damage. They had come, Eoin was certain, for the children, and had not imagined that those childrens' mothers would fight. They had struck Megan down, breaking one of their few sacred laws, and yet had not thought females who had chosen motherhood and exile over the clan might disregard those other ancient laws as well. "Róisín had no skin to save her."

Megan closed her eyes. "If she hadn't been so brave, I don't know if the rest of us would have been, ourselves."

Eoin's fingertips found new scars across his body, and thought they would heal more quickly than the sick emptiness in his chest. "You would have been. For the children."

"If Róisín hadn't been so quick, there might not have been children to fight for. She was...you had better come to see, Eoin. You'd best come and see." Megan offered a hand and Eoin rose with her help, moving stiffly and knowing he shouldn't be walking at all.

Glendyr and his brother and sister waited in the next room, pale faces streaked with tears that flowed anew when their father joined them. He knelt and held them all, wordless with the same shock and sorrow they shared. Megan left them for a long time, but finally said, "There's more, Eoin. More you need to see."

They went together, Megan ahead and Eoin with his children hand in hand behind her. She stepped aside as they left their home, and for long moments Eoin did not understand what he saw.

Selkies, male and female alike, working to restore the village, patrolling the nearby water's edge, laughing and playing with children. Faces he knew and face he didn't: strangers from other clans, *dozens* of them. They slowed as they noticed him, facing him with respect, with hope, with pride, and Megan whispered, "They've been arriving since my father's defeat. They're telling tales of schisms within the clans, of the battle here being a breaking point. They've come to see our people survive, Eoin. They're here to fight for us, because other warriors will think as my father did and will come to try to wipe us out, because this isn't over, it can't be over, not until those like my father change their minds or die away. They're here for the children, Eoin. For the hope of children, when we've had none for so long."

He was nodding, had been nodding since before she began to speak, understanding not just what the new arrivals meant, but what Róisín had meant as well. She would be the death of him, he had thought, but no. Instead, he had been the death of her, and she, she, his bright and clever Róisín, *she* had been the life of him.

The life of him, and of all their future to come.

MOUNTAIN'S DAUGHTER

IN SO FAR AS YETI names translated to human words, her name was *Little Patch of Darkness Against Snow Shadowed by the Great Mountain*, and in the tongue she had grown up speaking, it sounded quite beautiful. When, as a young adult, she left the mountains to learn about the people she'd been born to, she was sufficiently appalled at the ad-hock translation that she had chosen to simply take the last of it, the mountain's name for her own: Denali. But in her heart she thought of herself as Little Patch, and it would be the name she was known by in the long memories of the Old Races.

She did not, of course, remember the incident that had separated her from human parents, or at least not clearly. It came to her in dreams: a slide into crystallized snow, shadows blue and deep and dangerous all around her. The air was thin in those dreams, snow pressing on her, taking her breath away; she could not, try as she might, claw her way free as more snow piled up around her, above her, taking the world away until she wrenched awake with a gasp. She would lie awake, then, feeling air fill her lungs again until she trusted it hadn't abandoned her, and then she would shift in the furs, trying to find a space different enough from how she had been sleeping that the nightmare couldn't return. Even so, she would often go back to sleep with that shade of glacial blue burned behind her eyelids, never quite releasing her from its grip.

It had been an avalanche, late in the season, that spawned those dreams. Her mother, Rekka, still spoke with surprise when she mentioned it: the human tribes rarely risked the mountains at all until the brief northerly summer had settled well in and what rotten snow that intended to fall, had. Perhaps the winter had been unusually harsh, or the summer before, unusually sparse; for the mountain-bound yeti, who survived, in truth, more on magic than on food, it made little difference, but something had driven Denali's tribe to the mountain pass weeks before it was truly safe. Rekka did not know, to this day, whether any of the older humans had survived, only that Denali herself had been thrown clear, and that against all wisdom, Rekka had crossed the broken snow field to collect the shivering, sobbing human child: the little patch of darkness against snow shadowed by the great mountain.

The others, deeply disapproving, had dug through the snowy rubble in hopes of finding survivors so Rekka could be forced to give the squalling baby back to them. They found bodies, seven of them, swiftly, because no other creature on earth could sense heat or sound beneath the snow as the yeti could, but there were no living humans to be found, not all the way to the avalanche's leading edge. Nor were there footprints to suggest anyone had gotten away, but even the elders would not discount the possibility; perhaps a cloud of snow had snatched someone up and flung them a far distance, or perhaps the cold between, the space where yeti stepped to hide from prying human eyes, had seized a few humans and cast them out again elsewhere. It happened; the Arctic peoples had legends of the cold between, and how it sometimes saved a hunter in a storm, or a child lost on the tundra.

When Denali returned to the human world, that was where

she told them she had been: the cold between, caught there for so long that she had grown up from an infant into a child, and from a child into a woman, all under the watchful eyes of the spirits who lived there. It was not even a lie, but it was not until much later that she understood that the people to whom she had returned did not, quite, believe her. Not when she had, with unintended arrogance, taken the Great One's name as her own, and not when she had been raised by spirits. She was old before she understood that human tribes half-believed her to be the spirit of the mountain itself, given mortal flesh and come to judge whether the People were respectful enough of the land they lived upon, the beasts they hunted, and the spirits who guided them, and that she would grant them the mountain's bounty if they were found worthy.

They *were* worthy; within the range of human fallibility and generosity, they were, but she could no more influence the caribou run or the berries flowering than any mortal, and perhaps less than some; and the Great One's weather did as it wished no matter what a human might do. And like a good spirit, she went back to the mountain, in the end: but that *was* the end, and she had so many years between.

She was too young, when she became Rekka's daughter, to remember much of the world she had left behind: growing up in the Great One's shadow was all she knew, and the gentle, enormous shaggy creature who had adopted her was the only parent she could recall. Her earliest memories were of combing through Rekka's fur, laughing with delight as she found threads changing to summer brown and grey, for the yeti changed coats with the seasons like ptarmigan or hares. In winter, Rekka was white with blue shadows; in summer, beautifully patterned and mottled to walk unseen against the bare stone.

To Denali's practiced eye, all of her adopted tribe were distinctly individual, easy to tell apart, though if she tried very *hard* to think as a human, she could almost imagine they looked alike. Almost; it was easier to think the humans she'd seen from a distance all looked alike, with their black eyes and black hair and brown skin. Sometimes whole tribes of them looked generally different from another whole tribe: that group was taller and darker of skin; this group, more broadly built and more golden than brown—but within them the individuals were difficult to distinguish, and she had no idea if she looked more like one group of them than another, or what people might have once been her own.

It didn't distress her, the wondering. She could imagine no happier life than running, in clothes woven from fur shed by the whole tribe, across snowscapes, or scaling cliff faces that her fingers adapted to, the tips flattening and widening as she pulled herself from one tiny ledge to another. She could hold her body's weight from any fingertip, although not from the last two for *long*, as she had discovered the hard way more than once. Her finger and toenails were thick and strong, accustomed to being jammed into small spaces so she could climb, and at night she would compare her own funny, small hands with their blunt thick nails to Rekka's long graceful hands and claws so filled with power. The yeti were too large to look as though they moved quickly; large enough that they should seem ponderous, but instead they looked like dancers, every motion effortless, even—as happened far too often—when they were lurching to save Denali from her own latest antics.

There was no fear in falling, when she knew the tribe would be there to catch her. She grew strong and bold and tall, or at least, she *thought* she was tall. It was hard to tell, when surrounded by adults of a species that grew half again the height of men, and there were no other children. She had asked why, once, guilelessly, and Rekka had frowned at the Great Bear glittering in the sky and said, "I think we must live on more than magic, to breed. We Old Races," for she had long since told Denali of the different ancient, magical races that peopled the world along with humans, "breed slowly anyway, in exchange for our long lives. But I think we yeti are especially slow to have children, perhaps because we live so close to the edge of the world." She had put her hand out then, like she might reach into the cold between, and Denali had grabbed her long fingers and held her in place.

Denali could herself travel into the cold between; she had learned how when she was too young to know she couldn't, which was, she imagined, the way of all magic. But she wanted Rekka to stay, then, to tell her more stories of the yeti people, and her mother obliged, as she always did. "We do not fight," Rekka murmured. "Humans fight so much, and the Old Races in general, somewhat, but we yeti have eschewed conflict. It's easy, perhaps, when we can always step into the cold between and avoid it, but even if it was not easy..." She shivered, which yeti rarely did.

"You're too big to fight," Denali said with airy confidence. "Too much energy to bother."

Rekka laughed, a warm whuff of sound. "Dragons are much larger, and far more combative."

"But they go out into the world, too," Denali replied shrewdly. "We don't. Maybe if we did we would fight, too."

"I hope not. I think it would lose us what we are. And *you*, my daughter," Rekka said with a gentle nudge, "are not yeti, no matter how much you look like one in your cloak of our fur and your clawed snowshoes that mimic our feet."

Denali extended her toes, wiggling them, then tucked them back under Rekka's warmth. "I'm not human, either. Perhaps someday I'll bridge the worlds, if I can do it without sending them all into the mountains to hunt you."

"They've hunted us before," Rekka murmured. "We simply step away."

"Do you ever step to another mountain?" Denali demanded. "Is the cold between a gateway between one place and another? Could I visit yeti who live in low green mountains far away, or the very tallest mountains in the world, or on the walls of the smoke-spitting mountains? Would they be brown and grey in the summer too, or would the ones who live in forests be brown and green, and only grey in the winter? Do they live on magic alone too, or do they gobble rock and thank the spirit of a fallen deer when age or accident has taken it, and eat its flesh? Or leaves? Do they eat leaves? We eat leaves and berries and fish and—"

Rekka laughed louder, a rumble that made rocks shiver, and Denali gazed at her with surprised innocence. "*You* eat fish and berries and thank the spirit of the caribou when it falls and feeds you," Rekka said. "I think no yeti needs those things. We haven't partaken of them in aeons, not since humans came to our remote lands and hunted *us* when they saw us."

"You should try," Denali declared imperiously. "Maybe you would have a baby, and I would have a sister."

Stone rattled in its setting with the power of Rekka's laugh, that time. "It takes more than a meal to make a child, child. But perhaps you're right. Perhaps it would be worth trying, if we wish to continue on in this world."

"I'll go fishing for you," Denali volunteered. "With the bears, when the salmon spawn. It's not hunting at all, Mama, not when they just jump right into your hands. They're offering themselves, just as the caribou does when it falls, or the blueberries when they drop from the bush into your hands. Except the berries don't mind if you give the bush a shake."

"The rivers are a long way away," Rekka said, but they both knew it for an excuse. The yeti took Denali to the rivers for the nourishment *she* required; if they did not, she wouldn't even know about them. Denali shrugged, confident of herself.

"Nothing is far away, through the cold between."

"Everything is far away, through the cold between." Still, when the salmon runs came, Denali was allowed to go, accompanied by more than one of the tribe, and when she brought back more than enough to feed herself for the winter, after much quiet discussion, a few among the tribe began to take meals with her. Mostly berries, or tea brewed from spruce needles, and honey from the bees and milk from the caribou; sustenance obtained without the taking of life, even if there was enough frozen fish in a mountain crevasse to feed the whole tribe for a full turn of the seasons. Denali didn't care: her delight in sharing meals with others was palpable, even if she ate different food than they did, and for the yeti, the food itself, after so long an absence, was a curious pleasure.

But there were no children, not that season and not for many after. Denali grew, and grew thoughtful, watching her yeti family and the world beyond, judging one against another. She stepped into the cold between—and cold it was, always: the sun shone unending on white snow there, or the moon sank deep into bare tundra, soft and springing underfoot, and in neither case was there ever any wind, which made the cold bearable. Nor was there life beyond the yeti who traveled there, and the occasional lost mortal: no mosquitoes buzzed, no wolves howled, no foxes yipped or eagles cried, and certainly no talkative ravens bounced around full of commentary. The tundra lay brown when exposed, winter melted away but no sign of spring breaking through yet; that was the cold between, barren but survivable, even when the living world was hostile and murderous. Denali crossed through that cold place time and again, exploring all the land in sight of the Great One, vast distances indeed. She watched humans and bears and wolverines, moose and caribou, following their tracks and studying their ways, and came back, in time, to say, "Animals strike out on their own, Mama. They find mates from other herds and flocks and tribes."

Eyebrow ruffs rose, giving Rekka a comical look. "Are you saying you want a mate, Little Patch?"

"*Mother,*" Denali said in horror. "*No.* I'm saying *you* need to find one somewhere else. Through the cold between, to the cold *beyond.* To the low green mountains or the volcanic peaks, if you want there to be children."

"*You* want there to be children, my sweet."

"I want my family to live," Denali replied.

"We're in no danger of dying, little one."

"Not dying," Denali said slowly, "isn't the same as living."

She began to watch the humans more after that, perched on some high place the cold between could bring her easily, until Rekka joined her in the twilight of a late summer day, when the sun had fallen enough that their forms couldn't be picked out against the horizon. "What do you see in them, Little Patch?"

"Your future. And mine. You can hide forever, Mama, but even if you do, some of them should know about you. Be ready to protect you. My children could do that. They could help. Not just the yeti, but all the Old Races. The others are less reclusive, you've said so before. They must need help, from time to time."

"That's a great burden to put on your children, to bear them into the world so they can carry a secret? There's no telling who any child might grow up to be. Not all of them will be suited to knowing about us. It could put us in greater danger. We do well enough, hiding in the shadows. It doesn't chafe, not for yeti, at least."

"Not now," Denali murmured. "But the bold among them explore a little farther each year, Mother. What happens when they push all the way into the mountain's heart and discover you? Will you live in the cold between for always, then?"

"We have other recourses," Rekka said uncomfortably.

"Do you?" Denali's voice softened. "Do you, Mama? I know from your stories that others among the Old Races can cast off their immortal forms and appear human to the eye, but I've never seen any of you do that. Can you, still? And if you can, what then? Live among them, in their brutal world, with their short lives? Feed on the beasts they've slaughtered and betray your souls, or on nothing at all and betray yourselves? You'll need *something*, Mama. Something or someone, to help you hide in plain sight."

Rekka shook her head. "They might come to explore the high remote cold places, but they will never live here, not so long as they have any other choice. We will remain in the mountains, hiding in the cold between when we must, to avoid them. Perhaps this is why we don't have children anymore, Little Patch. Perhaps to bear the world as we old ones have chosen to would be too much for the young, as it is too much for you."

Denali stood, looking down over earth gold and faded green with dying summer; at the twist of a mud-brown river as it found the easiest passage through flat lands, and at the mountains ringing the valley, hundreds of miles distant. "Not all mountains are cold and tall and remote, Mama. Even if they don't come to live in *these* mountains, they'll go to live in others, where the brown and the green of your people live. If you won't go into the cold beyond to warn them, to at least tell them the distance can be traveled and that the winter mountains can hide them, then I will."

"You worry too much, daughter. We can't be followed into the cold between. We're safe there, even from the most ardent pursuers. Do you not trust your own kind?"

"Why would I? I know almost nothing of them. And no. I don't, because if I, who grew up with you and know almost nothing of their ways, can see and think and feel that they would hunt you and fear you, then how much more violently would they, who know nothing of *you*, respond? I will go," she said with reluctance and eagerness both, "and learn more of them. Maybe I'm wrong. But if I'm not I'll find a way, Mama. I'll find a way to help protect you, no matter what else I might do."

She went into the valley then, traveling by the glimmer of moon and early-rising sun, while the only parent she had ever known watched from far above. Rekka would watch her forever, she knew that, and only hoped she would do it from a safe distance. It was enough, more than enough, for a strange lone human woman to walk out of the scrub forests and bug-infested swamps; for that woman to be accompanied by a nine foot shaggy shadow would be too much.

It had not occurred to her, until she met the first humans, that she would not know a word of their language, nor they of hers. She learned swiftly, claiming the name Denali as her own, and thought nothing of the fascination the People showed when she said she had come from the great mountain. Some few hated her for the name; she knew that, but didn't—not for many years—understand why, and when she did, she regretted the monumental arrogance that taking the name displayed, but it was far too late then. That she did not hunt, or weave bark, or work leather, or any of the skills that were necessary for living, only set her apart from them farther; in retrospect it was no surprise she was given to the shaman, a big-eyed, grey-haired old woman who sniffed at her as if she stank of something strange, but was reluctantly, then eagerly, willing to teach her.

The shaman could very nearly step into the cold between at will: she drew the sick and injured to its very edge, calling spirits through it to guide them back to health, and from time to time, standing on its border, Denali saw Rekka, ghost-like, watching her mortal daughter ford the mortal world. "There are other beings in the cold between," Denali told the shaman, and was rewarded with a look of scathing approval: scathing because that was obvious; approval, because she had seen the obvious. "I know them," she said to the shaman, and the old woman's gaze sharpened until Denali felt she was being seen through.

The longest night came on them soon after that, the sun rising over the horizon for less than a hand of hours, the sky glorious with gold and the white frozen earth reflecting blue shadows for all the time the sun shone. The shaman put Denali in a musk-ox-hide tent at sunset, filled it with smoke and smells and a heated stone, and told her not to come out again until the spirits of the cold between had spoken to her. Denali, freezing, tried twice to step *into* the cold between before she realized there was magic in the hide, and that she was as tied to the mortal world as she had ever been. Fear boiled up in her, warming her more than a little, then faded again as the scented smoke began to do its work. Her shoulders, then her eyelids, relaxed, every breath growing deeper and slower until she felt that she floated just above herself, looking down at the hot stone and the top of her own head. There were a few white threads at her crown, promise of wisdom to come.

She expected the yeti to come through the fog, travelers of the cold between that they were. Instead a woman unfurled from the earth like a swiftly-growing sapling: in mere moments she stood before Denali, examining her with quiet reserve. Denali studied the woman in return, too hazy to feel surprise at the earth sprouting people. The woman was small, round-faced, and while not wrinkled with age, gave the impression of it anyway. She looked like the elders of the tribe, with straight black hair and brown eyes, clear as water despite their darkness, although she dressed in nothing like Denali had ever seen: a robe of woven material that looked soft to the touch. It shimmered when it moved, as if a river, or perhaps the wind, had been captured in its making, and its color changed with every breath: blue and green and brown, with touches of black deeper than the night sky in its shadows.

The yeti are beloved to me, the old-not-old woman said after a while, and without words. *They are the gentlest of all their kind, the least imposing upon the earth and the most forgiving of spirit. They are in some ways right: their discretion lends them a certain lack of vulnerability that some of the others do not share, but you are also in some ways right: humanity has met very little it could not capture and kill when it was minded to. I cannot give you time with which to right that fault in your own people. All I can offer is guidance through the cold between, that they might follow in your footsteps if they should choose to gather, an event you are unlikely to live to see. You need not decide now—*

"Of course I'll do it," Denali said with such certainty that the spirit-woman smiled.

Of course you will. Impetuous humanity, so much greater than itself, and so much lesser. Remember that time does not move as smoothly in the cold between, Little Patch, and watch where you step out, that you do not lose yourself in the world.

She faded then, or perhaps she had faded long before the words even began. Denali stared in astonishment at where the little woman wasn't, at where the place she had stood blossomed with forget-me-nots, their delicate blue turning purple as a sliver of rising sunlight forced its way under the hide tent's lip. Denali, shivering, pushed herself out of the hide, all too mindful of the image of a child exiting its mother's body, and followed a dozen steps' worth of blue flowers before the shaman spoke in a voice of power: "If you walk this path, I will not see you again, Child of the Great One. Carry with you the blessing and the strength of the People; tell each shaman that you meet that you have been my student, and ask for their teachings as well, if they will share them. You carry a burden, daughter of the mountain. I do not envy you your task or the sorrows that lie in front of you, and yet if I had the strength I would join you, to see the wonders you will see. Be strong. Return often. Remember all of those who have been your family."

Denali looked back, but the cold between rose around her, taking her as it might take a truly lost soul, and in it there was no one but herself.

Herself, and a trail of greenery, of blossoms, that led a path across the barren between.

They changed, those flowers, from forget-me-nots to pink dogwood, from dogwood to daisies white and yellow, and to dozens, blooms of innumerable colors, as Denali followed them through the cold between. When the flowers changed, the trail stopped and she left the cold, sometimes to find herself on the outskirts of another settlement or roving tribe, others, to stand in the heart of a camp full of yeti who vanished, panic-stricken, into the cold between themselves. The first few times, Denali chased them into the cold, only to have them pop back into the world again; after a while, she learned to sit down and wait quietly, as eventually someone would come back.

It helped that all the world over the yeti spoke the same tongue, and that once they were no longer running, they could listen and understand. It helped, too, that in the cold between they saw the singular track of flowers that guided Denali, and that the curious among them followed those tracks a little distance until they themselves came upon others of their kind. Denali often left with the conviction she was offering them a stronghold in the cold between, a place to gather in safety and remain forever if humanity pressed them too hard, but even that, she thought, was better than losing them to knives and slings and spears.

The humans were harder: *their* languages changed from

tribe to tribe, and her purpose with them was more difficult. Study with their shamans, yes, but more, to find among them those who might be trusted with the yeti's secrets, that the people might be guided away from the mountains and the monsters said to lurk in them. She stayed long enough to learn languages, to learn all the human magic they had at their fingertips, and moved on, always searching, never satisfied. From time to time she lurched back to the shadow of the Great One, sometimes to visit her mother, always unchanging, and others to search out the shaman's heirs, for the old shaman had been right: Denali never saw her again. Only when adults with children of their own recognized her as the spirit of the mountain who had visited when *they* were children did she begin to understand that she lost not just weeks or months in the cold between, but years and even decades.

The world changed around her, subtly, as she traveled: for a time it grew much colder, the years harsh even for the yeti, who spent many of them nearly asleep; she woke more than one tribe from a near-hibernation with her visit, and not even the most adventuresome among them chose to follow the flower-laden path through the between, not during those cold years. Human tribes became scarcer for a time, until the cold between had taken her so far south that even the frozen expanses could no longer touch them. In some places she found yeti who weren't even mountain-bound: they dwelt in deep jungles and had short soft fur like a cat's, rather than the long hollow hairs that Rekka's tribe had. Those warm-weather tribes used their human forms on occasion, either to avoid humans or, once in a while, to trade with them. Had they been unable to walk into the cold between, Denali might have thought them some other kind of Old Race entirely, but the one thing all the yeti, no matter how disparate, had in common was the ability to reach the between.

She was not yet old, but neither was she young, when the

flowers at last stopped blooming, stopped leading her along new paths. For the longest time she hardly understood what it meant, that she could stand in the between and have trails of greenery behind her but not in front. She retraced her footsteps then, never stopping to see how the world outside changed, intent only on returning home, spirit of the mountain. There were footprints along the way now, much larger than her own: the yeti traveled amongst themselves, sharing, visiting, making their large world smaller, and every step accompanied by the evidence of others making the same journey made her smile.

She had not, in the end, been able to trust humanity enough to tell them of the yeti; not even the shamans and the dreamwalkers, though the latter traversed something so close to the cold between that Denali wasn't sure they didn't already know. But there were witches in the world, too, human magic born of unfiltered evil, of hate and fear and anger whispered as secrets into the earth until the earth itself gave birth to a witch. Witches hunted magic, be it Old or human, and Denali feared too much what might happen to the gentle yeti if a witch should hear of them. So theirs was a secret that would go with her to the grave, but at at least they could reach one another now; that was a worthy lifetime's work.

Rekka met her in the cold between, so close to the shadow of the mountain that its weight could be felt even in the between. Rekka, who had not changed at all over the years, save for a sadness in her gaze as she looked at what time had done to Denali. Denali settled onto the tundra beside her mother, nestled as small as she'd ever been against the yeti's warm white fur. "Perhaps I'll have a sister," she said after a time, and felt her mother draw her closer.

"More likely now than ever before," the yeti murmured. "We are able to be together now, our people, few as we may be. Perhaps you will."

"You shall," said a voice, half-familiar, as if from a dream, and from the blooms rose the old-not-old woman again, more vibrant in the cold between than she had seemed in the musk-ox-tent so very long ago. "You will, but if you return to the world you won't live to see her, as she'll be a long time coming. The Old Races have asked a great deal of you already, Little Patch. Whether they may ask more is your choice, as always."

"As long as there's breath in my body," Denali said.

Rekka made a sound of protest, but the other woman smiled. "Impetuous humans. The cold between will hold you, unaging, as it has done all the time you've traveled in it. You may go out of your mind with boredom; that is always a risk. But your yeti family will visit, and you can...rest." The word itself was nearly a gift, sending a wave of weary relief over Denali. "Even humans can nearly hibernate, in the darkest months of winter, and it is never anything but winter in the cold between. You may be roused, from time to time, to eat, to speak, but you may rest here, and if you're willing..."

"When have I not been?"

The old woman smiled. "Then I'll wake you when you're most—influential. It won't be when your sister is born," she warned. "Not for decades, centuries past that. I can't even promise you'll ever know her. But there is a world waiting, Little Patch. There is a world waiting for you and for your kind, your family of spirit. It's a long, long journey to reach it, and there are so many things that could go wrong between now and then. But we all must act as though it is inevitable, mustn't we? That's what you've done all these long years, and without you, without those like you, we never *would* reach it. I'll do what you wanted to," she added with a sparkle in her clear brown eyes. "I'll find those humans who will help, and set them to helping."

"How will you trust them?"

Another smile, more wicked than the first, crossed the

woman's lips. "Your magic is only human, Little Patch, but mine is so much older than that. Now say good night to your mother, child. She'll check on you often, and you'll sleep safely here in the cold between." She moved away as Denali clung to Rekka's side, silent with tears and hope; it was Rekka who, in time, brushed Denali's hair aside and placed a kiss on her forehead, then helped her to settle into the tundra, with a promise of watching over her, and eternal love.

The old woman returned, drawing springy earth up over Denali as if it was a blanket, and smiling as forget-me-nots rose and bloomed. In moments Denali's breathing steadied, her eyes drooping closed. As Rekka had done, the old woman bent to kiss her forehead, and to murmur, "I'll come to wake you, my dear, after the apocalypse."

LONGEST NIGHT

CHILDREN WERE RARE; FOR ALL the Old Races, they were rare, always had been, and were precious for it. Amongst the gargoyles they were perhaps not quite so rare as they were for some of the others; the dragons had not hatched an egg in four centuries, and the last before that, some twelve hundred years or more gone. Selkies had been driven to mate with humans to breed, and in diluting their blood had lost their way; no one knew how many were left, only that they had faded into the seas, and were mourned by the Old Races who both remembered and survived. Siryns, yeti, sea serpents; no one had even *seen* a serpent in centuries, save in human stories of oceanic monsters, but humans and their tales were hardly to be trusted. The djinn, perhaps; they were deliberately insular, not unlike the gargoyles in that way, and they might yet bear children in their roving desert camps. But not the harpies, not the cold-loving yeti; all the lost races, and no one had ever seen a vampire's child anyway. So children were to be celebrated, perhaps especially by a people who spent half their hours as stone.

This one had come into the world at the longest day, or near enough, and had been born pale even among the gargoyles. In the half-year since then he had acquired a little ash-white hair and a shout that echoed against the mountains until rocks trembled with it; Biali muttered and winced with each bellow, while his mate Hajnal laughed, asking, "What did you expect of an infant, my love? Has it been so long since one has graced us, that even a gargoyle can't remember how noisy they are?"

He said, "Yes," with a scowl that got another laugh from her; Hajnal laughed easily, and made decisions quickly, for their kind, which was much of what he loved in her. She leaned toward adventure, eager to travel; that was how she had come to their cold Germanic mountains at all, when she had been born to a range farther south, where the stone ran darker and shone with veins of obsidian that had influenced her coloring. Biali himself was nearly as pale as the infant, with unrelentingly white hair and stone-blue eyes, but Hajnal's hair grew dark and thick and her skin tinted toward deep gold, whether in human form or her natural gargoyle shape. She had crossed half the world in her travels, from her Italian mountains south into the depths of Africa, exploring the world a night at a time, and after centuries of collecting memories, had returned to her native Europe, and come, in time, to find the small northern tribe Biali was a part of.

They had known each other at once, of course; gargoyles did, spending so much of their time in their great gestalt, where not only their memories, but the collected memories of the Old Races, were kept safe. Even so, he hadn't expected her—*enthusiasm*; gargoyles tended by nature to be a reserved lot, and Biali was no different from the many, in that. But curiosity drove Hajnal, sent her searching the world and finding amusement in it, and if she had settled long ago with Biali, it had not changed her inherent fondness for the new and interesting. Once she had drawn him north, out of the mountains they called home. For over a century, they had traveled to places where in winter the sun barely rose at all;

there, they had met others of their kind who traded away a summer's sleep for a winter's wakefulness, though the danger of sleeping for months on end sent Biali's skin to crawling. Hajnal laughed at that, too, at the image of stone shuddering against itself in revulsion. Earthquakes were like that, she said, and Biali was satisfied to be an earthquake.

"It has been a long time," she said now, under the light of stars and a rising moon. "The last who were born here were born long before I came."

"I was one of them," Biali agreed, for he was less than half Hajnal's age, although he had seen some eight hundred years. "I don't remember my own shouting."

"You're choosing not to," Hajnal said with a smile. "It's in the memories."

"If we have a child," Biali said dryly, "I'll go into them and remind myself."

"If only we could, as easily as that." It wasn't a regret; stone mostly had little use for regrets, but there were few enough amongst the Old Races who didn't wish, at least sometimes, to become parents. For some it was a personal yearning; for others, an almost-unacknowledged admission that humanity was outpacing them, that they were all a dying people, and without children they would simply fade away from a world that already barely remembered they were there. Biali fell among the latter, though for Hajnal he would want anything.

"If we could," he said, not unkindly, "we would be human," and Hajnal laughed.

"What a trade, my love. Barren eternity or a brief span of years littered with children."

"And illness, and a paltry physical strength, and—"

"Enough! Enough, you convince me that the trade is a bad one." Hajnal shook her wings, then settled beside him, looking down into a hollow in the mountainside. It would fill with moonlight soon, glowing blue and purple in the soft brilliance, and then the child would be brought by his parents, while the rest of the tribe came to crouch around the hollow's rim, as Hajnal and Biali already did. A few others had gathered already, too, waiting for the rituals of the longest night, the halfway mark of a gargoyle's year. Humans counted it otherwise, Biali knew, but for a people consigned to night, the year began at the summer solstice, waxing through the autumn equinox and reaching its height in the long dark nights of winter, when they were free to breathe and move and live unfettered by the strange shaping of their lives. No others amongst the Old Races were so constrained, but then, no others were the living memory of so many peoples, either; to be bound by stone in daylight hours was the price of safekeeping that history, and that was as it was.

The children were not born into the overmind, into the memories shared by all the adult gargoyles. That would be too much for them, too overwhelming; the solstice rituals began the carving of the paths in malleable minds that would permit them the ability to access the memories as they aged. The first memories would be of the child himself, shared by his parents, then by the tribe, to solidify his place within it, so that he would always know his home and his family and his friends. It was done solemnly, bringing the infant into the pool of moonlight—auspicious, the elders said; to have moonlight fall on the hollow meant the child would see clearly throughout his life, although Biali had never heard of anyone saying a child brought into the memories on a foggy night would stagger blindly through life, and when he muttered as much to Hajnal, she knocked his ribs with a jutting elbow, and told him he had no poetry in his soul. Nor did he, but her castigation was enough to make him smile.

Solemn consecration or not, the child himself had no interest in sitting quietly while memories were built around him, softened to lead him into the first low hills that were the gargoyle overmind. No: he rolled over, he squirmed on his belly, he put effort into and succeeded in crawling away, until his mother's patient hands fetched him and put him back in the circle of light. The game began again, until Biali was exasperated and Hajnal amused. "I'm sure you sat patiently through it all," she murmured, and he snorted. So those were the memories they offered, in the first gentle moments of his presence in the gestalt: fond delight from Hajnal and modestly tempered irritation from Biali. Well, no one was universally liked: better the child should learn that now.

A spark of certainty, of self-awareness and confidence, lit up in the mental space they all shared, and into it, the child announced himself, sure of the name his parents had given him: *Alban.*

He grew quickly, as even the children of Old Races do, hurrying through childhood toward the strength and stability of an adult form, and when he *did* grow, it was all at once, from one sunset to another, as if the hours spent encased in stone were to be thrown off to reveal him at greater height and breadth than he had gone to sleep as. He grew *tall*, until he bore teasing about sharing height with the mountains themselves, and when he proved gangly and awkward with his height, Biali, who had himself been burdened by size as a youth, took pity on him and taught him, step by step, how to control a body outpacing its mind's ability to control it comfortably. They were an odd pair; Biali knew it even if Alban did not, for Biali was squat to Alban's ever-increasing height, but there was still satisfaction in teaching a boy who was all elbows and knees how to become graceful, and he was the first one to see the youth take wing, on a night where a bad tumble sent Alban into a ravine someone his age shouldn't risk.

Biali launched himself after the boy, torn between alarm

and laughter; the laughter won, when Alban's oversized wings snapped open, easily able to carry youthful weight, and he *almost* didn't crash-land, which for a first flight was high praise indeed. Half a somersault landed him on his back along a stream-and-stone-littered crevasse, and he stared into the sky, watching Biali come to a tidy landing beside him. In as close to sullen a voice as he possessed, Alban muttered, "It's hard to believe you were clumsy once too."

"I wasn't," Biali said unrepentantly. "Not like you. I was too strong." Muscle flexed in his arms and thighs as he spoke, physical recollection of his own youth. "It seemed like I broke everything I touched. Trees. Occasionally mountains." Alban gave him a quick look and a smile pulled at Biali's face. "Not entire mountains, but pieces off them. There's a—I'll show you, when you're better at flying. At *landing*. A ridge, a ways from here. The gestalt will show you how it used to look, before I ran into it. It took a long time to learn to control it. I'm still strong, even for one of us."

"How did you learn? You couldn't have—" Alban stretched an arm out, then brought a fingertip back to touch his nose, a gesture that took more time and concentration than it ought to; if he hurried he was inclined to poke himself in the eye, or the cheek, simply from not quite knowing where he *was*.

"No, but I had to slow down, too. I went into the memories." Biali sat on his haunches, gaze fixed on distant stars. "I found stories about humans, there. Some of them were strong for their kind, too. Wild and angry, feeding on their strength in battle until it burned out, and that suited me, save for the fact that I would have to go fight human battles to get any use out of it. We don't fight among ourselves." He shrugged. "So I looked farther, until I found stories that showed me how to control the strength, use it when I wanted instead of accidentally. Finesse instead of force. Slowing down. I don't break things anymore, and you won't either, in time."

"You learned all that from humans?"

"From memories of them in the overmind, yes. I had to. There weren't stories of our own kind being beleaguered with too much strength, not as children."

"You can't be the only one." Alban rolled off his back, shaking his wings before folding them down. "Any more than I can be the only one who's too tall and clumsy."

"No, but their lives may have been different. More conflict with humans, or pursuits that let them use their strength or size in a way that taught them to control it without ever realizing that's what they were doing. It can be difficult to find something like that in the memories, when the result is the consequence of an unnoticed action." Biali curled his lip. "Humans are simpler. Can you fly back out of here?"

Alban's wings stirred. "I don't know. I've never tried taking off from a low point before. But I can climb the walls if I can't fly out."

"There's no updraft, this deep. You'll have to jump to get the height to fly. Aim for the wall," Biali said with a brief grin. "That way if you don't fly at least you'll have a head start on your climb."

Alban pulled a face. Biali's grin broadened and he sprang upward, wings beating rapidly to catch air, and moments later he landed on the ravine's edge, watching Alban crouch to leap. He could tell from the instant the youth left the ground that he wouldn't make it: he lacked the necessary height. But his aim was true enough, and he caught the wall, scrambling up with more ease than Biali would have had; those long arms and legs were good for something. His expression was sour as he pulled himself over the edge, and Biali cuffed his head, still grinning. "Nobody makes the first try."

"You would think we would, though. That we'd learn from the memories."

Biali pursed his lips. "You'd think. But it's not the same.

Come on. There's a mountain to climb, or we won't make it home before dawn."

"I won't. You could."

"The entire tribe would take turns chiseling bits off me if I left you out here on your own." Biali hopped upward, using wings and strength to scale the rocky peak far more rapidly than any human might, with Alban moving almost as quickly behind him. Night after night they went out, Alban's size turning slowly to grace, his speed to measured thoughtfulness, and before he had seen twoscore years he had grown not only to his height, but a breadth bettered only by Biali, who looked all the more squat beside him. In their natural forms Alban towered over him by nearly two feet, and in their rarely-used mortal forms, the difference wasn't much less. Hajnal, who was small to begin with, looked ridiculous beside Alban, save for the way he would sit at her feet, enraptured, to listen to the tales of she told of the world she'd seen. He vowed often to see it one day himself, an ambition Biali could not, in any serious way, appreciate: *he* had traveled because Hajnal wanted to, and was content to leave humanity to itself, and gargoyles to their remote mountaintops.

Stranger still than *wanting* to visit the human world was Alban's fascination with *words*: they were what the young gargoyle valued, not the shared experiences the gestalt could offer, but the stories Hajnal told, memories filtered through the words she chose, rather than the clarity of being *there*, as the overmind meant memory to be shared. Humans, not gargoyles, shared memories that way, but gradually Biali came to understand that was the point, for Alban. Humans—stories of them, at least—engrossed him, and he had hardly seen his first score of years when on a longest night he said, "We won't survive this way," with a deep certainty better suited to an elder than a youth. It had silenced the gathering for a moment, everyone from his parents to the oldest of all looking askance at the young gargoyle. Only Hajnal had smiled, though she said nothing. In the end, none of them did, either because it was a truth too hard to bear, or a lie they could find no way to refute.

The comment refused to fade in Biali's memory. It seemed to define what Alban became: thoughtful and reserved, not that gargoyles were prone to great shows of emotion. But Alban watched his own people from a distance, recording them not in the gestalt, but in ordinary, mortal memory. He left their tribe for the first time when he had seen barely half a century: went to human villages in the mountain, learned their language, returned to tell stories that no one save Hajnal wanted to hear. *She* sat curled on a rock, or nestled into a hollow of stone, listening to tales of human children climbing Alban as if he were a tree, and laughing so hard they cried with delight when he would suddenly rise or run or toss them into the air, making the most of his size and strength; of the adults being more cautious of the stranger in their midst, but warming to him as he struggled to learn their language and laughed at his own mistakes. He traveled in winter, of course, so the long nights offered him more time to spend among the mortals, and often he found that when he emerged at sunset there was some task or trouble that needed his size and strength to finish. It had come on him slowly that a village woman had taken a liking to him; that, he confessed, was what had driven him home again. Learning about humans was one thing, but explaining himself to them was—

"Against our laws," Biali, who had come to listen after all, rumbled, and Alban spread a big hand in agreement.

"Their lives are as encapsulated by the sun as ours are," he said. "They draw closed with the sunset, with only a few hours, at most, of time stolen beside their fires and with their candles. I had to tell a story of living deep in the mountains, working on my own, to excuse the hours I kept, and then protest that I needed no help to clear land or chop wood."

"No doubt once they saw you chop wood they accepted that was true," Hajnal replied, amused. "How quickly could you reduce a tree to cuttings, Alban?"

"Faster than any of them, once I learned *how*. They have so many tools we don't use. We live lazy lives, compared to many of them, don't we? We eat almost nothing—"

"Why would stone need to eat?" Biali grumbled, earning smiles from Hajnal and Alban both.

"But that's it," Alban said. "Unless we spend our hours in mortal form, we survive as living stone, with no great need for sustenance, no time wasted in hunting, no energy expelled in staying warm. We ought to be great artists, or thinkers, or inventors, and instead we spend so much of our time hidden in the memories, looking back instead of forward."

"What would you have us look forward to? Pretending at being human, living in the shadows of their societies, as you've just done?" Biali shook his head. "That's no life for a gargoyle."

Hajnal arched an eyebrow. "Whereas hiding in the mountains watching them encroach ever further is ideal?"

Biali snorted. Hajnal and Alban exchanged a smile, and Biali harrumphed again, making the other two laugh. "There are no good solutions," Alban said easily, and for some little while the topic lay fallow, through the change of seasons. It became easy to forget that Alban was young, yet; he had become part of the always, a known mark in the memories, and one of the few of whom Biali was truly fond. Alban's tempered enthusiasm balanced Biali's dour gruffness well, and Hajnal flew alongside both of them, so they were large and strong and small together, and one was rarely seen without the others.

Rarely, but not inevitably: Alban left twice more before his seventieth year, years he could count more closely than most because he had come into the world in the same year as one of the human royalty, a girl who grew up to be queen for so long that even the Old Races noticed, and marked it in their memories. In his seventieth year—in hers—she died, and he left again, to see the land that had been hers to rule. Hajnal went with him; Biali proclaimed them both insane, and watched the memories they added to the gestalt prove him right. London, full of humans and animals, *stank*, and no theatre performed in the round could convince him it was otherwise worthwhile.

No one else followed them, in the memories, not with the attention Biali did. Hajnal asked more than once that he come along behind them, but the distance was as close as he had any desire to encounter humanity in. *But they live so brightly,* Hajnal said through the memories. *Brutal, short, ugly lives, yes, but with so much passion, Biali. It might rub off.*

I don't want *it to rub off,* he protested, and the memory of her laughter stayed with him as dawn stole their lives away.

They returned just before winter, flying at night over the narrow gap of water between England and France, hiding in woods and hills and once in a while on a church top for the daylight hours, then taking advantage of the increasingly long nights to wing their way home. They arrived dangerously close to sunrise one morning, risking a fall from air-borne heights, risking shattering on the mountains below, to be home. Biali waited for them, awake, pacing, watching the sky, demanding they show some modicum of sense and land before dawn caught them; they could come the last little distance at night, in safety. But no, they both insisted on wasting no more time in arriving home, and with the sky dangerously grey on the horizon, they landed together with the grace of long practice. Biali, cursing their foolishness, caught them in a hug, and woke from daytime's stony prison in the same embrace, still scolding, until Alban threw him over with a laugh, and they pounced and wrestled and tumbled in the snow like children. Earth-shaking children, to be sure, able to knock small rockslides loose, while Hajnal leapt lightly into the air and watched from above, where she wouldn't be caught in their wrestling.

Their antics drew the attention of a handful of others who ended up caught between amusement and disapproval; the eldest of them, sternly, said, "You've spent too much time with humans, Alban," and, "Biali, you should know better."

"Surely you ought to be reprimanding me," Hajnal replied. "They're both striplings, compared to me." But Biali disengaged from the game, brushing snow and dirt away, and suffered a sting of chagrin, that Alban's youth and playfulness should be so infectious. Alban, for all his size and propriety, seemed unscathed by the scolding, though he too shook off the snow and spread his hands in a show of apology.

Not enough of one, though: he said what he had said before, with more conviction. "We need something of humanity, to survive. The more time I spend with them the more certain of it I become."

The elders landed, at that, scowling around at each other and then, together, at the youngest of them. "Then you spend too much time with them, Alban. Humans are dangerous to the Old Races. We need have nothing to do with them."

"Humans are dangerous to us whether we deal with them or not," the big youth replied with quiet confidence. "They're eager to explore their world, finding new corners of it every day. Eventually they'll find us, whether we want them to or not. What would you have us do? Lock ourselves away in stone forever, hoping we might be mistaken for sculptures and statues? Hoping their casual destruction of the unknown will pass us by and we'll emerge unscathed from their hammers and wedges? The Old Races haven't survived for untold millennia through willful ignorance of our situation. We're going to have to adapt, one way or another."

So much of the tribe had gathered by then, all but a handful. Thirty or forty of them, as many as would be seen on the longest night, though that was weeks away yet. They stood against Alban, a gathering of relentless stone, and despite his youth he looked neither afraid or uncertain, as if his conviction ran as deep as the mountains. Hajnal came to the earth finally, landing by his side, and if she didn't take his hand, the gesture of solidarity was still clear, and made Biali look to see where he himself stood in the throwing of lots.

Neither with nor against; closer, perhaps, to Alban and Hajnal than to the gathering of their elders, but not *with* the two itinerant travelers. Hajnal's gaze on him was patient, loving, but not pleading; she didn't need him to stand by her, though she would welcome him if he did.

He knew it at the time, recognized it as a moment of schism, and still did not move. Could not, perhaps, move; the path Alban stood on the precipice of was too unwelcome to Biali, even if Hajnal stood there as well. There was a chance, still, that they could be drawn back; that was what he believed, or told himself to believe, even then, and the most that he could do was stay rooted where he stood, with neither faction and wondering at the cost of solitude.

"Come with us." A ritualized request by now, after a dozen leave-takings and returns. Hajnal crouched on the mountain's ridge, looking out into sky turned blue with moonlight, and snow that paled the horizon. "For a little while, Biali. Come see a little of the mortal world with us. A month or two, no more."

"Stay," he countered, and that was as habitual as the rest, by now. "They can't find every hidden space on the planet, Hajnal. We've been safe in our quiet corners for a long time now. Stay, and stop tempting them."

"Once you would have come with me."

"Once you didn't have a more eager young idiot to accompany you."

She looked at him, the corner of her broad mouth half

turned up. "Were you an idiot, then?"

He was one now, and knew it, to stay behind, but it had become a line of foolish stubbornness he would not, or could not, cross. "I was always happy to stay behind, Hajnal. I traveled because you wanted it, not because I had any need to see their world, or even more of ours. It's all there, in the overmind."

"But it isn't the same, experiencing the memories once removed. The scents, the colors, the textures. They're distanced, in the gestalt."

"Not very."

"No." That, at least, she granted him, with little more than she smile she'd offered before. "Not very. But enough. I'd go so much farther, if our wings would stretch that far, Biali. To the New World, to the frozen poles. Doesn't it bother you, that we gargoyles, especially, are so limited in our terrain? Only as far as we can fly in a night."

"But night lasts for months, when you go far enough north, and the gestalt shares stories of those who have crossed the ice in the darkness. You could reach the New World, if you wanted to."

"Would you come with me?"

"Wouldn't Alban?"

"That," Hajnal said quietly, "is not what I asked. Come with us," she said again. "To Spain, to Portugal. There are places where gargoyles can live, Biali. Cities where so many torches are lit that the night seems as bright as day, and men and women live their lives late at night. We could be part of that."

"Where *humans* live their lives late at night. We'll never be part of that, Hajnal. We're not human."

She transformed suddenly, an unexpected burst of air as her gargoyle form gave way to the slighter human form that all the Old Races could cultivate. Her transformation wasn't as dramatic as some: Alban lost half a foot or more of height, and Biali, some of his breadth, but Hajnal, small to begin with, was hardly any more delicate as a human than as a gargoyle. Her hair whipped around her, long black tangles the only clothing she wore, and her eyes were dark and luminous in the moonlight. No gooseflesh marred her skin, despite the cold wind; that was perhaps the greatest sign of her alien nature, that even in human form, gargoyles were largely indifferent to the elements.

"We're not," she agreed, and her voice was lighter in this form. A human might call it sweeter, but to Biali it sounded thin, as if she had lost something of herself in the transformation. "We're not human, but we can go among them as if we were, and revel in experience. Where's the profit, Biali? In staying true to our first forms, if most of what we do is let the world glide by below us without ever touching it? Come with us," she said one more time. "Come see the world with me again, Biali. There must be ways to belong in more than one world at once."

Softly, wondering if there was regret or only inevitability in the word, Biali said, "No," and Hajnal sighed. Maybe this time, he thought, without believing it: maybe this time she would choose to stay, choose the safety of isolation and the quiet life of the mountain gargoyles. She had, a few times, at the beginning, but no. Tonight, as she had done most of a dozen times past, she stood on the mountain ridge, human form bare and fragile in the darkness and the wind, and stretched her arms as if she could embrace the world.

"Look for us in the overmind, then, my love. I have to go. Alban is waiting for me."

She leapt, inexpressible strength flowing even through human limbs: leapt high, and long before a descent began, transformed again, with wings flared to catch the air and glow pale in the moonlight. A sense of joy touched him through the overmind, joy in flight, joy in exploration, tempered only faintly by the sorrow of leaving.

Spain, 1608

New memories flooded the gestalt, at least the places Biali haunted: the lingering scent of sunlight hot on bricks, the warmth of a hand placed against those warm stones. Human laughter, so bright and easy, and human friendships. A woman who looked very like Hajnal herself, with bright black eyes and long loose hair, and dresses in red and yellow and blue, trimmed with equal brilliance; Hajnal herself enthralled by the textures of those dresses, the smooth fabric, the delicately worked lace. Her absolute ineptitude at *making* those laces, to the great hilarity of her mortal friend. Alban, quite solemn in comparison, but easier and more open than gargoyles ever were, a glass of wine almost as white as he was held delicately in his big hand; a determined Spaniard, hardly seeming half Alban's height, teaching the big gargoyle the steps of a quick-footed dance, and Alban's fond memory of Biali's patience with an awkward youth that now paid off in his ability to join in a human celebration.

Food of rich depth, spices and warmth, paired to the wines and applied, assiduously, to see what the Germanic pair—for that was how the Spanish peoples saw Hajnal and Alban, the accents of their native tongue rendering a liquid language more guttural than it was meant to be—to see what they could hold, what they liked, and whether, after a series of wagers, it was possible to get either of them drunk. It wasn't, and none of the wagering humans really thought that giant Alban couldn't hold his drink, but tiny Hajnal's ability to partake endlessly without becoming incapacitated delighted them. Laughing mortals, hassling two gargoyles out of their seats and onto a square of dirt kept clear for dancing, and Alban's lessons being worthwhile as he effortlessly spun a laughing Hajnal across the square.

Biali visited those memories often, studying them, searching for the differences between mortal and immortal, and finding far fewer than he might have hoped. The hours they kept, yes, because gargoyles could do nothing other than retreat at dawn and rise with the sunset, and the length of memory; the humans told stories of childhoods that had been a mere span of years in the past, while Alban and Hajnal were careful to say little about their own pasts, or to elide the details of *when* an event had happened, but the content of the stories was not so very different. The children were: there were so many human children, even in the evenings that Hajnal and Alban partook in. Babies at their mothers' breasts, little ones scrambling between legs and under tables, protesting bedtimes and wheedling for treats, older ones trying to be grown-up, sometimes with eerie success and other times with laughter-inducing failure, even youths who reminded Biali very much of Alban, all elbows and knees, if with less height and strength than the gargoyle lad had possessed. Memories of their enthusiasm filled the corner of memory that Hajnal frequented, and if she still harbored no regret over having none of her own, she was very fond of the small humans she encountered.

They were none of them dangerous, not really; even deep in reluctance Biali could hardly dispute that. Not so long as the gargoyles excused themselves before dawn, and if their hours were a source of interest to the humans, they were also, perhaps, a source of envy. To not rise and work with the sun; well, they were clearly wealthy, then, and the friendship with higher classes surprised and delighted the mortals, who half-imagined that the nobility were an entirely different people than themselves, so rarefied did they seem. *If only they knew,* Biali said one night into the overmind, as Hajnal's memories of the day built new hillocks and bumps in the vast range of memories, and she laughed, echoing in the growing hills.

Perhaps you'll come with us next time, she said again, with a hope more familiar to human optimism than gargoyle nature, and for once Biali only grunted noncommittally, rather than refuse her outright. She and Alban stayed in the warm south longer than they had planned: years, rather than a month or two, reveling in the days and nights of nearly equal length, that left them feeling more part of the world than the short summer nights farther north. Time flew so quickly for immortals it was easy to forget how much of it had passed, even for Biali, left behind; it was only when some lingering moment in the gestalt showed him a human child who had been an infant when they arrived now reaching girlhood that he thought of the years they had been gone, and wondered into the overmind if their unchanging aspect would undo them, after too long in one place.

Startled by the thought, they reluctantly left the sea and the warm salty air, but then returned home eager to see the tribe again. Hajnal flew into Biali's arms with a laugh, knocking him rough-and-tumble as if they were human children themselves, and Alban, amused, drew them both to their feet. He had gained his full breadth in the years they had been gone, shoulders wider than Biali's and his presence implacable. When he argued in favor of joining the human world this time, more of the tribe listened, though, like Biali, they didn't go so far as to join him where he stood—as ever, now—with Hajnal, against the tide.

The tribe spoke of them together now, when they spoke of them at all: Hajnal and Alban, instead of Hajnal and Biali, as it had been for centuries before Alban's birth. If they had become lovers that was absent from the memories, kept carefully to themselves, though there were moments in the overmind where the possibility could be seen: Alban's hand covering

Hajnal's against a sun-warmed wall, or in their laughter as they danced, or in quiet nights in the mountains above human cities, though any of those could be the comfort of friendship as well. But Hajnal came back to Biali with the joy of long-delayed unification, and if Alban had become so human as to learn jealousy, there was no sign of it.

Still, they stayed for so little time it could only be seen as a visit. Their world was beyond the mountains now, and Hajnal hesitated this time, before leaving, to make her familiar plea: "Come with us. To the east, we think, this time. To India, perhaps even to China. There's so much world to see, and it will take years, Biali. Decades. Come with us."

For the first time, Biali shook his head, not to say no, but to object to the scale of her ambitions. "That's too long, Hajnal. Maybe not for you, who are accustomed to traveling, but not for me. I left for that long once before. I don't want to do it again. Not the first time, not in so long."

Surprise and pleasure lit her face. "Then we'll go somewhere nearer. London again, or even Paris. It doesn't have to be for so long, if you'll come with us. Where would you like to go?"

He laughed, gruff sound. "I'd like to stay here, but you never will, will you?"

"No." The answer needed no consideration, though she managed a note of apology in the simple word. "I could contain the urge to travel when no one else wanted to, but with Alban..." She shifted a shoulder, obsidian shrug. "The world is there for us to explore. To learn how to belong to it. Come try for a while, with us, Biali. If you hate it you can always come home again."

London 1653

He did hate it, despite his best intentions. Paris, laden by its stinking River Seine; London, worse than that with the slaughterfields filling the Thames with offal. Innumerable humans, sometimes appealing with their swiftly changing lives, but mostly smelly and violent; the theatre that drew Alban and Hajnal bored Biali, melodramatic representations of the human condition only throwing into relief all the reasons he preferred to stay away from them.

Moreover, his mortal form got him invitations to a different aspect of the human world than Hajnal or Alban, one delicate, one tall, both beautiful by human standards, were offered. *He,* squat and muscular and roughly handsome, looked to men like a fighter, and they were eager to encourage him into a pit or a ring to see who could come out the best, himself or some poor human fool thrown in against him. He only participated once in a while, when he could slip away from the more genteel life the other two pursued, and he won more rarely than that, simply because it would be too easy to win all the time. That coins were tossed at his feet, that wagers were laid and livelihoods lost on the fights, only served to increase his dislike for humans and their cities, but they were so *easy,* and his skill and strength so superior that to disdain the opportunity seemed a waste.

A waste and a danger, because no human could be that strong, or should come back from taking a blow as easily as he did. That *he* might be the thing that betrayed his people to humanity loomed large in his mind, and after some months in London's stench he found Hajnal, far too close to dawn, to say, "I don't belong here. I don't *want* to belong here. Come back to the mountains with me, Hajnal. For a while, until the scent of humanity isn't in our bones anymore, until we're less than human, again. Or more than."

Stone didn't regret, not much, not often, but deeply, when it did; that was the pain that spasmed over Hajnal's features. "I don't belong there, Biali. Not anymore, if I ever really did. This is the world I've chosen. This is the world I want."

"And Alban."

She looked away, into the grey light of dawn, the closest thing to day that any gargoyle could see another in. Moonlight was kinder to them all, brighter, more flattering on the shadows and angles, but brightening twilight and its unkindness suited the sorrow on her face. "And Alban. I didn't expect that, but then, I didn't expect you would be so rooted, either. I thought that I loved you so much that you must be more like me. I think it's that you aren't like me that I do love so much, but in the end, I want someone to travel with."

"If I had known that," Biali said in a low voice, "I would have pushed him off a mountaintop before he could spread fledgling wings to save himself."

A surprised smile flashed across Hajnal's face. "No, you wouldn't have. If not out of nobility, then because killing each other is against our edicts."

"You may think better of me than I deserve."

"No." She reached up, put her hand against his cheek, and was caught that way by the dawn; when sunset's shadows reached them she finished, "I know you better than that. You're not even angry, Biali, much as you might want to be. This has been a long time in the making."

She was kind enough to not remind him that it had been of his making, too, as much as hers or Alban's; that he could have chosen, long ago, to join them on their travels. That he might have made things of himself, or them, that were not what came naturally to any of them, and had not, but that was what stone did, endured as it was, with little change save the great breaks that changed everything. She was right in that he wasn't angry, but that left room for regret, unfamiliar as it might be to their people. "Be careful in the world, Hajnal. I *will* take it out of his hide, if you come to harm."

Amusement flashed in her eyes. "As if I cannot keep myself

safe. What nonsense, Biali. You're right. You've already been too long among the humans, if that kind of absurdity is what you've learned from them."

"Still."

She shook her head, but smiled. "I'll tell him. Unless you want to."

Biali glanced skyward, shaking his head. "If I leave now I should cross the Channel well before dawn. Come home soon, Hajnal. I'll miss you."

"And I you." She stayed where she was, watching until he had disappeared with distance, and still he felt her in the memories, watching where he had been, wishing him farewell, with a sense of loss that salved his pride more than he cared to admit.

Hours later, Alban's shock was palpable, a reverberation in the gestalt, and *his* loss was as acute as Hajnal's. Biali had landed by then, found a safely ruined old human building to take shelter in, and drew silence in around himself, detaching from the overmind to nurse regret and sorrow and a blossom that could be anger, if he tended it long enough. But that would be human, and there had been enough of that already.

He returned to a tribe on the verge of splintering, and, in returning alone, in rejecting the human world, unintentionally drew them back together. There was satisfaction in that, as if he'd struck a blow against Alban and his dreams of living in the world. That it was a blow against Hajnal as well was easier to ignore; perhaps without Alban's influence she would never have gone out into the mortal world again. But that became circular, because without her stories Alban might never have explored it in the first place. Biali put a stop to those thoughts and questions, burying them in the gestalt, and watched the stories that Alban and Hajnal added to it from a distance, never with the intimacy of earlier decades. For forty years or more those memories grew, and then abruptly, as if death had taken them, they stopped, but even death didn't cause a *breach* in the memories. Whatever had not been added to the gestalt, in death, settled into the minds of the nearest gargoyles, so that nothing would be lost; it was a sacred duty to then bring those last memories to the overmind, but no final hours were recorded, and only a very little while after that, Biali left the mountains again to learn what had become of them.

LONDON, 1667

London had burned, in his absence. The tribe had known that, of course; even they were not so removed from the world as to miss the burning of a great city. Knowing, though, and seeing the startlingly scarred remains, the black marks where flame had flown, and the resurgence of humanity into those empty spaces, were different. Biali spent a handful of nights walking what remained of streets he had known, and flying above them to gaze without recognition at a city reshaped by fire. He searched for Alban and Hajnal in that time, as well, but it was the ruined city that captivated him, and woke a spark of loss in his chest. He wouldn't have imagined that he would care, but perhaps too much had been lost from his own world already; to see even a human city in ruins seemed a waste.

Hajnal and Alban were not—Biali believed—dead: their final memories had not come to the gestalt, as happened with all gargoyles at their time of death. The few other gargoyles who lived near London knew there had been a dragon in the city before it burned, but it had not approached them and they, distant in the hills, had been content to leave it be, in turn. Nor were there any humans to be found who had known either Alban or Hajnal; they had not, it seemed, had so close a community as they'd built in the south. They had traveled from England, though, never staying put as long as they had in Spain. Ireland, Scotland, even farther north than that, leapfrogging from one tiny weather-beaten rock to another until they reached places where the sun neither set nor rose, before returning through more conventional paths; Biali knew that, and yet expected, somehow, to find some trace of their presence in London. But perhaps it had been there, and had burned. The dragon might have known, but it was gone too, and if any other Old Races were near, they had nothing to say to a solitary gargoyle searching for two lost members of his kind.

The world was too large; any direction he chose was almost of necessity the wrong one. He searched regardless, feeling their absence—Hajnal's absence—in the gestalt like a wound; death would at least have sealed itself behind her, finishing her story in the overmind. They were not *dead*; Biali was convinced of it, but could hardly prove it. Could not, either, stop searching, not when the tribe quietly gave up hope; not when the elders began suggesting, then commanding, that he return. He argued; he was not in the world for its sake, not for the experience of humanity that had driven the other pair. He was there only to find them.

They do not wish to be found, the tribe told him. *They have chosen to Breach. They are exiles, both of their own choosing and ours; we cannot forgive those who turn their backs on the memories, when the memories are all that we have and all that we are.*

Return, Biali, they said to him, *return before you too are exiled, in spirit, if not in body.*

"Yes," he heard himself say to them, aloud, not within the surrounds of the overmind, "that would be wise." Then he continued on, learning to fight as men did to earn coin so he could feed his mortal form, which he used more and more, until his winged shape seemed almost alien to him. He never left the gestalt, not the way Alban and Hajnal did, but he lived in it less, grief giving way to fury at the empty place where they had been. The tribe became quieter, less important than finding the lost ones; had they spoken more loudly, they might have told him when the quest became a hunt for vengeance, when it was no longer worry, but rage that drove him.

Humanity suffered for it, if Biali did not: he was rarely in a place long enough to bother losing fights, and brutalized those who challenged him. Once in a while a mob of gamblers would turn on him, horrified by the violence he'd wrought; those occasions ended poorly for the mortals, and those who survived found themselves both bloodied and penniless for their efforts. Years went by quickly; decades, he could almost notice, pacing Europe and Northern Africa, Russia and back to Europe again, trusting that they would never leave their home continent for too long. St Petersburg rose; Lisbon drowned; between them wars staggered on, the endless effort of human domination. Biali, disdaining, profited from it, and searched.

He found Alban in the heart of revolutionary France, and by then it was too late.

FRANCE, 1785

Blood and rain lay puddled together, bootprints filled with both. Mostly bootprints: a few half-smeared prints were not human at all, and Biali crouched beside those ones, dipping his fingers in the muck. Massive width and depth at the ball, sharply arched toes. Claws. Little hint of the heel at all: a gargoyle's forward-leaning stance. He could all but see the crouch, the preparation for leaping upward. There were bullets lodged everywhere, some in the mud, others in buildings nearby. A few were bloody, the scent nearly washed away by unrelenting rain, but he knew even the hint of it: Hajnal's blood, spilled by humans in the storm. Her footprints, but not her body. Not even the broken remains of a statue shattered by axes and hammers. Either she still lived, or they had been thorough.

Alban's blood, too, and his footprints, deeper than Hajnal's. And then in the incessant rain, under the cover of night and clouds, the familiar sound of wings. Biali rose, and saw in the darkness a blur of white, with no smaller shadow in its wake.

He didn't fly, only launched himself into a cannonball to smash into Alban's gut, bringing them both to the ground. His fists rose and fell without compunction, not so much as a question asked, though he would beat the answer out of Alban if he could. The larger gargoyle blocked, arms crossed to catch Biali's blows, and shouted Biali's name, but refused to fight back. Biali leaned back to gain greater momentum for another massive blow, and Alban, given the space to breathe, flung him off and leapt to the air, fleeing like a coward.

Biali, roaring, gave chase, though within a handful of wing-beats he knew it was useless: Alban had the wingspan and strength to outpace him, and would never be caught unwillingly. He came to earth, though, well outside of the town, and settled into a preparatory crouch, waiting for Biali to renew the attack even as he shouted, "She is either not dead or has sealed herself off from the overmind more thoroughly than I thought possible. Her memories haven't come to me, Biali. We can find her."

"You stupid, naive—" No words could suffice. Biali never slowed his headlong rush, slamming into Alban with all of his airborne velocity. They skidded across mud and half-frozen puddles until a rocky outcropping—a fence—stopped them. Alban's head hit with a satisfying crunch and pieces of stone fell around him as Biali wrapped his hands around his throat and began to squeeze. Dust ground from between his fingers, from the sides of Alban's throat, and the sound was a glorious inexorable scrape of stone weakening stone. "You've been absent from the overmind for over a century, you faithless *breach*, and now you want me to believe she lives because she hasn't returned to it? No one leaves the memories for so long, no one knows what happens when you reject everything that we *are* for ever. You've lost her to all of us, you—"

Alban's hands were around his wrists now, tight enough to hurt, but not as much hurt as Biali did to Alban. Even gargoyles could be broken, even stone could shatter. Biali lifted Alban a few inches and shoved his head back down, hearing it crunch against stone again. Alban's grip loosened, then fell away entirely, and a vicious grin curved Biali's mouth.

It was the last whole expression he would ever feel. He didn't see Alban's hand close on another piece of stone, on a sharp-edged chunk of the fallen fence. He saw, perhaps, the flash of movement, turned his face toward it when he should have flinched away; the rock's edge caught his cheekbone with a sculptor's precision, and stone, which could, after all, shatter, did. His cheek, some part of his jaw, his *eye*: ordinary earthen rock stabbed splinters into shockingly tender stony flesh as shards that had once been his face fell into the mud and were swallowed. The pain went so deep he could hardly even scream, only make a wrenching sound of sickness that scraped from the bottom of his gut. He could hardly see: one eye didn't work at all, and the other swam with blackness as he fell away from Alban, gasping agony beyond comprehension.

It woke voices in the overmind, fear and concern and horror flowing through him so quickly he hardly knew which was his and what came from without. Gargoyles didn't take damage, not like this, not in their immortal forms; that they even *could* terrified the gestalt, and Biali's unfiltered thoughts spared no blame: this was the work of the exile, of the breach, of Alban Korund, and Hajnal had died at his hand, too. Disbelief swept him, but he pushed back with his conviction, and slowly the overmind reminded itself of Alban's strangenesses, his fascination with humans, his certainty that humanity's way was the future for even the Old Races, his departure from the gestalt; all of these things, fed by Biali's pain and rage, began to create a cohesive whole, a narrative that would stand in the memories forever.

Neither the overmind nor Biali latched on to the other truth, that as he writhed in the mud Alban, soft with shock, found what fragmented pieces of stone he could reassemble and crouched above Biali, pressing those shards back into place, and whispered, "Transform. Change, Biali. To stone and back again. Quickly, to heal."

Even the transformation was shocking, in its agony. There was will, deep in the silent heart of a gargoyle given fully to stone, else they could never take on their most immobile form without risking never returning from it, but will was almost always *all*: there was no sensation of relief, no reluctance to return to the living stone, no awareness of time's passage. But in this transformation lay all of those things, and a fundamental rage that knew Alban was right, that he must change again and again if he hoped to heal at all. That he had to go back to the pain, in order to find any release from it.

He came out of stone still roaring, anger and anguish perfectly paired, and went back into it so he no longer had to hear his own howls. Again, again, again, until the pain was, if not gone, at least bearable, and rage could drown it out. But Alban was wisely gone by then, leaving Biali nothing but the elements to take his madness on. He left the field in ruins, his hands battered from fighting Alban and even more so from mindlessly thrashing stone and wood and whatever else could be reached; cows and sheep died that night, and it was only fortune that no humans did. Fortune not just for mortals, but for Biali himself, whose passion and the thick grey clouds conspired to make him ignore—for no gargoyle could not *know*—dawn's approach, and he ended the night half buried in muck, hoping in his hate that it would obscure him enough from any human gaze that might glance over the landscape.

It did, or no one came seeking those particular fields that day; he awakened filthy and still enraged, but with a modicum of sense reasserting itself. He fled the fields and the carnage under cover of pouring rain, and was, at least, clean again when he finally found somewhere safe to huddle against the storm. He had almost no sight in one eye; a faint distinction between light and dark, that was all. His jaw, at least, held, but his cheekbone, the eye socket, they felt craggy with wreckage, sharp gaping wounds where stony flesh had once been. The next night it cleared, moonlight pooling in ditches, and that was where he first saw the ruin of his face, looking back at him from water turned blue by the night.

If this was what Alban had managed to repair, what had gone before must have been horrific indeed. A seam ran along his jaw and lower cheek, deep and pitted with marks where shards of flesh had had broken away and, having not been replaced, had gone unrepaired. The cheek and eye, though, were worse by far: gouges that went far beyond bone-deep, and which revealed inner workings, striations of stone-like muscle, pitted structure that looked nothing like mortal bones but could be seen as nothing else. His eye was clouded, a crease lying over it where, perhaps, a slab had been pressed back into place, and all of it glistened like raw mortal tissue, not like gargoyle flesh at all.

He shifted, taking on his human form with a shudder. It was somehow less shocking, that face, perhaps because he was less accustomed to it, but the scarring seemed less deep. Silvered skin instead of pitted, the bones crushed but the original angles less dramatic, and so not *as* dreadful in comparison. Even his vision seemed better, less occluded, and the bitter thought that he would prefer, now, to wear this face to his natural one arose. Alban had taken everything as relentlessly as time wore away stone, as implacably as water could crack it.

In exchange Biali hunted him relentlessly, harassing him whenever the opportunity arose, taking a certain bleak gladness in the regret shadowing the younger gargoyle's features when they met closely enough to speak, or even simply see one another clearly. When Alban left Europe for the New World, the elders of their tribe asked, though they hardly had to, that Biali follow the exile, settle where he did. Unspoken was the reason: there were other gargoyles, certainly, in the Americas, but it was Alban who held his own and Hajnal's secrets apart from the gestalt. Should he die—a prospect no one held in any great concern, not because his safety was in question but because it seemed better for everyone if he and his radical thoughts met a tidy end—it was thought best that those memories ought to return first to a member of the tribe, for examination before releasing them into the overmind. Memories were gathered by the gargoyle physically nearest to the one who died; in order to fulfill the tribe's needs, Biali of course must stay close to the Breach.

Very little distracted him from that duty; very little indeed, and what did distract him only fed the circle of loathing that burned in his heart. There were strictures against killing him, but time would offer an option; of that, Biali was sure.

YEAR OF MIRACLES

LONDON'S SLAUGHTERFIELDS STANK OF BLOOD and fear and
regret. Mostly blood, of course: it sank into rough-woven wool,
caked beneath ragged fingernails, traced muscle in arms and
soaked the ground underfoot. Cattle and goats, sheep and
chickens, dogs, cats—any kind of meat could be dressed out in
the fields, and every kind of animal seemed to know it.
Frightened bawling and thin screams were part of the air.

Once in a while, a man lay in the streams of blood,
damming them with his stiff, smelly body until the guards took
him away, or impatient butchers kicked him toward the river.
More often the river: wealth rarely came to the slaughterfields,
and so neither did law.

It was better that way, mostly. There were rules in society.
She didn't know much about them, except to know women
were traded and bet on and bred like horses. In the
slaughterfields she at least owned herself. It would have been
different if any of her brothers had lived, maybe, but they
hadn't, and her father had needed someone to lift carcasses, to
bend over them and strike flesh from bone, after the stroke
had weakened his left side. The second one had taken his life,

but by then she was the face of the family business, and folks just moved on with that. Two years had passed now, and she wasn't rich, but she wasn't whoring, either.

"From whom would I buy two dozen cows, a dozen pigs and as many sheep, and, oh, a flock of chickens for dining on?" A man's voice, behind her. She had a table with wares, and a stretch of canvas to keep the sun off and prevent the meat from spoiling too fast. Some of it, the expensive stuff, was salted already. The man might want that, since his request was unheard of. Nobility might ask for that much meat, but nobility didn't come to the slaughterfields themselves. They sent servants, though this man sounded too cultured to be one.

There was no hope of schooling her voice to match his. It made her uncomfortable in a way she was not when servants came around. Many of them had risen from low places and still sounded like the country and street folk they were. This man made her aware of how broad her accent was, and how refined his. Made her aware of the differences in their worlds as only the rich could do: thoughtlessly, effortlessly. It was clear enough, and always had been, that those born to a cheapside life were considered by the wealthy to deserve it, somehow. The poor knew better. There was no deserving or worthiness. There was only fortune, good or ill. Mostly ill.

She shaded her eyes, taking the sun's glare down enough to see the man. A stranger, someone she'd never seen before. Someone who shouldn't have looked comfortable in this part of town, but he was fearless. He was also tall, slim, ginger-haired and green eyed, and in a cloak only a fop would wear, its colors striking and bright. Layer after layer of fine cloth, reds and golds in no fashion she'd seen before, and the vest beneath it of cloth softer than she would ever touch. Just seeing it made her wipe hands on her skirt, uselessly; the fabric was stiff and black with blood. She squeezed it as she curtsied, feeling red dampness ooze between her fingers.

"I could get you that, sir. Not for tonight, nor tomorrow, but for Sunday dinner, aye. Slaughtered and dressed and brought to yer table, m'lord. I'd need payment in full up front," she added boldly. Even payment for half that lot would fill her belly for three months, but the rich didn't always know to bargain.

His eyes widened with mock dismay. "Slaughtered and dressed and brought to my table? Now why would I want that, when it's so much more fun to make the kill myself?"

She rubbed a finger in her ear, squinting at him. "My lord? You'll want a farmer with lands for that, if it's for hunting them yourself...." Hunting boar: the wealthy did that, she knew. But hunting cows and pigs was an oddness, even for the rich.

"Oh no." He kicked a foot up, displaying a boot of dark red leather, rich and beautiful and covered in the worst a slaughterfield could offer. "Hunt cows? And ruin these boots?"

She stared at the muck and offal already staining the fine leather, then lifted an uncomprehending gaze to the bright-eyed man whose foot rested on her table. "M'lord?"

"Your name, he said gently. "What is your name, slaughterfield's daughter?"

"Sarah," she said after a moment. "Sarah Hopkins, m'lord."

"Sarah." He took his foot from the table and bowed, deeper than she imagined a man would give even the queen. When he straightened again it was with a wicked grin. "All I wanted, Sarah Hopkins, was an excuse to speak to you. My name is Janx."

"My lord Janx," she said when it became clear he expected some kind of response. Up and down the way, others were staring now. Pausing in their salting, in their butchering, in their gossip, and leaning to get a better glimpse of the dandy at her table. He had better buy something, she thought: bad enough to already hear cat-calls and whoops, but worse by far if all the man wanted was to return to his monied friends and laugh over befuddling a slaughterfield girl. "Will I find the cattle and the sheep for you, my lord Janx?"

"What?" He looked surprised, then recalled himself and waved a hand. "Oh, no, no. Have dinner with me instead."

She stared at him. There was no other possible response, or none that wouldn't have her arrested by the rarely-seen guards. He waited, though, with unconcerned expectation that slowly shifted toward uncertainty. "You don't eat dinner?"

"Not with the likes of you, m'lord." The words weren't quite insulting. Sarah judged her tone was, though, by the astonishment flitting across the redhead's face. No one, she imagined, had ever referred to him as *the likes of you*. That was reserved for people of her class and below.

Janx, who was tall and slim and quite beautiful, sounded honestly confused: "Am I not pleasing to you, Sarah Hopkins?"

It was something a doxy might say to a man indifferent to her wares. This time Sarah looked both ways, up and down the alley of blood she and others worked. Waiting, she decided, for the others to show themselves. The men who had made the bet with red Lord Janx. The bet that he had lost, to be standing here asking silly questions. When it became clear—*again*—that he actually expected an answer, Sarah said, "Of course you are, my lord Janx," because first it was true, and second and more important, it was the answer that might keep her from being beaten or worse, should his friends push the jest too far.

"Then why not have dinner with me?"

He was a very good actor, this Janx. If he could look this bewildered, as if he really didn't know the answer to his question, then Sarah thought he would do well in one of the theatres in the round she'd gone to once or twice when she'd had a penny to spare.

He would have made a convincing, handsome face up on the stage, but it seemed the good looks hid a simpleton's mind. Sarah was crass and loud and bold, as all the butchers were, but as a child she'd been quieter. She had learned brassiness to survive instead of learning more numbers and letters as her father had hoped she could. She had learned to write her name when she was eight. It was the little girl who'd loved learning those four careful shapes with the "a" repeated who answered, much more gently than the cleaver-bearing woman she was now. "Because you are a lord, my lord, and I am a slaughterfield butcher."

He snorted a puff of blue smoke, though there was no pipe in his hands or even visible in the lines of his clothes. "If that's your only excuse, couldn't I insist by rights of being a lord?"

She nodded, and when he looked pleased, had the nerve to ask, "But why would you?"

"Oh," he said after a moment, and this time it was his turn to gentle the answer. "You really don't know, do you?"

"Know what?" Her mind danced, light and full of twists and turns, like she'd taken too much of the poteen.

Janx, tall and ginger and fine, said, "That you are the most beautiful woman London has seen in this side of twenty years, my dear."

Her burst of sound was not a beautiful woman's laugh. Raw and sharp, it hurt her throat, but tightness hurt it more as Janx's smile faltered. The slaughterfields stank of regrets, and that smile gave all those regrets a face of their own. It hurt him, Sarah thought, that she didn't believe him. That she *couldn't* believe him. It took time to find her voice again. "Thank you for the kindness, Lord Janx. Go home now, my lord. Find another woman to..." *Mock:* that was the word on her lips. But she said "Woo," instead, and wondered at herself even as Janx gave her another slow, deep bow, then walked away with thoughtfulness written in his features. He was hardly a dozen steps away when her fellow butchers came, laughing, teasing, wide-eyed with envious wonder. A few of them angry: angry that she had caught the eye of a lord, even if that lord had no business being in their part of the city. "A wager, a wager, that was all," she said more than once, and let her blushes be mistaken for modesty or pleasure. This would feed the gossips for months. Years, even. Any time someone with a hint of wealth came to the slaughterfields, the ginger lord's attention to Sarah would be remembered.

"Small enough price to pay," she said beneath her breath, and more clearly, "A pity he spent no coin. What good's a lord if his purse is tight?"

That earned laughter and a degree of forgiveness, and little by little the day faded toward normalcy. Cuts of meat sold, enough to cover the cost of a table along the row, and a bit left over for a pastie and beer before sunset took her home.

There was no looking-glass in the two-room street-level house that had been her parents' and now was hers. Of course not: glass was for the rich, and a copper was better spent than pounded flat to make a reflection. But a wooden bowl of water showed Sarah her face in barely-moving ripples, and she really looked at herself for the first time since childhood. Children were interested in such things, in making faces and seeing them copied back, and in learning the shapes that made up themselves. Adults had no time for that, not with bread to put on the table and butchering to do.

She didn't look like the child she remembered. That girl had been as clean as any slaughterfield's child could be, and a little spoilt. There had been curl in her dark hair, but it had been so many years since her hair was let loose of a tight braid that surely the curl had been choked out of it. She had been pretty, perhaps, in the way of children who are not yet broken by the world, but she had grown up strong, and that was a far better thing. Much as her father had loved her, a beautiful daughter would have made him more money by lifting her skirts than wielding a cleaver.

For an instant—only an instant—she thought of using the water to clean herself with. To see if, beneath the dirt and blood, some of the girlhood prettiness remained. The thought left as quickly as it came. It would be noticed if she was clean, tomorrow, and those who had been angry would turn cruel. Giving herself airs, they'd say; airs, because a lord had spoken to her. Making herself better than they, they'd say, because only their betters would bathe and perfume themselves. Never mind that there was no scent that could drown the smell of blood: even letting the idea take root was dangerous. It was no way to survive. The water went into a pot for porridge, and Sarah put the ginger lord out of her mind so he could not disturb her rest.

He came back in the morning.

She knew it before she saw him, a cold sick excitement in her stomach as whispers and sharp looks scattered her way while she prepared her table. A chicken leg stretched *so*, the cleaver slammed down to separate it from the body. Slammed too hard: it stuck in the table, and harsh laughter followed as she yanked it free. She would not, *would not*, look up in anticipation. Would not smooth her rough-spun skirt like a nervous maiden. Would not do anything but her duties, though her hands were cold and she split the other curséd leg in half when she took the knife to it. She was still staring at that, counting up the damage to her earnings, when Janx stopped before her table a second time.

"You'll get me gutted, my lord," she said to the chicken, and forgot to curtsey. Janx drew breath as if to speak, held it, and then held his silence too. Unexpected, that: she thought he was one who spoke just to hear his own voice, and wouldn't have imagined she might still his tongue.

But she had, and that was invitation of its own, so she spoke to the chicken again. Safer than looking at the red lord's light. She might let herself become fanciful, if she looked at him again. "There's naught as unforgiving as the poor. They'll see me dead before they see me rise, and you coming here twice hints I could." Not that she would. Not that she might. Not either of those things, not ever. Saying that, *thinking* that, was beyond her. Mad enough to say as much as she already had. "You do me no favors, my lord, by coming here."

Silence again, long enough—loud enough: every table near them, every passer-by, stood arrested, breath held, straining to hear every word that passed between them—long enough that the chicken's blood spilled to the table's edge and over, and made a pool around her shoe. That was long enough to wait on a man's answer without seeming bold about it. Sarah looked up, a dry swallow moving her throat, and found Janx's unreadable gaze on hers.

"But you won't come away with me," he said. Not a guess. Not even—quite—an invitation. Because he knew better, and while the answer he gave was true enough, it twisted a queer knife in Sarah's heart.

"Of course not. How could I?"

He nodded, slow and thoughtful as he'd been the day before. "I'll have that order from yesterday. Slaughtered and dressed for my table for Sunday dinner. You can do that?"

Sarah, hoarse with disbelief, whispered, "Payment in full."

Laughter sparked in Janx's green eyes. "One third, slaughterfield's daughter. A third today, a third when I come to inspect the meat before it's delivered, and the final third—"

"On delivery," Sarah said, swiftly. "On delivery." Janx dropped his voice and stepped closer. So did everyone within a stone's throw, heads turning and tilting the better to hear them. "Are you really in danger because of my attention, my dear? Will they come at you in daylight?"

"Yes," she said, "and no. Probably not."

"Then I'll arrange for protection at night. When will the meat be ready for inspection?"

"Protection?" Her thoughts were slow, slower than the river choked with winter ice. This went beyond a jest. Beyond a wager. A man of means couldn't possibly think her worth protecting. She thought of the water bowl and the woman it reflected, and wondered what he saw that it hadn't shown. Or maybe he liked blood and filth: a man who offered to hunt herds of cattle might. Heart sick in her chest, she shook her head. "If I'm worth protecting I'm worth killing, sir. Don't do me that favor. Whether it's the guards or a hired man, they won't look right around here."

"The man I have in mind will go unnoticed. The meat, Sarah Hopkins?"

"Saturday sundown." If she lived that long.

Janx smiled. "Saturday sundown. Until then, my man will come to watch over you at dusk. The first third in full," he added, dropping a bag of coin onto her workspace without bothering to count it out. Then he went away with no look of care or concern. Sarah watched him go, then turned a helpless gaze down the row.

One among many met her eyes with regret instead of resentment. Jacob, a miller's son who didn't stink of blood and shit, and who had come courting her of late. He was stopped three tables down, as if he'd heard tale of yesterday's scene and come to talk or tease about it. But the red lord had returned, and that, perhaps, changed everything. Sarah said, "He will cast me away," and Jacob smiled. Not a happy smile. A smile of loss and acceptance.

"Maybe," he said, "but maybe not. And if he does, if you

come back, I'll never say a word about it. Reach high, Sarah. Hold tight."

He left then, a better man than she might have ever dared dream of having. It wasn't fair, Sarah thought. It wasn't fair that life played games like this. Offering two men, one who was beautiful and impossible, one who was steady and sensible. One who would burn and one who would hold.

It wasn't fair that she was just foolish enough to reach for fire.

At least she had coin to spend and an order to fill. Even better, almost, was the gossip fodder she offered: twice she drove bargains laughably to her advantage, so eager were the vendors for details of Lord Janx's smooth voice, of the cut of his coat, of the fall of his hair. That word of all those elements had rushed ahead of her didn't matter. She was the very source of the particulars, her word to be trusted above all others, even if the moment her back was turned claws lashed out. There were no blades; that was all that mattered.

She was still out as the sky turned red and then grey with evening. Lord Janx's man would never find her, if he even existed; it would be her own neck getting home. Not that his man would likely find her small cottage, either, packed as it was between countless others. The red lord had not, after all, asked where she lived. Nor would she have had an address to give him: her alley had no name, and no signs to point the way. You knew, in London's back ways, or you didn't, and if you had to ask you were likely to be knifed and left for dead, your boots and coin stolen.

"Sarah Hopkins." Another man's voice, another new voice, though as unlike Lord Janx's as it could be. *He* sounded like he was always about to laugh or maybe sing, light and cheery. This one was deep and solemn, no humor to it at all, and it belonged to a man who stepped out of shadow to tower above her.

Janx, she thought clearly: the lord Janx was tall. This man

was taller, perhaps the tallest she'd ever seen, and so broad across the shoulder she moved her head to look from one side of him to the other. His hair and eyes had no color in the dusky light, and he was not nearly so finely dressed as the red lord had been. Only far better than herself, or anyone who might normally walk this part of town after nightfall. Her voice broke between laughter and disbelief: "He thought *you* would go unnoticed?"

A rumble came from the big man's chest. Not quite a laugh, but amusement. There was humor in him after all. "Janx only notices beauty, so to him, I'm unremarkable. My name is Alban. I'll keep you safe, Sarah Hopkins."

"I think you could keep the whole of London safe," she murmured, and let him follow her home that night, and for two more besides. When they spoke, he called the red lord *Janx*, no deference shown, though nothing in his clothes or bearing said he too was a lord. It was only on the third night that she dared ask about that, and the white guard—if Janx was red, Alban was white, paler than any man she'd ever seen—rumbled again.

"We're brethren, he and I. The titles I might use for him mean nothing in a—" He hesitated, and finished carefully, a foreign accent more clearly marking his words: "In an English court. Don't be too impressed with him, Sarah. Anyone can buy fine clothes and learn a noble's accent."

"I couldn't." They were at Sarah's home by then, and Alban stopped at the threshold as he had each night before. For the first time, Sarah gestured inside. "You could come in."

"I think that would threaten your reputation. Or mine."

Sarah laughed. "Am I as dangerous as all that?"

"If you've earned Janx's attention, you are almost certainly more dangerous than you know. Beauty often is. But," the big man said more lightly, "even if you are not, my wife is."

Surprise burst in Sarah's chest. "You're married? But you're here all night every night with me!"

"She understands. We are...protective by nature, she and I. A few nights to assure a woman's safety is nothing, in the face of the years we have together."

"Be careful of that thought," Sarah whispered. "The years are always shorter than we hope."

Color came into Alban's eyes for the first time since she'd known him, yellow in their depths. "There, you see? Wisdom: and wisdom, Sarah, is as dangerous as beauty. Go now. Sleep well. I'll see you at sunset tomorrow."

"I'm to meet Lord Janx then. No one will be bold or foolish enough to come at me."

"True enough." Alban smiled, brief but not teasing. "But you may need protection from Janx."

Coldness settled on Sarah's shoulders, a cloak that pushed away springtime warmth. "Will I?"

As cold had settled on her, stillness settled on Alban. He didn't seem to so much as breathe, though finally a sigh was pulled from his lungs. "I don't know. I only met him when he hired me to protect you. He won't deliberately do you harm, but he may forget how fragile you are, and that this is your life, not a game. That's the way of his...ilk. Hajnal—my wife—would be better able to advise you."

"Perhaps she could come see me tomorrow," Sarah blurted. "Before I see Lord Janx. I would be grateful for advice, my lord."

"Alban," he said gently. "Always Alban, Sarah. I don't pretend to Janx's airs. And...I could bring you to her tonight, but she can't see you tomorrow."

"Is it far?" She hadn't been tired until he made the suggestion, but weariness rose in a sudden war with curiosity.

Alban, for some reason, looked to the sky before his face wrinkled in a frown. "Farther than I think of it as being, yes. I could hire a carriage."

A smile twitched Sarah's lips. "You're as blind as he is. No carriage would take me, Alban. My skirts would stain the seats."

His frown deepened and he examined her as if he'd never seen her before. Acceptance slowly cleared his expression, though a touch of surprise still remained. "A cart, then."

Sarah shook her head. "I'll seek your lady's advice another time, if I come to needing it. Thank you, though."

Alban nodded, then turned his attention down the alley. "Would you leave this place if you could, Sarah Hopkins?"

"Only a fool wouldn't." She spoke without thinking, but then followed his gaze along the narrow cobbled path between leaning buildings. At windows covered with cheap cloth, or more often not covered at all, and at doors hung crooked in their frames. Upward, at the strip of sky visible where ever-larger upper stories almost touched, their thatched roofs poking straws at one another. She had been born in this alley and would likely die there, having spent all the days between walking to the slaughterfields to sell the meat she bought bleating, then butchered for those who could pay. She hadn't imagined more until Janx spoke to her, and even now she knew that imagination failed her. There was no life beyond the slaughterfields that meant anything to her. So she answered again, more honestly this time: "I would like to try."

"I wish you luck." For all his size, Alban nearly disappeared when he settled into place beside her door. He would be there until dawn, or just before. She never heard him leave, but he had always been gone when the sun edged into the sky. A night-time guardian, just as Janx had promised.

For the first time, she wondered what else he might promise, and whether she had the courage to accept.

* * *

A streak of foolish hope and vanity made her look at her Sunday gown when the sun rose. Practicality defeated the thought: the larger beasts were bought, slaughtered, butchered and hung to age, but there were chickens a-plenty to prepare for Janx's table, and they would bleed on her one good dress as easily as on her slaughtering clothes. More, Janx would neither notice nor care what she wore. Her neighbors, though, would, and would rightfully mock her for wasting good clothes to catch the eye of one so far above her.

Especially, she thought with unusual confidence, since she'd caught his eye already.

He came to the market before sundown, when she was elbow-deep in guts and feathers and blood. She wiped sweat from her forehead with a forearm, smearing blood instead, and straightened to stretch her spine and squint at the red lord. "You're early, my lord."

"I couldn't bear to see you only in dusk's faint light. What is life without the sun's gentle touch shining in your hair and bringing a blush to your fair cheeks?" Janx put a hand over his heart, eyelashes fluttering, and looked insulted when she laughed. "Do you not believe me, Sarah Hopkins?"

"How could anyone?" She directed his attention with a thumb over her shoulder. "Your chickens, my lord. The rest is hanging for inspection, and I'll have it packed in a cart and brought to your kitchens when you're satisfied."

"My dear," Janx said in pretend dismay, "do you think it's well-hung meat that satisfies me?" His dismay turned to a shout of laughter as Sarah thinned her lips at him, and he bowed, gesturing that she should lead the way. She had a step or two in which to fight down laughter of her own before he was beside her, walking as if they were equals. He should not be encouraged, she told herself fiercely, but it was hard not to fall into his catching sense of play. He asked her questions—sensible questions about the preservation of meats and about the strength and skill necessary to cut through bones and joints—as she brought him through the market to the hanging room where she most often hired hooks.

Janx's nostrils flared as they entered. The scent here was different: saltier and more intensely of meat rather than blood. There was that, too, of course, but the drying flesh had a deeper smell to it, one that lingered in the throat.

"Yes," Janx said. "This will do. Don't have it packed in salt to be delivered, slaughterfield's daughter. There's salt a-plenty already."

"You'd best hope the night is cool, then, or it'll sour. You must have very large kitchens," Sarah added, then winced. If there was a skill to smooth conversation, she lacked it.

Janx only nodded, absent answer given as he stepped closer to a hanging side of beef and sent it gently swinging. "It would take an army to cook all of this. Can you have your man deliver it before dawn, Sarah Hopkins?"

She would never see the coin, if it was paid to the man and his cart in the middle of the night. Still, two-thirds of the price she'd named for all the meat would see her through the summer. Beyond, if she was careful and lucky enough to not be robbed of it. "Sure enough. At which bell?"

Like Alban, he glanced to the sky before answering. It was darkening now, spring's late dusk coming on. Dawn would be early, too. "Three bells," he decided aloud. "No doubt it'll still be dark then."

"And do you live in Westminster, m'lord, or a country estate?"

"Oh, God, an estate. I would itch my skin off in the city's close confines. Bad enough to walk below the jetties—" He fell silent at Sarah's expression, then offered a rueful apology. "Which is of course where you live. I meant no insult, Sarah, but don't you find it...distressing? The way the houses...?" He tented his hands, echoing the dangerous lean of buildings toward one another.

"I wouldn't know anything else, my lord." She'd been easy before, but stiffness filled her now.

Janx's face fell. "I'm a poor suitor, aren't I?"

"No." Sarah shaped the words carefully. "You're a wealthy one, and that, my lord, is probably worse. I'll need to pay my man tonight, if he's to deliver the goods in the small hours," she said, feeling clever. "It'll be half of the final third, and I'll come tomorrow to collect the rest." That was spoken like the truth, though she doubted herself the moment it was said.

Janx dropped a purse of coin into her palm as carelessly as before, never counting it, and Sarah never doubting it contained at least as much as she demanded, perhaps more. But he dipped into the purse, bringing up a shining bit of metal between two fingers: the last of what she was owed, the money she claimed she would come for on the morrow. "Will you truly come?"

Sarah looked away and Janx chuckled. "I shall wait with hope regardless. What might I do or say to entice you?"

"Nothing, my lord." The money felt heavy in Sarah's hand, like she'd been bought and sold already. "I thank you for your custom."

"I believe you've been dismissed, Janx." Alban spoke from the meat hall's door, startling Sarah and sending a mild look of irritation over Janx's changeable features.

There was a woman with Alban tonight, small and dark-haired, with faintly golden skin tones that made him look all the paler by comparison. His wife, Sarah guessed. Her heart clenched with pleasure and nervousness that he'd remembered.

"Master Korund." Janx bowed less deeply than he had for

Sarah. "I didn't retain your services for the night, nor the lady's at all."

"You cannot imagine the coin you offer is what causes him to be here," the woman said. Her voice was deeper than Sarah expected: warmer, and marked with the same accent as Alban's. "As for myself, I'm generally wiser than to truck with the likes of you, but Mistress Hopkins asked for me, and so here I am."

"Goody Hopkins, Mistress," Sarah whispered. She would lay no claim to a gentlewoman's title, even one so modest as *mistress.* Not while nobility stood among them, and from Janx's naming of Alban as *master*, he and his wife were of gentle birth, too.

Mistress Korund, with as much regard for class as Janx showed, waved away Sarah's objection. "I don't care for the sound of that word. Mistress will do. You may go, Janx. Leave the girl alone."

To Sarah's astonishment—to *Janx's*, clearly—he stepped back, entirely obedient. Then a sulk pushed his lip out and he closed with Sarah again, suddenly all jade eyes and injured hope. "Would you have me go, Sarah?"

"I've told you already," she said. "I'll come tomorrow for the rest of the payment."

"That," Alban's wife offered, "means yes. Go on. I need to speak with her."

Janx's easy humor fled and he crossed to the Korunds so quickly it made Sarah's head ache. Something was wrong with the way he moved, the action more like an unbroken ripple across a pond than a man crossing space with so many steps. Softly, softly enough that Sarah thought she was not meant to hear, he said, "Watch what you say."

Hajnal Korund, who stood head and shoulders smaller than the ginger lord, showed not a whit of concern at his too-close presence. "I know what can and cannot be said, Janx. It might do you well to remember what can and cannot be done."

"Laws," Janx murmured, "are for the law-abiding." Then, more clearly, and peevishly, "Yes, yes, I've been dismissed, very well, I shall take my leave of you all." Quicksilver in temperament, he was suddenly smiles and charm as he bowed once more to Sarah. "I do await tomorrow with anticipation, my dear. Don't destroy my hopes."

He left them all behind, the Korunds at the door and Sarah standing amongst meats hanging in springtime warmth. The hall was emptier than could be accounted for by his leaving, and a chill of loss crept up Sarah's spine. "He didn't say where his estate was."

"It would never occur to him that someone might not know. I'll tell your man which streets to take," Alban offered, then hesitated. Made another offer in that hesitation, one that could be heard even if it went unspoken.

Sarah looked to his wife, to a woman she hadn't even met yet. Sympathy curved the other woman's mouth, and Sarah wondered if she had found Alban both appealing and impossible, when he'd first come courting. "When you are old," Hajnal said, "which will you regret more, the going, or the staying away?"

Sarah closed her eyes to admit the truth without facing it. "The staying away."

Hajnal's voice deepened further with understanding, if not surprise. "Then Alban will tell you which streets to take, too."

She wore her Sunday dress, of course. Even scrubbed herself in water heated over an otherwise-unnecessary fire. Scrubbed until the water was brown with old blood and her fingers wrinkled. Took her mother's bone comb to her hair, leaving tangled snarls of it on the floor. Taken from its braid and combed, though, it shone in waves. Janx, who had no evident regard for social standing, would like it down, she thought. But only children and harlots wore their hair loose, so she bound it back up again and counted having thought of what he'd like at all a mark both for and against him. She didn't want to think such things, but if it didn't matter, she would have kept to her workday clothes and not bathed at all. He had won something from her already, then, and it would be false to say she wasn't glad of it.

The road there was long enough, and then some, to strip away her rabbit-heart excitement and cold nervous hands. A ha'penny bought her a cart ride down the longest stretch, and she left it behind with straw stuck in her skirt as a reminder. She shook it free before reaching wrought-iron gates with a monstrous dragon worked in the metal. They stood open, perhaps awaiting her, and she crossed through wondering how Janx had ever come so far afield as to even see, never mind speak to her. He was landed, not just a lord in name with no property or money: she couldn't yet see the house, though she'd passed by a gatehouse already. Unmanned, that, which was strange, from what little she knew of the wealthy.

"You came." Janx, impossibly, crested the low rise in the road in front of her. A very low rise: she could see over it, see the path beyond. He had not come up it. Sarah gaped, and he spread his fingers, dismissing the oddness in favor of a brilliant smile for her. "You came," he said again. "I thought you wouldn't. Especially after Hajnal had a word with you. What did she say?" He all but pranced forward, offering her an arm.

She was astonished enough to take it. Janx's smile, already broad, widened further. He squeezed her hand against his ribs, murmured, "You look lovely, my dear. For me?" and gestured down the drive. "We have a carriage coming. Would you prefer to sit and wait, or walk to meet it?"

"How did you get here before the carriage? I didn't...see you." Sarah let go his arm to climb the rise, satisfying herself that there were no hollows or depressions large enough to hide him at the roadside. She turned back to face him and caught thoughtfulness in his eyes before he gave a tiny shrug.

"I couldn't wait on something so slow as a carriage and four. The wind carried me, Sarah Hopkins. What do you think of that?"

"I think you're mad." More, she thought she should be angry at his playfulness, but it pulled a smile to her lips instead. "Is there really a carriage coming?"

"Of course."

"Then we'll wait." Bold decision, but he'd asked and seemed determined to treat her as an equal. She would likely never see such regard again, and Mistress Korund's words lingered in her mind: *which would she regret more?* Surely anyone would regret not taking the mad and wonderful moments as they were given, that those memories might linger on cold nights in the future. Sarah sat on the ground, tucking her skirts around her ankles, and Janx clapped his hands with childish delight.

"I should have brought a picnic."

"Is the wind kind enough to carry that, too? But your cook would be furious, my lord. She must be working her fingers to the bone preparing a feast from the meat. Will there be a...a ball?"

Janx sat beside her, arms looped over his knees and bemusement on his face. "No, I'm afraid not. Not tonight. Would you like one? I could host one for you."

Sarah laughed. "I wouldn't know how to dance at a ball, my lord, even if I should be allowed to attend such a thing. What, then, with so much food? Oh." The last was spoken to the distance as the promised carriage and four appeared. Matched horses, all bays with white stockings, and stars on their foreheads when they were close enough to see. The carriage itself gleamed, black wood and shining trim, and a liveried footman leapt down to offer her a hand to rise from her seat in the dirt.

She only stared at it. At his tidy fingernails and clean hands, much cleaner than hers had come, even with scrubbing. At the cuff of cloth beyond the hand, no doubt more costly than what she might earn in a year. It wasn't Janx who was mad, after all: it was herself, for having come here.

Janx brushed the footman away, standing and taking Sarah's hand himself. He was finer by far than the footman, of course, but she expected that. Knew her place in comparison to that. It was easier to have courage facing the ridiculous than facing a servant who would only see her as getting above herself.

"Trust me, if not yourself, Sarah." Janx kept her hand in his, steady and soothing, but made no effort to tug her toward the carriage.

She wavered and finally whispered, "This is not my life, my lord. This is not who I am."

"No," he said just as quietly. "But it could be."

"Because I'm beautiful?" She still didn't believe that, but it was easier to accept he saw beauty in her than any other possible explanation for the madness that had entered her life.

"Yes, but more because you're brave. A beauty drowned in cow's blood has done you very little good so far—"

"It caught your eye," Sarah said a little dryly. "I don't understand *how*, as certainly your like was never seen in the slaughterfields—"

"Not mine, no," Janx said as if surprised, "but servants. I listen to servants, Sarah. They have a great deal that is interesting to say, and I had heard tale of the beautiful butcher from more than one source. And beauty may have brought you to my attention, but it's your bold spirit that brought you here today. That makes far more difference than mere loveliness. One catches the eye. The other—" He broke off and Sarah's eyebrows rose.

"The other?"

One corner of his expressive mouth crept upward. "The other catches the soul, I was going to say. But then I thought it might be too much."

"Two dozen cows, a dozen pigs and sheep, and a flock of chickens, and *now* you worry about too much?" Confidence restored by humor, Sarah made the smallest move toward the carriage, and Janx leapt to provide her support as she stepped in.

She could not speak, once within. The leather seats were finer than she'd ever touched, even knowing and trading with tanners. There was *glass* in the windows, large panes without leading. She couldn't begin to imagine the cost. And the road was smooth enough, but there was no jostle at all as the team of four turned and brought them back up the drive. Fingers clenched against the seat's edge, Sarah watched spring-green land grow into shaded woods before a turn in the road revealed a house larger than entire London blocks. Stairs as wide as her alleyway was long led to doors of impossible height, all of it reflected in a long pool stretching before the house. A squeak broke from Sarah's throat and Janx beamed, clearly pleased with himself.

"Do you like it?"

She nodded, finger pressed to her mouth. "How do I not know you, my lord? Is 'Janx' a prankster's name? Are you..." Imagination failed her: the king's oldest son was new to England and still barely more than a boy, even if he should for some reason choose to hide his name. "What is your family name, sir?"

"Nothing that would mean anything to you. I'm no one special, Sarah, but I do have outrageous amounts of money. When the opportunity arose to let these lands after the family who owns them fell on hard times, well." He gestured, taking in the landscape. "I could hardly refuse such a glorious setting, could I?"

Owning such an estate was difficult enough to imagine, but that, at least, might come through family and inheritance. *Renting* them meant incomprehensible wealth. Sarah swallowed, fingers still against her mouth, then dared a tiny smile behind them. "I didn't charge you enough for that meat."

"Not nearly enough, no." They were at the broad steps by then, and Janx waved the footman away a second time, offering Sarah his own hand after jumping free of the carriage. She hesitated in taking it and he curled his fingers, coaxing. "You're here. You might as well enjoy the day. And there's no one here to worry about your rank or your garb save you yourself."

Sarah, under her breath, said, "And the servants," but took his hand and climbed from the carriage. The house rose so high and solid that the clouds racing above made her dizzy as she looked upward. Janx put a hand in the small of her back, steadying her.

"I'll have them dismissed, if you wish."

Alarmed, Sarah took her gaze from the dazzling sky. "The clouds?"

Janx laughed and waved his hand again—he liked to take up space, make big gestures, and his clothes and cloak moved beautifully when he did. "The servants, Sarah. For the day only. I have no intention of running an estate this size by myself. Or at all."

Her shoulders dropped in relief. For a moment it hadn't seemed impossible that he might shoo away offending clouds. Nor, upon thought, did it seem beyond him to dismiss every servant for good as a thoughtless gesture of comfort to her, without ever understanding what that would do to their reputations and their families. "Let them be. I wouldn't want to spoil your cook's good work."

"She certainly isn't cooking it all. Which would you like for your meals today? Beef? Chicken? Lamb? Pork?"

Water rose in Sarah's mouth. "Beef is a rare enough treat, my lord."

"Beef it is. May I show you the house and grounds while she prepares it?"

This man got what he wanted far too easily, Sarah thought. The ease of wealth, and of charm: even as she thought he should be challenged, she had no real desire to ruin his fun herself. She did, though, ask, "Could I stop you?"

"With a word, my dear. With a word."

Curious, she looked up at him, fine and red-clad and as serious as she'd seen him, which did nothing to hide a twinkle in his green eyes. "You mean that, my lord." Half a question, and Janx stepped back to offer another of his theatrical bows.

"With all my heart. So: *will* you stop me?"

"Well, if she won't, I certainly will." Another man; another new and cultured voice. The humor fled from Janx's face for real, eyes flat and black and mouth thin for one bleak moment before the mirthful mask returned. This time, though, Sarah could see it *was* a mask; that beneath it, he was displeased with the new arrival.

So many men to change the shape of her life. So many educated voices and expensive clothes and deep rivalries. So many small moments, embedded forever in her memories. The world had smelled of blood and sorrow and regret when she met Janx.

It smelled of warm dust and sunshine and new grass the morning she met Eliseo Daisani.

He stood at the head of the stairway, made small by their enormous size and by the tall pillars and doors rising behind him. His hair and clothes were dark and conservative, but he came down the stairs with the same lightness of foot the red lord showed. He was swarthy and not handsome, certainly not by comparison to Janx, but he took Sarah's hand and kissed her inner wrist, shockingly intimate and with as little regard for propriety as the other man showed.

Sarah's heart knocked in her chest. Both men looked at her as though they'd heard it, and the small man smiled. "No wonder he was trying to keep you to himself. The honor is mine, Sarah Hopkins. I am Eliseo Daisani."

"I'm..." He knew her name already, and she could think of nothing else to say. She hadn't been flustered by meeting Janx, but then, he'd only spoken sweetly, not kissed her. Nor should he have, rank with blood as she'd been. Nor should this Eliseo Daisani have, either, of course, only that was a thought hard to keep in her head as a blush mounted her cheeks. She finally retrieved her hand and curtsied, still unable to speak.

Janx, less reserved, muttered, "What a pleasure to see you, Eli," in a tone that said it was not. Master Daisani's nostrils flared and he gave Janx a sour look.

"'Eli'? Really, Janx? Must you?"

"Yes," Janx said, after the appearance of all due thought on the matter. "Yes, I think this time I must. Eli."

A smile pulled at Sarah's mouth and she glanced down, trying to hide it, as Master Daisani turned to her with a sigh. "He's annoyed that I've come today. Oh, but we've amused you. That's something, I suppose."

"Eli," Sarah murmured to her shoes, "is a very nice name."

"Now see what you've done," Daisani said to Janx, but all the irritation had gone out of his voice. Sarah's smile widened and she glanced up again, hardly daring to rest her gaze on the smaller man. He was *not* Janx: not so handsome, and therefore somehow less alarming, despite the liberties he'd already taken. They should both be alarming, Sarah reminded herself. They were both far beyond her in birth, and in truth she could only end up damaged from their interest, but for the moment...

...for the moment, it was glorious. Oh, she should be wiser, but wisdom was for the old, and she was young. Nineteen summers, or maybe twenty. Old to be unmarried, but having taken over her father's business had kept her unwed. She didn't mind: children were a different kind of work, just as tiring, and had she been a wife and mother she never would have drawn Janx's eye.

Or Eli Daisani's.

A blush heated her cheeks again, but she squared her shoulders to make herself feel bold. She drew breath, but Janx spoke before she could: "May I make an outrageous offer, my dear?"

"More outrageous than meat to feed an army, overpayment and a carriage sent to get me at the gate?"

Janx cast his glance heavenward, thoughtful, then flashed a smile upward before nodding happily. "Much."

Sarah spread her hands in invitation, and Janx clapped his. "I've retained the entire staff from the owners of the estate. There are at least three ladies' maids desperate with boredom. Perhaps you would permit them to dress you for dinner?"

"All I have is what I wear, my lord." She brushed her palm over her skirt, certain Janx would have an answer to that, too.

His quick smile lit up his features yet again. "I may have also retained several wardrobes full of gowns. Surely something will fit you."

Peculiar emotion filled Sarah's chest. Neither offense nor anger, but some cousin to them, and to rue besides. "Am I a doll, my lord?"

Daisani hissed softly, admiration in his gaze when she glanced his way. Janx rocked on his heels, muttering, "A palpable hit," before shaking his head. "No, nor would I wish you to be one. I would, though, like you to see what I see in you, and I think only dramatic measures will accomplish that."

"And when you've made me pretty and dressed me in fine

clothes, I'll still return to the slaughterfields, my lord, where they'll name me your whore and throw only rotten fruit if I'm lucky."

"You could stay," Janx said, and in those words hung the balance of her fate. She knew it, even in the moment. In the silence that weighed heavy in the air; in the stillness both men took on, and in the length between her own heartbeats, as if even they waited on her answer.

Which will you regret more? Hajnal's voice asked, and Sarah heard herself say, "You will buy me a home in London. Something sensible, not an estate. You will put money into a lender's hands for me and me alone. Enough for a year or two, more if I'm careful. And when you cast me away, those things will both be mine, and you will never return to claim interest on them. Because if I stay, even for a night, and let you make me fine, then I can never go back to what I was without endless jeers and perhaps danger, and I will have *some* manner of surety set aside before I do that."

Janx's eyes were bright. "And how do you know I'll do those things if I promise them today? I might lie to you."

Sarah shrugged. "It's no loss to me to return home now and wait on the papers and the lender. This is your game, my lord, not mine."

"Go on," Daisani said to Janx. "Lie to her. Let me promise her what she requires instead. I already own the house to suit." He turned to Sarah, expression serious. "Stone built and near the city wall, but within it. There are modest grounds and a small staff. All yours, Sarah Hopkins. The banker I will have to speak with tomorrow, but the account can be opened and filled by dinnertime."

"That's not fair," Janx protested. "I only have this estate. Sarah, I would hardly lie to you—"

"I told you to invest in houses, Janx. How am I to blame if you never listen? Miss Hopkins, you are a clever woman and drive a solid bargain. Will you accept your requirements from me?"

She had known. Deep inside, she'd known when she made the terms, that Janx would agree. Not that Daisani would; that churned surprise inside her, though it wasn't so hard to understand. They were friends, the sort who couldn't get on without each other and showed it through unending arguments and rivalries. She knew other men—and women—like that, though none nearly so immoderate as these two. *She* didn't matter so much, not to them. It was the winning that mattered, and somehow she had fallen into their sights as a prize.

Men had always seen women as prizes. There were worse by far to be sought after than two gentlemen, and the promise of a better life lay before her no matter how else it might end. "You'll have to teach me to speak," she said softly. Anyone could learn a noble accent, Alban had said. *Not me,* she'd answered, but that, it seemed, had been yesterday.

"To speak," Janx said before Daisani could. "To dress, to dance, to charm, to arms! Does this mean you accept our offer?"

Our offer. They hadn't planned it this way: that much Sarah was sure of. But she was sure, too, that they knew and accepted each other too well to not take advantage of the other's generosity.

She said, "I accept," and delight blossomed on both men's faces.

Three determined maids, a shining brass tub, and more hot water than Sarah had ever seen did what she had been unable to: removed the stains and stenches of the slaughterfields from every part of her body. She had never been bathed before, not by someone else, and never so

thoroughly. They were efficient but brutal, and Sarah felt
bruised and raw when they took her from the tub, her skin
bright red. Tangles of hair stuck to the tub's sides, and more
came out, turning to rat's nests as all three women took a part
of her head and worked first wide, then fine, toothed combs
through her hair. She was pulled this way and that, their fists
against her head to reduce the yank. When she was dizzy from
the pulling, she held up her hands, pleading for a pause, and
they slowed, then stopped. Sarah pushed her fingers against
her skull carefully, trying not to undo their work, and asked,
"What are your names?"

The girls looked at one another, and the oldest of them
shrugged. "Colleen, miss."

Laughter caught her off guard. "All of you?"

"It's what the mistress called us. She don't care beyond
that we're Irish, so that's what she called us."

"Well, I'm not the mistress, so you are...?"

They were Rose and Mary and Bridget, and they were less
grim in their duties after that. A fourth girl, younger than the
ladies' maids, knocked at the door and entered with watered
wine, cheese, meats, and a message Janx had clearly made her
memorize: "So that you don't perish, my lady, whilst you're
made even lovelier than you are by nature."

Sarah protested, "I'm nobody's lady," but knew it as a lie
even as she spoke. It amused Janx to elevate her, and so to the
servants she was a lady, whether her voice and hands showed
it or not. These ones would hold their tongues, at least within
earshot, about what they thought, because they would be
grateful to the ginger lord for keeping them on when the
family lost the means to maintain the estate. They would bow
and curtsey to Sarah, and so by their ends, she was what they
named her: *lady*. Lady from the slaughterfields, she thought,
but forbore to object a second time.

She did, though, cough on the watered wine when Rose

and Bridget laid out the dress she was to wear. Pale yellow, a springtime color, and more fabric to it than in both her own dresses combined. The waist was narrow and long, and the shoulders were completely bare. Rose set a lightweight wrap inside the open shoulders and made a small apologetic movement. "This might do you best, my lady. You've strong shoulders for a..."

For a noblewoman, Sarah finished, but was no more likely to say it aloud than Rose was. There would be no pretending her frame, built through years of hard work, could mimic one of the delicate ladies of the court.

"For a woman," Rose said with determination, as if she'd meant to say it all along. "You'd best not eat anymore. The corsets will be tight. We'll finish your hair, mistress, before we dress you, so please sit back down..."

"Leave it simple," Bridget ordered. "Her ladyship don't need a peacock's feathers. Not like the mistress," she said, far more slyly than she should. Sarah laughed even as she wondered if the maid would have spoken so if Sarah's accent had been more like Janx's and less like Bridget's own.

The springtime sun had moved past the high mark in the sky before they were finished, and that, Sarah thought, was *simple.* She could breathe more easily in the corsets than she expected—Bridget made another sly comment about the mistress's aging waistline—but when they brought her to a mirror, she still looked behind herself for the woman reflected there. All three maids stood behind her, hands clenched in their own skirts and barely-disguised delight brightening their faces. *They* were visible enough in the mirror—real glass, not polished metal—and Sarah looked back, barely understanding that the fourth woman there, the one prominent in the reflection, was her.

There was no sign of the slaughterfield's daughter in the mirror. A young noblewoman stood there instead, dark brown hair drawn back and held with pearls. Her eyes were very large and very green, and her skin less marred by sun than she'd expected. More pearls were at her throat, three short strings that made her neck look long. The wrap poking up from under the shoulder trim softened the breadth of her shoulders, and the long narrow waist gave her a height she'd never aspired to. Wide satin skirts fell in beautiful ripples over artificially wide hips and brushed the floor: Sarah had refused the tall boxy shoes on the certainty of never being able to walk in them. She wore slippers instead, their color just a shade or two darker than her gown.

"His lordship will be agog," Mary said with satisfaction, and they released Sarah from their clutches.

His lordship was agog.

Flatteringly so, both men, not just Janx. They stood when Sarah, dry-mouthed with nerves, silently entered the hall they occupied, and neither of them spoke until she twitched with worried anticipation. Then Janx took two quick steps forward, his hands extended toward her. She took them—hers were clammy and his cool and soft—and he bowed, kissing the knuckles of each hand. The maids had tried giving her rings to wear, but her hands were larger and rougher than their mistress's, and so her fingers were bare. Clean. Impossibly clean, for a butcher's daughter, but bare.

"Am I right?" Janx murmured over her hands. "Do you see now what I saw in the market?"

Sarah wet her lips, unable to answer with more than a stiff nod. Janx straightened, looking unutterably pleased with himself, and that loosened some of her worry into a shy smile. "You are a gem," Janx murmured. "A rare bloom set to unfurl its petals. An unparalleled beauty. You—"

"You look lovely," Daisani said dryly, and Sarah blushed. Janx's mouth flattened and he threw Daisani a dark look, one which the smaller man ignored as he, too, came to kiss Sarah's knuckles. "Janx," he told her, "sometimes doesn't know when to stop. Restraint isn't a word in his vocabulary. Will you join us for supper?"

Sarah pressed a hand to her stomach, flattened by the strong corset. "I'm not sure I can eat, in this."

"Well," Janx said, all wide-eyed innocence, "we could remove it for you."

Panic lurched Sarah's heart into a race, the hand over her stomach pressing harder against a rise of sickness. The cost of all this was certain, but she had thought it might be longer in coming. Had thought this game of theirs might play out more slowly, so she might have time to accustom herself to the idea of whoring. They were polite men, clean and wealthy, and there would be—this she believed—a house and security, after. There were far worse fates for a slaughterfield's daughter. But she had thought it might come on her more slowly.

Daisani, without changing expression, made a scant turn toward Janx and kicked him in the shin, as one boy might do to another. Offense as childish as the action flew into Janx's face, but Sarah laughed, fear released in the burst of sound. "He really *doesn't* know when to stop," Daisani said with genuine apology in his voice. "You haven't been brought here and made lovely and offered food so it all might be stripped away from you, Sarah. There's no price to this, despite what Janx's ill-advised words might suggest or threaten."

The redhead looked abashed. "Forgive me, Sarah. Eliseo's right. I'm sorry if I've made you afraid. I only meant to tease. There is no cost for this," he said more softly. "No cost at all, such as you might fear. There would be no pleasure in that, and truly, my dear, I wish to please you."

The hammering of her heart slowed and her hands came warm again. It was unwise to trust them, but she did. Maybe because they had so much power, and she so little, that refusing to extend trust was laughable, but more, she thought, because they somehow made her feel as though she *had* power. As though they meant everything they said, unlikely as it seemed. She didn't lack confidence—no woman running a butcher's table in the slaughterfields could—but they strengthened it in her, somehow. There was no use asking why. *Why* Janx wished to please her, or why any of this was happening. She would only get the answer she'd been offered so far: because she was lovely, and these two men liked pretty things. And so, trusting the clothes, the grand hall, the eager men, she drew herself up and found enough humor in herself to attempt an accent as high as theirs: "Then it would please me, my lords, to dine with you."

Janx, who had no dignity, cheered and offered his arm. Eliseo took her other, and together they went to feast.

That first meal was not a lesson in manners. Far from it: instead the men out-did one another offering her savories, all of them laughing as she pursed her mouth and winced and coughed on the more exotic flavors and reached eagerly for the best of new delicacies. The servants clearly thought they were all mad, but served up plate after plate, never minding that no more than a few bites were taken from each. Sarah was sparing with the wine despite Janx's encouragement, and still by the end of the meal she had drunk enough to call him by his name, and to do the same with Eliseo. *Eli*, she called him, and he looked secretly pleased.

She did not, in truth, know when the lessons began, only that her manner improved: that it became easier to manage a wealthy woman's skirts, and that she began to dare the tall boxy shoes that put her eyes level with Eli's. That she became accustomed, even comfortable, with the maids dressing her and styling her hair, and that her speech, by slow measures, became more gracious. None of it was learned in the way of studying, as she did with letters and numbers, but it seeped into her until one afternoon she spoke with a stranger's voice.

It stopped her, that cultured tone, and she glanced across the hall to another mirror—Janx's home was littered with them, his own vanity or the landlords' reigning supreme—and found she knew the woman there.

No one else would. No one, certainly, from the slaughterfields. Not even Jacob, who might have married her. He would bow to the woman in the reflection, as Sarah herself would have once caught her skirts and scrabbled a rough curtsey. The mirror showed someone high-born, someone wealthy, and yet there was no surprise, no discomfort, in knowing that image as herself.

Oh so softly, Sarah murmured, "Excuse me," and left the hall for the outside world. She abandoned her shoes at the drive's edge and, not caring that her feet might be stained, ran across the grass until there were hills between her and the house, and until London's mark could be seen on the horizon. A breeze picked at her hair, patiently taking it from its pinnings. She tucked the stray pieces behind her ears as they came loose. Perhaps a noblewoman would do no such thing, but that was something she couldn't know. She'd met no other highborn women: she and Janx and Eli had delved into an existence of their own making, undisturbed by outsiders. They could stay that way, a world out of time, forever. There were moments when Sarah thought she wouldn't mind that, which, like the glimpse in the mirror, made her wonder what had become of the woman she'd been.

"May I join you?" She hadn't heard him approach, but it was Eli: Janx would have assumed she was bereft without his company and made himself comfortable without asking. She had wanted to be alone, but that difference between the two men amused her, so she was smiling as she looked back at Eli and nodded. Janx had found her, and made her laugh easily, but a disloyal part of her preferred Eliseo Daisani. He was neither so handsome nor so outrageous, and those things made him more...*suitable*...for the slaughterfields girl.

Eli sat, which she, mindful of her expensive dress, hadn't done, and looped his arms around his knees. "Have we made it too hard for you? Alone out here, away from any society?"

"Too easy, I should say. I almost wish it could stay this way forever."

"It could," Eli said idly.

Sarah breathed disagreement. "Nothing lasts forever."

"You'd be surprised."

They had plucked her from blood and grime and muck and brought her here, gentled her manners and improved her dress, fed her fine foods and finer wines, and smoothed the butchery from her voice. All those things were at least as impossible as their idylls lasting forever, so Sarah smiled again and sat. "I'm not sure I would be."

He glanced at her, seriousness in his dark gaze. Always more serious than Janx, of course, but Janx was a silly creature. She wondered, not for the first time, how they'd come to be friends, and this time asked, cutting Eliseo off to do so: "How *do* you know each other? You're nothing alike, you and he."

Eliseo slid his jaw around, looking as if he bit back his first answer. "What would you say if I said we'd known each other since before time began?"

"That you've aged well," Sarah said dryly, and Eli laughed.

"It's true. We have. We liked the same woman once, a long time ago. That's how we know each other."

"And she liked neither of you?"

His eyebrows rose. "How did you know?"

"You're both here with me."

"Ah." Eli turned his attention to the distant smudge that was London. "As it happens, you're right. She fancied someone else entirely. But that was a long time ago, and she's dead now."

"Oh. I'm sorry."

"Don't be. I'm not even sure I remember her name. No." The denial came swiftly, almost angrily. "I remember. Pandora. Pandora and her box of mischief. Do you know the story? Open it and let the demons into the world."

"Close it so hope remains."

"Remember," Eliseo said, "that the box was said to hold all the evils to plague mankind. Hope was in there along with all the other devils. I've often wondered if it was meant to countermand or exacerbate them."

Sarah gave him a hard look. "No wonder she didn't like you."

Eli blinked, then laughed. "I am scolded. Forgive me, Sarah. I didn't mean to be gloomy. But you're out here on your own, so perhaps you want to be gloomy. Is everything all right?"

"I didn't know myself in the mirror earlier. Or, no. I *did*. That was..."

"Even worse? What would you do with hope if you found it, Sarah?"

"Cling to it," she said softly. "As I have done. She may not have liked you, but she did me a favor by bringing you together so you could find me. It's a cruel name to give someone, though. Janx read me the story. What kind of mother would name her daughter after a woman who let evil into the world?"

Eli's silence lingered a moment before he shook himself. "She had no mother save all of humanity, and perhaps demons aren't necessarily evil. Perhaps they're just not human."

Sarah peered at him. "And perhaps they fit in a box, too. That would be tidy. We could rush around scooping them back into their prison."

"They would fight tooth and nail not to go."

Cold crawled into Sarah's throat, making her voice small and cautious: "Are demons real, Eliseo?"

"Demons? No, I think not." He spoke with serene confidence, but there was an oddness in the words. A lightness that suggested he knew more than he dared say, and that the knowing caused him a hurt that ran so deeply it had to be touched on delicately if at all. "Shall I tell you how I think Pandora's story really went?"

"Please." Cold stayed upon her, despite the summer heat. They kept to their banter, Eliseo and Janx, and never let anything rise from below. Something lay close to the surface now, though, and Sarah dared say nothing else for fear Eli would change his mind.

They sat together under the sun for a long while before he spoke. "There was Prometheus, who brought fire to man, and his brother Epimetheus, who lacked foresight. And there was Pandora, who, the stories say, was the first human woman. She wasn't, but that's not this story. She was, though, beautiful and curious and clever, and both Prometheus and Epimetheus cared for her very much. In the stories, the brothers are called Titans, the children of gods, but they weren't so much children of the gods as simply extraordinary beings themselves. Prometheus *could* make fire, and Epimetheus...well, he wasn't wise. He acted too often before he thought, and one of those actions was to tell Pandora the truth about himself and his brother, and about many others besides. Stories of dragons and of gargoyles, of siryns and sea serpents, of selkies and djinn. Of *vampires,*" he said, soft emphasis on a new word. "Creatures that lived on the blood of others. And of many more, until she knew all the tales of all the ancient races that had once peopled the earth. He did it to win her heart, but instead he frightened her away.

"Pandora told the stories. Told them far and wide, until

the things that the brothers were became a part of the human consciousness. Until they were the demons which frightened people; the dark things in the night. That was the evil Pandora released: the knowledge of the other beings. And the hope that was left behind, that was the hope that the Old Races might find a way to live with the new. It has stayed in the box ever since, and taunts the brothers from time to time."

"And which of them," Sarah asked slowly, "which of them are you?"

"Epimetheus, of course," Eliseo said to the horizon. "Could Janx be anything other than the fire-bearer? But I learned, Sarah. Oh, how I learned. I had always acted without thought, acted on impulse, done what felt and seemed right in the moment with no eye to the consequences. No longer. Not since Pandora, and she was so very long ago."

Her heartbeat came in slow thick pulses, doing nothing to ward off the chill still settled in her hands and cheeks. "I don't understand, Eliseo."

"Are you ready to?"

She looked at him there in the meadow, at his hair so black the sun could find no red or blue highlights to it; at his skin sallow but unburned. At the weary patience in the slump of his shoulders and the cautious hope in brown eyes.

Hope, which taunts the brothers from time to time.

"No," Sarah said carefully, slowly, and got to her feet with as much deliberation. The world smelled of sun-heated grass, and enthusiastic robins trilled songs in the near distance. There was a breeze, warm against her nerves-cool face, and the sky was relentlessly, intensively blue. So many moments burned into her memory, crisp and clear, and all of them to do with Eliseo and Janx. Her heart hurt for them and she barely understood why. They had given her too much already; she did not need this new ache, this pain that reached deep inside her and made a living space. It was difficult to breathe around that place already, and in a moment of clarity she knew it would only grow worse. "No. I'm not ready. Not yet."

Eli nodded.

Sarah, cold, afraid, excited, walked away.

A storm came up suddenly, driving her inside the manor house, and washed away again as quickly. Sarah escaped the house again before the last drops had fallen, and, searching for a place where she might be alone to think, followed a groundskeeper up a narrow stairway as he went to the rooftop to sweep away water and leaves after a storm. Sarah delighted by the the expansive roof and the endless view of the countryside, kept herself out of the way until the man's work was done, then found a protected space where she could sit quietly and watch the changing afternoon air. She liked the roof's remoteness. It made thinking easier, though she wasn't certain *thought* was what she did. Mostly she sat, gazing at darkening horizon and *feeling*: feeling wonder, fear, hope, awe, bewilderment, and other things she was unprepared to name. There had been subtext to Eliseo's story, impossible subtext, but in her core she believed it.

"Have I lost you to Eliseo, then?"

Sarah startled, Janx's cautious voice unexpected. She turned to watch him approach, his hair purpled by the moonlight and his gaze cast downward. Diffidence did not sit well on his shoulders, but he was trying. Sarah had to give him that: he was trying. For a moment she didn't understand why, and then clarity swept her: her absence at through the day, at dinner, all of it hearkened to a change, and the obvious guess was passion. Hence Janx's diffidence, his caution in approaching her: he would not want to be rejected, and perhaps thought restraint would win her back more quickly than anger or jealousy.

"He told me a story," she said instead of answering

directly. "The same one you read to me, about Pandora. But he told it differently."

Janx breathed, "Ah," and came to stand beside her. The storm might have passed from the skies above, but not so much from within her. Sarah thought that was a tempest that might never settle. There were stars above now, glittering more clearly than they ever did in the city. Brighter even than usual in the country, now that rain had pounded mist and dust from the sky. Thin moonlight-silver clouds tried to mask them, but they were fierce enough to gleam through.

Like hope, always shining. "Why did you not tell me that version?"

A faint smile danced over Janx's lips. "Because I'm not the intemperate brother, of course."

"You aren't really brothers at all."

"No. Only in arms, though that encompasses too little."

Brothers in arms, in love, in fate, in anger, in fear, and at the moment, she was the source of their concern. It was a heady thought, one she could become intoxicated with. Surely there was a kind of power in attracting men such as these, even if she wasn't yet sure what sort they were. There were too many things to say, and none of them seemed right. She finally said, "Pandora is a story from thousands of years ago," to the stars, and waited.

"Yes." Janx was rarely gentle, but he was gentle now, all the patience and calmness in the world resting in his voice. Sarah was cold again. She seemed to always be in a state of flushed or freezing with these two, as if a steady temperature was an affront to their pull. They would probably like that.

She put her hands together, trying to warm her fingers, and Janx put his hand over hers. They were cool. Not icy like hers, but Eliseo radiated heat and Janx merely warmed her hands a little more than they were. Looking at them, she said,

"I thought you were the one who brought fire."

Oddly enough, he understood, and there was a smile in his voice as he answered. "I know. I should be scalding to the touch, should I not? But Eliseo is the one who runs hot. It has something to do with his quickness, like a raging fire that burns white with heat."

"Is he very quick?" Sarah asked distantly. Her body hurt, an ache that ran through her most private places and pulsed in her chest. They both did this to her, these men and their secrets. Jacob, sweet kind Jacob, had never stirred her this way, and surely there was a wrongness in being drawn so strongly to two men at once.

"Yes," Janx said again, just as gently. "Yes. Eliseo is very quick indeed."

All the cold flushed to heat within her, until her hands burned under Janx's cool ones. Her question came from a parched throat, a broken whisper of two words: "And you?"

Her hands spasmed as she asked. Janx looked at them, smiled, then lifted his gaze to hers and her knuckles to her lips. "I," he said, "I fly."

She didn't know, later, why she had the wit to release his hands and back away, only that he smiled in rueful approval, and did the same himself. Sarah stopped at the roof's high edge, but Janx moved to its center, then a little farther still. "Don't be afraid, Sarah."

"I'm not." It was no more the truth than it was a lie, but the words were buffeted away by the winds of change.

Literal, physical, astonishing winds of change, accompanied by explosive sound, as if even unseen air could be shoved out of place and was affronted by so being. Janx was swallowed whole by that burst, and the impossible was left in his place. Red even in the night's dark, and long and twisting, with four powerful short legs—short compared to the length of him, at least—and wings that spread once to announce their size, then tucked back down against his sides.

Sarah, blankly, said, "*Baner Cymru,*" and Janx gave a sound very like a dragonly laugh.

Eliseo, who had not been there a moment before, said, "Don't give him airs," and spread his hands apologetically when Sarah yelped. "I heard him change. Half of London probably heard it. It's a good thing you pay the servants so well that they are selectively deafened to your behaviors, Janx. I thought *I* was supposed to be the intemperate one," he said to Janx, and then back to Sarah, "He can talk in that form, but it's difficult."

Sarah said, "*Baner Cymru,*" again. "I've seen it at the cathedral. He's—he's—are you—?" The last she said to Janx, who did not, in fact, *look* like the red dragon on the Tudor flag, the Welsh flag: that beast stood more upright, its neck and head lifted high where Janx's stretched out. More, though, Janx had an astonishing ruff, with whiskers that splayed around his face in long dancing threads.

"No," Eliseo said sourly. "He's not. That's someone else."

"There are *more?*" Sarah's voice broke and she laughed, high and excited. Her heart caught up to what she was seeing, leaping to a too-fast rhythm, and finally her hands began to shake. She'd known after Eliseo's story that there was something extraordinary about the men, but her imagination had failed her. There was no shame in that: even staring slack-jawed at the man-turned-dragon on the rooftop, her imagination was still inclined to fail. She didn't disbelieve, but neither did she quite *believe.* She felt the same way about God in his Heaven, though surely if a man could become a dragon, God had a hand in that. "How many more? You said—you said gargoyles and sea serpents," she said, grasping for the monsters of some familiarity. "And—and...*vampires.* How many more, Eli? How many more?"

"A dozen or fifteen true Old Races once walked this world," Eliseo murmured. "The ones I named and others besides. There are so few of us left now, though, Sarah. There are dragons and vampires, of course. Selkies, who are seal-people from the far north and Ireland. I never understood that," he said absently. "Why they spawn in such different places, when most of us call one birthplace home. There are a handful of siryns and sea serpents left, but like the selkie, they're dying. Your people are hard on the oceans, Sarah. Hard on the magnificent beings that live within it. And there are djinn in the deserts, and the gargoyles, like your friend Alban Korund."

"Alban? Alban is—?"

"It's why he only came to watch over you at night. His people are bound to stone during the daylight hours." Eliseo spoke evenly, as if steady words would help calm her racing heart. "It's a terrible limitation, but they carry the memories of all the Old Races. Stone binds them safely for all our sakes. Without them we might forget the ones who have faded away."

"And if they're forgotten you're all lost?."

"We are." Eli's voice remained soft, reassuring. "We are not human, Sarah. You are ephemeral, ever-changing, ever forgetting and ever learning. It is a pity when you lose what has gone before, but you discover it anew, in time. We are too static for that. We depend on one another, even as we turn our backs on each other and walk our own paths. Our secrets belong to all of us, and we become less with each of our various kind who slip away. If we lose what has gone before, we become nothing as we face the road ahead. Worse than nothing, perhaps. In the end it may make us...human, and then we are truly lost."

"It is not flattering," Sarah whispered, "that I should be 'worse than nothing' to you." She could not tear her gaze from Janx, could not waken offense in her breast at Eli's words.

Faced with an eternal dragon, she *was* less than nothing, a fragile seed already lost in the wind.

"No." The word was almost a sigh. "Humans, the best of you, are equal to the best of us. More than, for your flexibility and daring. But you are also different, and if we let ourselves become like you, we have nothing left at all. We must hold our memories tightly, and remember what we are."

Sarah was not listening, not in truth. She nodded, but she also crept toward Janx, even as she wondered at her own boldness. She should be afraid. She *was* afraid, but not for her life. Excitement thrilled her instead, so sharp it was a kind of fear in itself. But the fear was for losing what she stood on the brink of understanding, not of the two men: they would have done her harm long since, if they'd meant to at all. Janx lowered his head to his paws—enormous paws, nearly as large as she was, from heel to claw-tip—and watched her with jade eyes bigger than her head. She touched one of his whiskers and it twitched, making her laugh with breathy nerves. It took long minutes to work her way around him—the roof looked smaller with a dragon ornamenting its center—and when she finally reached his head again, he pushed up and extended a front leg in clear invitation.

Her heartbeat soared, but she looked toward Eliseo. Even with only the moon's light, vexation and acceptance were both clear in his expression. He was quick, Janx had said, but Janx could *fly*. He nodded once, scant motion, and as if released, Sarah kicked off her shoes and scrambled up the scaly forearm offered to her. Her skirts and the long point of her corset were poorly suited for riding a dragon astride, but she wrenched them around—her maids would never approve—and huddled down low against Janx's spine.

He sprang upward in a surge, wings snapping open behind her. Sarah shrieked with glee, casting one panicked, delighted glance back at Eliseo, whose faint smile faded into the distance within seconds. Then she was among the clouds, catching at them in amazement. They felt nothing like they looked, their downy softness entirely imagined. Instead their thin mist left droplets on her face and soaked her dress, but the night's warmth and Janx's heat were enough to keep her from being cold. A wingbeat or two more and they were beyond the clouds, nothing between Sarah and the stars but moonlight. She reached for them, too, clear light making blue shadows on her skin before she buried her fingers in Janx's ruff again and let him take her where he would.

London sped by beneath them, torchlight marking streets and showing her the jumbled city in beautiful lines. A few tiny people moved between the lights, but she was invisible so far above them, just a cut-away against the sky. Another few minutes' flight and they soared above the Channel, and then over land again: France, which she had certainly never thought to see. The earth curved into black distance, starlight on broad rivers and rolling mountains. She had the wild impulse to fling herself free of Janx's back: to fly alone, unbound and untouched. The dragon would catch her, if he could.

If. It was that which prevented her from being a fool, and instead Sarah ducked her face against plate-sized scales and laughed with delight. The world could be hers to see, with this impossible beast of burden, and she had little doubt he would willingly carry her across oceans.

The eastern sky was bluing with dawn, and the whole of her body bluing with cold, before the view became the manor grounds, and the broad rooftop a familiar landing-place. The roof was discolored, though, even from the distance, and when they landed it was in a riot of flowers, purple and red buzzing everywhere in the rush of Janx's wings. Sarah slid from his back, so numb she could hardly stand, and gaped at what awaited her.

Eliseo Daisani, not to be outdone, stood with waterfalls of flowers overflowing his arms. Daisies she knew, though she'd never seen red ones, and the other blooms were thistle-purple, elongated, and entirely unfamiliar. He knelt, scattering them amongst the hundreds of others already burying the roof, and murmured, "Red daisies for beauty unknown and amaranth, for love everlasting."

"Nothing lasts forever," Sarah replied, but not even she believed that, not now. For some reason there were tears in her eyes as she knelt and gathered blooms into her arms. They warmed her and smelled of summer heat greater than any England knew. "How far did you go?"

"India." Janx exploded back into human form, answering when Eli would not. "Amaranth is from India, Sarah. Half the world away."

"A quarter," Eliseo said disagreeably, and Sarah, arms full of flowers, laughed through her tears.

"You are mad. You are completely mad, both of you, and I love you for it. What are you?" She raised her face to Eli, petals brushing her jaw. "Prometheus who brings fire is a dragon, of course, but what is Epimetheus? What is the impetuous brother?" *Impetuous:* a word she hadn't known, not until these two men had come into her life.

"A vampire," Eli said. "Fast but not wise. Such is the fate of my kind."

"You said...*vampires*...drink of blood. Men's blood?"

"And women's. Not, however, when I'm courting. Not unless I'm asked." Eli glanced at Janx, then back to Sarah, taking a deep breath before he said, "But I would offer you a sip of mine."

Janx made a small motion, enough to indicate surprise, and Sarah looked at him, not Eliseo. "He offers you the gift of health, Sarah. That all your years you will be strong and fit. It is not," Janx said carefully, "an offering he makes lightly. Or often. And I think perhaps never to one who isn't already a lover."

"Occasionally," Eliseo said, and bit his own wrist so blood welled up. Horror squeaked in Sarah's throat, but he chuckled. "It will heal in an instant. One taste for health, Sarah. Will you take it?"

This was not a time to think. She stepped forward and seized his wrist, brought it to her mouth and tasted a shock of too-sweet blood, its thickness coating her tongue. Eliseo hissed, then broke away with a deep-throated sound of pleasure. "Enough. One sip alone is enough. You should feel it quickly enough."

"I do." The words came roughly as the remaining chill spilled from her body as if chased. Aches she'd been unaware of disappeared from her spine, her hands, her legs. She'd had no trouble breathing, though the air up high had seemed thin, but her next breath came more deeply and fully, straightening her shoulders and bringing a sense of vitality. She came to her feet with an armful of flowers and spun, flinging the blooms in the air. They rained down around her, soft scents dashing against her cheeks, and when she opened her eyes, smiling, it was to find both men watching her eagerly.

They stopped her where she was, their gazes so bright and intent in the coming sunrise. Again, again, the moment burned into memory: Janx's fiery hair turning gold, Eli's sallower skin coming to life in the forgiving light. Flowers everywhere, petals catching and drifting on a curious breeze, and herself in the midst of it all, a focal point when she had never dreamed of such a thing.

"I have never," she whispered, and now she was afraid again, with the same overflowing, heart-aching excitement of revelation. "Not at all, much less with..." With men of the Old

Races. With a dragon, with a vampire. With two. There were too many ways to end the fumbled explanation, and so she finished with silence.

Janx and Eliseo shared a complex glance of befuddlement before Janx, with less grace than she'd ever seen, mumbled, "Yes, of course. But which...which of us would you prefer?"

She looked at him, at them, in astonishment. Looked at constraint and caution in two men who had uprooted her life with hardly a thought, much less a show of uncertainty, and asked them, "How could I choose? How could I ever, ever choose?"

They were old. Very old, and she was very young, but she had surprised them. They looked at one another again, no longer confounded, but perhaps judging. *Brothers,* Sarah thought, though they were not, and she could hardly imagine what more, or less, they might be to one another.

It was Janx, of course. Janx who was bright and easy and full of laughter, who finally looked away from Eliseo to smile at Sarah and to promise, "You don't have to, my dear. In the end, you will never have to."

Sunlight, gold and soft, warmed the amaranth to a rich scent that tickled Sarah's nose. *She* was warm, far warmer than the flowers; Eli's skin was hot to the touch, more than enough to keep all three of them warm, even with Janx's cooler temperature. She, still tangled between them, felt soft and content and calm. The manor house staff would be shocked. Sarah laughed, and the men surrounding her stirred.

"That," Janx said into her shoulder, "is not the sound of a woman facing the day and the cold light of reason with misgivings in her heart. I, for one, am grateful. What's so funny?"

"I thought the staff would be shocked," Sarah murmured. "And then I thought the slaughterfield's daughter should be shocked. And then I thought of a man who is a dragon, and another who can run to India and back in the space of a night, and I wondered how the slaughterfield's daughter could ever be shocked again."

"Like this," Eli said very softly, and offered his wrist with the words. Sarah's heart jumped. Janx drew a sharp breath, then was still, so the three of them were as statues in morning sunlight. "Two sips for life, Sarah Hopkins. Will you risk immortality? This," Eli added, confirming what she'd thought Janx's indrawn breath might mean: "This I do not do."

He was right, then: she could still be shocked after all. She didn't take his wrist, not yet, though thick blood, dark blood, welled and prepared to drip, only said, "Then why?"

Eliseo met her gaze, then looked briefly, almost bitterly, at Janx. "Because no one has ever dared to love us both."

"They were all fools." Sarah caught Eli's wrist and drank again. Drank without thought, one sweet sip before he pulled away.

"One for health. Two for life."

"And three?" she asked playfully. "Three for love, perhaps?"

Eli closed his fingers around the wound, though it healed already. "Three for death, Sarah. That's the price of a vampire's gift."

A shiver rushed her and she looked away. He saw the tension in her and sighed. "Not easily. It's the third bloodletting, usually, though if you broke away and came back to the same cut it would kill. Swallowing away the taste of what's left in your mouth is not the danger, Sarah. Do not fear." She nodded, feeling small and for the first time in weeks, afraid. Not the delighted fear of exploration and passion, but of being out of her depth and little more than a trinket to astonishing men. Janx put his mouth against her shoulder and murmured, "Don't. Don't retreat from us, Sarah. Not now.

Not...not when so much possibility lies before us. We might have..." He lifted his gaze, though not his head, and Eli responded to the unspoken query.

"Decades, certainly. Decades of youth, Sarah. Decades of strength and beauty and wit. Perhaps longer. Perhaps centuries."

"You don't know? I thought you had given...this...to others."

"From time to time, yes, and it's lasted decades. It depends on the woman. On her health when we met, on her age, on..."

Clarity fell over Sarah, not entirely welcome, but it somehow lessened her fear. "On her wish to survive. How long do they—we—usually last, Eli?"

"Decades," he said a final time. "Often over a century. Never two. Not yet."

Sarah closed her eyes, breathed in the scent of amaranth, and smiled at the warmth of close-pressed bodies. "I think I would like to be the first, then."

"In that case," Janx said, suddenly bright and irrepressible again, "we had best be prepared to let you out in public."

He had not meant the slaughterfields, when he said that. Indeed, his expression had been one of comical horror when she announced an intention to return, and had only worsened when she said she'd go alone. "They won't know me," she told him blithely, "and even if they did, and hate me for it, Eli says I'm very hard to hurt, now."

"Not hard to hurt," Janx muttered. "Hard to kill. There's a difference."

"I'll take the carriage," she promised, and for the dozenth time thought of the arrogance and unlikelihood of that simple phrase passing her lips. Thought it from the carriage seat, watching the city's cobblestone streets pass beneath the wheels and turn to hard-packed dirt, then to blood-streaked mud. The horses disliked that, snorting and tossing their heads.

Faces Sarah knew glanced or gawked at her carriage and at the fussy matched set pulling it. Some looked away rather than curtsey or tug a forelock, while others offered smiles desperate for a thrown coin. She had some—Eli had thought of that where she would not have—but she kept them clutched in her purse, in her palm, as she was drawn through the streets and fields that had so recently been her home.

There was no light of recognition in anyone as she passed by. She was a fine lady in a fine coach, and even if they had more than a glimpse of her, they wouldn't know her. She had come to prove that to herself, though the proving left a score across her heart. These had been her people, after all.

But she had decades, even centuries, ahead of her, and with a lifespan of so many years, no one could ever quite be her people again. No one except Janx and Eli, perhaps, but she would never be what they were, either.

"Stop the coach, please." A tap against the front panel caught the driver's attention and he reined in the fussing horses. Sarah started to open the door, then, fingers clenched around her purse as a reminder, let the footman do it for her. He held his mouth pinched and his nostrils flared, unspoken but clear opinion of the muck he had to walk in to do so. Sarah, with a solemnity that would do Janx's most outrageous theatrics justice, lifted her skirts enough for the footman to see the sturdy slaughterfields boots she wore under a gown of silk and brocade. His eyes popped and she grinned, then nodded toward his coach-side perch. "Get back up there. You needn't ruin your shoes. I'll only be gone a few minutes."

"The master will have my hide if I let you go alone, my lady."

"I won't be alone." Sarah lifted her voice to call, "Jacob!"

Two dozen men who weren't named Jacob and one who

was looked up at her call. Those who weren't lit up with the same gossipy expressions they'd had when Janx first called on Sarah, but Jacob himself slowed in his work, then stopped, staring down the small distance to Sarah. After a moment he wiped his hands clean of flour and bread, then cast aside his apron and came to her, ignoring the calls and whistles from the other men. "They don't know you," he said when he got close enough to speak. "How could they know you? You're well, Sarah? You're...safe?"

"I am." It had been spring when she'd left the slaughterfields. It was the heat of summer now, and the harvest would be on them soon. In another month the fields would lie fallow for winter, and then a year would be gone. The first of many spent in immortal youth: a year that would slip away and be nothing in a life counted in decades and centuries. That was why she had to come back now, before she was someone else entirely. "I wanted to see you. I wanted to thank you."

"For letting you go," he said, and gave a crooked smile at Sarah's nod. "You weren't mine to keep, Sarah. I think even if we'd been wed, you wouldn't have been mine to keep."

"But you might have hated me. You might hate me still." She no longer sounded like him, though with his rough accent in her ears, her own was less polished than Eli had made it.

"For escaping? No. It's good of you to come back. To tell us you're all right."

Sarah cast a look at the others. Some had recognized her now, and wore expressions from sneers to wonderment. Not all of them would be glad she prospered, and it would be made worse if she offered the purse in her hand. She turned back to Jacob with that purse at the ready anyway, and made an awkward gesture. "I am. More than all right. I wanted to give you this. I have so much now, and we might have..."

Jacob gave the purse, then Sarah, an odd look. Not insult;

that was a fear she'd had, but he only seemed perplexed. "A dowry for a promise never made? No, keep the coin, or give it to God if you must give it away. You owe me nothing, Sarah. I might have wished it otherwise, but the world's not made of wishes."

But it was. Sarah pressed her eyes shut, then took Jacob's hands and folded the purse into them. "For the children you'll one day have, Jake. For an education or a guild. For me, because I'll have no babes of my own."

Shocked, Jacob blurted, "Is the flaw in yourself or in him?", then flushed red enough to make Sarah laugh.

"Him." *Them,* but she could never say that aloud. "He is...too different."

Now consternation twisted Jacob's face, and Sarah could all but name the perversities that the miller's son imagined. She touched his arm, meant to be reassuring, but he caught her hand with concern writ large across his features. "You're sure you're all right, Sarah? You look well. You're—you're beautiful." He stuttered the compliment, as if the word was not enough, then forged on. "But if that lord is unnatural..."

"He's my heart's desire. I could never have dreamed, but now that I know..." She was making it worse: now Jacob looked as though he thought *her* perverse. "I'm happy," she said firmly. "I'm well. Take the coins, Jacob, please? Take them and wed and have a family, and think of me from time to time."

He swallowed, eyes on the purse. "You won't be coming back."

"No. I came to say goodbye. To say that you'll be remembered." Remembered for far longer than he might think, but that was a thing he would never know. "Goodbye, Jacob. Thank you." She turned away before he spoke again, and, to the footman's gratitude and horror, let herself into the coach.

She carefully did not look back.

* * *

The city estate Eliseo had arranged for her was modest only by his standards. The grounds were longer and deeper than the streets and houses she'd grown up in, and their back against the city wall made them feel impenetrable. There were no rickety buildings hanging dangerously over the pathways, and the driver brought her coach and two to a coach house.

Staff awaited her; Eli had arranged that as well, though she hadn't known it until she arrived. She had thought she would come to a quiet, dead house, and found a bustling one instead, as if she was a landlord who had only stepped out for a moment rather than one who had never attended the premises. If they were surprised to see her, they didn't show it, though how they could have expected her, Sarah had no idea. She hadn't forewarned Janx that she would stay overnight in town; the idea had only struck her as they left the slaughterfields.

A steward showed her the house, larger by far than any one woman could need. There were three sitting rooms and a dining hall in the downstairs alone, with the kitchen hearth backed against the dining hall's inner wall so heat poured through. In summer it was sweltering, but it would be cozy when skies turned grey. An equally unnecessary number of bedrooms made up the second floor, and the one she was shown into as her own had a discreet necessary closet to one side and a brass tub as tall as her hip to the other. "I shouldn't have given him coin," Sarah said to the house. "I should have given him this. He could fill it with a family."

"My lady?" The steward looked attentive and Sarah, with a sense of unreality, waved him away. He disappeared out the door and she laughed, quiet sound of disbelief. Janx's expansive manor had awed her, but she'd grown accustomed to its size. This house, by all accounts less grandiose, was more overwhelming simply for being *hers.* She sat in one of the windows—leaded glass in small diamonds—and watched the sun set, golden fire reflected dozens of times. She hadn't been alone in weeks, and the silence was welcome, though already she missed Janx and Eli. A messenger would have to be sent to tell them where she was. Perhaps there was someone at the house who filled such a role. Reluctant, she uncoiled from the window seat to ask, but as she did, a knock came at her door. "A visitor, my lady. Are you home?"

Sarah stared at the door, bemused. Neither Janx or Eliseo would bother with formality, and she knew no one else. She stood, shaking her skirts, and came to the door. "I am. Who is it?"

"A Master Korund, my lady. Shall I have the maid prepare a parlor?"

Not because the parlors were unprepared for company, but so she, a fine lady, would not be alone in the room with a gentleman. Sarah swallowed a laugh and nodded, allowing the steward to guide her downstairs.

Alban waited in the parlor, watching the maid fuss unnecessarily with the fire. He turned as the door opened, a smile creasing his face. "Sarah Hopkins. I wouldn't have known you."

Sarah, with no regard for propriety—Janx was a dangerous influence—dashed across the room to hug the giant blond man as she had not dared to greet Jacob. "Then how did you know I was here?"

"I've paid a boy to watch the house since you went to the country," Alban said with no apology. "He fetched me when you came here."

"But I came in the day!"

Alban's eyebrows rose slowly and he glanced at the maid. Sarah covered her mouth with one hand, apologetic, then dismissed the girl, who had the sense to disregard propriety and close the door behind her. "And yet Janx warned Hajnal to hold her tongue," Alban said then. "I should be surprised."

"Why?" Sarah sat and gestured for Alban to do the same. "I suppose it's dangerous, but I'm not Pandora. Even if I was, I knew from the start that my life was a trinket to them. They were always going to be the death of me. Why not tell me the truth?"

Alban stayed on his feet a moment, studying her. "You've changed, Sarah Hopkins. Not just your voice and education, but your certainty. It suits you. And it is against the laws of our people to tell humans the truth. We have very few laws that bind us all, and it seems neither Janx nor Daisani consider themselves bound by them at all." He finally sat, his breadth and height making his chair look under-sized, as if made for a child.

"What happens if the laws are broken?"

"Exile. We shun those who risk exposing us all. There are so few of us that no one wishes to be excluded from the whole, and so the threat is a legitimate one."

"But they have each other." Sarah spoke without thinking, dismissing the depths of that threat without consideration. Her easy assumption changed Alban's expression, though; it seemed that he did not leap to the belief that Janx and Daisani would be enough to one another that exile might mean little to them. Nor was he greatly surprised, once the newness of the idea settled in. He nodded thoughtfully, and, emboldened, she pressed for more answers: "What other laws do you have?"

"There are to be no half-breed children. Not with each other as a rule, and not with humans at all. And—"

"You can *have* children with us?" Hot and cold flooded Sarah in turns, blushes scalding her cheeks while her hands turned to ice. "I thought—I thought—"

"But we can take human forms, so we are perhaps not that different. Our own half-breeds we call chimeras, children who have aspects of both parents. They tend not to be bound by the same constraints their parents are, and they are almost always dangerous."

Sarah's heart slowed its lurching, though her stomach still boiled with nervous shock. "I think you must all be dangerous."

Alban said, "Yes," after a pause. "Which is why our third law is that we must not make war among ourselves. We do not kill one another. The results would be catastrophic to our peoples. What *did* they tell you, Sarah Hopkins?"

"What they are. What you are. That I might live—" She hesitated over *forever* and said, "a long time, with them," instead.

"A very long time, if Eliseo has given you that gift. Are you happy, Sarah? You're here, and not with them."

"Oh." She stood, hurrying for the door. "I forgot. I need to send a man to tell them I'm here."

"Hajnal has already gone." Alban shrugged a big shoulder when she turned back to him. "My contract with Janx may be ended, but we've kept watch for you. When you came here without them there were three choices. One, you'd run away. Two, you'd been sent away. Three, you'd dallied in the city and were unable to return home before dark. Of those, two need Janx and Daisani to know where you are, else they might tear London apart searching for you. So Hajnal went to tell them, just in case."

Sarah's hands found her hips and rested there indignantly. "If I'd run away I would hardly want them to know where I'd gone."

"Do you think you could lose them by running?"

"They promised," she said after a moment. "That if I chose to leave they would honor my wishes."

"Sarah." Gentle regret tinged Alban's deep voice. "They may even have meant it when they said it, but our world doesn't easily let humans go once it's captured them. I think that may be the greatest cruelty in sharing our secrets with mortals: you can never go back, and you can rarely escape."

Sarah thought of Jacob, of the slaughterfields, and smiled a little. "I don't wish to."

"And that," Alban murmured, "may be the other cruelty of discovering our world. Sarah, should you ever need it, Hajnal or I will be there to help you. Remember that."

"I will." She made the promise lightly, and Alban accepted it with a nod.

Janx's matched set took her back to the country estate in the morning. She was greeted by an agitated vampire with ruffled hair. Sarah touched it, curious, and Eli's mouth twitched. "I went to the city in the night. It may have left its mark."

Sarah's eyebrows rose. "Why did you do that?"

"I couldn't decide if granting you the city house unconditionally meant it was inappropriate to arrive on the doorstep unannounced. I changed my mind...several times."

"What he means to say," Janx drawled from deeper in the foyer, "is that he has run back and forth dozens of times, never crossing beyond your gate for fear you wouldn't want him there. I," he said with a superior air, "have waited patiently, certain of your return."

"You," Eli snapped, "can't transform in the city without betraying your origins. Don't pretend it was nobility and trust that kept you here."

Sarah's smile died on her lips. "You don't trust me?"

"I trust you implicitly," Janx replied. "I trust the men of London not at all, particularly when they might catch a glimpse of such unexpected and unescorted beauty. I would be..." Playfulness turned to discomfort on his changeable features and he glanced away with a frown. Sarah's own frown deepened and she looked at Eliseo, accustomed now to one of them completing thoughts the other would not.

"You are peculiar to us, Sarah. It would be...distressing if something happened to you."

"'Distressing'."

"I would lay waste to the city," Janx said softly, almost not to her at all. "I would count the costs in thousands of lives and call it worthy if the man who harmed you was among them."

"His living flesh would feed crows for a dozen days," Eli said in very nearly the same voice. "We swore to you we would not stop you from leaving, but should someone take you from us..."

They were mad. That was the thought that rose in her mind, though it tempered itself quickly enough, and brought a truth to light: they were inhuman, and mens' lives meant nothing to them. She was a spark, a brief and brilliant interest set apart from the rest of her kind. It made her precious, and made those around her all the more worthless. She should, as so often, be afraid.

Instead she was painfully glad she had said goodbye to Jacob, and cool with an anger and a comprehension. "Alban was with me. I was safe. And Hajnal told you where I was. You do not own me."

"Yes, and yet. We cannot own you, Sarah, but I beg of you—"

"Tell us next time," Eli finished in a murmur. "If you intend to stay away. The hours before Hajnal's message were...uncomfortable."

Irritation sharpened Sarah's voice: "I hadn't planned at all. Epimetheus should understand that well enough."

Janx's remoteness disappeared in a rush of laughter. He was on his feet, crossing the foyer and catching Sarah's hands to bow over them in uncontained glee. "A hit! Oh, we are put in our places, my brother! Sarah Hopkins, I shall throw a ball for you in thanks for your skewering wit and your cold anger. This," he said to Eli, "this is such a woman as we so rarely find. Why can they not all be so bold and wise?"

Eliseo proved his own humor to be restored by saying, "Because we would be left broken and exhausted if they were," as dryly as he could. "Shall we do this for you, Sarah? Hold the event of the season? Present you to the gathered courts, and make them wager on where you've come from?"

"Only if I collect the winnings." Sarah smiled, though. "You'll have to teach me to dance."

It had seemed simple at the time. If she could be taught to speak and dress, she could certainly be taught to dance. "Like a bear," Sarah said under her breath, but there was no mutter her men couldn't overhear. Eli laughed aloud and released her while Janx slid from his chair to sprawl, snickering, on the floor, putting both himself and his lute in danger of Sarah treading on them. She took more care avoiding the lute than Janx: it was a beautiful instrument, and he would catch her if she fell.

"The astonishing thing is not that it dances well," Janx said to the ceiling, happily, "but that it dances at all. Sarah, my dear, I assure you you have more grace than a bear. You're simply concentrating too hard. It will come more easily if you have more fun. How did you never learn to dance? Is it not what the simple folk do?"

"I learned. I can dance you a poor jig if I must, but I was never any good. I thought it was..." Sarah waved an impatient hand, and felt suddenly as though the men had altered even the way she spoke with her body. "Disinterest, or lack of practice, or—but we've been practicing for hours every day for three weeks now. I'm not a good dancer. I don't suppose you've some kind of magic in your blood like Eli has in his. For grace instead of life, perhaps."

Curiosity quirked Janx's eyebrows. "I have no idea. Not being a vampire, I've never been inclined to feed anyone my blood. We could try, though I doubt it would impart grace." He pushed up on his elbows, suddenly delighted. "Does this mean you think I'm more graceful than he is?"

"You are," Eli said without rancor. "I've always thought the selkie or djinn, people of water and air, should be the most graceful of our kinds, but it's the dragons and even gargoyles and harpies. I think it's something to do with the wings."

Janx, sounding genuinely pleased, said, "I hadn't thought you'd noticed," and in a rash movement sat up and tore his wrist open. Sarah, as thoughtlessly, moved forward, knelt, and drank.

Bitterer blood than Eli's, with a taste of smoke. She swallowed and coughed and wiped her mouth, eyes watering. Janx laughed. "You didn't do that with Eliseo's. I never thought it tasted that bad."

"You drink a lot of your own blood?" Eli wondered.

"Like anyone, I cut myself from time to time, and the injured digit finds its way to my mouth. We don't all heal as quickly as you do, Eli. Sarah?"

His blood sat at the back of her throat, dark and sharp. Sarah exhaled through her mouth, trying to push the flavor away, and finally swallowed repeatedly, rapidly, but the bitterness lingered. Through a face distorted with distaste, she rasped, "I hope that did something, because...*bligh!*" Her tongue protruded, still trying to rid itself of the lingering sharpness, and Janx got up, rueful, to find and offer her wine. Sarah drained a glass gratefully, coughed again, and lifted the cup for more. After the second, the worst of it had faded, but she took a third cup and drank it before standing to begin her lessons again.

The dancing got easier, after that. Less to do with Janx's

blood, she mumbled into his shoulder much later, than the three cups and more of wine. But the ease of finding her feet lasted: the next day, even with a bad head, she showed more grace and skill on the ballroom floor, and in another week she was no longer certain of embarrassing herself. Janx took full credit, though Sarah showed no evidence of increased poise anywhere but the dance floor. Less of it, in fact: weariness dogged her as the summer nights grew longer, and she blamed those longer nights spent tangled with both men for her indolence.

"Indolence," Eli said with admiration. "Your vocabulary has improved, Miss Hopkins."

She curtsied. "Thanks to you and Lord Janx, Master Daisani."

Eli shook his head, unexpectedly serious, and caught her fingers with his own. "The opportunity is thanks to us, perhaps, but you've embraced it. One cannot tutor an unwilling pupil, not to any meaningful degree. You've done yourself proud, Sarah. I should think you're ready for anything."

"It's easy to believe that when I'm here with you. Harder, when I think of facing the rest of your world. Of the courts and society, I mean. The other part..." She fell silent a moment, tracing a pattern on Eliseo's hand. "I won't ever be part of that, will I? Not really. Alban told me about your laws. You should be exiles already, you and Janx. Just for telling me you exist."

Eli echoed something Janx had once said: "Laws are for the law-abiding. It's easier, I think, for some of the other races. The gargoyles and djinn still live in tribes, and the selkie who are left survive in pods. But there are very few vampires to begin with, and dragons have always been solitary creatures. Exile means less to us, perhaps. And besides, who will tell?"

"Alban might."

"No." Eli spoke with such certainty that Sarah peered at

him. He shrugged. "We've spent a little time together these past few months, he and I and Janx. He's young, hardly more than a hundred years old, and he has an interest in the world beyond the Old Races. Otherwise he and his mate would still be hidden in the mountains with the rest of their kind. So he may not approve, but he won't tell tales. The cost is too high."

"Would he be exiled too?"

"Not that." Eli's gaze slid off hers, and a chill took Sarah's breath.

"Me. I would...I didn't think to ask what happened to Pandora, did I?"

"Suffice it to say she did not live to a ripe and happy old age," Eli murmured. "The Old Races take their secrets seriously, and count human lives as little cost to the keeping of those secrets."

Sarah closed her mouth on the next question: *and you?* She knew the answer already, had known it for weeks, ever since Janx and Eli had made it clear they would stop at nothing should she ever come to harm. She had no need and more particularly, no desire, to hear the sentiment explained in plain language. Fear might lie down that path, and it was a price she was unwilling to pay. "Will they not hunt for me?" she asked in time. "If I live at your side for decades, even centuries, the rest will know I've been told. Would they not act?"

"It would be too like an act of war. One does not casually murder the...wives," he finally said, cautiously. "Of one's acquaintances. Not without expecting repercussions."

"Wives," Sarah echoed. She would have expected her heart to lurch at that word; it would have had Jacob used it once upon a time. Instead amusement rose, as much at Eli's discomfort as anything else. "Have I missed the ceremony, then, or *is* all of this the ceremony?"

"I thought you might take offense at 'mate'," Eli mumbled.

"And 'lover' seems so transient, in human terms. You take husbands and wives when you mean to spend decades together. Only the wealthy or bold retain long-term lovers without marriage."

"We take *a* husband or *a* wife, not two of one," Sarah said. "I think 'lover' will do, Eli. I don't believe I need to be a wife. I don't believe I ever did." The thought surprised her and she kissed Eliseo's knuckles as gracefully as he'd ever done hers, then released him to walk away, lost in her own contemplations.

She'd been too busy with her father's business to worry much about marrying, though she'd have had Jacob if he'd asked. Marriage was security, warmth at night, children to care for and finally to care for you. But that had been before the Old Races; before a vampire's gift ensured she would have far less need of any of those mortal concerns. Eliseo had probably not intended to free her by offering her health and life, but he'd done so, and the truth was a bright place within her. She had no need to be a wife, and no pressure to become one, not anymore.

Later, she wondered if it had been a proposal: if it had been Eliseo's way of asking without exposing himself too badly. If, even more, it had been a sly way of determining whether she would take him over Janx. He had not followed her, perhaps taking her dismissal of the word as a rejection. It had been the right interpretation, if that's what had gone on in his mind: she had meant it when she'd asked how she could ever choose. Janx came to her in time. It was a dance itself, these two, always careful not to push too hard for too long with her alone, nor to overwhelm her with their constant presence. She danced, too, trying not to show favoritism—easy enough, because their different aspects appealed differently. She was more comfortable with Eli's less-striking looks and quieter manner, but outrageous Janx was the one who most often made her laugh. Evenings almost always saw the three of them together from supper until retirement, and in the morning they broke a little ways apart to begin the dance again.

But it was afternoon now, and she had left Eliseo, and so it was Janx's turn to steal time. He was quiet for once, only taking her hand and leading her into the steps of a silent pavane, one of the dances she'd struggled to learn. It was easier trading steps with imaginary partners and coming back to touch fingertips with Janx than it had been with bemused servants and staff playing the parts of other dancers. Perhaps it would be easier still with the lords and ladies and gentle folk born to the classes that did these dances as a matter of course. Sarah came to the end of the five-step pattern and curtsied so that Janx had to stop and bow, himself.

Only then did he finally say, "You're ready, you know. You're ready for a masque or a feast or any such manner of meeting."

"Then you had best have a Lammas Day masque for me, my lord, so I might prove to myself that you're right."

Janx, delighted, swept another bow. "As my lady commands."

Her ladyship, Sarah thought nine nights later, was mad and a fool besides.

Even the poor celebrated Lammas Day, with the first of the harvest in and fresh breads and fruit and grain to be dined on. There were rituals of gift-giving and of thanking the earth and a long night of dancing before the summer sun began to slip away in earnest. Sarah had fought mock battles over loaves of good brown bread and poured watered wine on the ground all her life, and had thought nothing of it until Janx had smiled when she'd done it that morning. The wealthy, perhaps, did no such thing. And it was the wealthy who were coming to the Lammas Night ball: Janx had shown her the list of names, told her who they were. They did not reach quite so high as dukes and princes, but every rank below them was invited, and in truth the king's bastard sons were only not expected because of their youth or distance from London.

Alban and Hajnal, though, were not on the guest list, nor, upon asking, were any others of the Old Races. "The nearest dragon is in Wales," Janx said with a curled lip. "We do not enjoy one another's company, Sarah."

"And vampires?"

"This is to be a ball, my dear, not a bloodbath."

Perhaps not in actual terms, she thought now, as she sat dressed and lovely and determined not to leave her room. Not in actual terms, but from the coldness of her hands and the swift beat of her heart, she already felt she would be a sheep for the wolves in the ballroom. It would be bloodbath enough for her to leave this room. She watched the long drive from a window, carriages coming down the drive to finally pool like a school of dark fish at the steps. Stunningly dressed men and women stepped free of them, and the sounds of music and laughter began to rise from the halls below.

A tap came at her door. Sarah scowled down the road, knowing to open the door was to lose a battle that was already ridiculous to fight. Still, she remained where she was, stubbornly insistent on not joining the party, until Eliseo pushed the door open and stepped inside. "What do you see when you look at me, Sarah?"

That surprised her. Surprised her enough to look at him, and then she was lost indeed. He tended to wear sober clothing, even for a masque, and so his ribbons and half-coat and breeches were all black over white stockings and a white shirt. But even without the riot of color Janx would be in, there was no imagining him to be *conservative,* not with the sheer, absurd yardage in the breeches and shirt or the dramatic poof of his cravat, which was red.

So was Sarah's dress, and so would Janx's entire outfit be. There would be others in red, of course, but the keen-eyed among the guests would notice that the three of them all wore the same red, the same fabric, the same shade. It would cause speculation, curiosity, interest—all the things Janx thrived on.

That was, of course, if Sarah agreed to leave the room. She closed her eyes against Eli's repeated question, "What do you see when you look at me?" and answered less than honestly: "More than I should."

Because she saw the quicksilver speed that was Eli's to command. She saw the mass that Janx hid in his day to day mortal life, and the shadow of wings around him always. More than she should see, and yet never enough. That was the dishonesty in her answer: it suggested she saw too much, when she would never, never be able to see deeply enough into the two men who had become her world. "Always," she said quietly, and opened her eyes. "Always, more than I should."

"And they," Eli said with a subtle emphasis, meaning the gathered courtiers and nobles in the ballrooms below, "see less than *they* should. They'll see a woman of wealth and beauty, Sarah, no matter what you feel lies below. Scratch their surface, and they're much like you. Not bold enough, perhaps, to pour wine as openly as you did, but they'll break bread and feed it to the earth as well. They know where their food comes from."

"Serfs," Sarah said, bitterness rising from fear.

Eliseo smiled. "And slaughterfield daughters. Perhaps what you should be thinking is not that you'll be found out, but how agog they would be to find the finest masque of the season is hosted by—"

"A dragon," Sarah interrupted dryly, and Eli, who had clearly not been going to say that, laughed.

"Very well. By a dragon. Do you think any of them would accept that easily?"

"I think they'd try to kill him. As they would probably try to kill me, if they knew."

"In that case." Eli offered his arm. "Let us all three go into danger, Sarah Hopkins, for we belong with the king's elite no more than you do."

By all reason, it ought not have given her any confidence. Eli and Janx were no more endangered by a ballroom of courtiers than they might be by little girls with daisies. It was the equality, though: offered, granted, assumed. To Eli, she was no more and no less in danger of being found out than he was, and nothing save Pandora could possibly expose *him.* Buoyed, she took his arm and let him bring her to the masque.

The music stopped when they entered.

Whether it was Janx's theatrics or uncanny timing, the music stopped and three hundred souls turned curiously toward the doors Sarah and Eli passed through. There was no herald to call out their names; this was a party, not the king's court, but in the silence there was no need for such a man. Recognition rippled over them in a whisper of shifting silks as women curtsied and men bowed.

They straightened again with recognition satisfied and interest alight in their faces. They knew Eliseo, but Sarah was new to them, and she saw in their gazes what Janx and Eli had told her time and again: that she was extraordinary herself, even in such company as she now kept. They were eager for her, eager for what new gossip and talk she would bring, this woman who had been hidden for weeks—months!—at Janx's country estate, with no visitors to make society any the wiser.

In the moment before Eli introduced her to the nearest couple, an astonishing thought came clear. They *had* to hide, the two men in her life. She did not, and it seemed a sudden and peculiar gift she might give them, the gift of her own honesty and true self. As Eli drew breath to speak she made a choice, and thrust her hand forward as any man in the market might. "Sarah Hopkins," she said, and made no effort to keep the cultured accent her men had lent her. "Not Goody, for I'm no one's wife, and not Mistress, for I'm no one's lady. Just Sarah will do. You are?"

Eli went terribly still. Distressingly still, the way only he and Janx could do, and then he smiled so broadly Sarah almost laughed to see it. "Lord Bothswaite, and the Lady Cecilia, Sarah. Second cousins to the Duke of York, I believe? We're honored to have you here tonight."

Bothswaite had taken Sarah's hand and now held it with an expression of not knowing how to release her politely. "It's," he said. "We're. I'm. It's...."

"You too, yer lordship." Sarah extracted her hand from his dull grip and beamed at Lady Cecilia. "Your gown's beautiful, my lady. Would it be imposing to ask who your seamstress is?"

Lady Cecilia drew herself to her full height and said, as coldly as she could, "Yes."

Sarah, brightly, said, "Oh dear," and turned to Bothswaite again. "Would ye care to dance, melord?" She'd have sworn an actual chill blew off Lady Cecilia as Bothswaite, unable to refuse without being a boor, accepted the offer as gracelessly as he could.

Sarah danced beautifully.

She was handed from one partner to another, hasty and uncomfortable introductions made each time, until Janx stepped in barely able to contain his laughter. "What are you doing, my dear? The Bothswaites have left, but I think new attendees are arriving even still, as if rumor draws them here."

"That's what I'm doing. I can't possibly go back to where I've come from, Janx, but it suddenly came to me that I didn't *have* to pretend to be one of them, either. I've probably cost you your place in the courts," she said with a hint of apology.

"There are other courts, if it comes to that, but fear not. We will be wildly popular for months because of this, Sarah. They're shocked, horrified, and will be entirely unable to stay away. The idea of talking with a butcher's daughter in a lord's house will be irresistible."

"It's not that the bear dances well," Sarah said, and Janx's quick grin flashed across his face.

"Precisely, though it happens that the bear dances very well indeed. I knew we had given you a voice and clothes, Sarah. I had no idea we'd invested you with a sense of theatrics as well." He laid a hand against his chest, modestly, as they stepped apart and came together again in the pattern of the dance. "Or dare I say *I* invested you with a sense of theatrics."

"Dare all you like. I have." Sarah curtsied as the dance ended and was passed away again, this time to a group of women flushed by excitement. They hadn't been dancing: it was Sarah's presence and coarse tongue and their proximity to her that made the occasion heady. Before she was called to dance again she had secured and offered half a dozen invitations to tea, and she was merry as Eliseo took her away onto the ballroom floor.

"They'll turn cruel, you know."

"They're cruel already," Sarah said. "It's voyeurism, not friendship, that guides the invitations. But it works both ways, doesn't it? We watch them with their fine gowns and mincing ways even as they watch me and my rough ones. Perhaps we'll all learn something from one another."

"You, at least, will," Eli murmured, and Sarah nodded. People were leaving, and the musicians began a mournful tune meant for goodbyes rather than dancing. The room emptied, remaining individuals scattered like fallen petals, and Sarah turned to Eliseo.

"Would you have wanted me, if something else had lain

below? If I was one of them, and not a daughter of blood and guts and gore?"

Eli tilted his head, bird-like, and remained silent a moment before giving a considered answer. "I think he wouldn't have noticed you, then. You would have been an ordinary sort of beautiful, rather than a beauty hewn from muscle and sinew. Janx has never had an eye for the ordinary."

"And you?"

"I," Eliseo Daisani said blithely, "would have had you for lunch."

Sarah shouted with laughter, and the Lammas Masque came to an end.

She had worked hard every day of her life until Janx had taken her from the slaughterfields. There was no sense in mere socializing being exhausting, not after the girlhood she'd known, but she slept even in the hard-bouncing carriage, and retired early when callers came to her. Her rude upbringing was excuse enough: she could hardly be expected to behave in a more civilized fashion, and besides, sudden departures from polite company gave her visitors all the more to gossip about.

Janx was as happy as she was to sleep, especially in a south-facing room where the afternoon sunlight poured in and warmed the bed to baking. "Cool blood," he mumbled into her shoulder when she asked. "Lizards of all sizes like to sun themselves."

"What an unfortunate thought."

He chortled and she drifted into sleep again. Eli was there when she awoke, concern in his dark eyes. "Are you well, Sarah?"

She rolled over to catch his fingers with hers, hair tumbling in her eyes as she did so. "I've never been so lazy in all my born days, Eli. It's tiring, that's all. I would be better with back-breaking labor as I'm accustomed to."

"Perhaps the groundskeeper would give you a ditch to dig." He smiled, kissed her fingers, and stood. "Supper will be ready soon. You haven't been eating well, either."

"I'm fine," she promised. "I'll dress for supper and see you soon."

He nodded and left Sarah sprawled on the bed, sleepy eyes watching the sun slide toward the horizon. She'd been tired since Lammas Night, since the aftermath of the ball, as if it had taken all her energy and nothing had replenished it. Food had smelled too strongly of late; that was why she'd eaten little. It would pass soon, as summer illnesses did. She sat up, reaching for a dressing gown, and winced as she compressed her breast with the action.

Winced, then went still, her heart and breath stopped between one beat and the next. Her hands turned to ice and goose bumps swept her despite the lingering afternoon heat.

It was not a summer illness, and it would not pass in a little while, not if fatigue and tenderness and scent-sensitivity meant what it usually did. And it did, she was sure of it. Her blood hadn't come for weeks, a detail unnoticed in the fullness of her new life. It *should* have been on her during the masque, red as her gown, and that meant she was more than a month gone. Almost two, by all likelihood.

Two months gone with child, when she had believed she would have no children at all. Two months gone with the child of a dragon or a vampire, when the Old Races forbade such unions entirely.

She chose a simple gown that needed no assistance for donning, and dressed herself with cold hands so she might go to supper.

"There was another story," she said over the meal. "Another one you read to me, Janx. About the statue who came to life?"

"Pygmalion's statue," Janx said. "Elise. A gargoyle, of course."

Sarah stopped herself before she spoke further, staring in astonishment at the red-haired man across the table from her. He blinked, mild expression, then smiled. "You're surprised. Should you be, my dear? So much of human mythology and magic can be laid at the feet of the Old Races. Surely you know that by now."

"I hadn't thought." That changed the story. Changed the truth of it, but not the thrust that had prompted Sarah to ask. She nearly went on, nearly asked more, but Janx continued instead.

"A statue by day, a woman by night. Only the touch of the gods could make it so, by human understanding, but in truth? One of us."

Sarah sat with lips parted, questions ready to fall from them, but a whisper of wisdom held curiosity in check as wonder raced through her mind. Had she known? Not Elise, of course, but the woman Elise had become in the stories? Had the statue known she'd been carved of ivory and brought to life by a sculptor's love and a god's gift? Had she known, as Sarah did now, the difference from one life to another?

And had she, as the story claimed, had children? Had that gargoyle female called Elise birthed babes to a human man?

And if so, what, what, oh, *what*, had the Old Races done about it?

"I didn't mean to stun you into silence," Janx said in amusement. "Are you all right?"

"Of course. You'll have to tell me what other Greek myths the Old Races are responsible for. I begin to think no part of humanity has gone untouched by you." Sarah left that where it was, smiling and nodding as the men began to out-do each other in tales of times long past. She heard almost none of it, though, consumed with the idea of an impossible child.

She had not meant to leave them, not ever. But nor had she thought to be a mother to the extraordinary, and her thoughts came slowly clear as Eli and Janx bantered.

They would never, *never* give this child up, no matter what it might do to the politics of their people. They would never allow it to be taken away or harmed, even if they themselves had to fight the Old Races. They would fight as hard for her, too, as the mother of their child, and there was no mistaking in Sarah's mind: it would be *theirs,* no matter who the father was. No matter, indeed, who the mother was.

Inside a breath, the life that she had been offered, the long years of her own, became something very different.

"I think tomorrow I'll stay in the city house when I'm done visiting the Lady Rathbourne," she said when Eli and Janx's game of sharing outrageous stories as done. "I've been invited for tea, and it seems a long journey to come home again before morning."

"If only I could fly you there and back," Janx said in a mockery of sorrow. There was genuine regret in his green eyes, though, and Sarah shared that regret. They hadn't flown again, not since that first night, and she wanted very much to come so close to touching the stars again.

"If only I had the strength of ten," Eli said, much more dourly. "It's never seemed entirely fair to have speed but no commensurate strength so I can carry things as I dash around."

Sarah laughed. "Oh, yes. You're much abused, Eli. You can only go to India and back with arms full of flowers instead of carrying a tiger across the world for me."

As one, he and Janx straightened, their interest piqued. "Would you like a tiger?" Janx asked hopefully. "I could get you one."

"The poor creature would expire of fear if you captured one and brought it to me. I'll settle for going to India someday to see one myself."

"When London tires of the slaughterfield's daughter and her paramours," Janx promised. "Should we join you for tea with Lady Rathbourne?"

"Don't be silly. I saw her at the masque with you. She could hardly talk for tripping over her tongue. I think she actually drooled."

"Janx has that effect on women. I'm far less exciting," Eli said. "So if you require an escort..."

Sarah reached across the table to take both mens' hands. "I'll be fine. It's only a single night. You wouldn't want them to think I'm your prisoner, would you?"

Janx gave Eliseo a considering look, and Sarah, laughing, aimed a kick at him under the table. "You would *not*," she told him. "No matter how it might add to your mystery."

"Oh, very well. But we'll be bereft without you, so you must come back to us in the morning."

"How could I not?" The promise made an ache in her chest, but she smiled as she spoke, and they thought no more of it.

Tea with the Rathbournes was a trial, but at least it wasn't supper: Sarah escaped before sunset, and at her own home found the boy Alban had set to watch the grounds. He scampered to find the gargoyle, hand fisted around a coin that would see his family through a year of living graciously, and Sarah retreated to her parlor to wait.

Alban came, which she expected. So did Hajnal, which she did not, but the female gargoyle took a sentry post at the windows without speaking. Janx and Eli wouldn't come; Sarah had told the boy to pass on that message, and so wondered a little what devils Hajnal stood guard against. She didn't ask, though, and instead turned to Alban and spoke without preamble, for fear she'd be unable to speak at all if she did otherwise.

"I can't live with it." Whispered words, words that hurt her throat, her heart, to speak them. Whispered lies, because she *could.* Oh, she could live with the magic and mystery that were the two men she'd come to love. She could and was eager to, but not at the inevitable cost. Not at the price of her child lost to them all, or of her beautiful men lost to war. She was human. Mortal, for all that Eli's blood might stretch those mortal years out beyond imagination. She was meant to die, and they would, in the end, live with that.

"I look at them and I tremble." Her voice did too, shaking with what Alban would hear as fear, though in fact it was truth and sorrow. "They are such great creatures, and I cannot breathe when I am near them. I am so small."

Hajnal looked away from the window, her gaze deeper with sympathy than Sarah had imagined possible. She knew, Sarah thought: she knew what Sarah was doing, and would let Alban misunderstand.

And misunderstand Alban did. "That is the cruelty," he said, as he'd said once before. "There is so little in the memories, Sarah. So few instances of humans learning our secrets, and it always destroys them, in the end. I fear we're too much for mortals to grasp. How will you do it?" he asked more softly, and Sarah sat with her face in her hands.

"I'll have to die. They'll have to see it, or think they do, and...perhaps even think themselves to blame."

"Choose one," Hajnal said, her only contribution thus far to the conversation. Sarah startled, looking at her, and the dark-haired gargoyle shrugged. "Choose one. It will enrage the other, and a battle will be fought. The aftermath will be your best hope to escape their long reach."

"How could I choose? How could I—"

"How could you let one be the victor? Let one think he is less loved than the other? You must, or you and that child will never be free."

Alban's gold eyes widened and he shot a hard look at Sarah, who curved her hands over her belly protectively. "You didn't say," he accused Sarah, and in much the same tone, said, "How did you know?" to Hajnal.

"She has the look about her."

Sarah clenched her hands now, still keeping them in front of her belly. Rash hope ran through her, hope for an answer she had been unable to see. "Is there any way?" she asked Hajnal. "Any way for this to be made...possible? What happens to *us*, to we humans caught up in your games, if we are found to be complicit in the breaking of your laws?"

There was no softness in the gargoyle woman's voice. "You already know, Sarah. Daisani and Janx will survive, ultimately. Exiled, perhaps, but they seem to have some bond of family in each other, and exile may mean less to them than it would to others of us. But you and the child will not be permitted to live. You knew that when you called to us for help."

"And even if we should all flee together, my lovers and I..." But she had rejected that already, though the idea of so many long years with them was far from unbearable. It was the thought of the child being *theirs*, the thought of how precious and secret they would keep it, and how she would be brushed aside in its care that she could not bear. Not that they would lose regard for her: no, they might hold her in all the more esteem. But she wanted the child to be *hers*, as greedily as they would, and in the end she would be only human. She would never be able to keep up with the fathers in what she could offer the child, and so would far too quickly fall behind.

It was selfish, greedy, unkind. That, too, perhaps she had learned from Janx, from the bold creature who had singled her out and taken her from the world she'd known. He had not thought of what it would mean to her if he then rejected her; she, at least, thought of him. Of them. And then she chose for herself, as they would have done, and met Hajnal's eyes. "I knew when I came to you," she agreed. "Will you help me?"

"If you are ruthless, Alban will help you to escape, Sarah. There is no other way. Can you do it?"

"I must."

"Children are..." Alban barely gave voice to the words, shock and hope in his features. "Sarah, this is a great danger. Do they know?"

"Of course not. So it has to be soon, or this will all be much worse." Sarah's strength returned, though her heart ached with every beat. Quicksilver Janx or conservative Eli. Choosing one was worse than the betrayal of leaving them. They were brothers, and no one had ever dared to love them both. She could not take that away, not from either of them.

And yet she would have to. Sick with despair, she left the gargoyles behind, entering the gardens that surrounded her city house. The night sky glittered diamonds , sharp reminder of how close she'd flown to them. She would never reach close enough to the stars again to find answers written in them. She knelt, numb and cold despite lingering daytime heat, and let tears slide down her cheeks. So many moments of brightness and hope in these past few months, and they would all come to such a harsh and bitter end.

Hajnal joined her as the horizon began to blue, and stood quietly for some time before speaking. "Alban," she said as the sky grew golder, "Alban is very young. Very...romantic, I think, even by human standards. My people hardly know what to do with him, with his wild ideas and that romance in his soul. It's much of why I love him and chose him as my mate for life. But he sees the world through that romantic glass. He sees a human woman overwhelmed by extraordinary men. A woman whose only hope for survival is to escape those men."

"That's what he needs to see."

"It is, but do not let his perception alter yours, Sarah

Hopkins. Do not let yourself imagine that it is fear which sets you on this path. I see otherwise in your eyes."

"It is fear," Sarah disagreed softly. "Fear for them, not of them. And fear for my child. Your world would not welcome it." Those were true enough things; she did not need to confess her own selfishness as well.

"You're right. And you put me—and Alban—in a difficult place by sharing this with us. Our memories are shared by all the very moment we enter the repository that links us. To keep your child safe, we cannot ever again join with the rest of our kind."

Dismay clenched Sarah's stomach. "Would you do that?"

"Yes. Because Alban is romantic, and because I...am not." Hajnal smiled, barely a crease across her stern face. "I will perhaps be led to believe you have died, so at least one of us might stay connected to the memories. But Alban will stay apart. It's a great gift he gives you, Sarah Hopkins. Savor it. Savor the life you will lead, for it comes at a cost to all of us."

Sarah nodded, unable to voice a promise so large, and the gargoyles went away with the dawn.

She could not, in the end, choose, so what she did was worse. No easier, but certainly no kinder to take an afternoon in the sunshine with Janx and to say in a small and shaking voice, "I am afraid."

"Of what? I shall savage that which alarms you, my dear. I shall protect your virtue—very well, not your virtue—your stalwart heart from all comers! I shall—you are not playing," he interrupted himself, and all the humor fled from his face. "What on earth could frighten you now, Sarah? After you've seen so much with us?"

"I dream of being drained of blood," Sarah whispered. "Every night, worse and worse as his heat lies next to me. I dream of a cold death, my body empty and unwanted with its spirit and flavor fled."

Janx sat, eyebrows drawn down in concern. "You fear Eliseo? Sarah, he would never hurt you. He would..."

She raised her eyes to his, and whispered, "Wouldn't he?"

So easy. So terribly easy to sow a seed of doubt. So wrong, too: she wanted to cry out in protest as uncertainty and then angry caution changed the shade of Janx's green eyes. He spoke clearly, precisely: "I will not let him harm you, Sarah Hopkins, slaughterfield's daughter. Not ever."

"He's so fast. How could you stop him? I could be dead before..."

"I will not let him harm you." Brothers, and brothers could be driven apart by jealousy and hate. Sarah crushed her eyes shut and turned her face against a pillow, loathing what she did and seeing no other way forward. Janx sprang free of the bed and stalked away, anger and distrust in his actions. When he was gone she rose and went to find Eliseo.

To say to him, as she'd said to Janx, "I am afraid, Eli. Janx seems angry, and he's so fiercely *other*, when he changes. I'm afraid his anger, his size, his differences will be the end of me."

And as Janx had done, Eli shook his head. "He wouldn't hurt you, Sarah. He would never do you harm."

"Not intentionally," Sarah whispered, and watched a darkness come into Eliseo's eyes too.

"We are not meant to fight one another, his kind and mine. His size is too great, my strength too small. But he cannot match my speed, and I may not be strong, Sarah, but I can carry you from danger. Do not fear," he said, low and angry. "I will not let him harm you."

They slept separately that night for the first time since she had been unable to choose. All of them separate, each to their own rooms, though Sarah, wracked with exhaustion, rested very little at all. Daytime was worse, herself unable to meet either of their gazes and the men glowering at one another until at tea she burst out with, "Excuse me," and fled not just the table, but the estate.

She was astonished they let her go, though Eli was at the city house when she arrived. Janx would be just behind her with a coach and four, or would wait for nightfall so he could come by sky, his most favored way to journey. But Eli had no such need for discretion, and so waited for her at the home she called her own. He offered her a hand out of the carriage, his fingers hot against hers.

"Has it all changed so quickly?" he asked with regret. "It's been a beautiful summer, Sarah. If you're afraid of him, come away with me. He'll forgive us in time."

"Would you?"

Guilt replaced regret, Eli's gaze sliding to the ground. Sarah nodded and stepped away, only to have his voice follow her: "You're afraid of me now as well, aren't you."

She looked back. Looked at the distance she'd put between them, and the pain etched in Eliseo's features. There was no answer she could give, no answer she *wanted* to give: lying to them each separately about the other was a cruel enough trick. The thought of doing so directly took her breath so sharply she was left with nothing to speak with. But Eli took the exhalation for admission and bleakness came into his face. "How might I regain your trust? It is...unfair, Sarah. I think I've done nothing to lose it."

"Trust is a fickle mistress," she whispered, and Eli, blackly, said, "As are you."

A palpable hit: one of Janx's favorite phrases. Sarah closed her eyes with the blow, then drew tattered dignity around herself and went silently inside her home. Eli didn't follow, and she had the bitter thought that he didn't care enough to persuade her, and then an idea of fanciful anger: perhaps the Old Races couldn't cross a human threshold without being invited, and surely if he wouldn't fight for her she wouldn't wish to invite him.

She did not, in truth, want anyone to fight for her. Weary and heartsick, Sarah went to the back parlor, where she could stare out a window without exposing herself to Eliseo Daisani's watchful gaze. There was no better way, nothing she could think of to keep herself, her men, her child, safe. She whispered that promise to herself until the words were meaningless, and in time slept cradled in the window seat.

The sounds of destruction woke her. She jolted awake, unsure of her location, then came to her feet before thought could make sense of the roaring outside her home. She hurt everywhere: her narrow corset was not suited for sleeping in. Nor for running, but still before thought was fully engaged she *was* running, skirts gathered in her hands so she wouldn't trip as she rushed through the house and into the gardens.

A dragon and a vampire did battle there. Sarah screamed, useless sound of protest: the whole of London would see them if they weren't careful. Certainly all of her staff would, and gossip would spread from there. But her voice was lost beneath Janx's infuriated roars and tossed away by the wind brought up by Eli's speed.

They could not touch each other, not in any meaningful way. She saw that even in the dark, even with one too quick to watch and the other huge with rage. Janx slammed massive paws down, trying to skewer or crush Eli, but the vampire darted between the blows as if Janx fought under water, slow and clumsy with it. Neither, though, could Eli damage Janx: the dragon's scales were too hard to penetrate, and he had nothing like the strength or size necessary to rip one free so he might reach tenderer flesh below.

It didn't stop them trying. Sarah screamed again, and this time Janx heard her. He stopped mid-motion, wings flared to shelter half the estate grounds, and then snapped long teeth in obvious fury.

Half a breath later he was in the sky, taking the fight away from Sarah. Taking her out of danger, as he had promised he would. Sarah put fists against her mouth, trying not to sob, and Eli gave her one angry, helpless look before disappearing in a blur of speed.

Fire gouted through the sky, chasing after the vampire. Sarah ran for the garden walls, scrambling up trellises so she might see. She caught a glimpse of Eli swarming up a building wall as a swath of black against lighter brick, then lowered her head to watch where she put her feet. Fire roared again.

Sarah looked up, and London began to burn.

It seemed a long time before she realized she might be in danger. The fire spread quickly, leaping from one wooden building to another, and the heat became impossible long before she thought to save herself. Impossible, because she saw others running from it, saw them burning, saw them fall and die as she sat rigid on the wall, staring through smoke at the battle continuing on. She should have felt the heat, should have roasted from it, long before Alban separated himself from the night and landed beside her.

She had not seen him in his true form, so much broader and taller than he stood as a man. Paler, too: she could barely pick him out within the smoke, though his wings sent eddies swirling away from them both. He had no tail, which she thought odd for a flying creature, but his feet were huge and rudder-like. One could sail him, perhaps, she thought, then let go a sharp sob as he offered his hand. "This is your chance, Sarah. Come now, while the fire rages and the smoke hides us. Come while they're still fighting. They must not think to search for you until your scent has been burned away."

Sarah put her hand in his, astounded at her delicacy beside his size. He drew her up, then lifted her in his arms as if her weight was nothing. "Hold tight, Sarah Hopkins." He sprang upward as he spoke, wings catching the air more effortfully than Janx's had done, but in seconds they were within the smoke, and stayed there as the fire leapt and spread below them. She heard its crackle and Janx's bellows as they left London; those would be the sounds that stayed with her always, drowning out every other memory of childhood and youth spent in the burning city.

They flew until dawn, when the gargoyle's curse set in, and Sarah stayed at his side, silent and appalled as she watched the city burn in the distance. Come nightfall they flew again, until they reached a house set by itself in a small wood. Alban landed there and put Sarah down to gesture around. "You can grow food here, and I'll bring you pigs for meat. Will it be enough?"

The land, the freehold, was more than she had ever dreamt of, only a few months earlier. It looked now to be not insufficient, but perfect: hard work for good gain, in its way more satisfying than the easy pearls and silks Janx had offered, though she could never regret having sampled those. "It's beautiful," she whispered, then looked up at the sharp planes and angles of the gargoyle's face. "Will they be all right?"

"In time. Will you? Is your fear lessened now?"

Sarah smiled through tears that had only just begun to fall. Her fears *were* lessened: there would be no war amongst the Old Races over a child they forbade, and her men would find a way to forgive one another. "In time."

"Good. I must go, Sarah. It's a long journey home, and they'll be looking for me when the fires go out. But if you should need us again, we always find one another at the highest point in a city. Search there and we'll be waiting."

Sarah turned a tear-blurred gaze at the orange horizon; at the town that had been her home and which now burned out of control. "There are no high places left in London."

Alban touched her shoulder. "There will be other cities."

She shook her head with the protestations and innocence of youth. "No. Not for me. Goodbye, Alban. Thank you for what you've done."

"Be well, Sarah Hopkins. For you and your child both, be well."

She was wrong, of course, as she'd been wrong about so many things, but there were no cities for long and long again. London's faintly visible presence on the horizon proved too much reminder, and Sarah left the quiet cottage Alban had found for her after her daughters were born in the spring. Red-haired Kate and black-haired Ursula, each of them their father's daughter and no other. Year of miracles indeed, Sarah thought, though the poet who had so named it had known nothing of the wonders Sarah had seen.

She did leave Alban a note, a rough sketch of the British island, with a marker at the very top: the highest point in the country. He found them in Scotland many years later, children of the moors and wild seas. The girls were seventeen by then, and Sarah looked barely older than they were. He left them there, but came back to watch over them from time to time, and when a century had gone by, offered passage on a ship to newborn America. Eliseo and Janx came and went from the new world, he said, but it was vast beyond imagining: they would never find her if she didn't wish to be found.

New York City

It was unfair of Alban, Sarah thought. Unfair of him to send a lovely young woman to her doorstep in search of the twins, when she had been so careful for so long to keep them hidden. She knew, *knew*, when the young black woman rang her doorbell, that it had to do with Alban. She opened the door, already in a temper, and snapped, "Well?"

The girl—they were all girls by comparison, of course—blushed in surprise and glanced up and down the street before speaking. "Hi. Sorry, my name's Margrit Knight. I'm a friend of Alban Korund's and I'm looking for Kate or Ursula Hopkins...?"

"Never heard of 'em." Sarah began to push the door closed, heartbeat higher than it had been in decades. She was old now: she *looked* old and she was careful to sound American. This Margrit could never imagine her to be the Sarah of the story. Still, the girl slapped her hand against the door, holding it open and startling them both. Sarah's eyebrows shot up and she swallowed a sound of glee. After so long it was hard to surprise her, and after all this time she still loved moments of theatre.

Margrit Knight's blush intensified, coloring mocha cheeks to a delicious burnished red. "Wait. I'm sorry, but I'm looking for two sisters who used to live here. I might have the names wrong, but—"

"I've lived here since 1962," Sarah snapped, perfectly honestly. "Now go away."

"Oh." Bewilderment filled the girl's face and she fell back a step. "I'm sorry. I must have gotten the wrong address. I'm..." She glanced at her watch, at the rising sun, and sighed. "Sorry to have disturbed you. Thanks for the information. I'll go now."

She did, and Sarah closed her front door with a resounding thump before scurrying down the hall to snatch up the telephone and dial swiftly. "Katherine? There's a young woman out on the street looking for you and your sister. Alban sent her. I don't know if you want to talk to her or not."

Moments later she peered out through lace curtains, smiling as Kate strode out of the home she shared with Ursula less than half a block from their mother. Within a minute or two Margrit Knight had been invited inside, and Sarah retreated, letting the curtains fall back into place.

It had been more than three centuries. Longer by far than she had ever hoped to protect her children from their fathers and their fathers' world. It had *had* to come to an end someday: nothing, Sarah had said so often, nothing lasts forever. But they were grown now, and would very soon be part of the Old Races one way or another. It was inevitable, and more, it was necessary. Content, Sarah went to her dressing room, there to examine her reflection.

The woman in the mirror was no longer young. It was easy to see her as elderly, fragile, frail, though in truth she was hearty and hale, a youth spent in the slaughterfields lending strength to an ancient body. Time and again over the years she had caught glimpses of what Janx had seen that day in the market: beauty and boldness, and no one era had ever drowned that spirit. They had brought it out in her, and it had served her well for decades upon decades.

For centuries she had withheld the making of a promise, one that always lingered half-thought at the edges of her mind. She'd kept it there deliberately, not fully realized, so that it could never become the final devil in Pandora's box. So that hope would be unable to taunt her, as it had so often taunted two men who were in no way, and in all ways, brothers.

The twins would be discussing it now, and soon they would choose to leave behind the human experience that Sarah had given them. They would meet Janx and Eli—who was now called Daisani by almost everyone—and they would begin a new life.

As would Sarah. Finally she allowed that box to open, allowed the unthought, unspoken promise to take form. Allowed it to fly free on dragon wings and vampire speed, and smiled.

She would see them one last time.

EARTH-BOUND MISFIT

GARDENING WITH URSULA WAS WRETCHED. Her hands flew when she dug the soil, darted when she pulled the weeds, scurried when she loosened the vegetables, and hurried when she pulled them free. It was the same with picking berries or even catching fish: her quick hands made light of the work, but in a wonderful show of pedancy, she never, ever did more than her half of it. Kate was left to plod along doing her own half while Ursula scampered about, playing with birds and chasing rabbits, neither of which usually ended well for the animals.

She *did* collect all the honey; that was something, at least. Of course, she licked her fingers so clean of it that she might have drunk half the hive's work, and neither Kate nor their mother would know for sure because Ursula was so quick. Kate could have helped; her skin tended toward a certain imperviousness, but their mother sent Kate to collect nettles for tea and soup instead, and called it fair enough.

The best bit was when Ursula had to milk the cows, which required patience and slow hands, both so anathema to Ursula that Kate often finished that job, at least, before her. But none of it made up for the fact that her sister was light and lithe and quick, and had been since either of them could remember, whilst Kate was stuck plodding along the earth like an ordinary mortal. The twins were nearly fourteen now, and it seemed intolerable.

Their mother would have, Kate thought, protected them both from the knowledge that they were *not* ordinary mortals, at least as long as she could have, were it not for Ursula's inherent speed. But there it was, and so there too lay the answers to their heritage, that they were half human, and half not. Ursula, whose father was Eliseo Daisani, had inherited the speed and hunting skills that defined a vampire, and their mother Sarah wondered at times if, although Eli hadn't demonstrated it to her, whether Ursula's attention span, which could be brief as a single breath, was some part of that legacy as well. Perhaps not; children were often caught by one fancy and then another, but Kate could sit and watch a caterpillar cocoon and wait for it to emerge a butterfly without any need to move in the interim, and that, Sarah thought, was *her* father's legacy. Janx the dragon, drawn to beauty, and his daughter, able to wait on unfolding glory with a patience beyond mortal ken.

That was, in Kate's reckoning, all well and good, but her father could *fly.*

Sarah had seen it, had even ridden on his back so high into the sky the air grew thin; so high that the moon seemed within reach, and so high her breath had felt like ice in her lungs. She could hardly express the size of him: huge, vastly, absurdly huge, all serpentine and slender wings that might blot out the very moon he flew so near to. In its blue light his scales gleamed almost purple, though under the sun's brilliance he shone red, red as his hair; red as Kate's. He could transform from the dragonly shape to the human, but Kate remained locked with two legs and two arms and no wings, and it tasted bitter. Ursula could run; she, Kate, ought at the least be able to fly. She built a story in her mind that age would do the trick, and that on their fourteenth birthday she would come into that birthright.

The day came and passed without any such incident; so too did another birthday, until Kate spent long raging hours stalking the fields and frightening cows with her anger, which Ursula felt had to be a sign of impending dragonhood, as Kate's own self, slender and strong with youth as she might be, was hardly terrifying. Their moon's blood came, and *that* was not enough either, although Ursula grew faster and faster still, while Kate only became increasingly choleric.

Worse yet, aggravating her further, her skin began to itch, as if it needed shedding, or greasing, or both. Some days she would turn inside the house and something across the room would fall. Nothing ever broke: Ursula would catch it, no matter how far away she was when it fell, but Kate couldn't stop the crashes, any more than she could escape the itch. After a week of that she moved into the barn, where there was more room and less to break, and after a month, she stomped out to a northerly field overlooking the lashing winter sea, and dug a hole to hide in. Ursula helped, for once doing more than her own share of the work, then stood back with ill-disguised worry as her sister buried into the soil like an animal, and hunkered down as if planning to wait out the winter. In there she could writhe and scratch and thump without doing damage, and if the hole got deeper, so be it.

At a certain depth, its scent changed. It still smelled earthy, but metallic too. Kate dug down, not asking for Ursula's help this time, and found, in time, a chest of rotted iron, and inside it, Roman coins and jewels. Part of her, still a girl, thought she ought to drag it up to the surface and bring it to their mother; the other part of her, the dragon's daughter, coiled around it in the earth's cool grasp and went to sleep.

She emerged, gaunt and dirty and hungry, into spring air filled with the bleats of lambs and birdsong, and the scent of turning soil and new growing things. The chest of coins she dragged along behind her until a calf mewled and hunger turned her dizzy. A few quick steps, a launch upward and a landing hard enough to shake the earth, and the little beast crunched to the earth beneath her; she had taken three savage bites before thought caught up to action, and then it was she who mewled, and ran for home.

Ursula flashed out of the house shrieking and waving her arms, stopping Kate a dozen earth-rucking steps before the door. Clods of dirt spattered across the house as Sarah appeared in the door, less agitated than Ursula but with a scent of relief. Kate yowled, unable to stretch human words from a mouth shaped wrong, but Ursula mitigated her fear by seizing around Kate's neck and swinging herself upward, until her sister was an unfamiliar weight between Kate's shoulders. Ursula pounded her shoulder, shouting nonsensically, and, like a half-wild horse, Kate bucked and twisted beneath the ruckus. Huge and terrible feet rent the ground, and she arched like a cat, jumping up and down, but Ursula, laughing, hung on.

Her sides, along the spine, below the shoulders, felt strangely constrained, as if her arms were somehow bound against her. They weren't: what she thought of as *arms* were beneath her, supporting her weight, as were her legs, but *something* lay there, uncomfortably tight. Kate inhaled, pumping her lungs like bellows, and Sarah gave a shout of alarm and laughter as she made enormous throwing-away gestures with her tiny human arms. Pointing Kate in another direction, perhaps; thus guided, Kate turned and bellowed again before with a rip, her wings tore free.

It was not the uncertainty of a bird trying its first flight, oh no. Still mucus-covered, still sticky and new, Kate lowered her belly to the earth, banging wings against the house, the gate, flattening parts of the garden, knocking askew a carefully-built stone fence, and then leapt to the sky with strength and confidence and a joyfully shrieking sister upon her back.

The world below became patched pieces: Sarah smiling upward from the house, the new green of the garden around her. A distant road threaded through hills, and fields that were thought of as fecund seemed stone-littered and impossible to farm, from above. Sheep and cows made bright spots of color against brown tilled soil and grass-green hills; there lay the bloody spattered mess of the calf she'd half eaten, and behind it the chest of coins she'd dragged out *with her tail*. The gold was too small to be seen, but she knew it was there, as certainly as she knew the slate-blue sea that rolled beyond the cliffs and rocky shores. It seemed so orderly, and she had reached hardly any height at all: from far above the world would be a serene place, untroubled and untroubling. Her wings dried with every heartbeat, with every wing beat, and Kate, soaring in this new shape, this hardly-known form, felt satisfaction rising up from within, a confidence in her wholeness, and with that sensation thought that had she known how to laugh in this new body, she might have, for she had never felt so very *human.*

LEGACY

1840, NEW YORK CITY

A GERMANIC VOICE MURMURED, "A shame about the old church," and Richard Upjohn snorted.

"Not at all. There was nothing extraordinary about it, nothing memorable. It lacked even the respect of age, and moreover, it was poorly enough constructed that the weight of winter snow weakened it beyond repair. *My* church," he said with already-significant satisfaction as he examined the enormous hole that the foundations would be laid in, "will stand for the ages." Then he glanced sideways at the man who had spoken, and fell silent in surprise.

He was perhaps the tallest man Upjohn had ever seen, standing two meters in height, and had the breadth of shoulder to match. He was not old, but his hair glowed white even in the early evening moonlight, and his eyes were so pale as to seem colorless. His hair was unfashionably long, not coiffed at temple and top but rather smoothed back in a tail that fell between his shoulderblades, and his coat was of a cut not seen in a decade or more.

No one, Upjohn thought, would mock him for his lack of style. Not with the height and breadth of him, nor the warning rumble in the deep voice. He found himself searching for, if not an apology, at least a moderation of his strong stance against the old church, when a smile flickered across the huge man's face. "The snow was very bad that year," he said, defending the older building, "but it is true that it lacked age. The second church on this site, I believe. I never saw the first."

"Of course you didn't. It burned during the Revolution." The war between the colonies, Upjohn had been taught to call it in childhood: the Revolution, the Glorious Revolution, had happened more than a century earlier by English reckoning, but he had come to America by choice, and become a citizen only four years ago. In America the colonial war was the Revolution, and so too for Richard Upjohn.

Either way, the first church had burned a quarter century before Upjohn was born, and the giant German at his side could certainly be no older than Upjohn himself.

Another smile flickered across the tall man's face. "Yes, of course. Still, I had some fondness for the second church. I lived here, you know."

Upjohn's gaze sharpened, then fell into puzzlement. The man was not the vicar or the reverend, nor did Trinity employ a groundskeeper that Upjohn was aware of. And he could hardly be unaware of this man, who might well cow the grounds into growing tidy hedges and short grass with no more than his size and presence. "That's absurd. I've never seen you before, and I was commissioned to work here when the old church was so badly damaged."

"And yet," the big man said idly. "Walk with me a while, Richard Upjohn. I have a favor to ask of you."

Upjohn, curious and mystified, matched the German's steps as they left Trinity's grounds for the surrounding city. Three hundred thousand people lived there, a tenth the number in London, but its freshness was rife with potential. New York could be beautiful, if Upjohn and others like him were allowed their way.

The German, as if hearing his thoughts, said, "I've followed your career, Master Upjohn. You have a love for the Gothic. What is it that draws you to it?"

"I am a faithful man, Master..."

"Korund," the German said. "Alban Korund. The pleasure is mine."

"Korund," Upjohn echoed after a moment. "I'm a faithful man, Master Korund. I believe the Gothic churches carried the eye and voice to God, as they should. Their churches were manifestations of truth, truth made visible to purify the heart. To build and restore in their style is the work of God."

The German—Korund's—eyebrows lifted. "How deeply do your convictions run, Master Upjohn? Do you believe, as Hamlet did, that there are more things in this world than are dreamt of in your philosophy? Or are the answers to God's mysteries all plain in the light of day?"

"I would not presume to know all God's secrets," Upjohn replied stiffly, and Korund waved a large hand in apology.

"I meant no offense. There are many who do seem to presume such knowledge, and who close their minds to wonders because of it. I cannot help but think a man who seeks to bring Man's voice to God is not one of them."

Upjohn slowed, looking the length of the street they walked, up and down: Wall Street, once the city's outer wall, now swallowed by the city's expansion. Thin moonlight spilled down the long road, illuminating hand-painted signs and the home-going residents who lived at perpetual odds with the increasing business presence along the street. He had no particular sense of danger, not in such a well-populated area, but nor was it the appropriate venue for discussing religious leanings. "Master Korund," he said slowly, "you said you had a favor to ask of me. Perhaps you should ask it, and be done with these idle mutterings."

"Trinity will have vaults beneath," Korund said without further preamble. "I would like you to dig yet another room below them, one that I might reside in."

Long moments passed without the huge man's expression faltering in any way, no hint of humor or teasing in his countenance. Upjohn waited longer than that, even, before finally asking, "Are you mad?"

"I'm afraid not."

Upjohn stared at him longer still, then, thunderstruck, asked, "*Why?*"

"Because there are more things in life than dreamt of in most mens' philosophies." Korund waited a moment, then spread his large hands. "I require sanctuary, Master Upjohn, and you, as architect of this new church, are peculiarly able to provide it. I would prefer not to explain in detail, but if I must, then we should retreat to Trinity's grounds, where I might have a semblance of privacy."

"You cannot possibly imagine I would agree without a full understanding of why you ask."

Korund's brief smile filtered across his face again. "You might have. Men do extraordinary things for the strangest reasons. I *have* lived at Trinity since well before the old church fell," he continued as they turned back to the church grounds. "I take care not to be noticed."

"Forgive me," Upjohn said, fully aware his tone asked for no such thing, "but a man of your dimensions is unlikely to go unnoticed for any length of time. I find it sheerly impossible that you could live at the church and be unknown. The rector must know of you, at least."

"No." Korund said nothing more, and after a moment Upjohn realized he had no intention of explaining further. Irritation flooded him, then quieted under a sense of intrigue. A giant in need of sanctuary: that was a story suited for his children, and might entertain them a little if he had the whole of it. And there was an interest in the very idea, creating a hidden room in the heart of his first and perhaps foremost architectural gem. Trinity, with God's blessing, would stand forever: to have a secret built within it appealed.

"Very well," he said abruptly. "Convince me of its necessity and you shall have your sanctuary, but I must know the whole story, Master Korund. I will not build a safe house for a murderer or madman."

"I promise you that I am altogether more unusual than that." They walked together in silence to the church grounds, returning to the very spot they had begun. All lingering twilight was gone and moonlight barely grazed the foundation pit's muddy bottom. It looked more sinister than it had only half an hour earlier, and Upjohn wondered if refusing the German might find himself dead in its depths before midnight.

"I must have your word," Korund said to the pit. "That you'll speak of what happens here tonight to no one. If you decide against me, I assure you, you will not find me to prove the story you'd want to tell, but it would be easier—more reassuring—if you would make the promise regardless."

"If no harm comes of keeping the secret, I shall keep it."

"No harm will come of it." Korund, as if it were a natural thing to do, began removing his clothing.

Upjohn gawked, then turned away in a rush of embarrassment and offense. "What, sir, do you imagine you are doing!"

"The transition is hard on clothing," Korund said, as naturally as he undressed. "It can be done without destroying it, but my preference is to do without. Master Upjohn, I require sanctuary because although I appear as a man, I am not one. I was born in the same year as your Queen Elizabeth, and I have lived at Trinity Church since I fled France's revolutions in the 1780s. My family name is reminiscent of your *corundum*, the stone sapphire is made of, and I am a gargoyle, one of the last remaining Old Races."

A soft explosion accompanied the last words, and Korund's voice, already deep, dropped noticeably. Upjohn spun toward him, staggered back, and said with utter conviction, "Good *God*."

Korund awaited him in a crouch, his clothing set neatly to one side and his wings, his *wings,* wrapped loosely around himself in their lieu. He might have been carved of the pale stone he looked to be, save his yellow gaze following Upjohn's stagger. There was nothing remotely human about him, not from chiseled bone structure to a size that belittled his human height and breadth.

Upjohn, backing away, took one wrong step, and fell into the foundation pit.

A massive hand snapped out so smoothly it belied the necessary speed to catch his wrist and pull him effortlessly back to safety. Korund had not otherwise moved, nor did he once he was certain Upjohn had his feet under him again, only released him without ceremony. "My people are bound by stone in daylight hours," he rumbled, the sound of granite on granite, "and as such need daytime sanctuary. I have hidden myself—"

"In the graveyard." Upjohn's voice was thin and hoarse. "I've seen—you. I thought you were a...monument." He passed his hand over his eyes, unsurprised to find it trembling. He sat, shaking, and gazed wide-eyed at the pale thing before him. "I had never noticed it missing at night."

"Why would you," Korund murmured. "Most visitors are during the day, and no one thinks to look up when they come through at night. But the city grows larger, and I am—uncomfortable," he said, choosing the word carefully, "with the graveyard's exposure. When the decision was made to rebuild the church, when the architect was a man of Gothic inclinations, well. How could a gargoyle resist asking?"

"I might destroy you."

"No." As before, Korund gave no sign of intending to continue, though as silence stretched, this time he did. "You might at worst try, but I am stronger and faster than you, and can escape to the sky if I must. I have made Trinity my home, but will find another if I have to." The thin-skinned wings rustled, then settled again. "I would prefer the chamber beneath the new church, though."

"I could..." Words failed Upjohn, quavering voice disappearing into nothing. *Thoughts* disappearing into nothing: it was all he could do to not gape like a country child, not to shake like a leaf from a tree. "I do not dream?" he finally whispered, and Korund's smile, it seemed, was similar from one countenance to the other.

"You do not dream. I am as you see me, and I am confident of my secrets." Korund shrugged, a massive shift of absurdly wide shoulders. "You, after all, can tell no one, because they would think you mad."

"I think I may *be* mad."

"No."

Again silence, until Upjohn rubbed his face and nodded. Dreams were more accommodating, shifting and slipping to feel believable, while the thing before him sat solid and uncompromising; madness might present itself with such physicality, but if it did, he was lost already, convinced of Korund's reality. Whether he was God's wonder or the Devil's work: that was the question he barely dared to wonder. "Are you a creature of faith, Master Korund?"

Korund said, "No," so forthrightly it made Upjohn laugh.

"How is that? You must be God's beast or the Devil's, and so must believe in one or the other."

"Can one," Korund wondered, "believe in one without the

other? I believe in something else, Master Upjohn. I believe that my people came into this world before it had settled on the form its multitudes would take. My people are six-limbed, not four," he said, shuffling his wings in demonstration, "and we are few to your many. You are taking this very well."

"What choice have I? An acceptance of your reality or an acceptance of my own instant descent into insanity, and I do not *feel* insane. You frighten me," he whispered, then took a deep breath to allow himself the other admission: "And I am fascinated. I depend on planes and angles and perfect joinings for my livelihood, and you are those things made manifest. If you are the Devil sent to tempt me, you are..." Upjohn opened a hand and closed it again, knowing it to be a gesture of helpless admiration. "You are perfect."

Korund's mouth quirked. "As well for you, then, that I don't believe in your devil, much less come from him. Will you help me?"

"You said there are others," Upjohn said after a moment.

"Yes." This time the silence had humor in it, and Korund finished, almost apologetically, "But no, I won't tell you any more, only that they have their own sanctuaries. It's against the laws of my people to have told you this much, to have shown myself to you, but I am already exiled and they can do no more to me."

"Exiled? Why?"

Korund breathed laughter. "For keeping secrets, Master Upjohn. My people are the memory of the Old Races, and look poorly upon keeping secrets. Exile was the only way I could."

"Exiled by choice, then," Upjohn said, and for some reason found reassurance in that. Perhaps because he'd left England as a form of self-imposed exile, though in truth he was running from debts. Still, it seemed a commonality, if such a thing could be found between a creature such as Korund and a human man. "A room beneath the vaults would be all but airless. Dark. And ventilation would need to feed out at a distance, so you might have light and air without drawing notice."

"Darkness does not bother me, though light to read by would be welcome."

"You *read?*"

Korund's eyebrows, as white as his hair, shot upward, and he grinned, showing more fang than Upjohn expected. "I do. Books are an especial weakness, and I have a small collection that is dear to me. I will need," he added thoughtfully, "a bookcase. What a splendid thought. It's been most of a century since I've had a library of my own." He straightened as he spoke, and the air around him erupted again, leaving a man where the monster had been. As unconcerned for his natural state as before, he began to dress while Upjohn found somewhere else to look. "More important than a bookcase, though, is a bolt-hole. There are storm tunnels below the city, you know this?"

"Their depth determines the vaults' depth," Upjohn replied, then frowned. "And will determine the size of your chamber. I fear it will not be large, Master Korund."

"It needn't be. I spend my nights in the city, and largely only require solitude and safety for the daylight sleeping hours. Room for a single bed, a bookcase and a chair will be enough."

"My workers will know of the chamber's presence. Your secret will not be mine alone."

"My secret will be," Korund said with certainty, and came to stand beside Upjohn fully dressed. "The chamber may not be, but I doubt you'll mention the reason for it. Call it a flood room," he suggested. "Space to swallow water should it rise, so the vaults will have time to be emptied of precious contents."

"You're devious, Master Korund."

"Not particularly. One does tend to be quick at excuses after three centuries of needing them, though."

"You were really born the same year as the Virgin Queen?"

"I was. I knew Shakespeare in passing, and Kit Marlowe better."

"And did they know—?"

"No." Korund's grin flashed again, full and bright. "No, or all the world would know of the Old Races in allegory if not in fact. Kit kept secrets, but Will could not resist the slightest sniff of a story."

"And yet you trust my discretion."

"You," Korund said, "are an architect, not a playwright. Litter your creations with gargoyles and no one will think anything of it."

"I shall," Upjohn said dourly, and did.

1849, TRINITY CHURCH

The lad sent to deliver the letter thought the sender mad, but put it where he'd been instructed, atop John Atkinson's grave marker in one of the Gothic church's outer nooks. It was raining, but the letter was wrapped three times in waxed paper and the paper sealed along its outer edges. It could be thrown in the river, the lad reckoned, and would come out a century hence still dry.

He sat around for as long as he dared, watching the letter and the grave, half hoping a ghostly hand would reach up and seize it, but nothing so exciting happened. Finally, as it grew darker, he sighed and went back to the scolding he deserved for idling an hour away instead of couriering more letters across town.

Had he waited another half hour for the horizon to swallow the sun, he might have seen a black crack in the church's walls, and a white-haired giant of a man exit, stop, and crouch to collect the letter. He would never have seen, though, the words that brought a smile to the giant's face:

Should you wish to travel, the well-wrapped letter offered, *you will find accommodations in Raleigh, Providence, Boston, Buffalo, and may be assured of finding them in other cities in the future.*

Your friend and admirer,

Richard Upjohn, Architect

1858, QUEENS, NEW YORK

"I thought it unlikely you would be here," Alban Korund said in a voice unchanged by time, and Richard Upjohn turned from the chapel built to his design, smiling at first, then long-jawed with astonishment.

It was not only Korund's voice that had gone unchanged, but his features. His clothing was more fashionable than it had been twenty years earlier, but his hair was still worn long and he was otherwise precisely the man—or creature—he had been when Upjohn had last seen him in the eighteen forties. "I like to see them newly finished, if I can," he said faintly, then more strongly, "I think I hadn't believed you, about Elizabeth and Shakespeare and Marlowe. Now I do. Why does God grant you unchanging years while I—?" He gestured at himself, two decades older and greyer for the time.

"God," Korund said easily, though Upjohn knew he didn't believe, "has also granted you a son of talent equal to your own, and a family to have and hold. We each gain and lose things for what we are, Richard. One is no better than the other, only different. I had hoped to see you. So many of the other buildings are too far away."

"Have you traveled?"

"Some," Korund said with obvious delight. "Thank you for that, Richard. An unexpected gift."

"Come." Upjohn tipped his head away from the church. "We'll find a meal and talk. It's been a long time."

They spoke into the night, of course: through the night, and until dawn began to grey the eastern sky. Then Korund glanced toward the nearby chapel, and lifted his eyebrows in curiosity.

Upjohn smiled. "If they've built it to my designs, yes. Shall we see?"

Together they went to the chapel, to the same side and place where at Trinity Church a doorway was found, and Upjohn himself pressed the brick that should open a passage. The door shifted back smoothly, soundlessly, and, pleased, Upjohn swept a hand across himself, inviting Korund down. He followed the larger man deep under the chapel, unsurprised that Korund produced a tinderbox to light torches with.

The room below was empty, no bookcases or beds, which dismayed Upjohn. He paced the room and said as much, but Korund chuckled. "I'm sure you didn't specify what furnishings should be put in your flood rooms. No matter: the safety is all I need, not a bed."

"A stone floor is uncomfortable to sleep on."

"Mmm. Not for one such as I. Dawn is upon us. Thank you again, Richard." Air exploded, a sound heard only a few times, years before, but unmistakable. Upjohn turned, breath drawn to respond, and held it behind parted lips instead.

The gargoyle had become stone. Not the uncanny likeness that yet had life to it that Upjohn had seen so long ago, but stone itself, a statue of surpassing detail and quality. He stood frozen in motion; Michelangelo would have wept to achieve the naturalness of his stance and the delicate lines carving strength and power in alabaster. Planes and angles and joinings, Upjohn had said to him once, and that if he was the Devil's work, he was an excellent foil to draw Upjohn in. The Devil may quote scripture, he thought, but he could only warp and distort, never create beauty as pure as the unliving gargoyle.

There in the small room beneath a church of his own design, alone but for a living thing turned to stone, Upjohn

knelt and folded his hands, to give thanks and express wonder
to the God who had drawn Alban Korund into Richard Upjohn's
life.

1878, NEW YORK

"I am sorry," said Richard Upjohn the younger to the
extraordinarily tall and pale man standing in their doorway, "I
am sorry, but it's very late, and my father is very ill." His
politeness was strained by sorrow and offense: no considerate
soul would come knocking on the door so close to midnight
even if they had no idea a man was dying within the house's
walls.

"Yes," the enormous man replied in a lightly Germanic
accent, "yes, I know, it's why I've come. I'm sorry for the hour,
but I have little choice. Your father was my friend, a long time
ago."

"He won't know you," Richard said tightly. "It has come on
him quickly, this illness, but his mind is lost, his brain
softened. He speaks only of Trinity Church and secret rooms
and gargoyles who come to life. He is *dying*," Richard snapped,
and the big German lowered his gaze with a sad smile.

"I would still like to see him, if I may."

"Come back in the morning." Richard pushed the door
closed, only to have it meet the German's big hand, and stick.
No amount of subtle force could move it, and to try more
obviously would be embarrassing. Stymied, he glowered at the
man, whose expression remained apologetic and determined.

"I would have come in the morning if I could have, Master
Upjohn. Please, may I visit your father?"

Bristling with weariness and displeasure, Richard M.
Upjohn snapped, "Could I stop you?"

To his utter surprise, the big man stepped backward,
examining the outside of the house, at the large windows and
the trellises between them, then offered a brief smile. "Not in

the slightest. But it would be more polite and more usual to come in through the front door, and not be forced to peek into bedrooms to find where your father rests."

You wouldn't died on Richard's lips: clearly the German would, and evidently believed he *could*. Instead Richard stepped backward, leaving the door clear. The white-haired man inclined his head in thanks and came inside. "Which room?"

"Upstairs to the left." Richard swallowed. "Who are you? Why is this so important?"

"My name is Alban Korund, and your father gave me a home. Thank you, Mister Upjohn. I won't be long." He took the stairs quickly, leaving the son to frown in astonishment.

Not long proved far longer than he might have hoped. It was midnight when Korund went up the stairs; dawn was coming on when he came down again, his expression tired but gentle. He paused in the door, looking back at Richard, and said, "Thank you," quietly. "I would like you to know that while he is old, while he is dying, he is less touched in the mind than you feared. He has not lost his faculties, only his discretion, and even that is easily forgiven in an old man."

"Of course," Richard said bitterly. "I am so grateful for the reassurance of a stranger, that my father's mad tales aren't madness at all. I've looked through his records while you visited him. There's no mention of you, no house he built for a Korund. Who *are* you?"

"A friend," Korund said again. "Goodbye, Richard Upjohn. Thank you for allowing me to see your father one last time."

He left the house then, walking smartly across the streets toward nearby fields, and Richard stood in the doorway watching.

The distance was not that great: Korund must have known he could still be seen in the light of the oncoming dawn. Between one step and the next he *changed*, an impossible change, from one step a man to the next as a winged thing that seemed half again as large as the man had been. Blazing white in the pre-dawn light, he sprang upward and flew into the morning, and for an instant it seemed he looked back, angular face as inhuman as the winged body: a gargoyle come to life.

In a heartbeat he was gone, powerful wings taking him from view. Within minutes dawn burst over the horizon, golden light and golden light alone bringing tears to the younger Upjohn's eyes.

August **18, 1878**

Like the letter thirty years earlier, it was delivered wrapped in wax paper: the Saturday New York Times, and with it, a note.

Although aged, the obituary ran, *although aged, Mr. Upjohn enjoyed very good health until recently, and his death occurred after but a brief sickness of a week, from a softening of the brain.*

I would not have known, the adjoining note read, *had you not visited, and I would have believed him mad in his final days; would have believed the truth of what must be said in a public notice. Instead he spoke of you, and I have learned more of my father and of this world than I had ever before known. In my mourning, I thank you.*

Richard M. Upjohn, Architect

SALT WATER STAINS THE SAND

My name is Tahira Firaz Galia al-Shareef di Nazmi al-Massri, and today I have killed my brother.

He does not know it yet, but I see it as he limps away over desert sands. He is an exile, lost to his people, and because of that, he is dead. Because of me, he is dead.

It is not how I hoped this story would end.

"He is wealthy and powerful. Respected among the clans. You could do no better."

"He is old." A silly argument: I am old. There are very few young among us anymore, not since the Bedouins came to ride their horses through our sands and take the few resources we once called our own. The humans; my father and brother would not be pleased that I know their tribes by name, or that I care. They are all young, the humans, every one of them, even their most venerable sages. The most extraordinary see a hundred changes of the season, and I have long since lost count of how many soft desert springs I have witnessed. So: I am old.

But not as old as Amar, who is so old the desert sun has bleached the blackness from his hair. So old that the sandstorms have driven lines into his skin, so old that his scowl reminds me of young mountains, harsh and sharp with their newly-risen ridges. He is old, and has thirteen wives, and I will not be the next.

"Tahira," Malik says with a winsome note. "Tahira, you must listen to reason. Amar is powerful. He could destroy us if you refuse him."

"How?" Oh yes, I am young by comparison. Arrogant with my youth. Arrogant with my beauty, which I have been assured since childhood is incomparable. The appeal is in my eyes, green as the northern sea, when most of the djinn have eyes of desert gold and river silt brown. Malik's eyes are like that: brown, so brown that even in sunlight they are nearly black. Now they are bright with hope, though; bright with the conviction that he alone can convince his willful sister of her foolishness. And if anyone could, it would be he. I have seen that Malik treats other women with disdain, but that is the way of my people. Whether we learned it from the humans or they from us, it seems a mark of the desert tribes. Within our families, within the sanctuaries of our homes, we are priceless jewels, but without, we are for barter, like the horses the Bedouin sell.

I do not believe Amar would consider me a jewel, except as another one to parade through our short-lived desert cities, and I have come to think there is more to a life than being admired from a distance. I steal bits of knowledge from the world beyond the deserts, murmurs of gossip and of stories, and I hear of women—human women—who travel the world in search of adventures and equality. These are the things I dream of, though they are utterly forbidden.

"He is wealthy," Malik says. "Wealthy beyond the djinn, Tahira, you know that. You know that he—"

Silence. Complete silence, because though yes, of course, I *do* know, as does everyone, no one, not one of us, will admit aloud how Amar has broken the bonds of our people. We are djinn. We are an ancient and proud race, dancers with the wind, and one of the few, so few, remaining Old Races. Our ancient enemies, the water-born selkie, have disappeared, and dragons have not been seen in the skies for hundreds of years. Some no doubt still exist, eking out a worm-like existence beneath the sands, but their pride is gone. No gargoyle has come to record the histories of my people in a generation, and for the Old Races, a generation is long indeed. Nor do vampires haunt mortal nights, though they were never many to begin with. And we were all the most populous of our peoples, the ones who survived the longest.

And Amar has, in truth, betrayed us to the humans.

Not so boldly as that, no. He has not spoken our secrets to them; of that we can be sure. No djinn would, because although we follow our own laws within the clans, we respect the very few strictures that bind all the Old Races. One is to never tell humans who and what we are, for fear of being hunted out of existence. So, no: Amar has not gone that far.

But it is a well-known secret that his desert travels bring him not to the distant oases and rare growing fields but to the ancient buried tombs of the pharaohs and mortal princes. He guides humans to them for a fee, for a portion of the gold, which we have no especial use for. He has done this for centuries, aeons, but only in the past few years have the tomb raiders begun to ask for him. Only recently has he become known outside our tribes, and in becoming so known, become *powerful.* Humans are drawn to him, and now, ever more, the djinn look to him for leadership.

"And you would have me marry him?" I ask sharply. The wind outside our tent is as harsh, wiping away my words. This is not a safe conversation, even with much of it going unspoken. No one keeps a secret from the djinn. We ride on the air, listening in eager silence until we have learned what we wish to know. Only then do we dance away again to manifest in bodily form to eat and sleep and love. This is why my own desire to break the rituals of my people has gone unsaid: I can trust no one with such madness, not even my beloved brother.

"He could destroy us," Malik says again, more softly, and for the second time I say, "How? We trade with the other tribes as we all do. Father's eastern travels bring back silks and spices no one else can match. As long as there is a desire for those things, Amar cannot be our ruin."

"Unless he pays another to make the journey instead."

I am dumbstruck, so startled I let myself whirl into insubstantiality. Now I can feel the rising wind as part of me, can feel the grains of sand it carries as warning of an oncoming storm. I can taste the desert's grit and resolution, the promise that nothing can stand in its way. It substantiates me, brings me back to the speaking world, and gives me voice that is rougher than how I spoke before. "Only Father knows the trade winds over the mountains. They are our family's security. He would never share them with anyone, and the only other choice is by sea."

It is Malik's turn to shudder, though he keeps his grip on solidity better than I. Salt water is anathema to our people, the one thing that can bind us to bodies and force us to do another's bidding. No djinn travels by sea, even if the winds there are most favorable. They might die, too, and leave a djinni stranded over calm waters, waiting to see which lasted longer: his ability to remain incorporeal, or the quiet of the air. No: the sea is not an option, and there is no other way to China's riches.

"But what if he could be made to tell?" Malik's voice is low. He is kneeling, unusually supplicant for my brother. "What if salt water was used to bind him, and the routes commanded from him then?"

I stare. "Amar wouldn't."

Malik lifts his gaze, fear plain to see in his brown eyes. It comes to me that he was lying before. Lying with the brightness in his face, the humor and winsomeness in his an act for a doting little sister. He was masking fear, hoping I would bend to charm before his terror broke through. I rise, silk robes hissing against each other, and there is shrill demand in my voice: "Where is Father now?"

Malik looks away, and a shriek rips from my throat. We are mist, we are fog, we are dancers on the wind, but it is with concussive force that I dissipate. The energy expended rings in my ears, outrage and fear, and I use it to direct myself against the rising storm. Crosswise to the winds, chasing distance as though it is not there, and when I materialize it is within the very heart of Amar's tents: within the harem, where the women gather to wait out the storm.

I am a dervish, whirling through them. I hold a curved blade in one hand, seized from a table, and as I dance I cut and cut and cut. Screams stutter in my hearing, my ears catching the sound only as I take form long enough to slice and slice and slice again, and when I am done I fling the blade tip-down into the carpets. It quivers where it lands, but I do not share its hesitancy as I snarl, "It is me Amar wants. Tell him to release my father and come for me if he dares."

Then I am gone, and with me comes a thousand strands of floating hair, the prize and jewel of the women of the harem shorn away.

"I will not face a woman." Amar's scorn is staggering. He is furious, lined face flushed with rage, but he holds the tatters of his honor in place, as if it was not a woman who has humiliated him and his harem.

I spit, shocking waste of water in a desert land. There are few signs of greater derision among my people, and there is a collective indrawn breath from those who have gathered to judge our cases. "A woman should not dare," comes a voice from the crowd, and I spit a second time.

"Should not dare spit on one who is beneath contempt or should not say aloud what we all know? How dare this man claim to be honorable when we know, we all know that he does business with human treasure hunters? When we know he profits fr—"

"From their greed." Amar has controlled his anger and interrupts in his beautiful, rich voice. "Human treasure hunters who desecrate human graves. Why should I—*we*—not profit from their lack of respect for their dead? Why should we, who are part of this land's history from before humanity's rise, not be part of its future as well? Why should we not barter and bargain and shape our destiny, rather than hide and wait for our doom as the others have done? It is against the laws," he says, disgust rolling through the words. "Laws which assure our destruction. We do not have to confess all, to show ourselves to them, to become human, in order to control and manipulate them. The *laws* would have us die away, when we might do so much better."

My stomach slips. This is not the argument he is here to make. He is meant to face me in a fight for my hand. A fight for my father's safety, not twist the moment to make us look at the choices we have and are making. The worst of it, the worst of it is that impossibly, *impossibly*, I agree with him. We will die, we *are* dying, without bold action, and his are the boldest imaginable. But that is not the battle I meant to fight.

"Tahira al-Massri might do better, too," Amar murmurs. "She might stand at my side, first wife, as I lead our people into that future. I have her father's permission. Now I will have her."

"No." It is all slipping away from me. My father, my beloved father, stands beside Amar now. There are no marks on him, no dampness that threatens of seawater used as a weapon. His expression is serene, with no sorrow hidden in its depths. He belongs to Amar now, whether through fear or bargaining, and I am the price of that bargain. My hands clench in impotent fear. It does not matter that I agree with Amar's madness. I will not be bargained for: *my* future is worth more than that. To me, if no one else, and there is only one threat I have left to make. Not a threat; threats lack credence, and I mean what I say with every fiber of my being. "Then I will walk into the sea and be drowned, and the djinn will lose not only me but any children I might bear."

"That will not be necessary." Malik, Malik, darling brother, foolish brother, comes forward from the gathering, his dark eyes calm. "If you will not face her, Amar, then face me. If I lose, it is my life forfeit to your whim rather than Tahira's. And if I win, it is your fortune and place of power within the clans that is mine. But you cannot refuse my challenge," he says more softly, "unless you are a coward."

I do not even see the first strike, it is so fast. I do not see Amar dissipate, nor reappear, only that my brother is suddenly on his knees. In the next moment he too is gone, and every one of us gathered on the sands edges backward to give them room.

It is not like a mortal battle, a battle of djinn. Men stand and face one another, always seeing where his opponent comes from, always observing the coming blow. When djinn fight, it is a flurry of sandstorms, of wind given dire personality of its own. We can do each other no harm when we remain incorporeal, and so the dervishes whip around one another, throwing sand and spinning air until one, so suddenly, becomes something like a man, and there is a clash of swords.

Only the briefest clash, though, before they are both air again, neither having gained the advantage. Blade hits blade, no more. A test of strength and of speed, but never a killing blow. There are laws, among the Old Races, about killing those of our own. We respect that, outside the tribes, but within, oh, within.

Again sand sprays, blades smash together, and wind whips away. In time they will have the other's measure, and then will stand to fight; that is the only way an end can come. That is the manner in which djinn fight. My brother is younger, which may stand him well in the end: stamina will matter. But Amar is old and wily, and that may be Malik's undoing. I have no sense of it, only of my heart beating so hard it underscores the clash of their blades, and of the coldness of my hands despite the desert heat. Again they meet, swords ringing, and dissipate. Again. Again. Again.

I had not thought it could be done. No one watching thought it could be done: that much is clear from the gasp that arises. It takes such anticipation, such understanding of the opponent, such certainty, that no one save the most ancient of warriors would even try, much less succeed.

Amar is that most ancient warrior, and success is blood on his blade.

He is kneeling when he manifests. Kneeling, with his saber thrust backward, captured between his arm and body. It is a wicked curved line, deadly sharp, a low strike. Except he is motionless; there is no strike made.

Malik manifests *around* the blade.

It is his thigh that is pierced as he swings much too high, prepared for, expecting, an ordinary clash of swords. Color drains from his face, shock so great he cannot even scream. Two objects cannot occupy the same space, and Amar's sword was there first.

Amar twists. Yanks. Stands.

Blood, and then Malik, falls to the sand.

The bone is cracked: I have heard it, and the sand is swallowing the rain of blood. Amar looks over his shoulder, then shakes his blade free of blood. Once, twice, thrice. Then he walks to me. Says, "Your life for his. Let it be a worthy sacrifice, little girl."

He evaporates, as does every other djinn who is not by blood my kin. I cross the sand in quick steps to catch Malik in my arms. I dissolve. Come back. Dissolve again, holding him all the time. Again. Again. *Again.* Until finally he whispers, "Enough," and I cry out, relief hurting my throat. I help him to his feet, shaking with gladness. The shift from corporeal to wind heals.

But not well enough. Malik's face spasms as he puts weight on the injured leg. Only injured, no longer deadly. I catch him again, ready to take him to the wind a thousand times more. He says, "Enough," again, and I go still, heartache and confusion thrumming through my body.

"You've saved me," he rasps. "I could not have shifted. The limp is nothing, Tahira. You've saved me."

"For exile." My father, forgotten about but now implacable. I jerk toward him, sickness rising as he speaks again. "You will leave the deserts, Ebul Alima Malik al-Shareef di Nazmi al-Massri, never to return again. It is the law of the Old Races."

"But he would have been *honored*," I cry. "Elevated, had he succeeded."

"But he failed, and the price for trying to kill one another is exile."

"Outside the tribes!"

Malik puts a hand on my shoulder. Shakes his head when I look at him, and then without a word turns and limps away across the sand. I stare after him, emptiness gnawing a hole in my heart that grows ever-larger as distance takes him. Then he is gone, and I know that my brother is dead. For that cost, my future is my own.

Salt water stains the sand.

FALLING

"GET IN THE RING AND lose the fight. Make it look good. Can't have anybody suspecting."

No one ever does. Futile words, a waste of breath. Nearly a waste of thought, and gargoyles rarely bothered with wasteful things. But there was no fight Biali couldn't win. Not against humans. *Every* fight he lost looked good, and no one—not even the short, putrid-breathed manager he collected scant dollars from after the matches were done—had any idea he threw all of them. All but the few he permitted himself to win, usually against broad-shouldered blondes. None of them had the wheat-pale hair of his old rival, and none of them had Alban Korund's strength, either. Beating the pulp out of look-alikes was cold comfort, but at least it was comfort.

Tonight's bout was against a stocky Italian, hardly taller than Biali himself. He was missing two teeth and his nose sat askew, bulbous end mashed to one side. He'd never been pretty, but there were women who liked the rough edges fights brought out. Or at least women who could be paid to say they did, and for most fighters that was enough.

Not even the highest-paid doxies in the city looked at Biali without flinching. The left side of his face was scarred, eating his eye and flattening the cheek. It was nothing to the ruin of his gargoyle face, but he never let humans see that. Rarely looked at the marks himself, knowing all too well that they looked as if his very bones had been chiseled away. Or bludgeoned, more like, the weight of one corundum fist changing the shape of his hopes forever.

He wore his scars belligerently. It helped in the ring, frightening some men, making others bold. He didn't need the help, but there was no reason to try harder than necessary. Not when he fought humans. And he had no real use for mortal women, but their caught breath, their sliding gazes, stung him every time. Gargoyles were less taken with the physical form: stone chipped and wore away with time, and the wreck of his face was only age hurried along.

The Italian was in the ring already, snorting like a horse. Big slabs of marbled muscle on him, the solid stuff that would barely ripple when he took a hit. Biali might look like that someday, if all he ever had to fight again were feeble humans. The manager shoved his shoulders, hurrying him toward the fight, and because he played at being human, Biali moved. A few heavy steps into a ring made up of wooden slats and sweating men, dirt under all their feet. He could dig his toes in and become unmovable, win it that way, but then he would have to stop fighting.

And the fight was the only thing worth living for.

He let the Italian make first contact. A blow to the chin, hard enough to knock a man out. He saw it in the Italian's eyes, too, that he should have staggered, and gave a thin uncompromising smile. Fear and anger burst to life in the Italian's gaze, and for whole minutes there was nothing but ducking and jabbing, fists slapping against flesh. A bell rang. The Italian kept coming. Biali let him, took another hit that should have doubled him, and saw fresh anger erupt across the Italian's face. Then the Italian's manager was on him, hauling him back. Biali shrugged, returning to his own spot across the human-lined corral. Sweat and shit and animals and beer: they all stank, and no amount of washing got rid of the stench.

Perfume, though, disguised it. Perfume, but no man would wear that. Not here, anyway, not among the ranks of dock workers and street cleaners, not where a hint of effeminacy would get him killed. That was for dandies in the hothouses, for well-dressed young fops living life large as progress rolled on. Their kind would be killed, too—or at least beaten and robbed—down here in alleys and waterside warehouses.

It had to be a woman. A woman, where none would be welcome. A woman escorted by the sort of fool who would bring one here, and from the scent, she was beyond expensive. She smelled rich, like she hadn't been bought. The perfume was delicate, unlike what whores wore, and through the noise of betters and backers, silk shifted against silk. Humans would never hear it, but any of the Old Races would. A cowbell clanged, harsh flat sound as out of place as the woman's perfume. The crowd was moving, jostling, shouting, and finally broke apart enough to give him a glimpse of her.

Amber skin, black curling hair, large dark eyes. A free woman of color. Well, they were all free now, but the phrase lingered. Petite and curvy, or petite for a gargoyle, at least. Tall enough for a human woman, but it wasn't a human woman he was reminded of at all.

The name left his lips in an unvoiced whisper: "Hajnal."

It wasn't her. Couldn't be her. He knew it; Hajnal had died decades ago. But whenever he saw a woman like this he forgot, just for a moment. Forgot, too, that he'd lost Hajnal long before she'd died. Both remembrances always came back like a mule kick to his heart. He hated them for reminding him of her. Hated them for flinching when they looked at him, as she never had. Hated them for being human, when she had proved mortal too. Hate was easier.

She looked his way. Her brow furrowed, then smoothed, and she lowered her eyelashes. Less than a nod, but nothing coquettish. Just a greeting before the crowd closed and took her away again.

The ground shook, lumbering footsteps. Biali ignored it, still scowling into the crowd. Her scent lingered, but she was gone, not even a hint of what man she'd been with to give him a lead to follow. Behind him, the manager barked, "Fight!" and the thundering earth resolved into sense. He turned away, facing the ring again, and the Italian was there with a fist full of steel. It hit with a shattering boom, and Biali...

...fell.

It had been convincing enough. He'd gotten his pay. As he should have, for the only fight in memory he hadn't thrown. But he hadn't said that to the manager, only collected his dollars and shoved his way out through the gathered mass. Out and then up, pulling rickety ladders down high walls to climb them. He didn't need them. He could leap and dig clawed fingers into the walls more easily than take fire escapes to the rooftops, but there were always people watching in this city of millions. Better to transform closer to the sky, where fewer eyes watched.

The dull pain in his chin from the Italian's fist disappeared as he swung over a short rooftop wall and changed, explosively, into his natural form. Stone healed, or the transformation did; it was one of a dozen reasons the Old Races were hard to kill. A few quick steps brought him to the roof's far wall and he launched from it, stout wings catching the building's updraft and carrying him aloft. He was a blunt white mark against the sky, should anyone look up to glimpse him, but humans rarely looked up. And right now there was still a chance of catching the woman's scent again, following her. Of finding out who she was, why she had been at a place no woman should be. Of learning why she'd been brave enough not to flinch when she saw his scars.

Of exposing himself, as he sometimes did, to ridicule and rejection. Gargoyles would not by nature do that to themselves, but by nature they gathered in tribes or clans. Not Biali; not since he had chosen to follow the outcast to New York decades earlier. Not since he'd been asked by the elders if he would, because Alban Korund had not joined the overmind in centuries, and the only way to learn what he knew was by watching him. In a few minutes the air currents would bring him above Trinity Church, where Korund lived. If Biali was human, he might convince himself he had taken wing to check on the other gargoyle, but he lacked the talent for that depth of self-deception. He would look to see if Korund was visible, but he wasn't Biali's prey tonight.

Most nights, yes. Most nights, Biali was the best and worst choice for watching Korund. Best because he had reason above all others to want to catch him out. To find some way to punish him for Hajnal's death over a century earlier. She had been Biali's once, in so far as any gargoyle belonged to another. They tended to mate for life, though, and he had been more than happy with the tiny dark gargoyle whose family had risen from obsidian veins. But she had been distracted by Alban Korund when he was just a youth, still trying out his burgeoning wings. Had been taken by his fascination with the world outside the tribes and mountains, and in the end, had been taken away by that very world. Yes, Biali was the best choice to watch Korund, both of them exiles in humanity's cities.

And he was the worst, because desperation lay behind his willingness to leave the gestalt. He would do nearly anything to lay some avengeable blame at Korund's feet. Hajnal's death had not, despite her departure from safety with Alban, been his *fault*. He had not fired the guns that shattered her wings or thrust bayonets into her human body. He had murdered no one. He could be blamed, but not condemned, and even if he could be, they had no law to put one another to death. Exile was their punishment, and Alban had imposed that on himself long before Hajnal's death. No one knew why. Even Hajnal's memories, which might have answered the question, had been contained by Alban, who was closest at her death, rather than being restored to the overmind. To the precious gargoyle memories that kept all of them, every single one of the remaining Old Races, in mind. They paid a price for being the bearers of so many memories: every other Old Race could move through day or night in its human form. Gargoyles, though, were bound to stone in daytime hours. Stone endured. Memory, therefore, endured. Without the gargoyles, the Old Races themselves might forget who and what they were. That was a cost too high to pay.

Even if it meant the dawn was likely to prevent him from finding the woman who'd been at the fight. There was time yet, December nights as long as any. There were a few gargoyle clans who lived in the far north and equally far south, having traded mountains for months of night. They slept all summer in those remote climes, but winter was theirs. Biali felt a flash of envy for that.

More for the kinship, though, than the wakeful months. Perhaps it had been easy for Korund to leave the gestalt in the beginning. He'd had Hajnal then, so he was never alone. Perhaps near-isolation had become comfortable enough that the solitude after her death hadn't been a shock. Biali could not imagine it. Bad enough to be only one of two gargoyles in the city, even if he was the one who could and did linger in the community of minds accessible to them no matter where their physical bodies rested.

Wind kicked up, spewing dust down one of the city's long straight streets and bringing a hint of perfume with it. Maudlin thoughts cast aside, Biali sharpened his gaze, always more acute than human vision. He had come a long way from the docks, toward the Upper East Side, where townhouses and expensive apartments sprawled behind iron gates and well-paid police patrols. He'd moved faster than the woman would have, unconstrained by streets and certainly unthreatened by passers-by. Not that a woman willing to come to the fights would feel threatened by much. He wondered again who her escort had been, how she had been granted passage through the fights at all.

He came to earth in an alleyway north of the park, transforming before the sodden drunk amidst the garbage could focus. The man still shoved backward, disbelieving fear sobering his lined features. Biali bared his teeth and the drunk looked away, deliberately forgetting what he hadn't quite seen. The Old Races survived that way. Had for centuries. Would, if they were lucky, for centuries more, but even the unchanging gargoyles admitted in their deepest places that they were at the end, not the beginning, of their long history.

A carriage stopped up the block from him, driver leaning out to bray, "No further, lady. Walk the rest of the way, or get somebody dumber than me to drive."

His quarry opened the door herself, stepping down with more grace than pique, and paid the driver without speaking. He turned the carriage and drove south again, back toward wealthier streets, but the woman continued north. Toward Harlem, full of Jews and Irish and blacks. The undesirables, but she was too well-dressed, too genteel, to live rough. Biali had her scent now. He wouldn't lose her, even if he couldn't see her. It was easy to cut across a shorter block and come up a side street a few yards ahead of her.

She did startle this time, coming to a full stop with her hands clenched warily in her skirt. But he'd come out of the darkness without warning. Any woman might shy at that. Her first impulse of fear faded as she recognized him, and surprise wrinkled her forehead. "You are the fighter."

The fighter. Not the scarred one, the white one, the angry one. There were many descriptors she might have chosen. That she used only the one was somehow flattering. Unaccustomed to the feeling, Biali muttered "One of 'em."

She shook her head, a motion so small it might have been taught by the Old Races. "The others, they can be said to be something else. The one you fight tonight, the Italian. That is what he is. His name, it does not matter. The men after you, they are the Irish, the German, the Spaniard. Maybe you are the German too, but no. I see in you only the fighter. It is...pure, in you. Who are you? Why is this?"

"My name is Biali." He frowned, then shrugged, hard motion of broad shoulders. "Why is because I've got nothing to lose. You're Spanish." He'd expected her to be American, and from the South, or from Boston, where many of the freed coloreds had gone after the war.

"Mexican," she said, but with a smile. "My mother is a *don*'s daughter, my father a Buffalo soldier. *Mi abuelito,* the *don,* he does not approve, but he approves less of my mother being unwed with a baby girl. I have come here to see the land my papa fought for. I have left them there in the fine seaside *hacienda,* waiting for my return."

There. A woman's life, the whole of her history, given up to him willingly, yet he didn't know her name, and he had already lost her. Biali bared his teeth as he'd done at the drunk, angry at an unchanging world. "You're never going home alive if you walk through Harlem alone at night."

Her eyebrows quirked. "But I am not alone." With a gesture, she invited him to walk beside her.

Stupefied, he caught up after several steps. Her smile was genuine, but as brief as her other expressions. "There. You see?"

That was an almost gargoyle-like literalness. Except a gargoyle could be expected to protect herself. Most of the time. More than a human woman could, despite Hajnal's fate. Biali stole a glimpse at the woman beside him. The resemblance that had caught him initially was superficial: her eyes were more almond in shape, her nose broader, flatter than Hajnal's. Her skin tone was very close, though, and they shared a strength of jaw as well as the thick dark hair. Women like her—paler of skin, but otherwise very like Hajnal—had died recently. At least one had been acquainted with Alban Korund. "Not being alone doesn't mean you're safe."

Amusement touched her eyes. "Am I in danger?"

Exasperation as rich as her humor rose in Biali. It would be smart to frighten her. Instead, surprised by his own intensity, he said, "Not while I'm near."

They walked in silence a while, the woman considering that reply before she said, "But you do not know me."

"No."

She nodded, continued in silence, then said, "She was so special to you, then?"

She left him behind a second time, his footsteps ceasing to echo on quiet streets. A dozen steps before she turned, expectant, and said to his angry shock, "There are so many reasons a man might hurry across a great city to find a woman. Lust, love, loss. You do not have the eyes of a man who lusts, and you do not know me to love me. So it is loss, no? I remind you of her, and you will see me safe because of that. What was her name?"

No one should see that clearly. No human, anyway. Nor ask such questions, either, and no gargoyle should feel pressed to answer, but the name came unbidden for the second time that night: "Hajnal."

"Hajnal." She tasted the name, then smiled, brief and sweet. "A strong name, no? I would like my daughters to be strong enough for such a name."

"You have daughters?" The question came out before he could stop it. She was old enough, certainly, but there was nothing of the matron about her. The Italian had hit him harder than he thought, if his mind was so garbled. A human shouldn't flummox him half a dozen times in as many minutes. "Who *are* you?"

"My name is Isabel, and I think I have come here for you."

He should have walked away. Instead, somehow, he was at her doorstep, accepting the offer of a meal. Her house—rented, no doubt—was too large for one woman, even a woman with a Mexican manservant and maid who both looked disapproving as Isabel brought him into the house. Not *too* disapproving: they were no doubt paid by the *don* Isabel had mentioned, and no doubt sent letters back to Mexico detailing the granddaughter's exploits.

Everything about the house proclaimed wealth. Not outrageous wealth, not so much to buy a colored girl a place in New York's finest society, but more than expected even in this wealthier stretch of Harlem homes. The rugs were new and deep, the windows caulked and the shutters firmly set. Tapestries and paintings hung on the walls, keeping warmth in, and generous fires burned in both the dining hall and the parlor Isabel later invited him into. There, finally, assured of some degree of privacy from the staff, Biali asked what he should have before: "What did you mean by that? What were you doing at the fights? A woman who lives like this shouldn't be in the docklands at all. How did you get there unmolested?"

Isabel poured drinks, a task more suited for servants in the drawing room, not a woman in her own front parlor. Glass in hand, she settled near the fire, feet tucked under her skirts as if she kept company with intimates, not a stranger from the street. Maybe that was how the wealthy behaved in Mexico. Biali sat on the edge of another chair, safely distant, and scowled at her with interest as she shrugged. "A woman told me to go there. A tiny woman, with wrinkles and black hair, as I sat and had tea at a bookshop. She said the man I wanted would see me there, and no other would notice me."

"The man you wanted."

The woman smiled again, that brief tantalizing curve of lips. "I see how my mama looks at Papa, no? He is a fighter, a soldier, a strong good man. There are many men like this in Mexico, but I cannot look at them the way I see Mama look at Papa. So I think I am too, what is the word? Housed?"

"Sheltered."

"*Sí*, yes, sheltered. Too sheltered from the world, if my mama, the *don's* daughter, can find a soldier to make her eyes shine and I can find no one. So I travel. First to San Francisco, with so many hills and Chinese men. Then to Chicago, but there is still the scent of fire there, and I do not like fire."

"Fire? It's been twenty years since the fire."

"Perhaps it lingers in the air always." Isabel lifted a challenging eyebrow.

Biali sank back in his seat, more defeated by the expression than the Italian in the ring earlier. Humans were mad, vermin and blights on the earth, creating danger and discomfort wherever they went, and he preferred to fight them, not hold conversation over dinner and brandy. He hadn't touched the snifter she'd poured for him, but she swirled her own like it was a theatrical prop. Every action enthralled him. Human women were not expected to act so freely. She might have been one of the Old Races, unconstrained by convention, except there was nothing inhuman about her. Nothing except an uncanny awareness of things the mortal world moved past, like ancient races walking amongst them, and fires that burned out decades in the past.

"Maybe it does."

Isabel nodded, satisfied. "So I have come here, to this greatest city. And here I have seen a man like no other and he," she said with a spread of her hands, "sees me. No?"

"No. I mean yes." Biali bit down on further speech, staring at the woman. "You believed a prediction from an old woman at a bookshop?"

Isabel lifted a chiding finger, waving it at him. "Old women are wise. Everyone should listen to them. And she was right, no? So many men, and only you follow me."

Infallible logic that made no sense. Biali grunted "I should go," and left his brandy untouched on a chair-side table. Isabel remained still, nothing but her voice arresting him as he reached the door:

"You will come again tomorrow?"

That would be madness. He had what few answers he might need or want from her. Luck, that was all that had brought her through the night safely, both coming and going from the docks. Luck, unless the bookshop was the one he thought it might be, and the tea brewed by the old woman herself. And if that was so, then she was interfering, directing lives the way she liked to, and offered all the more reason he should refuse.

He said, "Of course," and closed the door behind him.

Giddiness was not for gargoyles. Not a word they would ever use, not an emotion they would ever experience. Nervous stomachs were not for creatures built of stone. Nor were cold hands or irregular heartbeats. Steadiness: that was the very purpose of his people. *To strive, to seek, to find, but not to yield*: the poet who had written those words had not done so with Biali's people in mind, but the last of them resonated.

He wondered if Isabel would appreciate that he knew Tennyson. That he had, in fact, *known* Tennyson, though not well, and not that he could confess to it, sixty years after the poet's death. It did not—should not—matter. Neither the knowing of the poem or the acquaintance of the man. Such accolades were for young men bent on impressing young women, not ancient gargoyles who knew better than to take themselves to a woman's doorstep not long after nightfall.

He knew better, and yet.

Isabel's smile when she answered the door—she herself, not her manservant or maid—her smile was secretive and pleased. Smug, as if she had known he couldn't resist. As if she'd been certain his promise to return was an honest one, when he hadn't been sure of that himself. And after that he was lost, knowing he would come back time and again until she sent him away, as she inevitably would.

It lent an edge to his fights, a desperation that made losing more difficult and the money riding on his bouts more worthwhile. Isabel came to the fights more often than she should, always with the same scent lingering around her. Sweet tea, not perfume after all. It was certain, then, that Chelsea interfered, but Biali couldn't bring himself to face her. To condemn her or to even comment. Not when Isabel's easy smile was for him. Not when she touched his scarred face without cringing. She was human, ephemeral, doomed, but for a few hours each night she was his, and the rest of the world faded away. It had been too long since gentleness had been in his life, and he could not quite make himself turn away.

Winter's long nights faded into spring's equal days, stealing minutes he could spend with her, but she never questioned that he came to her at sunset and left before dawn. New York could encompass such a life, as any large city could, if that was what a young couple dreamed of. She told him some of what she did during the day: sleep, of course, to make up for the hours they spent in the city at night, but in her waking hours, museums, tea, long walks, embroidery. None of it, she said, was her *life*. That, he thought, was what she shared with him. Certainly in the first days her smile when she greeted him in the evenings changed from smug to openly pleased and then, as days became weeks, to simple joy.

It had been decades, even centuries, since a woman had looked at him that way, and it was difficult to remember he could seem no older than she was, when they spoke of their histories. Of mountains, he told her one night. They sat together on the rooftop above the small apartment he had taken for himself when it became clear he was too foolish to walk away. Humans had to have dwellings, could not live on roofs, pitted and scarred by rain and sun, as gargoyles did. There was a view from the roof: a small park, a crossroads, and in the deep of night, when streetlights had guttered, a swath of stars across the skies.

"There were more of them in the mountains," he said to her one night. "There were no lights to dim them. They made a path across the sky. We would—" Try to fly that milky way; that was what gargoyle children did as their strength grew and allowed them to soar skyward for the first time. But he couldn't say that to Isabel, and she picked up the narrative before he found a variation on his own past to share with her.

"Run along it?" she asked. "It is like that where I am from too, a great streak of color and stars along the dark sky, reaching all the way to the water. We live near the sea, no? On *la playa del oro*, the beach of gold you would say. Only for the sand, though. There are no rough hills to dig precious metals from, not for many miles. The *don's* people tease crops from the land, and we delve deep for fresh water so close to the sea." Her heartbeat was quick, pressed against his side. Quick enough for worry, as if she missed her home so badly it set her heart to speeding.

Biali began to sit up, concerned, but Isabel stopped him with a hand on his chest. She shifted to do it, her skirts rustling as she knelt with her thighs pressed against his. His own heart knocked hard, sudden understanding taking him with human shock.

"I would give you precious things," Isabel whispered. "To tease and delve, Biali. Will you have me?"

"I've never with a—" Color flushed his face, almost an impossibility, but what he'd been about to say was absurd. *I've never.* True enough, when the sentence ended with *with a human woman,* but he could hardly say that.

Isabel, though, laughed, a soft shy thrill of sound. "That I do not believe, my Biali." She touched his scarred cheek, brushed fingertips over his ruined eye, and murmured, "You are not so fearsome as all that, and so that I do not believe. But you must not worry if you have never taken a maidenhead. The virginity is only once, no? And there will be many times after." Her composure left her abruptly, her skin darkening with a rush of blood, and she began to pull away. "Unless you do not wa—"

"No." Rough reply, almost harsh. He pulled her closer again, afraid to speak and drive her away. She softened in his arms, though her heart beat harder still, pulling eagerness and uncertainty taut. He could remember that, at least, from every first time with a new lover, though his people put no weight on virginity the way humans did. Isabel was brave, very brave, and very beautiful.

She tasted of sunshine, of the lingering warmth that was all he knew of daylight. That was a gift, one she couldn't know she gave, and for that, for all of it, he wanted to treat her well. He had no skill with women's clothes, but nor did he need it: she shed her outer layers breathlessly, then lost courage. Eyes large and dark, pulse in her throat quick as a vampire's, she waited in stillness as he loosened her corset, then touched his mouth to her breasts.

The sound she made then was liquid, and woke in him a

hunger that had been put away for more years than she could imagine. It would never do to be rough or quick, not with a mortal, not in the first moments. Not when desire was so fresh and new, and an exploring tongue and suckling lips could so easily drive her beyond the boundaries of what she knew. She didn't know what to do with herself, hips offering tiny plaintive surges as her fingers knotted in his hair. Petticoats were discarded and she lost her nerve again, but skin could come later. Bloomers were no impediment to thick, blunt fingers, and if her thighs crashed together at the first touch, they parted again with increasing willingness as his touch coaxed pleasure from unexplored territory.

He watched her eyes, gauging her need from the grip on his shoulders, to judge when to take her. To make the moment of peaking the same moment he slid within her, so that if there was pain it would at least be swept away by the shuddering, clenching rolls of release that came with his body fitting to hers.

And there was such bewilderment in her eyes at the cresting of pain and pleasure, such beauty in the vulnerability of her hands knotted against his shoulders. He waited, watching her. Stone could wait forever, if need be. It needn't, though: as the first wave passed she slowly softened again, until finally she nodded, a fleeting smile darting across her face. Enough to let him move again, to teach her, to guide her, and finally, some little while before morning, to find a release so exhaustive that he barely stumbled away, apologizing, before dawn took him to stone.

"You always leave me before the sun," she said the next evening. Not angry, but thoughtful, which was more than he might expect of any woman newly breached and then abandoned. "Do you not like it on your face?"

"I rest in daylight. I always have." True enough, if misleading. Softer confession, though: "I would stay if I could, Isabel."

"Will you ever?"

"No." There was no question, no chance. Not so long as the laws of the Old Races held. *Tell no humans of our existence.* It was a matter of survival.

Isabel, to his surprise, laughed. "I think a man should lie to a woman when she asks that question, Biali. I think he is meant to say yes, *sí*, of course I will stay."

"I'll never lie to you." *Gargoyles don't,* he wanted to say, but there were so many things that would go unsaid. A promise of truth would have to be enough.

Isabel pursed her lips, put them against his shoulder, then nodded. "Some women would not like that answer. I think perhaps I do. Truth can be terrible, more terrible than lies, but I am glad to trust what you tell me is always true. Tell me this, then. Do you lose the fights on purpose?"

Biali blinked. "Yes."

"The one the night we met?"

Rare humor rose. "I was supposed to lose, but not that badly. I didn't know there would be a beautiful woman there."

"Then tonight," she said firmly, "you will win a fight for me. And then we will come back to here, and be together, for if we have only the nights, my Biali, then we must have them with all that we are."

He won that night, and every night after that she asked. His bad-breathed manager was torn between delight and fury. Mostly fury, as Biali won fights his manager had bet against him on, but sometimes delight for the sheer brutality of the fights. And Isabel watched them, every one, and after the first night or two she went unmolested by greedy hands or greedier looks. Everyone knew, now, that Biali threw the fights he lost, and none of them wanted to meet him outside the ring for harassing his woman. Weeks passed, winter nights growing shorter but no less sweet for it. This, Biali thought: this was happiness. Isabel and the fights. He could ask for nothing more.

It had to happen, then, that Alban Korund would interfere.

Biali caught his scent after a fight, the big gargoyle in human form one of dozens of men pressing to see the match. Like Isabel, Alban dressed too well to frequent the dock fights: well-cut suits of good cloth, shoes that had seen less offal than most, and his long wheat-pale hair tied in a knot at his nape. Men were egging him on regardless, hoping to get him in the ring. They were fools: anyone fighting Alban would be undone by the gargoyle's long reach, never mind his inhuman strength. He stood the better part of a foot taller than Biali, with arms of according length, and Biali was already their master.

He bulled his way out of the wooden corral, other fighters and plenty of dockworkers making way for him. Isabel came to his side, joining him as he approached Alban, and for the first time in weeks he wished she might be somewhere else. Not because Alban was prettier than Biali—most things were—but because Biali wanted Isabel kept well away from the Old Races. They were dangerous to humans, whether humans knew it or not.

"You're doing well," Alban said softly. Most of the time, he was soft of voice. Compensating for his human height and breadth, which were still nothing in comparison to his true form. "Some reporters are starting to notice."

Isabel's face shone at the news. "You will become famous, yes, my Biali? You will be a prizefighter across the nation!"

"No." He and Alban spoke together, in agreement for the first time in centuries. Isabel faltered, looking between them, and Biali shook his head. "Fame's no good. Neither's too much money. I don't need it."

"*Mi abuelito* would like it," Isabel teased, uncertainly. "A famous fighter, better than a Buffalo soldier."

"He'll have to like me as I am." Not that Biali would ever meet the Spanish lord on the beach of gold, but it was too soon to think of that. It would always be too soon. "Why are you here, Korund? Why are you telling me this?"

"Because it's always too soon to lose something precious." The big gargoyle's phrase so closely echoed Biali's thoughts that Biali scowled. Alban had not joined the overmind, had not made any effort to abandon his self-imposed exile; he had not, therefore, heard a whisper of what went on in Biali's mind.

It was more offensive, somehow, that they shared a perception of the world. Biali turned away, his arm protective and possessive around Isabel, and when he looked back, Alban was gone.

"He is the one, no?" Isabel asked as they left the fight. "The one who took your woman from you."

A breath escaped Biali, astonishment so broad it touched amusement. "How do you do that? How do you know these things?"

"They are not so hard to read in your face, my Biali. You hide behind your scars, but I can see through them to the man below."

"Then I am lucky," he said roughly, and left her ever-more reluctantly come the dawn.

He awoke to a shocking connection across the mental void: *Biali!*

An image with his name, a place in the park, wooded, secluded, near the northern end. Sunset still colored the western sky, though grey, not gold, crept through trees and lent no warmth to the scene.

One word. One image. Alban Korund had not risked so much in the gestalt in three centuries. Biali should claw his way into that connection, force it open, learn what he had been sent to this city to discover. Expose Alban's secrets, touch Hajnal's last thoughts, and return, finally return, to the clan he had left behind.

He ran instead, launching himself from the window of his small apartment, still in human form. Transforming, wings snapping open, beating, straining, pushing him through the air as quickly as he could. Alban's presence in the gestalt was gone, his sojourn there so brief it left barely a sketch of memory, much less pathways into the secrets he kept. And after three centuries, there was no good reason for him to break silence. Which meant his reasons would be very bad.

Biali flew.

Alban crouched beside her, his wheat-colored hair falling around his shoulders and his huge hands reluctant to touch her. She was broken everywhere, beautiful lines of her face as smashed as Biali's. Her corset gave structure to ribs that no longer had enough, and her wrists were shattered. Biali knocked Alban aside, fury roaring from him, but the other man made no fight, only rolled and came to his feet several yards away.

"Isabel. Did he—who did this to you?" There was no blood on Alban's hands, though that was scarce comfort. Biali took his place, crouched beside the dying woman, his own expression glazed with shock. "Isabel..."

"A wo...man." Her brown eyes were huge with pain and bewilderment. "So strong. She hated..."

"Hush," Biali whispered helplessly, "Shh, shh. Save your strength. You'll be all right."

"Me," Isabel finished. "Hated...me. Hated...herself. We were...alike. Except...."

Except for strength. Hatred offered plenty of that. Biali should know. "Hush," he said again, but she smiled.

"I came for you, Biali. I did not mean...to leave like this."

"You won't. You can't. Not again." That made no sense, and all three of them understood. Isabel smiled again and let her eyes close, tears leaking from their corners. Biali made useless fists above her, as afraid as Alban had been to touch her and cause more pain. So *fragile.* Humans were so *fragile,* and he couldn't even lay the blame for this at Alban's feet. A woman, Isabel had said. What woman would have the fury to do this to another?

The same one who had murdered at least one other of Alban's acquaintances. He was the commonality between these women who looked like Hajnal. There was blame to lay at his feet after all. Biali's vision rushed red with rage. He balled himself, ready to pitch himself at Alban, to beat answers out of him and provide some sort of catharsis for himself.

"Daisani is in the city."

Biali lifted his head, staring without comprehension at the other gargoyle. Then understanding lurched through him, obliterating wrath. He bent his head over Isabel's, whispers fierce with determination. "Don't die. Wait for me. Wait until morning, Isabel. Live until morning. Promise me that."

"I'll stay with her." Alban's voice, so remote that sympathy barely touched it. That was as well: the last thing Biali wanted was his sympathy. "Go," Alban said. "Tell him I've asked for this."

Biali stood, lip curled. "You? Why you? What will that gain me?"

"Just do it, Biali."

He would, too. Without knowing why, he would. "Don't let her die. On Hajnal's memory, Korund. Don't let her die."

"Hurry."

He hurried, and it hardly seemed fast enough. Daisani was wealthy and men like Biali, rough and scarred and ugly, were not welcomed in the fine restaurants and clubs that Daisani frequented.

He was almost certain he'd killed only two or three of the fools who tried to stop him from entering the club he found Daisani at. Someone hit him with an iron bar. Biali took it, wrapped it around his own fist, and hit anyone who came near in the face as he stormed through the club. After a few of them fell, no one else got in his way.

Dapper, slight, black-haired and not particularly handsome, Daisani still commanded the attention of everyone at his table. Or he did until Biali found him, and then without a blink the mogul snapped his fingers and sent the others away. Then his eyebrows arched, mockery in their questions.

"A woman." Fumbling excuse, suddenly absurd in the face of the violence he'd used to approach Daisani. Words were not Biali's strength. "Alban sent me to you."

The questioning eyebrows shot higher, becoming exclamations. Daisani patted his lips dry with a napkin, then stood, turning to the only other person who hadn't left the table: a woman, narrow and reserved, with a hint of suspicion in her eyes at Biali's explanation. "Vanessa, forgive me. I seem to have pressing business with intimate acquaintants."

Sudden understanding eliminated the suspicion—the envy, perhaps—from Vanessa's eyes. She knew, then. That was clear. She knew about the Old Races, and that was an edict none of them were supposed to break. Tell humans nothing. An exiling offense, if discovered.

Biali didn't care what laws Daisani had broken, not now. Not tonight. Daisani marked that, a hint of satisfaction creasing lines around his mouth. "Shall we go, then? Or will I go on my own, which will be faster?"

"No," Biali grated. He wanted to—had to—be there, and though Daisani could be there inside a moment, Biali would take minutes. Minutes Isabel would be able to spare, because she *had* to. Because he would not be absent this time, not even if his absence might save her life. This Vanessa woman already knew what Daisani was. That was enough to let Biali say, "We'll take the skies," and within a minute to do just that, Eliseo Daisani's inconsequential weight carried in his arms.

The park was no distance, not when flight carried them there. Not as quick as Daisani, maybe, but quick enough. Alban was kneeling at Isabel's side when they arrived, his soft murmur of reassurance doing nothing—or perhaps everything—to keep her alive.

Daisani's pupils enlarged as he glanced Isabel over. "She's all but dead already. This is a meal, Biali, not a rescue. You've wasted my time."

A snarl erupted in Biali's throat, but Daisani walked away unconcerned. No reason for concern, not when his speed was such that Biali would never lay a hand on him. "Then why did you come at all!"

Daisani tossed the answer over his shoulder carelessly: "Because you said Korund had sent you. I thought it was for some plausible task."

"Eliseo." Alban spoke unexpectedly.

Daisani paused. Turned his head, not quite looking back, but listening. Waiting for a move in the game, Biali thought, though he had no idea what the game was. Alban, though, did, and spoke again. "If you do this, we will owe each other nothing."

Daisani's jaw came up, tension spreading through his shoulders, then fading. "It is not so simple as that."

"It can be."

An ache came into Biali's hands. Not from Isabel's weight; he could hold that forever. From rage at the game these two played, at the exchange that meant both nothing and everything to him. He wanted to bellow, to demand understanding, to command a stop to their wordplay, and yet he held his tongue. Barely breathed around the hurt in his chest, knowing a wrong word would mean the woman's death. *Hurry!* roared inside his head, so loud Alban should have winced with it, had he touched the overmind as all gargoyles always should. So loud Daisani, who was nothing of the gargoyles at all, should have heard it, and made haste to do as he was told.

"It can't be," Daisani said ever so softly, but he turned. Came back to Biali and to the woman held in his arms, a woman whose breath came in short, desperate gasps now. A rattle had begun in her lungs. "It's almost too late," the vampire murmured. "I will not have her in this city, Biali. One sip for health alone, but I will not have her here, glowing with fitness and beauty. I will not have her here to wonder at what happened tonight, or at what other gifts another sip might bring."

Biali nodded, curt, furious, desperate, and Eliseo Daisani smiled. He was not a handsome man, though he could be mistaken for one. Not, though, with that smile. Not with the brief flash of savage black teeth that opened his wrist's veins. Not with the fastidious way he wiped blood over Isabel's mouth. There was nothing handsome, nothing compelling, about him at all, as he did those things.

But she wheezed again and licked her lips, half-conscious response to wetness there, and with the convulsive swallow that followed, her color improved. From blue ashen to a touch of pink beneath the skin, and with each wetting of her lips, each swallow, strength and health returned.

"You will owe me," Daisani said, and Korund, strongly, said, "He owes you nothing."

Biali felt, didn't see, tension sluice through the vampire again. His gaze was only for Isabel, for the slow improvement in her breathing, for the crackling and straightening of bone.

But he heard the challenge in the vampire's voice as he faced Alban: "And I?"

"Owe me nothing."

Daisani made a sound. Distrust, disbelief, perhaps relief. Then he was gone, a whisk of wind where he'd been. Biali, still clutching Isabel, looked up. There were so many answers there, lingering in the air. Alban's silence in the gestalt had to do with the vampire. With all the vampires, perhaps; perhaps an answer to their dwindling numbers this past decade. It was something, at least. Something he could bring to the others, something he could add to the memories. It might be enough to excuse him from his own exile, from his own long watch over the outcast. It would certainly bring others to the city, others who would question Alban and even Daisani, working to worm their shared secrets into the open.

And there were the women, the ones Alban knew who had died or, like Isabel, had survived through fortune alone. But they were human, and had Isabel not run afoul of their attacker Biali would have thought no more of them at all. He could let them go, in exchange for Isabel's survival. In exchange for the sure knowledge that it hadn't been Alban who had harmed her, because what reason would she have to lie, even if her attack hadn't been just before sunset, at a time no gargoyle could be awake.

Biali's voice scraped as low as it went, raw words offering a compromise he would never voice aloud. A gargoyle could lock individual memories away from the gestalt, only offering them upon his death. And gargoyles were difficult to kill. For her life, he would not say aloud, for her life, this night had never happened. "This doesn't mean you're forgiven."

A smile touched Alban's mouth. "No." His yellow gaze softened on Isabel. "Take care of her."

Then, like Daisani, he was gone, though less dramatically.

Just a big man walking away, leaving a scarred gargoyle and a woman slowly coming back to life.

He looked human again by the time she awakened. It had never been a matter of debate before, never a matter of consideration. He had never shown his gargoyle face to a human who didn't already know about the Old Races, and they were far and few between. But for hours as Isabel's breathing had steadied, as her color had improved and her wounds had healed, he had held her in his natural from, and had thought often of maintaining it even when health was hers again. In the end, though, it was easier to send her away if she knew nothing, and he had to send her away.

Her waking breath was sharp, as if it searched for pain and found none. Moments passed before her eyes opened. Before she whispered, "Biali?" and smiled, the same small expression he'd grown so fond of. Then confusion etched it away and she pressed her eyes shut again. "I was hurt."

"Yes. But you're well now."

"I should be dead, yes?"

"...yes."

Silence, and a slow exhalation. "And you will not tell me how this has happened."

"No."

Isabel opened her eyes again. "Why not?"

"Because I love you," he said simply, foolishly, honestly, "and the thing that healed you would surely kill you if you knew how."

Astonishment and a smile filled Isabel's eyes. "I thought you did not know those words, *mi corazón*. Will we be happy now," she whispered, "together and happy, as we should be?"

"No." Biali closed his eyes in turn, then forced them open again to watch slow dismay wash the joy from Isabel's eyes. "You have to leave, Isabel. This morning, on the first train."

"Because of the thing that healed me." Her voice had

dulled, but hope still lingered. "You will come with me?"

"I can't." Implacable as stone, that answer.

Isabel heard it, too, and the remaining light drained from her face. "Why?"

There was no explaining. No possible way to hide what he was. No days to be spent locked away in solitude while his body turned to stone. No way to travel apart from her, hidden in a train compartment. It couldn't be done. He'd thought about it all night. The only way was to tell her what he was, and that would lead to questions about how she had been healed. And that would cross Daisani's will, and whether there were debts owed or not, if Eliseo Daisani imagined for a moment that Biali had betrayed the Old Races' secrets—*his* secret in particular—to a human woman, he would be ruthless in his vengeance. Never mind that Daisani had clearly broken laws himself with the woman Vanessa. Unless Biali was willing to involve her in warfare, to level the field between himself and the vampire, he could not risk Isabel's awareness of the Old Races. "Because I'm not what you think I am."

"You are my fighter, no?" Isabel sat up in his arms, pulling her dress into order as if she instead pulled the shreds of her dignity around her.

Biali murmured, "Yes," even as he shook his head. "But that's both not enough and too much. Go home to Mexico, Isabel. Go home so that I can at least know you're safe. It's all I can do."

She wouldn't look at him. "Will you remember me?"

"Always." A promise that meant more from him than almost anyone, not that she would ever know such a thing. "Always, Isabel. Always."

She stood and left him without looking back, and in the end, Biali thought, that was what he deserved.

"That's how it will always be, you know." A smooth voice,

one he hadn't heard in a long time. He'd known the dragonlord was in New York. He had to be if Daisani was, the two of them always mixing like oil and water. Couldn't stay apart, wouldn't stay together. Biali grunted, dismissing Janx without looking his way. Janx didn't belong up here anyway, on rooftops overlooking the city. They were a gargoyle's territory, and Biali had kept to them for the weeks since Isabel's departure. He'd checked: her belongings were gone, her house no longer rented under her name. A ticket west had been purchased on the rail line. She had gone home to safety, as he'd asked. It should not have left such an emptiness in him.

Janx clambered over the roof wall's edge, seating an expensive-clad backside on grimy concrete, and kicked his heels against the wall like a human child, pleased with the detritus that fell toward the distant street. Biali's grunt lowered to a growl. "I didn't invite you to stay."

"I know. Tremendously inconsiderate of you. Exceedingly rude. Hajnal would be appalled."

No one expected him to be fast. Not in the ring, not on the streets. He was too short, too thick, like a draft horse. Full of power, not speed. But that was humans, and he never wanted anyone to mistake him for human. A fist lashed out, backhanded blow at the dragonlord's face.

Janx, infuriatingly, caught it.

Not easily. Gargoyles were the only real threat dragons faced from the remaining Old Races. Their strength beggared even a dragon's size, if a grip could be gotten. Janx's pretty nose should have been shattered, a red mess across his face like the Italian's. But he'd known. Known invoking Hajnal would beget a response, and so he'd been ready. Had braced himself, dragonly mass invisible in human form, but still present. Flesh smacked flesh, sharp slap of sound. Janx's arm trembled, but held.

"Tsk, Biali. Tsk, tsk. You know the rules. No fighting

amongst ourselves." He released Biali's hand, both of them knowing the stout gargoyle wouldn't throw another punch. "But no one ever said anything against us fighting *for* one another."

Biali slid a glance toward the dragonlord. He was cocky, relentlessly cocky, and more beautiful than a man, human or not, had any right to be. He'd never been sure whether Janx's actual looks—handsome enough, with a slim strong jaw and straight nose, with high cheekbones and eyes jade enough to be the stone—if his looks were what made him arresting, or the sheer weight of his presence that lent compelling beauty to well-set features. Either way he used it to charm and frighten. Frighten humans, especially, but not even others of the Old Races were quite immune to the dragonlord's charm. Which was why Biali hadn't left when Janx arrived: there was a warmth to the dragon that not even stone wanted to resist. "You want me to do your dirty work."

"Is there a more appropriate calling for a man made of stone?"

"Stone," Biali muttered. "Not dirt."

"What is dirt but battered stone?" Janx flashed a look toward the ruin of Biali's face, gaze full of pointed innocence. Biali ground his teeth but stayed silent. After a moment Janx gave a moue of exaggerated disappointment and went on. "I'm society, Biali. I provide certain luxuries to the wealthy and curious."

Biali snorted. "You sell opiates to the weak and desperate."

"Well, yes. But I do it with *style.*" Wide-eyed injury rolled over Janx's expression when Biali didn't agree, but then he shrugged and began a third time. "I make my sales in the ballrooms and parlors, not under bridges and on street corners. I have people to do that for me." He sniffed delicately, as if he could smell the lingering stench of the unfortunates undertaking that work. "But whether in parlors or pigpens, there are those who cannot or will not pay, and they must be reminded that I own them. You loathe them," he said more softly. "That's why you fight. Why not drop the pretense and accept an opportunity to simply batter them on my behalf? It won't bring her back, but neither does this." He opened a hand, encompassing the fighting grounds below. "You're a thug, Biali. Embrace it."

"What do you get out of it?"

"An enforcer I can trust. One I don't have to keep secrets from. One who doesn't edge toward the door when I come into the room." The last words were dry as burning leaves, fire crackling in their depths. "You have no idea how tiresome it is to reassure big strong men that I won't have them for lunch. Particularly when I'm supposed to be threatening enough to keep them in line. Really, have you ever tri—"

"Janx," Biali said, "I don't care."

Janx's mouth snapped shut, affront flying across his face. It subsided again, the dragonlord as mercurial as Biali was stolid, and his eyebrows rose a fraction. "There, you see? None of them would ever dare. I'll pay you whatever you want," he added carelessly. "Introduce you at the finest parties, if you want to make them writhe. Name your price."

"Companionship." The word flew out before Biali knew he would say it, and a snarl followed. Before he could dismiss it, though, Janx smiled.

"As it happens, I have someone I want to introduce you to."

Biali grunted again, anger at his own admission keeping him silent. Janx leaned forward, examining the polished leather of his expensive shoes, examining the dirty streets forty feet below, examining the muck-filled river a few yards beyond that. Examining everything, and by doing so making it clear he could wait forever. A stupid game. Gargoyles could out-wait anything, especially a dragon. And yet it was Biali who broke the silence, begrudging curiosity defeating him. "Who?"

"Someone who won't leave you. Who won't judge or fear or flinch. Her name," Janx murmured, "is Ausra."

coda

The child came in the night: a sign of bad luck, the midwife said. Worse luck still, thought her grandfather the *don*, but he could not insist that Isabel marry as he had insisted her mother do. Mama and Papa were more forgiving, as they should be, and saw only beauty, not ill fortune, in their grandchild. They were happy, all of them. Happy until dawn, when terrible things came to pass.

Warm fleshy tones turned dull, then black as night. Stone, unmoving, uncaring, unliving. The midwife left, never to return, and if she made it no farther than the *hacienda's* long drive, then Isabel did not know it until many years later. Mama screamed until the vapors took her, and Papa stood ashen with grim horror, waiting for Isabel to give up the frozen body of her child.

She would not. Could not. Did not release it, only held its cold body against her breast and wept until nightfall, when the miracle happened.

Life again. Warmth, breath, shining dark eyes. Hunger and anger and charm and fragile, needy life, all in the body of a child who had turned to stone by day.

By the third night, the change was becoming familiar. After a week, Mama even joked that a child who slept so soundly during the day was a blessing indeed. And after a month, when a fit of infantile range triggered the other change, the one that sprouted wings and clawed fingertips from the baby's back and hands, then finally Isabel understood why Biali had not come with her. Why he could not, and what secrets he had tried to keep by staying.

She would not go back to him. Not yet, perhaps not ever. But she would teach his child what kind of creature its father had been: one who loved so deeply that he chose solitude over risk. She would teach the baby to love the story of its father, and if God smiled on them all, perhaps someday father and child would be united.

On its christening day, she named the child Hajnal.

FORETOLD

SHE HAD BEEN RUNNING FOREVER. Forever: as long as she could remember, even longer than that. A head start. That was all she asked for, it was all she needed, and it wasn't enough. Couldn't be. It wasn't that the price was too high. It was that it would eventually come home to roost. Had to. That had been the bargain. Assuming the bargain would be kept, but then, she knew it would be, even if the witch didn't. Hadn't. Still didn't, no doubt: why would a witch keep her word to any of the Old Races, especially when she drew so much power from their captured immortal souls? But Manto knew; Manto always knew, had always known since she was a hatchling, because the power of prophecy was hers, a gift and a curse.

Mostly a curse.

One foot in front of another, running. *Humans* could run forever, except they couldn't. They could walk almost forever, though. Long enough to run any prey into the earth. Steady pace, carry forward, one foot in front of another. Eventually their prey collapsed.

Manto didn't know any more if she was prey or predator. She only knew she'd made the bargain, shown the witch how to call blood, told the witch the words to whisper, and watched her mothers be drawn deep into the vellum pages of the grimoire. So many of them, screaming as they went, but then, the harpies always screamed.

They ran in flocks, snapping, nattering, picking at one another, boiling over with loathing for themselves, for the world they were made to live in, and most of all for humankind and its easy endless expansion. They turned on mankind even more swiftly than on themselves; woe betide a solitary traveler or even a small group huddled together for safety. Harpies took glee in swooping from the sky, in screaming until they could no longer hear even themselves over the cacophony, in rending flesh from bones and eating it raw and dripping. They spared the children; even harpies would spare the children. But few of the wild winged women, few enough indeed, ever rose out of the madness enough to wonder whether those children, scarred by fear, might survive to become leaders of the bands that came to hunt the harpies.

Because come they did, if not often then incessantly, inexorably, never truly stopping, as if the hunt was an itching, pressing need that drove humans just as it drove the harpies. Wary men armed with spears and nets, wise enough not to come too close: a harpy's strength could break a man, her claws could rend him, and her venomous spittle blind him. Those who were meant to be the prey of men watched sometimes, watch with the anticipation of madness, as small armies crept into their canyons and ravines and crevasses. They hung upside down like bats, tangled hair falling toward the earth and clawed fingers writhing around each other in hungry anticipation, until they fell upon the humans like the predators they were, screams mortal and immortal echoing off stony walls as the fight was brought to life. When they won—and often the harpies did—when they won they would take the choicest bits, the eyes and soft dense organ meat, back to their males, for the males, rare and precious, were neither able nor allowed to fight.

Nor were they afflicted with madness, the males, or at least, not so deeply as the females. No one knew why, though even the males rarely had the presence of mind to wonder. It was something in the making of them, something in the long dead history of the Old Races. The vampires were said to be first; the vampires claimed they were not of this world at all, but the harpies were thought to be second. At least, *they* thought it: children of the gods, humans might say, but in their wild hearts they believed themselves to be children of another world, born to this one too soon, not yet fit or suited for it, and thus mad. Why it clung to the females was a mystery, but cling it did, and worst of all were the few driven sane by their madness.

Manto was one such: Manto who was born to see and speak truth, no matter how bitter, and even the best among her people could not believe her; their madness was too great, and her tongue, too sharp. Nor did it help that as a child she had watched her wild mothers and said—with faultless truth—*this will be the end of us.*

She remembered that day, the first time she knew clearly that they would not, or could not, listen to her. She hadn't yet been able to fly, pinfeathers still ratty and scrawny, but she had gone on the hunt with her mothers. Nothing more than finding wild boar for dinner had been planned, in so far as the mothers could plan anything at all, but they had come upon a little tribe of humans, mortals by far more afraid of the howling, air-born harpies than the mothers were of them. They scattered, those humans, running to hide beneath bushes, under tiny outcroppings of stone, in shallow divots in the earth: anything that might offer the slightest hint of cover. The mothers descended on them, crying with inhumane joy at destroying them, at feasting on them. Manto, too small and perhaps, in the end, too sane to participate, watched bleakly as the mothers slew and ate and bathed in blood, and saw in the eyes of the mortals who died last that their souls would not go easy into the night; that their bodies, when found by others, would bear witness to what had happened, and their spirits would speak to the living, telling tales of the winged monsters who had done this thing.

Humans, the mothers spat, *have no magic: their dead cannot speak, they cannot tattle on us, we are free to do as we wish,* to which Manto said: *no.*

Humans had little magic, *that* was true, but it could never be said that they had none. Even the mothers knew of witches, those appalling creatures born from the darkest secrets that could be whispered into the world, and for harpies to find another being appalling spoke troublingly of witchery. Where the mothers left ground soaked in human blood was rife for secrets to be whispered and witches to be born; if it did not take so very *many* secrets, so *much* darkness, to make a witch, harpies alone might have peopled the earth with monsters of human-born magic, instead of monsters like themselves. And there were human magics beyond witches; Manto could taste them in the air, even if she couldn't name them, and so she would never say with certainty that the mortal dead could not speak. Instead she spoke the truth, that the mothers laid the groundwork for their own destruction with their actions, and not one among them heard her.

In despair, Manto crawled back to the nests: climbed the harsh rocky cliff faces, avoiding the excrement, and crept into the divots and depths where the harpies made their homes in the walls. There, in the finest and most open of spaces, she would watch the fathers. They were beautiful, the fathers: gloriously feathered, with strong limbs and voices like silk and water, soft and sweet and cajoling to bring the mothers to them for eager mating.

They were also very, very stupid, of course; almost all of them, and perhaps that was why the madness did not plague them. Manto went among them often, speaking the truths she knew and trying to coax a hint of wit from any of them. With the fathers supporting her she could perhaps convince the mothers to change their ways: the mothers would do almost anything for the beautiful males. From time to time, even Manto forgot all else save sitting and gazing at the fathers while they strutted and preened and sang. Their posturing almost always ended in fights, though: even with less than a handful of fathers for the whole of the flock, they became so agitated with one another that strutting devolved into battle. But where the mothers found that appealing, Manto could only see the cycle that led to their doom, and was helpless to stop it. Still, she spoke to the fathers, hoping to lure them toward the idea of peacefulness, and they at least listened, which was more than the mothers could do.

Manto grew: her feathers came in and she learned to stretch her wings, took to the skies and—time and again—found herself startled at the human reaction to her appearance. Harpies were not beautiful, by human standards; harpies were not even beautiful by their own, not when they had the fathers to compare themselves to. But the face she wore, with its aquiline features, with the huge golden eyes with slit pupils, and the ruff of feathers that no one could mistake for hair adorning her skull, did not seem *frightening* to her, only alien in comparison to humanity's blunter faces. The winged arms, though, arms that could be, with effort, peeled from the structure of the wings themselves, so that even in her harpy form she might have hands, albeit hands with strangely long and delicate fingers better for clawing than caressing; those wings, and the powerful legs that ended in massive taloned feet, all with something of a human woman's body in between; together they made up a horror, judging from the faces of the mortals who saw them.

Even in human form she disturbed mortals; she could not change the color of her eyes, or shift away the patterns, like owl feathers, of her hair, and so it fell from russet to white to black in narrow bands and speckles, and there was something of those markings to her skin as well. Worse than that, though, was the truth that fell from her lips whether she wanted it to or not, and with that, it was better to speak truth to her own kind. They wouldn't listen, but neither did they seem to remember, later, that she had warned them. Humans *did* remember, and hated her for it. So she felt that she could belong to neither, not the mad immortal race that had birthed her nor the humans whose sanity made her unwelcome. She endured; she could do no more, and she failed, season after season, to convince anyone, the mothers or the fathers or the humans, that there might be some other way.

Eventually it came to her that she would have to *make* another way; that she alone could force it, and that she alone would bear the burden of having done so. Humans were plentiful by that time, shockingly plentiful; they bred fast and though many, many of their infants died, many also survived and began another generation in the time a harpy might sit idly waiting for a single egg to hatch.

Not that any of the wild mothers sat idly on her egg, warming it until it cracked forth a shrieking angry infant. They abandoned them through boredom or ruthlessness or forgetfulness, and though no egg would hatch that went wholly unattended, neither was it likely that the mother sitting on it when it birthed a babe was the one who had laid it to begin with. Most mothers would sit a while on any egg they found, though the worst of them would slash the shell and feast on the flesh of the unborn.

The fathers, though; the beautiful, stupid fathers would sit complacently on an egg as long as someone fed them. The less crazed among the mothers would bribe a father into sitting on their eggs; the choicest meals would draw any father from the egg he sat upon to another, where he would stay until something better was offered. Manto had known her father, or at least the father cajoled into sitting on her egg, and he preened with pride over the thirteen years he had perched on her egg: no other father in their flock had ever been so attentive. Manto supposed the mother who had kept him sated for those many turns of the season had perhaps birthed her, but such dedication—such *recollection*—was unlike any of the mothers; it seemed more likely that the mother intended only to curry favor with the reliable father, that he might later sit on her egg. But perhaps she had known both her parents; it was possible, and, being not a matter of prophecy, unknowable.

It was easier now to be human, at least. In this time, in this era, the soft wildness of her natural skin, the strange patterns and the wild poof of hair: it was as if someone had finally taken pity on her, and made mortal fashion reflect an immortal-but-human form. Even her golden-slit eyes were adored, because they were assumed to be contact lenses. She was admired for her unending dedication to the role: no one ever saw her without the contacts, no one ever saw her at the hairdresser, having the patterns re-done, and no make-up artist would confess to being the one who painted her skin.

She had long since discovered that they would listen to truth if it came in song and stirred their souls, but it had been meaningless for centuries untold to try to speak it that way: she was one person, and alien at that; mortals were more likely to try to burn her than listen to the music she made at summer harvest festivals, or in the dark of winter. But that too had changed, not as recently as this decade of too-pretty, too-soft, too-outrageous fashion that suited her so well; for a hundred and ten years now music had been recorded, and for nearly half of that, radio had carried music into the homes of millions. Records became more accessible, then innumerable other ways to listen: 8-tracks and cassette tapes, then the burgeoning format called CDs, and Manto, in a fit of madness comparable to that of the mothers, began a rock and roll career, singing truth to the wild hearts and troubled souls of teenagers.

They loved her: stars above, they loved her, and she them. First in bars, then in clubs, her words rolling over them: bombastic lyrics, rock and roll fantasies, the price of dreams coming true. From clubs to parks and from parks to fronting for the biggest bands, until it was her golden, alien self on the stage in stadiums, singing as though her heart would break; singing as though *their* hearts would break, all of them, together, as the world fell down around them.

It enraged some and freed others, and both were better than the endless aeons of being hunted, hiding, running, being *prey*: harpies were not prey. Not for anyone save mortals, and, in the end, witches.

The youth ought not have taken her unawares, but perhaps he hadn't, at that. Humans didn't, not unless the Old Races wanted them to. Not with their preternatural senses, not with the necessity of knowing who was nearby, for their own safety. And yet she let him approach as she crouched on the cliff's edge, too-long arms curling into taloned hands that dangled between her knees. She could blame the sunset, as if it carried a song in it too mesmerizing to ignore, because it *did*: light's music, reaching back and forward through time, because light was an infinite and impossible thing and it knew everything it touched. It carried memories of then and now, of tomorrow and yesterday, and for Manto those memories became prophecy.

And maybe that was why she let him approach, too,

because she knew before he arrived, bathed in the evening's red-gold light, that it had to begin this way in order to end the way it must.

He carried a sword in one hand and a spear in the other. Enthusiastic, or efficient, or terrified, or all of those things. If he'd wanted to kill her, though, he ought to have flung the spear as soon as he saw her broad-spread back, the wings opening from it to catch the sunset. She saw that possibility rise and fade again, too fast for her to worry, and when he had come close enough to slay her with the blade, he instead said, "What are you?", which was a fair enough question.

"A seer," she replied, and stood, turning, to let him see *her*.

He did well, only falling back half a step, only tightening his hands around the haft and hilt of the weapons he carried. Beautiful play of muscle in his body, fear knotting his stomach, shock cording his throat, but he did not run. Sun-kissed hair, sandy colored; if he lived in colder climes it would be brown, but here the light took to it, as it did to the warm depths of his skin. Light eyes to go with the sandy hair, and whatever people he belonged to eschewed facial hair: his jaw was clean and smooth, though he was clearly old enough to wear a beard.

She was taller than he; somehow that surprised her. *Noticeably* taller: a palm's length or more, and the ground she stood upon higher besides, so that he looked up and up and up on her inhuman glory. And then—and this was when all the futures began to tumble together, twining and shaping themselves toward inevitability—then he knelt and placed his sword and spear on the earth. Spread his hands and showed his throat and said to her, "And what do you see for me?"

Manto didn't tell him, of course; no one, no matter how nicely they asked, wanted to be told their lives ended soon and in agony. Neither did she tell him of the brief weeks of ecstatic joy they would find in each other; he came to that soon enough on his own, shy and eager both, exquisite need overruling the difference between them, and her heart shattered when he spoke, softly, of the lives they would have together, quietly, away from the rest of the world, safe from his kind and hers.

And because she was a fool, this once she rebelled against the written future, and tried. Escaped to the mountains with him, and to her surprise—because not even she, it seemed, could see everything the light saw—she fell pregnant, and while she didn't lay an egg like her mothers, neither was the pregnancy done in a mere nine months as a human's would be. Gravid, bound by gravity: that was how she lost him, too mortal to protect him and too alien to be forgiven. Had it been humans who found them, she might even have forgiven them, but it was the mothers, and the mothers laughed as she screamed impotently while they ripped her lover apart. In her rage and fear and loss she told them a thousand times that they must slay her too or face her vengeance.

They left her living, and set their fate in stone.

Not just any witch would do. Manto went from dark place to dark place in the world, crouching low to listen to the secrets that had birthed a witch there. It took so many, such a weight of horror; it was a wonder that any witch could ever be born at all, much less that there were dozens the world over. That was humanity, though: craven and fearful, murderers and thieves. A brother's wife coveted, a killing in the dark of the night, a babe unwanted, an envy to blacken the heart. On and on it went, and nowhere, not one place anywhere, did she find a witch born of joy and hope.

Finally: finally, in the far reaches of the north, in a place where the summer sun never set, where winter's night lasted months at a time, that was where she found what she sought: a witch born with knowledge of the Old Races.

There should have been many, Manto thought. Surely part

of the bleak fear that gave witches life had been awakened again and again by the monsters in the dark, the gargoyles and the vampires, the djinn and the dragons. But not until the north, and the unaging hag who called herself Baba Yaga, could Manto be sure that she was not—entirely—betraying her kind to humanity's ugliest magic.

She could see, upon looking at Baba Yaga, that her knowledge of the Old Races was imperfect. That it was a boil under the skin, aching and pushing at her, not clarified enough to burst. She knew of them in the same way a child knew of teething: discomfort with no source, only eased when the tooth broke through the gum.

Manto was that tooth, and she came to Baba Yaga in all her inhuman, arrogant glory, wings spread and talons sharp, ready to eviscerate in her own defense, even if a witch could not die by any method Manto knew.

The witch's eyes lit with greed when she saw Manto, but even a witch knew the power of prophecy, and only quavered in loathing agreement when Manto said, "Of all of us, I am not for you."

"What *are* you," croaked Baba Yaga, half desperation and half demand.

"We are the Old Races," Manto answered, and a hiss broke free of the witch's throat, a long and terrible sound of release. She crumpled to the earth, scouring it in gratitude, in pleasure, and when she raised her eyes again it was with a need so deep it tasted of rage.

"We existed before humanity ever dreamed of evolving on this world," Manto whispered, and with each word watched the witch's power grow. "We are bound by blood to one another and only by blood can we be bound. I will give you the words, witch, and the blood of my own kind, the harpies, and you will draw my mothers and my fathers deep into the pages of your books of magic. It will give you strength such as you have never known, for they cannot die by your hand, only live captured so their magic is yours to draw on. It will not last," she was compelled to say. "Not forever. Not for always. There is no magic, even ours, even yours, that is eternal. But it will be long and long and long again, and you will have forgotten that the power is yours to lose aeons before it leaves you."

"Give it to me." Greed garbled the old witch's words, and Manto lifted one hand to slice her own palm open with a talon.

A book formed from her blood, pages of vellum covered with leather. Embossed monsters rose in the leather, sea serpents and harpies, great hairy yeti and the strong-bodied siryns. Words rose on the pages, all the histories and truths of the beings who came before humanity, and at the edges of those words writhed the potential for containment.

Manto hesitated, then thought sharply, terribly, of her lover's screams, and with that cut her other hand, pouring blood onto the pages. The blood shaped itself, drawing pictures, and then the screams began in truth: the mothers, pulled by magic across earth and sea and sealed forever—or nearly forever—into the pages of the grimoire. The fathers too, though they protested less; poor beautiful stupid fathers, never truly understanding their fate. For minutes the howls went on, then hours, into days and weeks and in the end months, and through it all Manto stood and bled, bled herself white but would not die, because to die would be to free the mothers and condemn all of them, the Old Races all, to memory, to legend, to myth, and to obscurity.

Mothers screeched and tore at her as they were swept by, opening new wounds; still she stood strong while Baba Yaga cackled and rubbed her hands together as greedily as any mother. The old witch shone with power, though already Manto could see it would never last, that she would lose bits of it to time and foolishness, and other parts to the cunning of other witches. But for now Baba Yaga was likely the strongest of her kind: could witches easily cross running water, she might conquer the world when humanity was still too unproven to hold against her, but even man's darkest secrets and ugliest dreams laid in protection and conditions, and Baba Yaga was bound by the magic that had made her.

Finally the last of the mothers tore into the grimoire's pages, and the book collapsed shut on itself. Baba Yaga pounced forward and secured it with an iron lock, then clutched it to her hollow chest and squealed with dreadful pleasure.

Manto, weary already, murmured, "In a book of my making, a book of my blood, you may bind any of our kind save myself and the vampires. That is because we harpies come second only to them in primogeniture; I cannot hold them with my blood, but I can tell you how to." She leaned forward to whisper the secret of catching a vampire into the ancient crone's ear, and then she rose to walk away from the terrible thing she had done. She could not even look at the book: it pulsed black to her gaze, accusing her of genocide, although the knowing part of her said *no*; that she had saved them all, with the book.

"Lose it," she said, almost as an afterthought, "and only another of the Old Races may ever fetch it for you again."

Then she left Baba Yaga behind, and although she did not know it then, began to run, a run that would take her down through the centuries as memory and guilt and those of the Old Races who grew to understand what she had done, hunted her without mercy or surcease.

The one called Daisani found her after a concert. She ought to have known—well, she did know; that was her gift and her curse—but somehow she was surprised anyway, to see his sleek swift form appear across the limousine from her, his arms spread against its wide seat, one leg crossed over the other, casual and arrogant.

She had never seen him before, for all she'd heard of him over the aeons. Brother in all but blood to Janx, the rebellious dragonlord, his closest enemy and dearest friend. Daisani was slight of build, unimposing of height. Not handsome, either, though even she, a harpy, wanted to let her gaze linger on him. That was charisma, and would do well for him if he ever wanted to stand beside her on a concert stage. Dark hair, poofed on top and longish in the back in the style of the decade; she tried briefly to imagine him with the loose, large permed rock star locks that her own natural hair mimicked, and laughed, which was not what one should do when faced with the vampire known as the master of them all.

His eyes, already dark, blackened. Manto lifted her palms in apology, a very human gesture: to animals, anything that increased one's size was construed as a threat, but she only meant appeasement. Fortunately, the Old Races were, if not human, at least people, and even a quick-tempered vampire knew a peace offering when he saw it. But she let him speak first, knowing that if she did, it would be in defense of her actions, and to blurt a defense was to admit guilt.

"You're not what I expected," Daisani finally said, which wasn't what *she* expected. "The last harpy. I expected something more...haggard." He shifted comfortably on the leather seats, glancing out at street lamps that threw light and shadow over him as they drove.

"That's all right," Manto breathed. "I expected someone taller."

"Everyone always does." The vampire sounded unperturbed, but then, if he could be needled about his height he wouldn't likely be called the master of his kind. "I attended your concert this evening. You told a story, and I've been there for enough of it to know it was true."

"That's all my music is. True stories."

Daisani made a dismissive gesture. "Find me a minstrel who *doesn't* claim that. But you're different. You told *our* stories. And they believed you. In their way, they believed you."

"They want to. They hear reflections of their own lives in our stories. Not many of them really *believe* they're dragons or—"

"Elves," Daisani said drolly. "So many human legends, and we failed to manifest ourselves in that particular manner. I wonder if it's our failing, or their magnificence."

"We are not shaped by their dreams." The sharpness in Manto's voice surprised even her.

Daisani's gaze cleared, curiosity pulling at the corner of his mouth. "That," he said. "That was a true thing, what you just said. I could hear it. Not like your songs, either. Those have a familiarity to them, a truth said over and over. This was fresh."

"I sing the songs every night."

"And you but rarely defend our origins as our own." The twitch at his lips bled into a brief, full smile. His canines, against every legend of vampires in the world, were flat, non-threatening. Dragons had pointier teeth, even in their human form, but it was said—although not by Manto, and therefore it was not necessarily accurate—that no one saw a vampire's true form and lived to tell about it.

That thought led her down a path toward a vision, toward seeing, and for a rarity she shut her eyes and turned her face away: vampires might be the progenitors of them all, and the harpies their first children, born too early into this world, but not even she wanted to see the faces of that which may have begotten her mothers and fathers. Just in case—just in case, even if she herself had not said it—just in case there was truth to the legend, and seeing it would mean tonight was her last night to live.

Of course, now that Daisani had found her, that seemed likely anyway.

"Why did you do it?"

"I had to," Manto replied without hesitation. "If you were at the concert, you know that. I told the story."

"Yes." A thinner smile slipped over his face, and to her utter surprise, he sang: "Madness of the mothers, ravaging the land / Simplicity of fathers, bound by war and strife / We're the saner children, lead them by the hand / The future depends on us, embrace both love and life."

Manto, amused, said, "You're a fan," and Daisani, with a sourness of tone that didn't match the brightness in his gaze, said, "I pay attention. But I do believe you, and that leaves me in something of a...quandary."

A knot loosened around Manto's heart, one she hadn't even realized was there. "Oh?"

"There's a death penalty on you," Daisani said frankly, and though she knew it, to hear it spoken aloud took her breath away.

"We don't kill each other. It's one of our edicts."

Daisani's voice went dry enough to be dour. "We don't betray our entire race to a witch, either. Laws are for the law-abiding, Manto; you must understand that by now, even if you look like barely more than a child. I," he said after a moment's pause, "am not among the law-abiding, and I did come here to kill you. To extract vengeance for a people. But when I came, I didn't know—didn't believe—you were a truthsayer."

"And now?" Manto whispered.

"Now I want to know what happens next."

"No," Manto said, almost before he had finished speaking.

"You don't. No one ever does. Not really. But I can tell you she's been born already, the human who will change our future. I can tell you that your path and hers have already been set to collide. And I can tell you that the things I have done *will* come undone, when all *is* done. That I would not have done them if they were not necessary to the future of us all...any more than you would have done what you have done, to ensure the future of us all."

She saw it then, a glimpse of what a vampire truly was. Rage flew through Daisani, sluicing the veneer of humanity away. For an instant, less than a breath, less than a heartbeat, barely a blink, she saw into the cold uncaring killing depths of space, and the burning endless distant heat of a star, all shaped into a creature that sustained itself on blood and fear.

Then it was gone, and the man sitting before her was hardly more than a man, no more than a tap of one fingertip betraying tension or agitation. His voice, though, carried the death of everything in it, as he said, "I believe you're about to suffer a fatal accident, Manto. Probably in an airplane; that's very popular for musicians."

"And if I don't?"

"Then you will most certainly suffer a genuinely fatal accident," Daisani said softly. "Come back in a generation or two as your own child or grandchild, but wait until this future you have spoken of comes to pass, Manto, because it is known that I have found you, and if you do not die at my hands tonight you will surely die at someone else's, soon. Leave your music as your legacy, but die, that you might live again."

He glanced out the window again, then said, with something almost approaching sympathy, "This world isn't safe for us to live in anyway, not if we live as large as you're doing. Even I live too visibly, and far fewer people know the face of a real estate mogul than a rock star. Janx has slithered low, taking over crime syndicates and underworld activities so that the world never sees his face. I believe it chafes him even more than it does me, as I lack his vanity. But you've chosen a lifestyle you can never sustain. They're young and foolish and beautiful right now, and I see why they called to you. But they'll turn on you, Manto, so you had best go now, before it's humans and Old Races both hunting you."

"Why are you letting me go?"

The vampire's gaze went bleak. "Because I *have* done the things I have done to ensure our future, and I am not—mostly—a hypocrite. I won't condemn you for taking the same actions I decided were necessary, particularly as I decided without the advantage of true foresight. But mostly," he said, and his gaze softened then, "mostly because I find you've given me a modicum of hope, and it's almost impossible to offer hope to a creature like me."

"Don't hope too much. There's a great deal of darkness to come."

Daisani's smile went almost fond. "Oh, child. What am I, but a thing of darkness?" The smile vanished. "Tonight, Manto. Die tonight, or tomorrow you will die for real."

Then he was gone, as suddenly as he'd appeared. The car door must have opened and shut: Manto could hear its echo, and feel the breeze of his passage, but he was incomprehensibly fast, and she, after sitting stunned for a moment, sighed and leaned forward to tap on the limo's separating window. "To the airport, please. I feel like seeing the sunrise from the air."

And so she did, hovering above the horizon in gold light, broad wings catching the wind as, below, the little plane she had rented spun and fell out of control, until it smashed, with a dramatic explosion, into the mountain tree line far below.

The heat of the fire would wreck most chances of finding a

body or hopefully even bones, though there would always be those—this, Manto saw, with as much clarity as she had ever seen any future—there would be those who would never believe she had died this day. Even some amongst the Old Races wouldn't believe, save that Daisani himself was the source of the promise of her demise, but enough would. Enough of the Old Races, more than enough humans, and those humans who didn't would always be thought of as slightly mad; that was the price of conspirators. If they were lucky—if Manto herself was—they might live long enough to see themselves proven right, but she doubted it: there were many years to go before that came to pass.

Wings spread, she turned toward the sunrise, flying into it as if a phoenix had been born of the harpy: fiery gold and red everywhere, spears of light illuminating her feathers, turning them precious in hue, and in the dawn she saw farther than she had ever seen before.

No ordinary human living now would see her return, no: not with the morning sun casting its shadow over a world that, all unknowing, awaited the Old Races' rising.

Acknowledgments

This collection has been a very long time coming, and I have a lot of people to thank for their support. Some deserve a special shout-out: Katrina Lehto, who has always been a tremendous supporter of the Old Races, and Brian Nisbet, who essentially yells shut up and take my money! every time an Old Races project is mentioned. Paul-Gabriel Wiener, who is a rock, and Joliene McAnly, who goes beyond the call of duty as a reader.

This book (and many others) wouldn't exist without the encouragement offered by Bryant Durrell and Carl Rigney. Fred Hicks got me through the first stages of learning book design. Tara O'Shea has made me some gorgeous covers, and I was thrilled to work again with editor Betsy Mitchell on the titular novella, Year of Miracles.

The war room, as always, keeps me going: Mikaela Lind, Robin D. Owens, Diana Pharaoh Francis, Laura Anne Gilman, Ellen Million, Michelle Sagara, and numerous others are there, writing with me across the world, day in and day out.

And then there's Ted, and our son, who keep right on believing in me. I love you boys.

Special Thanks

Sorry, that last page doesn't even begin to cut it.

The Old Races short story collections have been crowdfunded projects that have taken far longer to realize as a final product than any of us imagined. Over the course of six years, more than 400 people have helped support the creation of these stories.

My sincerest thanks to the following:

A. MARINA FOURNIER, A B WARWICK, ABBIE HEATER, ADRIANNE MIDDLETON, AILSA BARRETT, ALANI JOLI ABBOTT, ALENA FRANCO, ALENA M. CALLAGHAN, ALICE TYRELL, ALTHEA CLARK, AM KOENIG, AMANDA LANE, AMANDA PRIOLE, AMANDA SAMUELS, AMANDA WEINSTEIN, AMBER SALEM, ANDREA N KING, ANDREW AND KATE BARTON, ANDREW WALKER, ANDY MERRIAM, ANGELA BISCHEL, ANGELA KORRA'TI, ANGELA N. HUNT, ANNE BURNER, ANNE PASCALE QUINTY, ANNETTE BEECHER, ANTHONY JAMES, APRIL MACHOLTZ, ASHLEY CRUMP, ASHOK KUMAR BANKER, AUDREY SALICK, AXISOR, BARBARA EAGLE, BARBARA GALLANT, BARBARA HASEBE, BENAETS DORIEN, BERNADETTE, BETH RASMUSSEN, BETH SKAGGS, BEVERLY LEE, BREANNE MACDONALD, BRENDA JENIGAN, BRIAN & DIANE DUPEY, BRIAN NISBET, BRIAN STANLEY, BRIANNA AGNEW, BRYANT DURRELL, CAITLIN CROWDER, CAITLIN DEAN, CAMILLA CRACCHIOLO, CARAGH MURPHY, CARINNA FILES, CARL RIGNEY, CAROL, CAROL GUESS, CAROLINE LEBEL, CAROLINE VALDEZ, CAROLYN BUTLER, CAROLYN CURTIS, CASSE WILLIAMS, CAT DEMIRA, CAT WILSON, CATE HOWARD, CATH STEVENSON, CATHERINE SHARP, CATHIBEA STEVENSON, CHARITY HIROSE, CHARLEE GRIFFITH, CHARLENE HAMILTON, CHARLES WATSON, CHARLOTTE CALVERT, CHERYL PRENTICE, CHIRAY KOO, CHRISTI PANCHYK, CHRISTINA BOUNDS, CHRISTINA DWYER, CHRISTINA SUTT, CHRISTINE SWENDSEID, CHRISTOPHER BUSER, CHRISTY HOPKINS, CHRYSOULA TZAVELAS, CINDY CURRY,

COBY HAAS, COLETTE REAP, CORI MAY, CORI WEISFELDT, CORRA, CORY W. TROTTER, COUTRNEY OSTAFF, CRYSTAL YOCUM, CYNTHIA WITKUS, DANIELLE INGBER, DANIELLE INGBER, DANIELLE WALTHER, DAVID BILLS, DAVID CAPON, DAVID LAUBER, DEB ALVERSON, DEBBIE MATSUURA, DEBORAH ALVERSON, DEBORAH BLAKE, DEBORAH ERICKSON, DEBRA MEYERSON, DEBRA ORTON, DEIRDRE M MURPHY, DENÉE ZAH, DENISE MOLINE, DIANA TAFT, DIANE DESAUTELS, DONAL CUNNINGHAM, DONIKI BODERICK-LUCKEY, DONNA ANTONIO, DOUGH MCGILL, EARL MILES, EDWARD ELLIS, ELISABETH PAIT, ELIZABETH, ELIZABETH, ELIZABETH CADORETTE, ELIZABETH COOK, ELIZABETH GARVIN, ELIZABETH MCDONALD, ELIZABETH NAYLOR, ELLA PEABODY, ELLEN MILLION, EMILY ERVIN, EMILY POOLE, EMMA BARTHOLOMEW, EMMA PITT, EQUUSTRY HANDCRAFTS & PRESERVES, ERICA OLSON, ERIN CATLEY, ERIN JAMES, EVANGELINE CHENG, EVIL HAT PRODUCTIONS, FARRELL MAGINNIS, FLYNN, FREYA WILSON, GABRIEL KRABBE, GARETH KAVENAGH, GARY LETEMPT, GEMMA TAPSCOTT, GEORGE RILEY, GEORGINA SCOTT, GLENN CASE, GLYNN STEWART, GRETCHEN SHANROCK-SOLBERG, HEATHER FAGAN, HEATHER KNUTSEN, HEATHER RONEY, HELEN KATSINIS, HOLLY TIDD, HUGH MCSWEENEY, HUGH MYERS, JACQULYNN UHRMACHER, JAI ADAMS, JAMES SCOTT, JANA LINDBERG, JANET GAHAGAN, JANICE DIMARCO, JANIS OSSMANN, JANNE TORKLEP, JEAN-MARIE DIAZ, JEFFREY D. KATZ, JENNIFER, JENNIFER CABBAGE, JENNIFER ERWIN, JENNIFER SIMPSON, JERI SMITH-READY, JESSE CUNNINGHAM, JESSICA NELSON, JILL VALUET, JOANIE SHEAFFER, JOANN CAPSER, JOE FERNANDEZ, JOHN BAKER, JOHN F. RICHARDS, JOLIENE MCANLY, JOSHUA JOHNSTON, JUDITH WEBER, JULIE KUHN, JUNE LUNDSTROM, JUSTINE BIRMINGHAM, K. GAVENMAN, KAELA WOOLSEY, KARI, KARIN MEACHAM, KARYL FULKERSON, KAT BONSON, KATE KIRBY, KATE LARKING, KATE SHEEHY, KATHARINE MILLER, KATHERINE MALLOY, KATHLEEN GAVENMAN, KATHLEEN HANRAHAN, KATHLEEN TIPTON, KATHRYN DUFFY, KATHRYN WEHNER, KATHY FRANKLIN, KATHY ROGERS, KATHY TRAXLER, KATIE BERGMAN-BOCK, KATRINA LEHTO, KATY WAGERS, KAYLA LOWES, KBREM, KELLY MCDONOUGH, KELLY MYERS, KELSEY THORNTON, KERRY AKA TROUBLE, KERRY COBEY, KERRY MALONE, KES YOCUM, KIELY OHMAN, KILSHARION KINSEY, KIM SMITH, KRISTINA RUMPFF, KRISTINE KEARNEY, KRISTY MIKA, KYNA FOSTER, LACEY R. RUBY, LARISA LABRANT, LAURA ANNE GILMAN, LAURA ATKINSON, LAURA BLALOCK, LAURA DENSON, LAURA HOBBS, LAURA

WALLACE, LAUREN DEVOE, LAURI WEAVER, LAURIE GAUGHAN, LAZYTEA CREATIONS, LEAH MACLEAN, LEAH MOORE, LEANN HAGGARD, LEANN PARENTEAU, LEIGH ANN MELLOY, LESLEY MITCHELL, LIANNE BURWELL, LIESBEHINDSTARS, LIMUGURL, LINDA ERVIN, LINDSAY STALCUP, LISA D FISCHER, LISA ELLEN SPENCER, LISA GINGERICH, LISA GUERTIN, LISA PEGG, LISA SOTO, LISA STEELE, LISA STEWART, LIZ SYREEN, LIZA HERNANDEZ, LIZA OLMSTED, LIZZETTE PILTCH, LOLA, LOLA MCCRARY, LORI LONG, LORI LUM, LOUISE SOUTHWICK, LUCY COX, LYDIA LEONG, LYN MERCER, LYNETTE MILES, LYNETTE TAIT, LYNN "LAZYTEA", LYNN CALVIN, LYNN LEHTO, LYNN SHULAK, M.A. OTTEWELL, MAGGIE MURPHY, MARCILLE RIPPERTON, MARGARET MENZIES, MARJORIE TAYLOR, MARNIE, MARSHA HANSEN, MARSHA SIMMONS, MARY ANNE WALKER, MARY BALDWIN, MARY D SLOAN, MARY GUSTAFSON, MARY HARGROVE, MARY KEEFE, MARY SPILA, MARY SPILA, MARYANNE SHOOBRIDGE, MATT GIRTON, MAUREEN GATELY, MAX KAEHN, MEGAN POKORNY, MELANIE COLLIGAN, MELISSA SIRIMANNE, MICHAEL BERNARDI, MICHAEL FITCH, MICHAEL NICKERSON, MICHAEL PERKINS, MICHELLE CURTIS, MICHELLE EDWARDS, MIKAELA LIND, MINDY MYMUDES, MING-LI KONG, MISS A. C. WALKER, MOIRA IRELAND, MOOD RING MEDIA, MORAG WATSON, NANCY WESTON, NATHALIE BOISARD-BEUDIN, NEAL LEVENSON, NELLIE BATZ, NICHOLE BECK, NICOLAI BUCH-ANDERSEN, NICOLE HALL, NORIKO SHOJI, NORMAN TISON, PAM HATLER, PAMELA BLOME, PAT KNUTH, PATRICIA DAVIS, PATRICIA LINDSELL, PATRICIA O'NEILL, PATRICK MALONE, PATSY TISDALE, PAUL ANTHONY SHORTT, PAUL-GABRIEL WIENER , PENELOPE MCCLAIN, PERSEPHONE, PETER MCCLEAN, PHIL STRACCHINO, PHILLIS ROSTYKUS, RACHEL COLEMAN FINCH, RACHEL GOLLUB, RACHEL MALONEY, RACHEL NAROW, RACHEL REITHER, RALPH HEBB, REBECCA LYSOHIR, RHONA, ROBERT FISHER, ROBERT LAMBERT, ROBERT TINSLEY, ROBIN BURTON, ROBINA LOWES, ROBYN HUFFMAN, ROSEANN FARBER, RUBBER SOUL BOOKS, RUTH LEON, RUTH STUART, S. ELEKTRA HAMMOND, S. INGRAM, SAIFA RASHID, SAM JUEDE & DONALD COOK, SAMANTHA CAMP, SAMANTHA DAILEY, SAMANTHA GREENALL, SANDRA JAKL, SANDRA MRAZ, SARAH F.W., SARAH BROOKS, SARAH FOSCARINI, SARAH GOSLEE, SARAH PALMERO, SCOTT DRUMMOND, SCOTT SHANKS, SEAN BLAKEY, SEAN COLLINS, SEAN COLLINS, SHANNON SCOLLARD, SHARIS INGRAM, SHARON CORBET, SHAWN CAPISTRANO, SHAWN TUMEY, SHEENA PENNELL, SHEILA LESTER, SHEL KENNON, SHERILYN

About the Author

According to her friends, CE Murphy makes such amazing fudge that it should be mentioned first in any biography. It's true that she makes extraordinarily good fudge, but she's somewhat surprised that it features so highly in biographical relevance.

Other people say she began her writing career when she ran away from home at age five to write copy for the circus that had come to town. Others claim she's a crowdsourcing pioneer, which she rather likes the sound of, but nobody actually got around to pointing out she's written a best-selling urban fantasy series (The Walker Papers), or that she dabbles in writing graphic novels (Take A Chance) and periodically dips her toes into writing short stories (the Old Races collections).

Still, it's clear to her that she should let her friends write all of her biographies, because they're much more interesting that way.

More prosaically, she was born and raised in Alaska, and now lives with her family in her ancestral homeland of Ireland, which is a magical place where it rains a lot but nothing one could seriously regard as winter ever actually arrives.

She can be found online at mizkit.com, @ce_murphy, and at fb.com/cemurphywriter

CPSIA information can be obtained
at www.ICGtesting.com
Printed in the USA
FSHW011916010920
73477FS